M.P.

THE GREAT ADVENTURE

"Each generation hands onto the next," Stanton was saying, "merging together to become a united force, beyond Europe and throughout the world. Tom Lambert is a young man of quite exceptional ability who will become the chief executive officer. I know you will give him every support."

Tom felt every eye turn to him. Watching the faces, Tom wondered who would be friend and who would be foe.

"A toast," Stanton cried. "I give you Stanton Industries."

With an answering murmur everyone rose, pushing chairs back from the tables, raising their glasses.

"To Stanton Industries," Amiens echoed with a sneer.

"To Stanton Industries," Desmond Edwards muttered with unconcealed disgust.

"Stanton Industries," Pohl barked, meeting Tom's eyes with a challenging look.

Feeling a hand on his arm, Tom turned in response to Melody's touch. "To your great adventure," she said softly, touching his cheek with her lips, her green eyes bright with excitement.

"[A] glossy thriller"
—*Chicago Tribune*

Also by Ian St. James

Winner Harris
The Balfour Conspiracy*
The Money Stones*

Published by
HarperPaperbacks

*coming soon

VENGEANCE

Ian St. James

HarperPaperbacks
A Division of HarperCollins*Publishers*

This is a work of fiction. The characters, incidents, and dialogues are products of the author's imagination and are not to be construed as real. Any resemblance to actual events or persons, living or dead, is entirely coincidental.

HarperPaperbacks *A Division of* HarperCollins*Publishers*
10 East 53rd Street, New York, N.Y. 10022

A hardcover edition of this book was published in 1991 by HarperCollins*Publishers*.

Cover photography by Herman Estevez

Stepback art by Pino Daeni

First HarperPaperbacks printing: December 1992

Printed in the United States of America

HarperPaperbacks and colophon are trademarks of HarperCollins*Publishers*

10 9 8 7 6 5 4 3 2 1

For Patsy
and other kindred spirits

BOOK ONE

1978

There was a ceramic look to the sky, as if it had been baked in an oven, unbroken solid blue save for the huge orange globe of the afternoon sun. Beneath the villa, the sea shone like polished glass, flat and still, without a discernible ripple. The air was listless, undisturbed by a breeze. In a world which slumbered in heat, even the cicadas were momentarily silent. On the terrace the pink marble paving was hot enough to blister bare feet.

In contrast, the room was refreshingly cool. Outside, searing white sunlight threw every line into stark relief, whereas there was shade in the room, even shadow.

Alone in the room, Tom threaded the ten-millimeter film into the projector. Depressing the switch, he watched the lurid images flicker to life. Two figures appeared on the screen, a girl with tawny Polynesian skin and a man who sat watching her, shielding his eyes from the sun. Both were almost naked; the man had a bath towel over his lap and the girl wore only the bottom half of a bikini. Yet it was not their near-nudity which drew the eye, but the masks which covered their faces. The girl's was frivolous; papier mâché glittering with diamante, the sort of thing worn at a fancy dress ball. Shaped like a butterfly, it covered only the top half of her face, leaving exposed her dimpled chin and full, pouting red lips. Apertures revealed dark Mediterranean eyes. Like the wisp of cotton over her pelvis, it decorated as much as concealed. Not so the mask worn by the man. His was ugly. Covering his entire head, the black silk clung to his scalp and fell loose to his throat, leaving eyelets and a gash for the mouth. Concealment was total, and with concealment came the whiff of corruption.

Tom braced himself for what was to come. He knew the film by heart. In eight months he had watched every frame a hundred times over. The shock had dulled, but never the pain. Pain and anger were permanent scars. On screen, the girl swayed rhythmically, as if to music. There was no sound track, no audible clue. The only noise was of the film clicking on sprockets as it unwound from one reel to the other.

She was dancing, the girl on the screen. A slow, sensuous dance. Her full breasts swayed in time with her hips. By now she was very close to the hooded man in the chair. He was leaning back with his arm on a table, a wine glass in his left hand. As the girl approached, he raised his drink in a toast. The girl smiled; her lips moved in speech or even in song, Tom was unsure, despite knowing every frame of the film. She threw her head back, laughing. Her pelvis was thrust toward the man in the chair; her hands fondled her breasts in obvious invitation; oil gleamed on her skin. Putting his glass aside, the man reached for her with his left hand. She came into his embrace; she held him in return, clasping the ugly hooded head to her body, shifting her balance to allow him to suckle a breast.

The towel fell away from the man's naked lap, revealing his right hand stroking his erect penis.

Tom closed his eyes. Beads of sweat stood out on his forehead. His hands bunched into fists, unclenched and clenched again. A vein throbbed in his throat. Opening his eyes, he forced himself to watch as the man slid his hand up the girl's thighs and into her crotch. She writhed and rubbed her body against him, one arm over his shoulder, her nails raking his back as he pulled her bikini down over her hips. Tom saw the pale moons of her buttocks. She turned to reveal a thick bush of black pubic hair. Stepping out of the bikini, she parted her legs. The man's arm moved like a piston, his exploring fingers lost from view as they went deep inside her. He tilted back even more, feet to one side of the chair, torso to the other, his penis thrusting upward. The girl stood over him, straddling him. Opening herself with one hand, fondling her breasts with the other, she lowered herself onto him.

Suddenly another figure appeared. A man danced across the picture, naked except for a grotesque mask made of skin and bone. It looked like the head of an animal, with savage, long teeth. Another man appeared, wearing the painted face of a clown, prancing into the picture, masturbating with both hands. The camera drew back revealing yet more figures—four, five, six, all nude and masked, one of them female, a negress squatting like a dog while a man sodomized her.

Tom no longer felt nauseous. Seeing the film the first time had made him ill. But the first time was long past. Disgust, outrage, a sense of betrayal had all gone, leaving only anger and an unquenchable thirst for revenge.

He directed his concentration less at the figures than at the background behind them. It showed the same terrace as was outside now. If he opened the curtains and slid back the glass doors, he could walk across the same pink marble and look down at the same sea. But he remained in his chair; his face clenched in anger, vengeance in his heart, watching the screen, remembering when he had first set foot on that terrace.

He was determined to remain unimpressed, which was far from easy; being driven to the airport at Heathrow by a chauffeured Rolls-Royce was not his usual start to the day. Neither was being flown to the Greek Islands by private jet. When Stanton had telephoned to suggest a meeting, Tom's reaction had been angry. "There's no point, I've resigned," he had said bitterly.

But Stanton had persisted. "Please, Mr. Lambert, I'm only asking for a few hours of your time."

Eventually Tom had succumbed. It was only later, when Stanton's secretary had called to confirm the arrangements, that he discovered where those few hours were to be spent. He had imagined the meeting would be in London.

"Oh no." Stanton's secretary sounded surprised. "Mr. Stanton is expecting you on Kariakos."

"Expecting me *where*?"

"Kariakos. It's an island in the Aegean. The Greek government leased it to Mr. Stanton years ago."

"You've got to be joking!"

"Not at all. Mr. Stanton was quite specific."

He struggled to overcome his surprise. "I can't believe it. I'm expected to go all the way to some Greek island? That's crazy. Why can't he see me in London?"

Stanton's secretary was not easily flustered. Her reply might have been a rebuke except for the tone of her voice. "Mr. Stanton rarely visits London these days," she said pleasantly. "Kariakos is more or less his permanent home. That's in the summer of course. He tends to winter in St. Moritz."

Tom *tended to winter* in St. Pancras and he said so. Well, why not? Stanton was nothing to him. He had no need to impress. He resented Stanton's intrusion. Everything had been fine until Stanton's involvement. He regretted agreeing to meet the man. He should have refused; he *would* have refused if he had the slightest idea of what to do next. As it was, his resignation had come about too abruptly for him to consider the future.

Stanton's secretary was as persuasive as her employer. "It needn't take long," she coaxed. "We could fly you out Tuesday and bring you back Wednesday if you like."

The flight reminded Tom of a James Bond film. Private jets were a new experience; private jets and private journeys, for it was obvious that the flight had been arranged solely for him. The ratio of two pilots to one passenger offended his instincts as an accountant, but there was no denying the comfort of the six-seater cabin. The carpet pile was two inches thick. Polished mahogany clad the interior. The decor was soft and subdued. Two semi-circles of deeply upholstered armchairs faced each other across a low marble table. The effect was of a foyer in an up-market club.

When they were airborne, the junior pilot came back to serve coffee. Earlier, at Heathrow, he had introduced himself as Gregg Richards in an accent that was faintly Australian. He was about Tom's age, twenty-eight, but age was the only similarity. Tom was tall, six feet two, whereas Richards was short enough for Tom to wonder whether cramped cockpits made lack of inches a prerequisite for pilots. And Tom's hair was dark brown, whereas Richards' was fair, with a prematurely receding hairline, made more obvious when he removed his uniform cap. "Would you like something else?" he asked. "Champagne perhaps, or a Scotch and soda?"

Tom shook his head. He replaced *The Financial Times* in the well-stocked magazine rack. For a moment his gaze remained on the newspapers. Most of the British dailies were there, together with the current issues of *Time*, *Newsweek*, *The Economist* and so on. Enough reading for a week, he thought drily, pondering Stanton's policy of no expense spared. "Just coffee," he said, settling back in his seat. "What time do we get there?"

Richards remained standing despite the five unoccupied seats. His manner was cheerfully attentive: polite without being servile. "We touch down in Athens at noon," he said. "I've arranged lunch for you in Piraeus." His smile became apologetic. "Nobody visits Greece for the food, but there's a place I know, run by a guy called Constantin. He'll look after you and I'll be ready with *Helena* by the time you finish."

"Helena?"

"Our flying boat. We keep her at Piraeus."

Until then Tom had imagined they were flying directly to Kariakos. He said so.

Richards shook his head. "Afraid not. There's no airstrip. Kariakos is tiny. Besides, I think Mr. Stanton prefers the island as it is. At one time we suggested a helicopter, but he wasn't interested. He prefers *Helena* or *Aphrodite*."

Tom cocked an eyebrow, "Is *Aphrodite* another plane?"

"Not likely, she's his yacht. You obviously haven't seen her."

Tom shook his head.

"Absolute peach. Eighty-foot. Real oceangoing sloop. Twenty knots and every facility imaginable." Enthusiasm got the better of Richards for a moment, stripping the years away until he looked about nineteen. Then his professionalism reasserted itself. "Kariakos is about an hour's flying time from Piraeus," he explained. "So allowing for your lunch and me to give *Helena* the onceover, we'll be there at about three."

Tom unbent a little. Some of the anger generated by his resignation faded. It was difficult to remain aggressive when confronted by well-mannered efficiency; and there was something positively relaxing about flying in comfort. Luxury was still new to him. Not that he trusted it entirely; it was like good whisky, he decided, very acceptable in moderation. Stanton was obviously intoxicated by it, what with private jets and oceangoing yachts. If Richards intended to kindle envy, he had failed. Tom had an in-built suspicion of self-indulgence and Stanton sounded self-indulgent in the extreme. Not that Tom knew much about him. Nobody did.

Declining cream in his coffee, he tried to draw Richards out, to learn what he could about Stanton. "I've yet to meet him," he said. "What sort of man is he?"

"Unique. There's no one quite like him."

"Oh? In what way?"

Richards had answered without thinking. A flush of embarrassment darkened his face. Reluctant to elaborate, he hemmed and hawed for a moment before saying, "It's just that he's got a different way of looking at life. He's developed a philosophy all his own."

Intrigued, Tom began to press Richards further, but the pilot clearly felt he had spoken out of turn. "You'll meet him for yourself," he said with a faint shrug. "We really don't see much of him. Most of our time is spent ferrying his guests back and forth. People go to Mr. Stanton rather than the other way about."

He clammed up after that and returned to the flight deck, leaving Tom feeling guilty about asking questions. The guilt irritated him. *Dammit, all I wanted was a clue.* Stanton wasn't listed in *Who's Who*; Tom had looked, just as he had asked around without finding anyone who had even met Stanton. He ran a hand through his hair, wondering yet again about Stanton's intentions. The man was going to a great deal of trouble. And expense. Tom shook his head. *It won't do any good, not if he wants me to return to Bolton Automation. Nothing will induce me to go back.*

Bolton Automation had been his whole life until the previous week. Or seven years of his life. Seven years of blood, sweat and tears—and eventual triumph. Without knowing, he had joined the company one step ahead of a receiver. Twenty-one years old and assistant company treasurer. The big break, or so he had thought. Within a week he had realized the company was going bust; within a month he had written his first report on reorganization. The memories came flooding back and with them an overwhelming sense of loss. The wound was still raw.

Even the name had been different in those days. The Bolton Typewriter Company Ltd: Britain's foremost manufacturer of typewriters and office machines. It actually said that on the stationery. Garbage. Everything was years out of date and falling farther behind. Profits had been made after the war—but only until German industry got going again. In the tire tracks of the first Volkswagen had come typewriters and everything needed for an office. All better than anything Bolton produced. Then came the Americans, with IBM leading the charge. Tom had worn himself out. On the factory floor they joked—"He gets everywhere—like a rash." It was no joke to Tom. He had poured his life's blood into the business.

Development engineers had been coaxed to produce better looking, more functional machines, and a wider range of machines—typewriters, adding machines, calculators . . .

Thinking about the past soured his mood. A frown creased his face as he remembered months spent on the factory floor, weeks spent persuading dealers to stock Bolton machines, endless meetings designed to turn loss into profit . . . only for the company to be sold over his head! Anger welled inside him.

The owners had sold Bolton to Excel Machines. Tom had not been consulted. The first he knew was when two of Excel's people turned up at his office. Boiling with temper, he had resigned on the spot. Stanton had called him the next day. Until then Tom had imagined Excel was owned by Sir Bernard Edwards. Edwards was chairman; Edwards was always writing pompous letters to *The Times*; Edwards conveyed an aura of ownership. "Actually no," Stanton had said on the phone, "my father founded the company and I've always maintained a controlling interest." That much was true, as Tom found out when he checked the files at Companies House. But who was Stanton? The man maintained a small suite of offices in Jermyn Street, but the secretary who worked there was discretion personified. "Mr. Stanton has various business interests in Europe," she said and no amount of coaxing would persuade her to reveal more. Tom had ferreted around. Excel had been founded in 1880, from which it was reasonable to assume that the father was long dead and the son was at least middle-aged. But beyond that Tom's ferreting had yielded nothing.

A yacht! Stanton owns a yacht. A real oceangoing sloop. And a Greek island. Shaking his head, Tom tried to imagine the sort of man he would meet. Onassis, the Greek shipping tycoon, came to mind. He owned a yacht and a Greek island. But Onassis lived in the glare of publicity, whereas Tom had never seen so much as a newspaper paragraph about Stanton.

Dismissing the man from his mind, Tom turned his thoughts to the future. He had to get going again. So why waste time with this meeting? He grew impatient to get it over and done with. *Tell Stanton what I think of him and get back to London.* Start from scratch, he told himself firmly, and was fidgeting in his seat by the time the aircraft began to descend over Athens.

He peered through the window and watched the ground come up to meet them. His only previous travels abroad had been three trips to Paris on business. He'd enjoyed them, except that, although different, Paris still shared the same climate as London; rain had fallen steadily during each of his visits. As the aircraft swept down over Athens, his biggest surprise was the light. Not the sunshine, he had expected sunshine, but the sheer quality of light was unlike even the sunniest day in northern Europe. The air was so clear that it sparkled. Sunshine glinted on a mosaic of rooftops, with every line of architecture etched clear. White stonework of centuries-old buildings dazzled. Despite himself, he was impressed. "Nothing to do with Stanton," he grumbled, resolving to remain unimpressed by anything connected with Stanton.

His gaze raked the airport as the ground rushed past. He stared out with curious eyes. He knew little of Greece, either ancient or modern. Absorbed by his work, he paid scant attention to politics even in Britain. But he did read the papers; enough to know that a military coup had taken place in Greece some time before. Three middle-ranking army officers had seized power. Vaguely he wondered what it was like to live under a military dictatorship. He remembered Stanton's secretary talking about Kariakos—"The Greek government leased it to him years ago." *Years ago* would be before the Colonels seized power. Yet Stanton was still there . . .

When the aircraft taxied to a halt, Richards returned, followed a moment later by Masters, the Captain. Older, and an inch or so taller than Richards, he was a similar type—another competent man whose polite manner did nothing to conceal his confident professionalism. Assessing the pair of them, Tom guessed they worked for Stanton because he paid well and it suited them, not because they lacked options elsewhere.

While Richards busied himself opening doors and lowering steps to the ground, Masters explained that he would remain at the airport. "Gregg will take you over to Piraeus and fly you on to Kariakos," he said, adding a shrug of apology, "I'm afraid you'll find *Helena* a bit noisy, but she's a reliable old girl. You'll get a good view of the islands, Mr. Lambert."

"Thank you, and thanks for a smooth flight."

The compliment was scarcely out of Tom's mouth when a thought occurred to him. "Will you be flying me back to London tomorrow?"

Surprise flickered in Masters' eyes, only momentarily, but the startled look was unmistakable. He was quick to recover. "We'll fly whenever you're ready, Mr. Lambert." His smile broadened into a grin. The expression was warm and friendly, but not enough to make Tom change his mind. He was quite sure that Masters had been unaware of his intention to return so quickly. Tom stared. He remembered Stanton's secretary saying, "We'll fly you out Tuesday and bring you back Wednesday if you like." It so happened that he did like. The meeting had been Stanton's idea, not his. He was keeping his end of the bargain, but the *few hours* had already been stretched. His priority was to get back to London. He had a living to earn.

"Until tomorrow then," he said, turning to follow Richards out of the aircraft.

Masters nodded amiably, but there was no telling whether the nod meant agreement or merely farewell.

Heat engulfed Tom as he stepped out of the Learjet. At the

foot of the steps, blistering tarmac burned the soles of his shoes. His shirt collar tightened and his gray worsted suit doubled in weight. Ahead of him the pilot walked over to a jeep parked at the edge of the apron. Grinning cheerfully, he swung Tom's overnight bag onto the back seat. "Don't worry, Mr. Lambert. There's never any shade in an airport. Hop in. We'll soon have you in more comfortable surroundings."

Tom levered his lanky frame into the passenger seat and Richards started the engine. As they moved off, Tom looked about him. A heat haze shimmered over the ground. He squinted at distorted images. The Lear had taxied a long way from the main terminus. The big commercial jets with their distinctive liveries were well away to the far side, surrounded by baggage trailers and red fueling tankers, looking like large toys attended by Lilliputian figures. Beyond them were various reception buildings, to which Tom assumed they were going. He was surprised when Richards turned off and drove in the opposite direction. They followed a service road parallel to the perimeter fence. The road surface was uneven and the jeep bumped from one pothole to another, making for an uncomfortable ride. Tom clung to the dashboard as they bucked and bounced for two hundred yards. Then they turned left into a small exit bay. A red and white striped barrier barred the way, spanning the road, to one side of which stood a single-story prefabricated building. Richards slowed to a crawl and put his hand on the horn. A door opened immediately. A man wearing an open-necked shirt emerged, quickly followed by a uniformed soldier with a carbine slung over one shoulder. As soon as they saw Richards, recognition shone in their faces. The soldier gave a mock salute, while the man in the white shirt hastened to raise the barrier, shouting a greeting to Richards as he did so. Richards responded with a word and a wave, and the next moment they were on the road into Athens. Silently Tom marveled at how easy it was—no passport control, no customs check, no jostling crowds—a convincing endorsement of the rich way to travel.

He absorbed little of Athens. All that culture was wasted—the Acropolis, the Parthenon, names vaguely remembered from history lessons as a kid. His impressions were of sun-drenched streets crowded with people; white shirts, dark glasses, bare, brown arms; traffic and noise, hustle, bustle—and troops—far more soldiers than ever seen on the streets in England.

Richards drove casually, steering with one hand while gesticulating with the other, pointing out landmarks with the cheerfulness of a tour guide. Perversely Tom's thoughts were elsewhere, still occupied by the look on Masters' face when they had talked about returning to London. It had been news to Masters, Tom was sure of that. What was more, his guess was that Masters already *knew* where he was flying the next day—and it wasn't to London. The suspicion irritated Tom, even though to return quickly was hardly of vital importance. He had no appointments, nothing planned; but he disliked people who broke their word. A deal was a deal, or it should be. Stanton's secretary had promised, and Tom expected the arrangement to be honored.

Piraeus turned out to be the port of Athens, with a dockside crowded with trucks and vans. Overhead derricks swung bulging cargo nets down to waiting stevedores who spilled into the road interrupting the traffic. Crates were piled high; the air was full of street cries and noise. Richards slowed to circumvent bollards and hawsers. As they lurched forward, Tom shouted his questions. Did Stanton own other aircraft or employ other pilots? Richards cocked an ear, shaking his head. "Nope, only me and Doug Masters." His sideways glance was quizzical. "No complaints, I hope?"

"None. I was just thinking about my flight home."

If he hoped for a revealing reply, he was disappointed. Richards managed to avoid any answer at all. Instead, craning his neck to see around the truck dawdling in front, he slammed into first gear and pulled out on the crown of the road. Further conversation was impossible. They progressed amidst blaring horns and threatening gestures, all of which Richards met with a good natured grin. And so it was for the next twenty minutes as they lurched up from the waterfront into a warren of back streets.

Using one hand to shield his eyes from the sunlight slanting down between buildings, Tom clung with his other to the door of the jeep. They passed a dozen tavernas with tables set out over the cobbles, several old churches, a man leading a donkey seemingly oblivious to the motorized traffic. Few tourists populated the pavement, instead the people were locals, mostly women and most of them elderly, their heads hidden beneath black shawls; soberly clad, sharp of eye and wizened of face. Another newcomer might have reveled in the *foreignness* of it, but Tom Lambert had a limited appetite for such things. The tingle of curiosity experienced in Athens was already fading. Like businessmen the world over, he worried about time and how quickly it passed. For years he had raced the clock; shaving production schedules, cutting delivery dates, pressing debtors to pay faster, delaying creditors by a few days. Time was a scarce commodity not to be squandered; even now, with Bolton Automation taken out of his hands, the habit to live by the clock was ingrained.

"Here we are," Richards shouted, as the jeep swung into a side street even narrower than the last. Tom was still looking at the old stone walls, pockmarked by age and graffiti, when the vehicle bumped to a halt on the pavement. Jamming his cap on his head, Richards leapt down, pausing only to grab Tom's carrying case from the back seat. "Daren't leave that. The thieving buggers will have the wheels if I'm more than five minutes. Come on, Mr. Lambert."

Tom followed, across the pavement and through a curtain of beads screening an open door. Inside was a cavernous room set out as a taverna with a dozen white-clothed tables on a stone floor. Light streamed in from a raised balcony at the far end. Overhead a large antique fan wafted air from one side of the room to the other. Only one table was occupied, by three men who looked up with startled expressions. The youngest rose to his feet when he saw Richards, but his companions pulled him back into his chair. Standing at the table, a young woman, dark-haired, olive-skinned, slim and pretty, paused in her task of pouring wine from a flask, her eyes narrowing with suspicion. To her left was a bar, at which stood one of the biggest men Tom had ever seen.

"Constantin," Richards greeted him noisily, swinging the overnight bag to his left hand in order to shake hands.

The big man's surprise gave way to a friendly grin. "Eh! Gregg!"

Seeing the stains of sweat on the back of the pilot's uniform Tom guessed his own clothes to be similarly soiled. He relished the cool air after the heat and dust of the roads. He stood back until Richards introduced him. Then his hand was gripped in a vise. "Welcome," beamed Constantin, "welcome to Piraeus."

The Greek had the girth of a Japanese wrestler. The blue apron around his waist could have served as a bedsheet. His white open-necked shirt must have been specially made. A giant of a man, as tall as Tom but three times as broad. His throat was as thick as a tree trunk. Fleshy of face and heavily jowled, black hair flecked with gray, he had bushy eyebrows above button eyes bright with intelligence. A gold medallion hanging from his neck tangled with the hairs of his chest. His lips parted in a smile as he released Tom's hand and turned back to Richards. "My friend, I confess I forgot you were coming—"

"Don't tell me," Richards groaned, "too busy putting the world to rights. Well, we're here now. You're to give the Kyrios Lambert a good lunch. Is that understood?"

"But of course—"

"Can't stop," Richards interrupted. He handed Tom's bag to the Greek. "Look after that and take care of our guest, eh?" He grinned at Tom. "I'll be about an hour, maybe a bit longer. Okay?"

"Fine," said Tom as the pilot turned on his heel.

Constantin put the bag behind the bar before taking Tom's arm. "Come, let me show you your table." Ignoring the curious stares of his other customers, he led the way up the short flight of steps to the balcony. "For you," he said proudly, "the best seat in the house."

The balcony commanded a breathtaking view. Peering over the balustrade, Tom felt as if the whole of Piraeus lay at his feet. He saw the waterfront and churches they had passed, and he half-recognized other buildings. "And over there," Constantin pointed, "is Passalimani." Turning, Tom saw another bay, occupied by hundreds of yachts. "There," said the Greek, pushing his shoulder close so that Tom could sight along his arm, "see?"

And Tom saw the seaplane, moored in the bay. For some reason he had expected the machine to be gray. Instead, *Helena* was painted bright orange, a vivid yellowy-red on shimmering blue water.

Constantin laughed, "What is the expression? Your carriage awaits? But first you must eat, eh? Up here you will be undisturbed, so please make yourself comfortable. The balcony suits you, eh?"

Tom looked around. The balcony was oblong in shape, about thirty feet by fifteen, covered by an awning woven from reeds. A vine climbed the inside wall, stretching leafy tentacles overhead, coloring sunlight golden-green as it filtered through the pale ripening grapes. Red geraniums overflowed from pots on the floor while purple bougainvillea decorated the balustrade. A cool breeze from the sea tugged one corner of the white cloth on the table.

"This is fine," Tom smiled, looking at the girl who had followed them. She was standing behind a chair at the head of the table. Catching his eye she responded with a shy smile before pulling back the chair, scraping its feet across the stone floor. Tom thanked her and sat down, while Constantin picked up an earthenware jug and poured wine into two glasses. He raised one in a toast, "Good health, Mr. Lambert. May your visit to Kariakos be happy and successful."

Following Constantin's example, Tom drank deeply, his attention caught by the reference to Kariakos more than the glass in his hand. It was only when he swallowed that he choked on the taste.

Constantin laughed. "Like turpentine, eh? Don't worry. It's retsina. Our vines grow alongside pine trees, the resin from the pines flavors the grapes." He shrugged. "You'll soon acquire the taste, believe me. Have some more, see if I'm right."

Smiling with abundant good humor, he refilled Tom's glass before returning to the bar. Once there, he exchanged a few words with his other customers. Tom had been aware of their interest. Ever since he had arrived they had watched with a curiosity which verged on suspicion. As soon as Constantin returned they plagued him with questions. Constantin replied in rapid Greek. Tom deciphered the word *Inglezos* followed a little later by *Stanton.* One of the men laughed and threw a furtive look toward the balcony. After which they turned their backs on him, resuming their meal, leaving him in a solitary state.

The girl served him, flitting back and forth from the kitchen. Her bare feet made small rustling noises on the stone floor. At some point, after the *taramasalata,* while she was serving the *pastitsio,* he tried to engage her in conversation, but she conveyed her lack of English with a blank look and a shrug, adding a small smile in case he was offended. He responded with a reassuring smile of his own and resumed his meal. More hungry than he had realized, the food good enough for him to overlook its strange flavoring. Besides, he remained preoccupied with thoughts of his future. He was sure of one thing. What he had done at Bolton Automation, he could do again. Take a down-and-out business, build it up, turn it into a success. All he had to do was find an ailing company, buy it for next to nothing, and get to work. The *next to nothing* was important. He had limited capital; his flat in London, his car, a few hundred in the bank. Even so, other men had started with less. . . .

Across the bay, *Helena* was moving, only a few yards, but definitely moving. Tom's interest sharpened. Straining his ears, he could hear the engines above the distant hum of traffic from Piraeus.

Constantin came up from the bar. "Ah! Won't be long now. He's testing the engines." For a moment they both watched the seaplane across the bay. Then Constantin looked at Tom's empty plate. "You enjoy? Good, eh?"

"Fine."

"And the retsina?" Constantin picked up the jug which was practically empty. "Ah!" He laughed as he poured the dregs into his glass. "You *did* get the taste for it." Turning away, he returned to the bar. Tom watched him collect another jug and start back. The three men were still at their table, talking earnestly. No more customers had arrived. The other tables remained empty. Even the girl was absent. Gone off duty, Tom thought, wondering about the slack trade. He allowed Constantin to refill his glass.

"Cheers," he said, "you're not very busy today?"

"Who is?" The Greek pulled a face, "The Colonels perhaps. Nobody else." He scowled as he filled his own glass, then cocked a questioning eyebrow. "Your first time in Greece?"

Tom nodded.

"I thought so. You come to a troubled land, Mr. Lambert." He drank deeply, giving Tom an uncertain look, as if trying to make up his mind. Then he said, "I will tell you my history. By profession I am a lawyer. By politics I am a Democrat. By inclination I am an honest man. On these three counts I am disqualified from following my profession. The Colonels gave me an ultimatum. Not in so many words, but . . ." He shrugged. "I got the message. Close my office in Athens or get out of Greece. I was given no choice in the matter."

Tom stared, unsure of how to respond.

Constantin continued with a wry smile, "So I opened a taverna in Piraeus. The problem is some people are frightened to come." He looked sadly at the empty tables for a moment, but the wry smile was quick to return. "It is better in the evenings. Many more customers. Darkness gives them courage, eh? There is plenty of good talk, lots of ideas, much boasting, much drinking." His good humour returned. "What's so different?" he concluded. "We saw off the Turks, we'll see off the Colonels."

The revelation was so unexpected that Tom was at a loss.

The Greek laughed. "Don't look so solemn. Eh, I'll tell you a Greek joke. A man on a crowded bus taps his neighbor on the shoulder. 'Excuse me, sir, but do you happen to be in the army?' 'No.' 'Perhaps you have a brother in the army?' 'No.' 'Or a son?' 'No.' 'Then in that case, sir, would you get off my foot!' "

Constantin threw his head back and laughed so hard that the gold medallion bounced on his chest. He slapped his thigh with a meaty hand. The three men looked up from their table, eager to share the joke. Tom laughed too, while at the same time thinking that such a joke would have no meaning in England.

His good humor restored, Constantin looked across the bay to Passalimani. *Helena* had returned to her mooring. Her engines were quiet. The big Greek sipped from his glass. "Not long now, Mr. Lambert. Soon you'll be on your way to meet your great English lord."

Tom was puzzled until he realized the reference was to Stanton. Smiling, he shook his head. "Stanton's not an English lord."

"Then he should be," Constantin said emphatically. "How can a man who lives like a king not be a lord?"

"Does he live like a king?"

"He fucks like a king. One beautiful girl after another. Sometimes two in a day. How else would a king live?"

Tom stared, suspecting a joke. Humor lit Constantin's eyes, but his expression was serious. Tom said, "You must have the wrong man. I'm going to see a man called Stanton."

"Of course! On Kariakos. The great Kyrios Stanton."

Tom had spent days trying to find out about Stanton. Nobody knew the first thing about him. At different times, Tom had imagined him as a recluse, a miser counting his gold, an elderly man, an invalid perhaps? According to Richards, Stanton was some kind of philosopher. And now this?

"It can't be the same man. I don't know much about him, but he must be about fifty—"

"So? You think all desire stops at fifty?"

Tom stared.

"Besides, you're wrong. He's older. Over sixty."

"Do you actually *know* Stanton?"

Before Constantin could reply, a cry came from the entrance. The girl rushed in from the street. She gabbled breathlessly to the three men, all of whom leapt to their feet. Kicking his chair back, the youngest ran to the balcony, calling the others. Alarm showed in their faces. One of them started for the bead curtain. The girl shrieked a warning. Clutching his arm, she pulled him to a halt. He turned hunted eyes toward Constantin. The big Greek shouted and pointed to the balcony. The first man was already over the balustrade, hanging by his fingertips before dropping from sight. Tom gasped and looked over the edge, aware of the second man at his shoulder. Looking down, Tom saw a narrow alley about twelve feet below. The first man was rising to his knees, hugging his elbow. The second man dropped.

Constantin was pushing the last man to the edge. Older than the others, gray-haired, the man was visibly shaking. Shouting, Constantin put one leg over the stonework while lifting the man off his feet, forcing him backward until he hung in thin air, held only by Constantin's outstretched hand. Gripping the balustrade with his other hand, the big Greek swung his entire body over the edge, lowering the frightened man toward his companions. One of them grabbed a dangling foot. They shouted. Constantin released his burden and heaved himself back up to the balcony. A groan came from below. Tom looked down. Half supporting, half dragging their limping companion, the men scuttled up the alley and around the first corner.

From the street came the sound of vehicles drawing to a halt. Doors slammed. Heavy boots clattered over cobbles. Constantin's eyes raked the taverna. The girl had already cleared the dishes used by the men. Quickly, with deft movements, she straightened the cloth and repositioned the chairs.

"What the hell?" Tom exclaimed.

Constantin hissed, "Keep your nerve, Englishman." Hurriedly he refilled their glasses. Then, to Tom's astonishment, he laughed as uproariously as when telling his joke earlier. He looked the perfect host, entertaining a guest, with a glass raised to his lips, relaxed and full of good humor. Suddenly the bead curtains were ripped apart. Soldiers ran in, carbines at the ready. Two in front continued the length of the taverna, stopping only at the balcony steps, pointing their guns at Constantin. Another soldier ran into the kitchen, two more remaining at the entrance . . .

The bead curtains parted again. Another uniformed man stepped across the threshold. Shorter than the others, he wore badges of rank on his cap. He stopped and stood there, surveying the scene.

Tom met the man's eyes; deep-set, dark, arrogant, accustomed to command. A thin-faced man with a cruel expression.

Boots clattering on the stone floor brought the soldier back from the kitchen, shaking his head. Simultaneously the girl began to mount the steps to the balcony, seeking Constantin's bulky protection. Suddenly the nearest soldier grabbed her, knocking her off balance. She stumbled and fell.

"Hey!" Tom was out of his seat without thinking.

The soldier swung around, pointing his gun.

There was no going back. Tom's mouth went dry. A voice began screaming in his head—*What are you doing? You'll get yourself shot!* But he was down the steps by then, on one knee next to the girl, helping her up for Constantin to lead, dazed, to a chair.

The officer advanced from the entrance. He spoke sharply in Greek. Constantin erupted with a torrent of words. Tom straightened up. The officer tugged his pistol from its holster. He pointed it at Tom, sighting along the barrel. In Tom's head the voice stopped screaming. Instead, terse and insistent, it shouted—*Stare him out. Stay calm. Don't show a flicker of fear.* The officer's cold eyes were unblinking. Constantin gabbled on, sounding indignant. Tom deciphered *Inglezos* and *Stanton*, followed later by *Kariakos*. Surprise showed in the officer's eyes; then a glimmer of doubt. He lowered the pistol and stepped back, his hostile gaze still directed at Tom.

Tom met the look without flinching. His pulse rate slowed to normal. Judging the moment, he shrugged and climbed the four steps back to his chair.

In perfect English, the officer asked, "What is your name?"

"Lambert," Tom answered, sitting down.

The officer slid the pistol back into its holster. When he spoke, his voice was still sharp. "You are a friend of the Kyrios Stanton?"

"I'm on my way to see him," said Tom, reaching across the table for his cigarettes.

The officer turned to Constantin. He questioned him in Greek, as aggressive as ever. Constantin shrugged. His reply was indignant, the aggrieved tones of the falsely accused. He waved a hand around the taverna, becoming excited, even angry. The officer sneered disbelief.

Tom sensed the accusations and Constantin's rebuttal.

"Enough!" The officer suddenly reverted to English as he held up a hand. "How long have you been here?" he asked Tom.

Tom glanced at his watch. "About an hour."

"Waiting for the Kyrios Stanton's pilot? Is that right?"

Tom nodded.

"Who else was here?"

Tom resisted the urge to look at Constantin. Even a sideways glance would have revealed too much. The girl was no help. She sat across the table, head bowed, eyes averted, still frightened. The voice in Tom's head asked—*What the hell have you got into? These people are nothing to you. Why should you lie?*

"Well?" the officer demanded.

Tom made up his mind. He laughed, "I was just asking this guy how he makes a living." He used the excuse to look at Constantin. The Greek responded with a blank expression. Not a muscle moved in his face. Yet deep in his eyes was a mute look of appeal. Turning back to the officer, Tom scratched his head. "I mean, you'd think there'd be lots of customers in a place like this. The food's good—"

"Was anyone *here*?"

"That's what I'm saying. Take this balcony. Look at the view. Yet I'm here by myself—"

"No other customers?"

"Exactly," Tom agreed cheerfully. Inwardly he was less cheerful; the voice was warning—*Stick to that. I was the only customer on the balcony. You can always pretend a misunderstanding* . . .

The officer embraced the whole taverna with a wave of his arm. "No other customers? All the time that you were here?"

The bastard's onto you. Careful.

The officer bristled. "Were you the only customer?"

He doesn't know. He's not sure. There's no evidence. . . . The girl dealt with the evidence . . .

"Well? Were you?"

"For Christ's sake, what is this? Stanton never told me about any of this. What's going on in this country? I'm sitting here, having lunch, enjoying the view when your bloody storm-troopers come busting in like there's a war on . . ." Once launched, he found it easy to simulate outrage. It was an outlet for fear. Fear made him contemptuous of himself, angry with

Stanton for dragging him across Europe, furious about being drawn into something that was none of his business.

The officer shuffled his feet. He continued to stare, but his indecision was obvious. Tom could guess why. The reference to Stanton had saved the situation. *Without that,* Tom thought, *I'd be out of here at the point of a gun. He's seething, but trying hard not to show it.*

With an effort the officer brought his temper under control. Finally he scowled. "Very well, Mr. Lambert. Perhaps we'll meet again under different circumstances."

"I doubt it. I'm going back to London tomorrow."

"Perhaps that's for the best," the officer said spitefully, salvaging what he could from the confrontation. He took a long look at the girl, who bowed her head to avoid his gaze. Raising a hand, he gestured to his men to withdraw. As he turned to follow, he paused to point an accusing finger at Constantin. "You," he said in English, "will *definitely* meet me again."

They watched him walk to the entrance and disappear through the bead curtains. Tom felt drained. Constantin was the first to recover, hurrying off in the soldiers' footsteps. From outside came the sounds of engines starting, gears engaging. Tom glanced at his watch, astonished that only ten minutes had passed since the girl had run back into the taverna. Ten minutes . . .

The big Greek returned, full of smiles. "They've gone—"

Tom's relief turned to anger. "What the bloody hell was that about?"

Ignoring the question, Constantin beamed. "You've a strong nerve, Englishman."

"Cut the bullshit! You owe me an explanation—"

The girl interrupted, talking urgently to Constantin while casting looks at Tom. Constantin leaned forward and whispered in her ear. Listening intently, she formed a word on her lips as if in practice. Then she turned to face Tom. "Thank you," she said in careful English, "thank you, Mr. Lambert."

The sentiments were so obviously heartfelt that Tom checked his harsh words. Constantin said, "You saved her brother's life. Those pigs would have killed him. Another political murder. We are in your debt."

When Tom opened his mouth, the words dried on his lips. The magnitude of saving a life, the girl's gratitude, left him with nothing to say.

Constantin was removing the medallion from around his neck. "I think you will come often to Greece from now on. Here, take this."

Tom was astonished. "I can't do that. It's very good of you, but I'll be back in London tomorrow. I've no plans in Greece. I'm seeing Stanton this once, that's all—"

"Please. You will come back. I feel it. And some day you may need friends."

"It's unnecessary. Really. I'm a businessman, an accountant. I know nothing of your politics—"

"And nothing of friendship?" Constantin looked reproachful.

Tom wanted to say it was stupid. He wanted to say they were acting like characters in an old-fashioned novel, something by Buchan, pre-war, when Europe was full of spies and dictators . . . He looked from Constantin to the dismay in the girl's eyes. Straining over her words, she repeated, "Thank you, Mr. Lambert, thank you."

Tom tried again, "I appreciate it, really, but—"

"Please." Constantin insisted.

There was no alternative but to accept. "Oh well, if you insist. I mean, it's very good of you. Thank you. Thank you very much."

The girl's face shone with pleasure.

The medallion felt heavy enough to be solid gold. Tom hoped not. A memento was one thing; something of value another. Examining the medallion, he turned it over in his hands. One side was blank. On the other was a line drawing of a man's head, below which were numbers: 469–399 B.C.

"Socrates," Constantin explained.

The girl interrupted, hurrying to the entrance. Outside a vehicle drew to a halt. Alarm showed on Constantin's face, but he relaxed at a word from the girl. "It's only your pilot," he explained, reaching for Tom's hand, closing Tom's fingers over the medallion, "best not to speak of what happened."

Tom allowed his hand to be pushed toward his pocket. It was

almost a reflex action to drop the medallion inside. The next moment the bead curtain parted to admit Gregg Richards looking reassuringly normal. "Sorry I'm late," he said, "took longer than usual. Not too bad though, an hour and a half, could have been worse. Had a good lunch?"

"Er, yes, fine."

"Right, let's go."

Slapping Constantin on the back, Richards collected Tom's bag from behind the bar. The pilot was too preoccupied to notice any lingering tension, too concerned about recovering lost time to sense the strained atmosphere. With a cheerful grin, he hoisted the bag into his hand and hurried back to the entrance.

Constantin and the girl came out to see them off, waving like old friends as the jeep lurched down the road.

"Right," said Richards as cheerful as ever, "next stop Kariakos."

Clutching the dashboard, Tom looked about him as they bumped down the narrow streets. London already seemed a long way away. A different world. . . .

Masters was right about *Helena*. She was noisy. Every nut and bolt in her frame rattled during take-off and the rush across the water was electrifying. Tom wished he had taken a back seat instead of sitting up front with Richards. Not that there were many back seats—only three—and behind them an open void for cargo.

Once airborne the noise diminished, but never enough to permit easy conversation. Tom was glad in a way; having agreed not to mention events at the taverna, the noise restricted possible questions. So he sat staring through the window until, gradually, the soporific effect of sunshine glinting on water, the throb of the engines, and the lunchtime retsina combined to make him feel drowsy. He dozed fitfully, starting awake now and then, to peer through the window at *Helena*'s shadow racing across the blue sea below.

An hour later, he felt a hand on his shoulder. Roused, he saw the pilot grin and jerk his thumb downward. Rubbing his eyes,

Tom sat up and looked through the window. And there was Kariakos. He took his first look at the island. From the air it was tiny, an emerald mound rimmed with occasional silver, rising from an azure blue sea. *Helena* was already low in the sky and dipping lower. By now Tom was wide awake, absorbing every detail. He saw a cluster of white houses huddled together in a small fishing village, with pine-clad hills rising behind. Twisting in his seat he sought a better view, but the aircraft had already swooped past, losing height all the time. He glimpsed another cove, another indentation in the coastline. *Helena* skimmed low over the water. Then the waves came up to meet them, faster and faster, as Richards brought the seaplane down in an unswerving straight line. Spray rose on all sides, falling away as *Helena* knifed through the water, her engines slowing, noise diminishing, still going forward but riding smoothly as she settled onto the surface.

Droplets of water streamed down the outside of the windows, distorting Tom's view. He could just about identify a bay backed by green-covered cliffs. He could see a sliver of sand. The place looked uninhabited, uncultivated, prompting thoughts of the world as it must have been before the advent of man. . . .

Next to him, Richards shut off various controls before unbuckling his seat belt and sitting back with a sigh, "Home Sweet Home," he grinned.

The noise of the engines faded, replaced by the sound of a gentle wind tugging around the cockpit outside.

"Nice landing," said Tom.

"I could put down here in my sleep, I've done it so often."

"I suppose so," Tom nodded, watching the pilot at his work.

Richards paused in the act of tapping a gauge above his head. "Well?" he asked with a sideways glance. "What do you think? Most people go bananas the first time they see Kariakos."

Tom turned back to the window. "Terrific," he said, before adding doubtfully, "but, well, sort of deserted. I feel like Robinson Crusoe."

The pilot laughed.

Suddenly Tom saw a wake of white foam trailing through the water. A speedboat was coming out to meet them. A figure stood at the wheel, steering with the assured confidence of a seasoned sailor. Tom's head swiveled as the tiny craft swept past. He glimpsed a white shirt and blonde flowing hair, saw an arm raised in greeting, then the boat passed beyond his view, going around *Helena* to the other side.

"Who was that?"

Richards remained silent, peering through his window. A look of admiration came over his face.

Tom unbuckled his seat belt and half rose from his seat, craning his neck, but to no avail. When he looked at Richards, expecting an answer, the pilot just sat there shaking his head until eventually a sound halfway between a sigh and a groan escaped his lips. "Jesus. What I wouldn't give . . ." he began softly before changing his mind. "Come on, Robinson Crusoe. Here's your Man Friday." He stood up, ducking his head as he moved back into the aircraft.

Tom watched him unfasten the bolts at the door before sliding it open. A breeze gusted in, bringing with it the smell and sounds of the sea.

In a semi-crouch, Tom collected his bag from the back seat, balancing as *Helena* rose and fell on the swell. Reaching the open door, he clutched the upright to steady himself. Then he looked down. The speedboat had drawn alongside. Looking up at him was a girl. She smiled and called out, "Welcome to Kariakos."

Perhaps it was other sounds—the sea splashing on the floats, gulls crying on the wind, the muted throb of the boat's engine—which gave a musical quality to her voice, or perhaps he simply imagined it. The eyes which met his were more green than blue, the color of the sea on the distant horizon. Her tanned skin bore the bloom of a ripening peach. The breeze tugged her golden hair, prompting her to raise a hand to brush it back from her eyes. She wore her clothes casually, as if she had dressed hurriedly to come out to meet them. Her white shirt was held by only two buttons, offering a tantalizing glimpse of her breasts, and when she stretched across to the aircraft, her lemon skirt parted to reveal a long shapely leg. "Pass your case, Mr. Lambert."

Dutifully he squatted onto his haunches to hand her the bag. Richards said drily, "Enjoy your stay, Mr. Lambert."

"Thanks."

Hurried into saying goodbye, he forgot the arrangements for his flight home. He was concentrating on lowering his foot to the float. The girl made it look easy, straddling the gap to the plane with feline agility. She swung the case into the boat while using her other hand to grip a strut linking the float to the wing. Tom clambered down clumsily, trying to gauge the motion of the boat before committing himself, only to land awkwardly.

"Okay?" she asked, putting a concerned hand on his arm.

He almost embraced her in his effort to balance. Close up she was enchanting. Her high cheekboned face was perfectly sculptured. A small mole decorated her left cheek.

"Hello," she smiled. "I am called Melody."

He wondered who she was. Did Stanton have a daughter? But Stanton was English and the girl's speech betrayed a slight accent. And her choice of words was unusual—*I am called Melody* instead of *My name is Melody.*

"Tom Lambert," he said, trying to shake hands while retaining his balance.

She laughed, "It is easier to say how do you do on dry land. Why not sit down?"

Defeated by the motion of the boat, he subsided onto the bench seat. Quickly he pushed his case aside to make room for the girl, but she remained on her feet and turned back to the dashboard, her left hand moving down to the throttle. The engine responded immediately, sending a tremor of vibration through the boat. With a farewell wave to Richards, she swung the small craft away from the seaplane. She steered standing up, head and shoulders above the windscreen, perfectly balanced, brushing the wheel with her pelvis. The wind tore her hair, streaming long golden strands over her shoulders. Water slapped the underside of the boat as it gathered speed. Spray burst over the prow. The girl seemed in her element. Behind her, he admired her trim waist, her long legs and bare feet. . . .

He was distracted by the shoreline, coming ever closer. The hundred yards gap was soon cut to fifty. He saw a villa perched on the cliff top. A sliver of white sand formed a narrow beach. Around the villa, spires of Mediterranean pines reached up to the sky. There was a total absence of people; nobody sunbathed on the beach or waited to greet them. The place looked deserted: isolated and remote. The small fishing village seen from the air was around the next cove and quite out of sight. The motion of the boat made focusing difficult. Squinting, shielding his eyes from the sun, he saw a white-painted jetty jutting out into the sea, with another boat tied alongside. Above the jetty, steps zig-zagged up to the villa, which was long and low, gleaming pink and white in the afternoon light, with a balustrade running the full length. A solitary building, as aloof as a castle.

The boat was already beginning to slow. The girl eased the throttle. Their speed fell away. Instead of rushing past, water began to lap both sides of the boat. They drifted in, bumping gently against the jetty. Cutting the engine, the girl leapt ashore, carrying one end of a painter. Once again Tom glimpsed long brown legs as they flashed from the skirt; half saw her breasts as she looped the rope over a bollard. Straightening, brushing her hair from her eyes, she gave him a faint smile before pulling the stern of the boat into the jetty. It was all done before he could raise a finger to help. The boat was tied up fore and aft, and the girl was standing there, hands on hips, appraising him with her unusual green eyes.

Gathering himself, he stood up and threw his bag onto the jetty. "Very professional," he said ruefully, clambering ashore, "did you serve in the Navy?"

"I grew up in a boat." She smiled, proffering her hand. "Now I can say how do you do properly, Mr. Lambert. Welcome to Kariakos."

She was tall, about five feet seven in bare feet. And perfectly built.

"Thank you. Did I catch your name right? Melody?"

"I'm Melody here on Kariakos."

Part of his mind puzzled about her meaning. Her words suggested that Melody was a temporary name and she used another elsewhere. The other part of his mind was confirming first impressions.

"Beautiful," he said, and then looked about him as if to suggest the compliment was meant for the island. The beach was a hundred yards long; a flat strand of white sand which widened and narrowed. Above, the cliff rose at sixty degrees, home to scrub and gorse at the lower levels, struggling upward in brave imitation of the trees on the skyline. Craning his neck, Tom traced the steps up the cliff face, realizing they were not "steps" at all but ramps which inclined first one way, then another. Here and there a white painted handrail had been erected to provide a safeguard against the drop. In England, with rough seas smashing the shoreline, the drop would have been fearsome. On Kariakos the sea nuzzled the beach and seeped under the jetty with the noise of a cat lapping milk.

The girl said, "Maurice has a siesta every afternoon. He will see you at dinner. If it is agreeable, I will look after you until then."

Tom felt a flicker of irritation, almost of anger—indignant to have come all this way to be told Stanton was having a siesta. The girl softened his temper. The message was aggravating but the messenger was charming. A man could drown in those eyes. She had a wide mouth which puckered at the corners, hinting at a smile even when her ex-pression was serious. He puzzled again about who she was. Would a daughter refer to her father by his Christian name? Some did. Suddenly he remembered Constantin. *"Stanton fucks like a king . . . one beautiful girl after another."* Tom stared, not wanting to believe; he had dismissed Constantin's words at the time. *Hell, Stanton is sixty for God's sake.*

"Also," Melody added, "Maurice thought you might like to relax after your journey."

Tom doubted Stanton had said any such thing. She had seen his irritation and was being diplomatic.

"Why not." He shrugged his acceptance.

A dimple creased her cheek when she smiled. "Then we go?" she said. "The villa is this way."

Walking beside her, Tom felt his heavy shoes dig deep into the sand, while the girl swung along with the grace of an athlete. "You journeyed well?" she asked politely.

Again he was aware of her curious phrasing. Most people would have asked if he'd had a good journey. "Fine," he answered, while reflecting on the lilt in her voice. Melody was a good name for her . . .

By the time they began the climb to the house, the heat was getting to him. The breeze which had made itself felt on the sea, even on the jetty, fell away across the beach. He stopped to remove his jacket.

Her smile was sympathetic. "Not so far now. There's a change of clothes for you up at the villa. And you can swim if you like." Her accent was more noticeable with certain words. Swim had been pronounced svim. The effect was charming.

"A change of clothes?" he echoed. Stanton took care of everything.

"You will be more comfortable, I think," she said, before asking, "you like to svim?"

"Sometimes."

They climbed the zig-zagged incline, pausing at the final bend to look back across the bay. *Helena* was making her take-off run, engines at full blast as she rose from the water. Watching the plane lift into the sky reminded Tom of his return journey, prompting a question, but before he could ask it Melody had set off up the last incline. "Come," she said, "we're nearly there."

When they crested the path, he stopped in his tracks. Stretching before them was a wide terrace, inset with a swimming pool and cascading fountains. The ground floor of the villa was revealed for the first time. What he had seen from the sea was merely the upper story. Below it, interrupted at intervals by wide Moorish arches, the ground floor stretched forty feet to the left and even more to the right. Long and low, the facade was covered by stephanotis at one point and bougainvillea at another, so that, what with the white shutters closed to the sun, the pink stone of the building showed only in patches. Flowers trailed from urns and spilled out of tubs. Set here and there were white marble statues. The overall effect was tranquil and gracious, and outstandingly beautiful.

He stared for almost a minute before realizing that Melody was watching him. She laughed. "Everyone is the same the first time. It took me ages to catch up with my breath."

He smiled, partly at the colloquialism which was so nearly

right, but mostly because her laugh was infectious. Her charm dispelled his earlier irritation. She was so natural, unspoiled by her beauty. The few really good looking women Tom had known had affected an aloofness verging on indifference. They wore beauty like badges of rank; compliments were expected, and received like bored officers taking salutes.

"We go first to your room," she said, grimacing at his shirt, "you can change into more comfortable things."

"Okay," he said, following her across the terrace. Skirting the swimming pool, they passed beneath one of the wide Moorish arches and entered the villa. The marble-floored hall was refreshingly cool, wide and high-ceilinged, and paintings decorated the wall. Flowers brimmed from vases, scenting the air. From somewhere far off came the faint sound of music. The place seemed empty, without housemaids or servants. Even outside, crossing the terrace, Tom had not seen any gardeners tending the flowers. The villa slumbered in the afternoon heat.

Melody led the way up the sweeping staircase. The corridor above was decorated with statues set into illuminated niches. Something about one of them made Tom check his stride. Like the others, it was a female nude, life size, cast in bronze. Sculpture meant little to Tom. The statues which he walked past in London's parks were merely garden furniture. He had never been to a gallery. Vaguely he remembered works of art seen as a kid: statues of Greek goddesses, partially clothed and demure of expression. There was nothing demure about this statue. Totally naked, the model was leaning back against a tree. One arm was raised and bent behind her, so that her head nestled in the crook of the arm. Her wide-eyed look was directed forward, and her provocative smile was one of unmistakable invitation.

He quickened his pace, sneaking sideways looks at the other statues. They were of different girls in different poses, but all conveyed an erotic sensuality. Suddenly it dawned on him that even the paintings downstairs had been more than usually explicit . . .

"We've put you in here," said Melody, opening a pair of double doors. She led the way and he followed across the threshold.

The room was big, square and high-ceilinged. A single feature dominated each aspect. To his left it was the sliding glass doors which led onto a balcony overlooking the sea. The view was interrupted by full length voile curtains. Behind the curtains, the glass doors were partially open, allowing the smell of the sea to waft in on the breeze. To his right was a vast four-poster bed, flanked by Chinese rugs which added patches of color to the pale marble floor. Beyond the bed was a door, half open, through which he could see the tiles of a bathroom; and on the near side stood a dark wardrobe, smelling faintly of polish. But what most drew his eyes was a statue directly ahead—life size, of a man and a woman, naked, making love on a chaise longue.

Vaguely aware of Melody opening the wardrobe he stood stock still, staring at the statue. There were three pieces in all, carved in different materials. The chaise longue was granite, anthracite in color, glittering with polished quartz. The girl was marble and the man was bronze. The figures seemed to move; an impression heightened by the interplay of materials—smooth pink marble for the girl; rough-cast golden bronze for the man. The man devoured her. His head was bent, suckling a breast. His right arm was behind the small of her back; his left hand cupped her right buttock. Muscles rippled across his shoulders as he thrust into her. Responding, the girl twined her legs around his body. Her left arm was over his shoulder. Her head was thrown back, hair falling away from her face, eyes and mouth open.

"I think this will fit," said Melody, holding up a white aertex shirt while gauging the width of Tom's shoulders. "There's more in the cupboard; slacks, shirts, sandals and things."

"Thanks."

Half turning, she waved a hand. "Your bathroom is there."

"Thanks," he repeated, wondering whether to make a reference to the statue; a joke perhaps, but the words in his head were vulgar, not funny.

She smiled, "Would you like to change? Have a shower? I will have drinks ready on the terrace in ten minutes."

"Fine."

Leaving the shirt on the bed, she advanced to the door. As she passed he caught a faint whiff of perfume and glimpsed again the shadowy cleft of her breasts. He was aware of her teasing eyes and the ghost of a smile. Then she was gone, closing the door softly behind her.

He sat down on the bed. His gaze immediately returned to the statues. The figures were hypnotic. Wherever he was in the room, he knew he would be drawn. It was like sharing a room with real people. Even as he looked, the man's arched back seemed to move. The girl's cry of pleasure could almost be heard. The effect was disturbing, erotic. "Christ, this Stanton must be really something."

The thought remained as he showered and put on fresh clothes. He had been asking questions for days. What was Stanton like? Why had he asked for this meeting? The girl had said, *Maurice will see you at dinner. If it is agreeable, I will look after you until then.*

"Look after me how?"

He stared at his reflection in the mirror. The borrowed shirt and white linen trousers fitted perfectly. *How did he know my size?*

Frowning, he fastened his watch. Mysteries irritated him. He hated to be outguessed. Business was all about outguessing the other guy.

Leaving the room, he walked down the corridor, re-examining the statues as he went. The villa remained hushed and sleepy. Without Melody, he felt free to peer and stare. Closer inspection was reassuring. Not all of the statues were erotic. Several were abstract, granite shapes with holes in the middle, reminding him of Henry Moore, the only sculptor he knew. And some of the paintings were impressionistic; great splashes of color which must have meant something to the artist but which conveyed nothing to him.

For some reason, he felt reassured about Stanton. After all, it was art. It was not unusual for a wealthy man to collect art. And yet . . . the underlying eroticism persisted . . . conveyed by a combination of things; the musky scent, the soft lighting, seductive far away music, and mingling in and out of the abstracts the parade of nudes in one inviting pose after another. He met the frankest of all at the foot of the stairs. On the way up, intent on following Melody, he had walked past it. On the way down he almost walked into it, or into them, for there were two; life size, a man in bronze and an ebony negress. Both were naked. The man was standing and the negress was kneeling between his legs. Cupping his balls in her right hand, her left hand was at the base of his cock, half of which was in her mouth. Her upturned eyes were met by an answering look in which passion and tenderness were inextricably mixed. The look spoke volumes, establishing a rapport of pleasure given and pleasure received which transcended everything else. The plinth below bore the single word—*Fellatio.*

Tom stared. Bloody hell, since when was a blow job a work of art? Then he laughed, remembering using those exact words to thank a girl in his past.

She was waiting on the far side of the terrace, looking out over the balustrade. Her back was to him as he emerged from the archway. Next to her a couple of sun-chairs had been arranged beneath a big orange shade. A small white cabinet stood between the chairs. She turned as he approached, her green eyes inspecting his choice of clothes. "You have decided not to svim, I think, Mr. Lambert?"

"I'd rather talk to you. Didn't you promise to look after me until dinner?"

Her smile widened. Her poise was flawless. "I promised you a drink. What would you like?"

The white cabinet was a small refrigerated bar. They sat beneath the sunshade and sipped iced lemonade made from freshly squeezed lemons.

Seizing the role of interrogator, Tom took charge of the conversation. He admired the swimming pool and the villa. He commented on the flowers and the blue sky. He said how different everything was from the London he had left only eight hours before. Polite small talk paved the way for more personal questions and gave him a chance to study her reactions. They pleased him. She responded to apparently idle chatter with enchanting candor; so much so that by the end of half an hour he was preparing to steer the conversation into more personal channels. He was stopped by the appearance of other people on the terrace. First came two men dressed in work clothes, carrying tables and chairs. Then three women, their arms full of white linen. Seeing them, Melody explained, "They get ready for your dinner tonight."

"*My* dinner?"

She smiled and instead of offering further explanation, asked if he would like to see the grounds. "You will like it better, I think. There is more cool under the trees."

There was too, even though their stroll involved a gentle climb around the villa and then up above it. Bushes of herbs flanked the path, and the scent of thyme and rosemary mingled with the pine trees to fill the air with a singular freshness.

Tom began to probe. "I know very little of Mr. Stanton," he said carefully. "You wouldn't be his daughter by any chance?"

Her laughter was reminiscent of her name; careless and happy with a music all of its own. "No, not his daughter. Just his friend."

The sea was visible through a break in the trees and they paused to admire the view. Sunlight and shade dappled Melody's face, accentuating the shadowy indentations of her mouth as it puckered at the corners. Above them, her green eyes shone with amusement. "Come," she said. "We go a bit further. The view is even more good. You will see."

He was about to follow her when a lizard flashed up a tree, making him jump. "God! Did you see that?"

She laughed. "They don't bite, Mr. Lambert. Nothing on this island can hurt you."

He looked at her, suspecting a hidden meaning before deciding that it was another example of her curious phrasing. Her clear eyes were completely without guile. They walked on for another thirty yards. The path twisted and turned until it crested a rise and entered a clearing. "See?" Melody turned with a smile. "Look."

The land ended a few yards ahead. The cliff fell away. Below them, the sea was a pure veronica-blue, stretching like silk into the distance. The clearing was about twenty yards wide, sheltered on three sides by the pines, creating the atmosphere of a cave.

From the sea it would have looked like a theater. Center stage was a wrought-iron bench, painted white and wide enough for two people. Next to it was a brass telescope, mounted on a tripod and fixed to the ground.

"Hey," Tom grinned, "let's take a look." He walked to the bench and sat down. Reaching for the telescope he spun it around on its tripod. "Don't tell me. On a clear day you can see forever."

"Crete," she corrected, "on a clear day you can see Crete."

"So," he indicated the bench, "come and behave like a tour guide."

Her amused glance made it clear that she knew he wanted to discuss more than the view. "Maurice said you would ask questions," she said, sitting beside him.

"Did he now? What else did he say?"

"That I was to answer them."

"That's a good start," Tom nodded. "Let's begin with you. If you're not his daughter, who are you?"

"I told you. Just a friend. One of Maurice's summer girls." Her mouth puckered mischievously, "That's our name for ourselves. You'll meet Jasmine and Velvet tonight."

"Velvet? For God's sake, what kind of name is Velvet?"

She laughed. "It's what Maurice calls her. You'll understand why when you meet him."

"Why can't I understand now? You tell me."

She shook her head, "No one can understand Maurice unless they meet him. I told him this. Explaining him is too much for me to do. He's like . . . he is one on his own . . ." Frowning, she searched for the right word, pouncing triumphantly, "Unique. Like a masterpiece. Never was there anyone like him."

Tom was neither blind nor deaf. He saw the admiration in her eyes and heard it in her voice. For a moment he wondered if she was in love with Stanton. It seemed improbable; a girl with her looks and a man old enough to be her father? Besides, she sounded more like a disciple than a lover.

"Unique is a big word," he said, remembering Richards had used the same adjective.

"Maurice is a big man. A colossus."

Presented with such an opportunity, Tom seized it with a series of questions, one after another. He probed for the next twenty minutes. And Melody answered without evasion, although the picture she painted created a certain confusion. Stanton began to sound like ten men. He was big physically—". . . I think as tall as you, but wider across the shoulders." Stanton was an art collector—". . . everything you see, he collected or commissioned. Have you heard of Manelli? Picasso? They are close friends . . ." Stanton was a connoisseur of wines—"Oh yes, in France he owns some vineyards." Stanton was friendly with many of Europe's leading politicians—". . . even your Harold Macmillan was here two years ago. There are photographs in the library . . ." Maurice Stanton was this, Maurice Stanton was that.

She seemed surprised at his ignorance and for the most part was happy, even eager, to repair gaps in his knowledge. However, once or twice a question brought a frown to her face. "These things I tell you are well known," she said candidly, "but something like that you must ask Maurice yourself."

Melody opened up a whole mine of information about Stanton. And she spoke with such charm and directness, that Tom was drawn to her. Her ready smile made him smile in response. He forgot about his adventures in Piraeus and basked in the pleasure of her company. Increasingly his questions concerned her directly. "How did you come here? How long ago? Where are you from?"

She was Norwegian. Her father worked in the Norwegian embassy in London. The previous spring she had attended an exhibition of watercolors at a gallery in Albemarle Street. It was a private showing; an exclusive gathering of collectors, bankers, and connoisseurs, mixed up with people from various embassies. Her parents had accompanied a man who was connected with a museum in Oslo. Melody had gone with them, along with a young man from the embassy whom her parents were pushing her way.

"Maurice was there. He and I got talking." She tilted her head with a look of enquiry, "I think you know only a little about painting?"

"Next to nothing."

"I thought I knew a lot. Until I met Maurice. He made me see everything differently. Like having . . ." She frowned, "what is that cloth for the eyes?"

"A blindfold?"

"Blindfolds," she nodded, smiling. "Maurice took my blindfolds away."

The day after the exhibition she had lunched with Stanton, alone in his suite at Claridge's. Trying to explain their long conversation, she said, "We talked not only about painting. There were so many things. With everything, he knows so much. More than anyone." She smiled proudly, "You will understand this when you meet him."

Her lunch with Stanton had lasted all afternoon. By the time they finished, she had been invited to Kariakos for the summer.

"I went back to my parents' apartment, packed some things, and flew out with Maurice that night."

"Just like that?" Tom said drily. "I bet your parents were ecstatic."

"My father was very angry. He was . . . like rockets exploding. But what could he do? I was twenty-four." The quirky smile tugged at her lips as she remembered. "He said Maurice had a certain reputation with women."

Tom nodded, "I heard. What about your mother? What did she say?"

"The same, but with a look, you know, she would have gone herself at my age. I wanted to learn and Maurice wanted to teach me."

Tom's perception of the situation changed at that moment. Until then, doubts had persisted. It was Constantin's fault with that remark about Stanton fucking beautiful girls. Even while disbelieving, part of Tom's brain had been assessing the possibility. Now he knew he was wrong. Suddenly everything was made clear . . . Melody admired Stanton for his knowledge.

"He teaches you about art?"

"Oh yes," she agreed, "he teaches me everything."

Tom remembered the other girls—Velvet and what's-her-name. Of course—they were pupils. Kariakos was a summer school. *Maurice's summer girls.* Constantin's misunderstanding of the situation seemed suddenly funny. Tom laughed. "Now I understand," he said. "Okay. So you spent last summer here. What about the winter?"

"Maurice is not here in winter," she said as if making everything perfectly clear.

"So what did you do?"

"Lived in Paris. Jasmine has a flat there. I worked in a gallery."

"And now you're back here."

"Now I am here," she agreed with a smile. Leaning back on the bench, she glanced up into the pines before looking out to sea, "A second summer on Kariakos. My last perhaps."

"Don't you know?"

When she shrugged the cleft deepened between her breasts. Tom dragged his gaze back to her face. She was still looking out to sea. Her puckered lips conveyed the hint of a smile. "Maurice says I will know when the time comes to go. Not yet, I think, but . . . yes, I think this is my last summer here. Then I shall be ready."

"For what?"

"For life." Her sideways glance was mischievous. "Ready to open my own gallery in Paris. Ready for great adventures . . ." She stopped. "Why are you smiling?"

He hadn't realized he was. He was just pleased; pleased that his earlier suspicions had proved so unfounded; pleased to be sitting among pine trees on a Greek island with this girl.

"You laugh at me," she scolded, "you already have great adventures, I think."

"Some hopes," he protested. "I don't have great adventures. I'm just an accountant—"

"Now I know you are laughing at me." She tossed her head as a faint flush came to her cheeks. "Maurice wouldn't have sent for his people to meet you—"

"What people? You're the only one I've met."

Her reproach gave way to a look of suspicion. "Edwards," she said. From her mouth it emerged charmingly as Ed-vards. "Sir Bernard Edvards."

"He's here?" Tom was surprised. "You mean the chairman of Excel Machines?"

Her cool look unsettled him. "I've heard of him," he admitted.

"And Gunther Haller. You've heard of him too?" Her sarcasm was unmistakable.

"No. No, I haven't. Who's he?"

"The First National Bank of Geneva?" she said with obvious disbelief.

"I've heard of that."

"Gunther Haller *is* the First National Bank."

"Oh! Well, good for him," Tom shrugged. "I still haven't met him."

His certainty softened her expression. Searching his face, her green eyes clouded with confusion. "Oh, I have been rude, yes? I thought you were making fun . . . with all these people come to meet you. Even Roddy is here—"

"Who's Roddy?"

"Maurice's son, also Pohl is here from Germany, Amiens from Geneva—"

"Wait a minute. Where are these people? The villa was deserted—"

"No," she shook her head, "not quite, but most of them are on Maurice's yacht—"

"I thought he was having a siesta?"

"He is. Maurice is at the villa. It is Roddy who took the others off for the day. They will be back for your dinner."

Her embarrassment gave way to curiosity. "So you see," she said, "I think you are much more than just an accountant, Mr. Lambert."

"Tom," he said, "please call me Tom."

"Very well . . . Tom," her smile returned, "but I think you are an important man. You are already having your great adventures, yes?"

It was a flattering concept to a man who had just walked out of his job. And the look in her eyes was good for his ego. He enjoyed the moment but decided not to prolong it. "I ran a manufacturing business," he shrugged, "not vast, but not so small either. Your friend Stanton bought it ten days ago. I resigned, now he wants to meet me. I don't know why, but if he wants me to work for him, he's wasting his time." Tom grinned, "Maybe I'll be like you. Start my own business. That's when I'll have my great adventures."

She listened attentively, watching him. When he finished she met his grin with a smile. "We shall see. Perhaps you will change your mind after a few days here."

"I'm not here for a few days. I'm returning to London tomorrow."

Her surprise was obvious, reminding him of the earlier incident with Masters.

Changing the subject, she asked, "Please, what time is it now?"

He looked at his watch, surprised to realize it was almost seven o'clock.

She stood up, smoothing her skirt over her thighs, "I have to bathe and change for this evening. Will you stay here or come back to the villa?"

The pang of disappointment took him by surprise, underlining how much he was enjoying himself. He rose, reluctantly, "We never did look through the telescope," he grumbled.

"Another time perhaps," she smiled, turning to go.

He wanted to prolong the conversation, to extend their time together; by now he was as curious about her as he was about Stanton.

He hurried after her. "When," he asked, "when shall we look through the telescope?"

She laughed, "Any time."

"But I won't be here. Neither will you at the end of the summer."

They had reached the clearing which offered the view of the sea—and then Tom saw the yacht. The long white vessel was moving very slowly, almost at a standstill, as if preparing to anchor. Even Tom, ignorant of seagoing craft, recognized something of beauty. "Wow! Just look at that. Is that *Aphrodite*?"

Melody stopped to give him time to look. "Yes."

Something in her voice caught his ear. He looked at her,

trying to decipher her expression. Distaste? But what was distasteful about a yacht? Especially to a girl who had grown up on a boat.

"Roddy is back," she said.

Ignoring her sudden coolness, he seized the chance to extend their time together. "Some boat. I was thinking of Onassis earlier. Until now I've never heard of anyone else owning an island *and* a yacht."

Melody shrugged. "The *Christina* is bigger and a hundred times more vulgar."

"The *Christina*? The Onassis yacht? Do you know him?"

"He was here last summer. We had dinner on board." Melody's coolness now verged on disdain.

Tom cocked an eyebrow. "You dislike him."

"There is a painting in the saloon on the *Christina*. The Madonna supported by an angel. Ari claims it is an El Greco. It's a fake."

Her indignation was amusing. The whole idea was amusing—one of the richest men in the world cheating over a painting and being caught by this girl. "Come," she said, "I must go." She turned away and continued on down the path.

He was still amused but over and above amusement was a growing attraction. His life had been empty of women for over a year. There had been a girl—Julia—and another before her, but both had grown tired of playing second fiddle to Bolton. Long hours, interrupted weekends, the priorities of the business had been perceived as neglect, interpreted as lack of interest. . . .

"Melody," he said, catching up with her, "is that what you'll do at the end of the summer? Open an art gallery in Paris?"

"Mmm," she nodded. "I think so."

"What about London?" he asked. "Will your business bring you to London?"

"Oh yes. Quite often I think."

"Perhaps we could meet? Have dinner or something? Compare our great adventures."

He made the suggestion casually, treating it as a throwaway line, but even as he spoke he knew it was important. She looked up at him. For a moment he was sure she would refuse. Her expression was serious, except for the puckering lips. Then she said, "Thank you, Tom. I think I would very much like having dinner with you."

He felt absurdly pleased. The whole day had been crazy. That jet, Piraeus, Constantin, that officer and the armed troops, this island. He didn't want Stanton's job. Stanton could stuff it. Crazy, to come all this way for a wasted conversation . . . but he did have Stanton to thank for this girl . . .

When they reached the villa, the terrace had been transformed. Tables had been arranged in a hollow square, glasses were being polished and silver laid out. He counted eight members of the staff all so engrossed that they scarcely looked up as he followed Melody across to the wide Moorish arch. "Looks like they're setting up for a party," he said.

"I told you. Everyone will be back to meet you at dinner."

He counted the chairs. "Twenty people?"

Smiling, she led the way into the villa, "I will come to your room to make sure everything is ready."

The atmosphere embraced them as they walked through the hall. The eroticism was pervasive. It was more than the sensuous works of art; they were the stage setting, significant in themselves but they alone did not create the mood of that house. Every sense was seduced. The perfumed air; the haunting, barely audible music; the soft lighting; all conspired to affect Tom even more than before. Time spent with Melody, under a warm sun with the sea and blue skies as a backdrop—looking into her eyes, surreptitiously examining her breasts—had heightened his sexual urge. And Melody seemed to respond. As they climbed the stairs her bare arm brushed his with the casual intimacy of a relationship already established.

As they entered his room, her face lit with approval. "Ah, good, Maria has laid out your tuxedo."

Tom's gaze was compulsively drawn to the statues. Their explicit eroticism was compelling, so that it took an effort to look at the bed. On the cover was a white linen dinner jacket, accompanied by a dress shirt, complete with bow tie and gold cuff links. A pair of highly polished black shoes stood on the floor.

Melody said, "Maurice forgot to let you know that we dress for dinner."

Advancing to the bed, Tom picked up the jacket and held it against himself. "How did he know my size?"

"Ask him when you meet him," she said, enjoying his look of surprise. "I will come back at eight to take you downstairs. Will that be all right?"

"Perfect," he grinned, pleased to know that she would be part of the evening.

As soon as she left, he ran a bath. "What a day," he grunted cheerfully as he lowered himself into the water. Scarcely thirteen hours had elapsed since the chauffeur had collected him from his flat . . . Relaxed by the hot water, eyes closed, legs outstretched, feet propped on the end of the bath, he contemplated his future with more serenity than for months past. Maybe he had needed a break away from London to see things in perspective? He had worked solidly for as long as he could remember. Work, work, work . . . only for the Brierleys to sell the business. Treacherous bastards! Trouble with dealing with double-crossing sods like the Brierleys was it destroyed your faith in the rest of mankind: you suspected everyone.

Shifting his position, he opened his eyes. He had left the bathroom door open. From the bath he could see into the bedroom. Suddenly he saw her. Realization hit him with almost physical force. Splashing upright, he grabbed the side of the tub and hauled himself out. He almost lost his balance, skidding on the marble floor. Naked, dripping wet, he rushed into the bedroom. Diffused by the voile curtains, the rays of the setting sun fell on the statues, turning the bronze man gold and the marble girl pearly pink. She shone in the light. Her long legs, parted and wrapped around the bronzed trunk, looked even more shapely. The sunlight picked out a dimple on one knee. Her back arched to show her tiny waist to perfection. But it was her face which drew Tom. Her head was thrown back; her thick hair fell away from the nape of her neck; her mouth was open in a cry of ecstasy. A mole decorated her left cheek. It was Melody.

For the next half hour he called himself every name imaginable. The biggest bloody fool under the sun. It wasn't even that his behavior was typical. He never acted like an impressionable adolescent, not even when he had been adolescent. There had *always* been girls . . .

Humiliation left a bitter taste. He was the victim of a joke, perpetrated by Stanton. *He set me up. Arranged for Melody to meet me, spend time with me, encourage me . . . and then this!*

He looked at the statues again, against his will. He despised them, but the figures drew his eyes. He swore violently. He could see little of the man, just a great bronze back and taut buttocks above muscular legs. The man's head was bent over Melody as he suckled her breast, his face was hidden, pressed into her flesh.

Hurriedly he dressed in the white dinner jacket and escaped out onto the balcony. He smoked a cigarette while watching the sky darken and the sea turn a pale gray. The cicadas, clicking in a ragged chorus, rasped on his nerves. He heard other sounds; voices from the terrace out of sight to his left. A man shouted, "Did you have a good day?" "Terrific," came the answer, "we went to Milos for lunch." A woman's voice called, "Darling, I *must* go and change." Laughter and shouted goodbyes rose above the sound of music. From elsewhere came the sounds of water running through pipes into bathtubs. He smoked another cigarette, cursing himself for being a fool, questioning why he was wasting time when he should be in London . . .

A while later, a knock sounded at the door. He turned to see Melody framed in the entrance. Her evening gown matched the color of her eyes; green silk cut daringly low. The upper slopes of her breasts were the same satiny brown as her shoulders. She had arranged her hair differently; lifted from the nape of her neck, it emphasized the line of her throat, around which hung an emerald pendant. She looked beautiful, and he hated her.

Her mouth puckered into a smile. "My word," she said admiringly. "You look distinguished. I am right, I think, you *are* an important man. I do not believe the things you said earlier."

She doesn't believe ME! That's rich. What nerve!

To avoid her eyes, he glanced at his watch. "You're punctual, I'll say that for you."

She gave him a quizzical look. "Something is wrong?"

Listen to that concern. And see that hurt look. Jesus, what an actress.

"No, nothing's wrong. Everything's perfect. Come on, let's get this over with."

In the corridor, she took his arm. "Tom," she said, looking up at him, "it is a party. Lots of people are waiting to meet you. Why are you looking so stern?"

"Business. I never allow pleasure to interfere with business."

She withdrew her hand as if his arm were on fire. They walked down the stairs, careful not to brush against each other, eyes directed straight ahead. Sounds drifted in from the terrace; the notes of a bouzouki band, the chink of ice against glass, the tinkling sound of a girl's laughter. Tom stopped at the foot of the stairs. Reaching for Melody's elbow, he pulled her around to face the statue. "Fellatio," he sneered, reading the inscription. "Is that art?"

"It is beauty," she said simply. "Look at their faces."

He knew what she meant. He had seen it earlier. He had understood. Sensual and erotic though the figures were, what passed between them transcended the physical. But earlier his mood had been different. "That's not art," he said harshly, "that's filth! Pornography."

He sensed her look at him. Instead of meeting her eye, he continued to stare at the bronze statue. The width of the man's shoulders was about the same as the bronze in the bedroom. It was the same muscular body. Instinctively Tom knew it was the same man.

Melody said softly, "I am sorry if that is what you think. It makes me sad for you."

She walked off, in the direction of the Moorish arch. He hurried after her, catching up with her just as she emerged onto the terrace. A man rose from his chair and turned to greet them. A tall, strongly built man with a shock of iron-gray hair and tufted gray eyebrows. His tan was enhanced by his white dinner jacket. Deep furrows ran from beside his nose to the corners of his mouth. It was a strong face, handsome, experienced, accustomed to command. But the most striking thing was the intensity of the eyes, as brown as cobnuts, staring with a vibrant penetration, conveying the impression of the shrewdest intelligence.

Melody said, "Maurice. This is Tom Lambert."

The tanned face split into a welcoming smile. Tom knew at once where he had seen it before. It was the face of the bronze statue at the foot of the stairs.

BOOK TWO

1978

The empty delivery spool on the projector free-wheeled, revolving mindlessly. The film was long finished. The screen was empty, save for the uninterrupted white light cast by the projector. Tom sat hunched in the chair. In three hours he had scarcely moved. Outside the afternoon drew to a close. The setting sun turned the sky a pale yellow, then a lustrous green. Soon it would be a deep velvety blue and the stars would shine down . . . just as they had that night years before.

Behind him the door opened abruptly. Heavy feet shuffled over the marble floor. A large hand reached for the projector, switching it off with such force that the spools jumped on their sprockets. "I was told you were working. If I'd known you were watching that garbage—"

"That garbage is why we're all here," Tom retorted.

"Now he tells me," came the sarcastic response. The man limped across to the windows and opened the curtains to the fading light. "How many times did you watch it today?"

"Not many. I got to thinking. Remembering back to when it all started. Even about when I met you."

"Hah! When I gave you the medallion?"

"Yes, and my first visit here."

Constantin sat down in the chair opposite. His movements were awkward and stiff. He lowered himself carefully, without bending his left leg. Tom looked at him. The years had taken their toll; the years and the Colonels' torturers. Constantin's history was now recorded in the files of Amnesty International. The opening paragraph proclaimed that ". . . the torture inflicted was as barbarous as any perpetrated by the Nazi Gestapo. . . ." Miraculously, Constantin had survived. Just. He had long since lost all his hair. One of the things Tom remembered was Constantin's hair. A thick abundance of black hair. Now it was all gone. Not just from his head which was as bald and bronzed as a duck egg, but even his eyebrows were now mere ridges of skin, bestowing upon him a look of surprise. His girth had halved; the big frame had once carried twice as much weight. Physically he was much changed, but mentally and in spirit he was tougher than ever. Watching, Tom saw him rub his left thigh.

"Leg hurting?"

"Everything hurts when I worry."

"So don't worry."

"Huh!"

"Where's Alec?"

"Telling *her* not to worry."

"It will be over by tomorrow."

Constantin sighed unhappily, "They have sent me in here to make one last plea—"

"No!"

"Everyone who loves you is here. Tonight you are safe, but tomorrow this place will fill with your enemies—"

"So what?" Tom's voice rose angrily, "Then it's over and done with!" Agitated, he rose and crossed to the windows, thrusting his hands deep into his pockets.

Constantin's expression was more sorrowful than angry. He rubbed his chin with a hand that was badly misshapen. First they had lit matches under the fingernails, then torn out the fingernails; next morning they had broken his thumb with a hammer, his forefinger the day after, his index finger the day after that. After which they had inserted the pulped mess into a vise and cracked all of his knuckles. Clearing his throat, he tried again, "If I cannot persuade you—"

"You can't," Tom interrupted harshly without looking around.

"Then I have a favor to ask."

Tom turned, surprised. "You want to go? I can fly you out—"

"No, no." Constantin shook his head. "You think I'd desert you? Now of all times. I owe you too much—"

"There are no debts between us."

"Not true," Constantin said flatly, leaving no room for argument. "Listen, my friend. You say this will all be over. You're wrong. If you go ahead, if you kill whoever did this—"

"I don't believe it! You're pleading for the life of a—"

"No! I'm pleading for nobody's life."

Tom stared without comprehension.

"Except yours," Constantin lowered his voice, "and perhaps hers." He jerked his head at the ceiling, indicating the bedroom above.

"Meaning?"

"Meaning you've never killed a man. It mightn't even be one of the men. It could be the woman. Have you thought about that?"

"I've thought about it."

"Have you thought what it will do to *you*? To kill someone. To kill in cold blood. You'll never be the same again. When they die something of you will die too. I know."

Tom turned back to the window.

"It will destroy you," said Constantin softly. "I've killed men. Another one won't matter. I'm beyond redemption—"

"For Christ's sake! If you're suggesting that you—"

"Listen to me. I'm agreeing with you. You want revenge. You want to find out who did this? Okay, okay. You be judge and jury. Let me be executioner—"

"It's not your business—"

"Was it your business to get me out of Athens that time?"

Tom sighed. He shook his head. "Leave it, Con. Knock it off.

You've helped enough. You *are* helping. Don't think I'm ungrateful—"

"Then grant me this favor."

"What difference would it make? You think I'm afraid—"

"No. *I* am afraid."

Disbelief lit Tom's eyes. "Rubbish! You've never been afraid."

"Wrong. I've been afraid all my life. Afraid things I believe in will be destroyed. Freedom, democracy—"

"That's different—"

"People I believe in. You're one of them. One of the things I believe in. That's why I'm here; why I'm helping, I'm afraid you'll destroy yourself. I'll fight to stop that. I'll even fight Tom Lambert himself."

Tom stared. When he finally spoke he sounded almost defeated. "What do you want, Con?"

Constantin smiled, an awkward, lopsided smile that revealed his false teeth. The surgeons who had reconstructed his face had done well, but even their best work fell short of perfection. The false teeth had never fitted properly. "I want to know what happened—"

"You *know* what happened—"

"Some of it. Bits of it. Even some of the people, though not all of them. We've been much to each other, my friend, but we've never lived in each other's pocket. There are years in your life that I know little about. I want the whole story."

"What good will it do?"

"You're doing it anyway. You said so. Remembering back to when it all started. Playing it through, sifting, delving, searching for clues. Am I right?"

"So what? I've been through it a hundred times—"

"And still the answer eludes you." Constantin put his misshapen hands on the arms of the chair and levered himself upright. "I've been questioned by experts. Interrogated. I've interrogated others. It teaches you things. You develop an inner ear. You hear things in a man's voice which contradict what he is saying—"

"Christ! You think I'm making this up?"

"Don't be a fool!" Constantin spat the words. "I want to

help. But I must *know.* Everything, understand? Whatever you can tell me about these people. When you first met them—"

"They were here the first night, some of the them. Roddy, Amiens, Haller."

"So begin there."

Tom left the window and returned to his chair. He sat down heavily, and ran a hand though his hair. Life had taught him to consider every option.

Constantin encouraged, "Like I said, you're doing it anyway. Going over it in your mind. Just talk aloud. Maybe my inner ear will—"

"We'll be here all night."

"Who cares? Nobody's going to sleep. Do you think she will sleep?" Constantin jerked his head toward the ceiling. "You think Alec will sleep? In twenty-four hours someone will be executed under this roof. Perhaps you're right, who does it doesn't matter, a court of law would find us all equally guilty—"

"No," Tom interrupted, "I thought of that. When the time comes, you must get off the island."

Constantin shrugged his indifference. He was at the side-board, pouring drinks, fumbling at the decanters with his crippled hands. He had his own views on the execution. He wasn't against it. If what had happened to Tom had happened to him, he would want vengeance. But he was Greek. It was the Greek way. A Greek could live with the consequences. Filling the glasses, he asked, "So what did you think of them?"

"Who?"

"Roddy, Haller, the people you mentioned." Constantin turned and shuffled to Tom's chair, handing him a glass.

"Bit early for brandy, isn't it?"

Constantin smiled. "There are worse ways to be interrogated." He approached his own chair carefully, watching the glass in his hand. Deliberately he set the glass down on the table before lowering himself into the chair to sit with his stiff leg stretched out and the foot raised from the marble floor.

Tom knew better than offer to help. Instead he sniffed the brandy appreciatively. "This was Maurice's favorite. He could be quite funny about it. He used to pretend to be angry. After all, he owned a French firm that made cognac. Never as good as this though. It's distilled in the monastery of Arkadin in Crete. It always reminds me of Armanac, but even smoother somehow."

Constantin nodded. Inwardly he drew comfort from the warmth in Tom's voice; the harsh bitterness was absent for the first time that evening. Constantin knew why. Tom could never talk about Maurice Stanton without affection. Strange, Constantin mused, the love that can grow between men. Not homosexual love, but love for all that, based on trust, respect, honor, and the total certainty that if help were requested it would be forthcoming without question. Such love was rare. Constantin had felt it for only three men, and one of those was Tom Lambert. He sipped from his glass, enjoying the liquid glow before asking, "Is this what you drank the first night you were here?"

Tom tried to remember. "Possibly. Not at the party, but later, when we had our meeting."

Constantin gave his lopsided grin. "That must have been quite something, your first meeting with Maurice Stanton."

"I hated him that night," Tom admitted. "I'd been with Melody all afternoon. I was knocked out by her. I know it sounds banal, but she was the loveliest thing I'd ever seen. More than that. There was a strength to her that I'd never come across in a woman. You could sense it. A strong will. I don't know . . ." He shrugged. "I'm not saying I was vastly experienced, after all, this was years ago, I was twenty-eight. But I wasn't *without* experience. I'd had my fair share of girls. I think that's it, the difference; they were girls, unsure of themselves, learning to be women. Whereas Melody . . ." He trailed off, dissatisfied by the explanation but unable to find a better one.

"I understand," Constantin encouraged, trying to keep him talking. "And then you saw that statue and became angry."

"That's right. By the time I met Maurice, I knew it was him. In *all* the statues. I didn't give a damn about the one on the stairs. Fellatio. Him and Velvet. But Melody . . ." Again he tailed off, his mind searching back over the years.

"So you hated Stanton?"

"Damn right. I was boiling. Not just because of Melody, God knows that was bad enough, but I saw it as deliberate. You know, get me excited about Melody, then throw it in my face that she was . . ." He shrugged, "I was furious."

Constantin waited before prompting, "But Stanton cooled you down."

"In a way. Partly I cooled myself down. I could hardly tell him why I was pissed off, could I? He sensed it, of course. Maurice could sense things like that at a hundred yards. He probably guessed. Not that he said so, not even later."

"So how did he calm you?"

"I'm not sure. I mean, I was as scratchy as hell; but he kept introducing me to people . . . and, of course, I had all that charm to contend with. No one had charm the way Maurice had charm. Even now, all these years later, all the people I've met, all the people I've done business with, really smooth operators, none of them could match Maurice for charm. It wasn't faked. It was real. Everyone reacted to it, not just women. He could charm anyone." Tom smiled ruefully, "I once told him he could charm snakes."

"What did he say?"

"He said he did. He said he'd been charming snakes most of his life."

Constantin heard the pride and let it pass. "So you were boiling mad and he kept you occupied meeting people—"

"Right. He and I sat at a table . . . Melody was there to start with, wearing a green dress that was driving me crazy. I scowled at her all the time. I hated her too. Anyway, she kept disappearing and coming back with this one and that one. Maurice said after I'd met everyone, he and I would go off for a talk."

"So you met Roddy and Amiens. Who else?"

Tom shrugged. "Most of them. Not that I took much notice. You know what it's like being introduced to dozens of people. You forget half the names. I remember Roddy though. He was only about nineteen then. He and Hugo came to the table together, though I didn't attach any significance to that at the time. What most struck me was that Melody disliked him. She covered it up, but at one point he put a hand on her arm and she shied away. Maurice didn't see it. Roddy was his blind spot, of course."

"What did you think of Roddy?"

"I don't know. He was just a kid. I didn't really get to know him until later."

"But first impressions?"

"For God's sake! This was ages ago! Can you remember what you thought of people when you met them for the first time?"

"I might," said Constantin, "if I intended to kill them."

1969

Stanton dominated. Naturally, being the host gave him an advantage, but Tom suspected that Stanton would have dominated in any surroundings. He had tremendous charisma. Physically he was big and strong, amazingly so for a man of his age, and he exuded vitality. His laugh was infectious. A laugh, rich and warm, which brought a grin to the face of anyone listening. Even Tom was affected, despite his resistance. And a single look from Stanton captured attention. His deep brown eyes conveyed such intelligence that any recipient was compelled to respond. By ten o'clock, after two hours on the terrace, Tom's mind was in turmoil. Stanton was urbane, civilized, charming—yet without doubt the man in the statues. Tom kept asking himself the same question about Melody. Was she just a high class whore . . . ?

He had met almost everyone by then. He and Stanton sat together while Melody brought people to the table to say hello. Even the muscles in Tom's face were confused—scowling at Melody one minute, smiling a greeting the next. Melody responded with puzzled looks which merely incensed him. *Good God, she must realize I know about her and Stanton . . . why pretend . . . why make it worse by taking me for a fool?*

The very atmosphere defeated him. Contradictions abounded. The scene was one of beauty and richness. Candles flickered on every table, flares illuminated the edge of the terrace; the balmy air was scented with jasmine. A number of women were there . . . wives, girlfriends . . . several of whom were exceptionally attractive, dressed in evening gowns of every color imaginable. Men were resplendent in white tuxedos which handsomely darkened the skin of faces and hands. The food was magnificent, the wines superb. The ambience was almost that of a family gathering . . .

. . . And yet, Tom tried to put his finger on it. Beneath the surface was an undercurrent, as if people felt threatened and saw him as the threat. He told himself he was wrong; that he was allowing his confusion about Melody to overflow into everything. Yet the suspicion persisted, heightened by some of the looks he was getting. When the Frenchman—Andre Amiens—was introduced, his politeness was positively icy.

With the meal over, men lit cigars and sat back in their chairs; while others were dragged up to dance by their wives. Which was when Melody returned to the table . . . bringing Roddy Stanton and Hugo Von Braun.

"Ah," Maurice Stanton pushed his chair back from the table, "Roddy. Come and meet Tom Lambert. You too, Hugo."

Tom rose, much in the way he had been doing all evening, extending his hand. But his hand was ignored. Instead Roddy responded by bowing low from the waist. "Mr. Lambert," he said, "we come to show our respect." Straightening, he turned to his companion, "So? This is father's new *Consigliori*. What do you think, Hugo?"

The other youth smiled, "Your father is famous for choosing as wisely in men as in women."

The simpering note jarred. So did the thinly veiled sarcasm. It almost overshadowed Roddy's use of *Consigliori,* a word Tom struggled to define as he appraised the two men. Both were good looking. Roddy was as tall as his father, but slimmer; fair-haired, with regular features, elegant and assured. Hugo was an inch or so shorter; dark with a saturnine look and a sardonic curl to his lips. The meaning of *Consigliori* suddenly clicked in Tom's mind. The word was Sicilian, the name given to the man who advised a Mafia Don; a hatchet man, even a killer. Startled, he glanced at Roddy, only to find him talking to his father about sailing to Milos. All of them had remained standing. Neither of the two young men had offered to shake Tom's hand.

"Not on *Aphrodite*," Stanton was saying.

"No, of course not. We're taking the sloop—"

"But you need a four-hand crew—"

"No, Hugo and I can manage her. If we leave in the next hour we can be there by morning. Hugo's got a bet with Bertie Gristwood. Bertie claims it can't be done by daybreak. Absolute nonsense, of course . . ."

Stanton hesitated, perhaps concerned in case his guest should feel snubbed. A look of severity crossed his face. Roddy was quick to respond, turning to Tom, "You don't mind, do you, Mr. Lambert? After all, you won't need me for your discussions, will you?"

Even without knowing what the discussions would be about . . . or perhaps because of *not* knowing, Tom felt nettled. His irritation was heightened by the supercilious look on Hugo's face, and the fact that Roddy caught Melody's arm as she passed. "Besides," Roddy purred, "so many people want to talk to you that I doubt I'll get a look in. Isn't that so, Melody darling?"

The words were honeyed and smooth. Anyone listening would have thought Roddy was being friendly. Certainly that was his father's interpretation. There was a distinct softening in Stanton's expression. But Tom saw what was hidden from Stanton—the pressure marks on Melody's arm as she pulled away and her look of distaste. She was quick to recover. She managed a strained smile in Tom's direction, which for once he met without scowling. "Everyone wants to meet Mr. Lambert," she said. "I have someone here. Jasmine wants to ask him to dance."

Standing aside, she made way for a petite Eurasian girl, as delicate as porcelain, almond-eyed, with jet black hair. Tom realized at once that she was the third of "Maurice's summer girls." He had already met Velvet—twice, counting the time he had seen her as a statue at the foot of the stairs.

"Mr. Lambert," Jasmine smiled, moving into his arms.

He had never been much of a dancer. He needed to be in the right state of mind to concentrate on the steps. Not agitated as he was then. Jasmine was lightness personified. She floated in his arms. She even managed to stay clear of his feet. But no amount of agility could enable her to escape the frown on his face. "Mr. Lambert?" she enquired in a puzzled, husky voice. "You are not enjoying yourself?"

"I never enjoy being taken for a fool."

Her bewilderment grew. Tom, who had never insulted a woman in his life, was overtaken by a sudden rush of temper. "What do you do then?" he asked harshly. "I've seen Velvet sucking his cock. I've seen him screwing Melody. How does he have you? Hanging from a chandelier—"

Her hand moved quickly to cover his lips, yet so gently that it might have been a caress. The next couple—the Frenchman Amiens and his wife—whirled past without even a curious glance, but Jasmine's dismay was betrayed in her face. Her dark eyes shone with pain. A blush rose from her neck. Removing her hand from Tom's lips, she took his arm and led him back to the table, her chin tilted high, her bearing proud. "Thank you for the dance, Mr. Lambert," she said with quiet dignity and turned on her heel.

Roddy and Hugo were on the point of leaving. Tom felt Roddy's curious eyes and glimpsed Hugo's smirk. He wondered how they had interpreted the scene. Regretting his juvenile outburst, he would have followed Jasmine to apologize, but Stanton was already beckoning. "Ah, you're back. I think you've met everyone now. Bernard was just saying it might be a good time for our chat."

Sir Bernard Edwards and Gunther Haller were at the table. Tom had already been introduced. Small and wiry, in his late fifties, Edwards was one of those spare-framed men who usually radiate energy. Except something was wrong with Edwards. Tom had sensed it earlier. There was a waxiness in his complexion which was unhealthy. An air of frailty. Even without being told, he guessed Edwards was a sick man. Haller was the complete opposite, big and beefy, heavily jowled, with a pugnacious inquisitive look to his eye. "Come, Mr. Lambert," he said, indicating the wide Moorish arch which led to the villa, "we have something to tell you that might be of interest."

Stanton opened with his warmest smile. "Now then," he said, cradling his brandy balloon with both hands. "Tell us about Bolton Automation."

It was an innocuous request, delivered in such reasonable tones that it invited an agreeable response. Unfortunately, Tom was still agitated. Thoughts of Melody and the atmosphere on the terrace jumbled up in his mind. He was still bringing his nerves under control when mention of Bolton Automation reopened a wound. Unable to disguise his resentment he retorted sharply, "What's to tell? You bought the company. I resigned. Bolton's no longer my problem."

If Stanton was surprised, not a flicker showed in his eyes.

The four men had settled themselves in the study, an elegant air-conditioned room on the left-hand side of the hall. Solid mahogany doors kept the noise from the terrace to a faint murmur. Two long leather sofas faced each other across a low table, and an elegant Louis XIV desk stood in one corner. Table lamps cast a soft glow. It was a comfortable den of a room, even restful if no attention were paid to the erotic paintings on the far wall.

"I agree." Stanton's smile conveyed genuine warmth. "Bolton is no longer your problem, but you were kind enough to accept my invitation—"

"I didn't expect any of this," Tom interrupted. "I thought we'd meet in London—"

"Much better here," said Stanton, "I wanted you to relax." He smiled encouragingly. "I do understand, you know, I can imagine us buying Bolton came as a shock. But I'd like to assure you that everyone is aware of what you did for the business."

Tom remained silent. *Here it comes,* he thought, *they want me to run it.* The anticipation gave him a certain dog-in-the-manger pleasure. He knew he would refuse.

Stanton said, "If it pains you to talk about it, perhaps it will be easier to listen. Why don't I relate my understanding of the situation?"

Tom shrugged.

"You joined Bolton seven years ago," said Stanton. "At which time the company was making substantial losses. Isn't that so?"

"I joined one step ahead of a Receiver. Another six months and the company would have gone under."

Stanton nodded, "And you made certain recommendations?"

"I was only twenty-one. The assistant company treasurer, that's all. They weren't too keen to listen to me."

"But they did."

"Not to begin with. Old Cummings was company treasurer and I had to submit my ideas through him. He said the board turned them down. I don't know whether they even saw them."

"But then Cummings resigned."

"Rats desert sinking ships. He was quite sure we'd go bust."

"And you took over his job, with access to the board."

"Access to a bunch of amateurs."

Stanton's eyebrows rose.

Tom said, "Not one of them knew his arse from his elbow."

Stanton smiled. "Perhaps you do them an injustice. After all, they appointed you chief executive a month later."

"Not willingly. The bank forced the decision on them. They'd strung the bank along with a pack of lies, changing their story from one meeting to the next. I gave the bank accurate figures. The bank came to trust me. The directors were given an ultimatum, either make me chief executive or the loans would be called in. They had no choice."

"Didn't it worry you? The hostility of your fellow directors?"

Tom shrugged his contempt. "They wouldn't have been fellow anything if we'd gone bust, would they?"

A look passed between Stanton and Haller which Tom failed to decipher. Then Haller said, "So you replaced them with competent people."

"I replaced Hunter who was supposed to be sales director. And got rid of Bob Thornton. I brought Alec Hargreaves in to be my right-hand man. But I couldn't do anything about the Brierleys, they owned the company between them. Not that they caused me much bother. They were non-executive directors anyway. All they did was attend board meetings and make stupid suggestions. After a while they didn't even do that."

Tom's manner changed as he talked, though he was quite unaware of it. Had anyone told him he would have been surprised. He thought himself much the same all the time. Yet even a casual observer would have noticed the difference. Ten minutes earlier he had been unsure of himself . . . unsettled by Melody, confused by the atmosphere . . . but when it came to business, his brain cleared. It always had, even years before when he had been studying accountancy, and later, when he joined Bolton. He analyzed business problems with such clarity that, for him, solutions became blindingly obvious. Common sense, he called it, common sense and dealing with matters in the right order of importance. Businessmen *without* common sense he regarded as fools, and few survived long in his company. Mastery of his subject gave his voice and manner an authority which did not pass unnoticed by the men in that room. Haller, in particular, glanced meaningfully at Edwards as Stanton continued, "So they made you the CEO and left you to get on with it."

"That's right."

"No easy task, I imagine."

Tom doubted Stanton could imagine any such thing. What would he know about nursing a sick business back from the brink? Tom compared the luxury of the villa to the mean streets around Neasden where he had spent seven years of his life. He had even moved his bed into the factory for five critical months, to be on hand to check every detail, working ninety hours a week, pleading with suppliers for credit, coaxing employees to meet new targets, juggling this, arguing about that. He smiled grimly. No, Stanton would never know what it was like. He shrugged and remained silent.

Edwards cleared his throat. "Remind me," he said, "how big was the work force?"

"Two hundred and eighty when I took it over, and it was touch and go if they'd get their wages. Now twelve hundred people work for Bolton." Tom shrugged. "You should know, they're your employees."

"And you didn't have a strike during the whole of that time?"

"Why should we? Everyone got a fair day's pay for a fair day's work."

"What about the unions?"

"What about them? Our people earned more than union rates."

Edwards snorted. "Six years ago we were paying ten percent above union rate. It didn't stop us from being shut down for three months."

"Didn't that teach your management a few things?"

"Yes," Edwards laughed wryly. "Not to trust the unions. We were shut down again the following year."

"People don't work just for money," Tom said flatly, "they need to feel part of an enterprise. We were a team at Bolton. When there was a problem, everyone worried. When we delivered a big order, everyone celebrated."

"Easier to do in a small outfit," said Edwards dismissively.

Tom shook his head, "I've heard tales of your place in Coventry. What you've got there is management and work force. Them and Us. They don't even speak to each other unless they have to. No wonder you've got problems."

Stanton raised his eyebrows, "You're on the side of the unions?"

"I'm on the side of the business. That's the whole point. It can't be Them and Us. The only *Them* are competitors. Weak managements blame the unions for everything."

Stanton smiled. "The fault, dear Brutus, is not in our stars but in ourselves."

Tom remained silent. He was unused to Shakespeare being quoted when he talked business. Glancing through the windows, he thought the whole setting somewhat Shakespearean. From where he sat he could just see the edge of the terrace. Flares spluttered and danced in the breeze, turning the balustrade into battlements.

Haller cocked an eyebrow. "The way you say 'weak managements' makes them sound dishonest."

"They are," Tom agreed, "and not just with employees. They cheat their shareholders too. Assets which have appreciated aren't revalued, so dividends are made to look moderately good, when in fact they're bloody awful. Shareholders think they're getting a good return, when in fact real dividends barely keep pace with inflation. I'll tell you this, British industry is ready for a hell of a shake-up."

Haller nodded, "I believe you. That's why we wanted to meet you."

"If you expect me to run Bolton, forget it. I poured my life into that business. The Brierleys promised me first option if they sold—"

"Forgive me for asking," Edwards interrupted, "but could you have paid their price?"

Tom scowled. "I'd have raised the cash somehow. Given time. The bastards didn't even tell me they were selling. The first I knew was when your people walked in."

Stanton had trouble keeping a straight face. "I understand you hit Tim Brierley. You fractured his jaw. He's considering bringing an action for assault."

"Big deal," Tom shrugged. A reflective look crossed his face as he rubbed his right fist. "I should have killed the bastard."

"Instead you walked out."

"Damn right."

"I can't say I blame you," said Stanton. "But it does give us a problem."

Tom shrugged again. He had warmed to Stanton, the man radiated irresistible charm, but Tom's sense of dissatisfaction persisted.

Haller cleared his throat; he looked at Stanton as if seeking permission to speak. Eyes twinkling, Stanton nodded, "Yes, Gunther, you'd better get to the point."

Haller addressed himself to Tom. "Apart from building a business, you built a reputation, Mr. Lambert. The fact is we didn't buy Bolton for a stock of spare parts. We bought it to get you."

Tom sat back in surprise. His eyes widened but he kept his mouth firmly closed.

Haller continued, "I'll put this as concisely as possible. Mr. Stanton has many diverse business interests which have been run as separate entities. For instance, Excel at Coventry has no coordinated policy with Pohl in Germany, likewise Bouvier in Geneva, yet all three are in the same industry. We think it's time they were amalgamated into one international company." He paused, testing Tom with a quizzical look. "What would you think of the wisdom of that?"

It was news to Tom that Stanton had links with Pohl. A sudden memory tick reminded him that earlier, on the terrace, he had been introduced to a Carl Pohl. "The man I met," he said, jerking his head toward the door. "Is he the Pohl of the Pohl Organization?"

Haller nodded. "Yes, that was Carl. His family owns a block of shares, but Maurice has a controlling interest."

Tom struggled to contain his surprise. The Pohl Organization was big, even bigger than Excel, and Excel was four times bigger than Bolton. "And Bouvier?" Tom asked in amazement. His researches had revealed a Swiss connection, but his enquiries had not led very far. "Do you own Bouvier?"

Stanton was enjoying the moment. He grinned with the vigor of a man twenty years younger. But it was Haller who answered, "You met Andre Amiens," he said. "Andre runs Bouvier, but Maurice is the owner."

"Bloody hell!" Tom exclaimed. He began adding it up—Pohl plus Bouvier plus Excel plus Bolton. *That lot together could be a giant!*

"The point is," Haller continued, "each business has been run independently in the past. We now want to merge them. We want to create an international corporation to be called Stanton Industries."

"I bet you do," said Tom, still struggling to absorb the implications. The scale of the operation would be vast—big enough to compete with the big German companies, even to take on the Americans. . . .

"Maurice also owns various other interests in shipping and chemicals," said Haller. "All of these businesses will form part of Stanton Industries."

"My word," said Tom, knowing it to be an idiotic remark, but still grappling with the size of the business interests involved.

Haller said, "Having decided on what will be a very large merger, we wanted someone to put the pieces together. That's why we bought Bolton. To get you. We want you to run it."

Tom had been toying with his glass. His fingers went rigid. Slowly he raised his eyes to look at Haller.

Haller smiled. "You can imagine our dismay when you resigned."

Tom glanced at Stanton, seeking confirmation.

Stanton met the look with a smile. "It will be a great adventure," he said. "*Your* great adventure."

Tom recognized the expression. Melody had used it, but even the pang of being reminded about her was swamped by surprise and excitement. He glanced at Edwards, who was studying his fingernails with exaggerated concentration.

Catching the look, Stanton said, "Bernard is retiring. We want him to conserve his strength for his old age."

The words carried more hope than conviction. Tom knew he had guessed right. Edwards was chronically ill. But any sympathy was rebuffed by the sudden hostility in Edwards' face. The look directed at Tom was full of defiance, the expression of a man in stubborn retreat.

Haller said, "It's a big job, Mr. Lambert."

Recovering some composure as questions formed in his mind, Tom nodded. "Why didn't you approach me direct? Why negotiate with the Brierleys behind my back?"

"You were totally absorbed," said Haller. "Approaching you would have been futile. Nothing would have induced you to leave Bolton, you lived for that business. We know that. You had tunnel vision. That's why you were so successful. Come now, surely you can accept that?"

"Okay," Tom nodded, "but why me? There must be someone in your organization."

They fell silent. Haller gave Edwards an uneasy sideways glance which Edwards met with a frown. Tom sensed disagreement. *Edwards didn't pick me,* he thought, *Edwards is against me.*

It fell to Stanton to answer. "The fact is," he said, "you're right when you talk about changes to come. Not just in British industry, but European and worldwide. What was that marvelous phrase? *The wind of change.* You see it everywhere; in politics, art, literature, the theater; everything's changing at a great pace. To capitalize on that we need someone of the right age at the helm. Most men over forty are too conditioned by the past, while few men of thirty have sufficient experience. That's what we found within our companies, so we had to look outside." He paused, marshalling his thoughts. "I'm not even sure it's a matter of experience. It's more a question of vision and determination. Dynamism. The sort of unswerving dedication which enabled you to turn failure into success. A man has only one destiny. I've seen too many struggle to make themselves something they aren't. They waste precious time. Finally they go disappointed to their graves, seeing too late the futility of their lives. If they'd given themselves over to what they were, they would have been happier and have achieved something worthwhile. You're one of the lucky ones, Mr. Lambert. You know what you are. The blood of commerce pumps through your veins. It's the stuff of life to you; more exciting than women, more sustaining than food, more intoxicating than champagne . . ."

The words were hypnotic. The full force of Stanton's personality was seductive. Tom's pulse raced while he did his best to remain level-headed.

". . . I offer you the chance," Stanton was saying, "to emerge as one of the most vital businessmen in Europe, even the world. A chance to fulfill your potential . . ."

It was heady stuff. Stanton went on at considerable length, describing opportunities involved in the way forward. He could have saved his breath. Tom was racing ahead of him. Even when he closed his ears to Stanton's fine words, the thrill remained. Tom could see the future—Pohl plus Bouvier plus Excel plus Bolton—and the future was exciting. . . .

"As for the immediate next steps," Stanton continued, "I understand you expect to return to London tomorrow?"

Tom nodded.

"We've arranged for that," Stanton said. "I can't offer you the Lear, I'm using it myself, but Richards could fly you to Piraeus in the afternoon and put you on the BA flight to

London. A first class seat has been reserved in your name." He smiled. "You'd be home for dinner if you want, but I'd be grateful for a little more of your time."

Haller stood up and went to the desk in the corner. "We've prepared some figures," he said, picking up a red leather brief-case. "We hoped you might look at them tomorrow. I'll be here to answer your questions, and when Maurice gets back in the evening we can discuss our conclusions with him."

As he listened, Tom understood the reason for the tension on the terrace. Amiens and the others had known something was in the wind. Tom had guessed right. They *did* feel threatened. They *did* see him as a threat. He glanced at Edwards. The sick man looked away, avoiding his eye.

The meeting was effectively over. Conversation continued for another twenty minutes, and although Tom answered various questions he could scarcely pay attention. His gaze kept straying to the red leather case. He grew impatient to examine its contents.

Eventually Stanton felt sufficient had been said, because with eyes twinkling, he announced, "We've worked enough for one night." He was of a mind to rejoin the others—musicians were still playing outside and people were dancing—but Tom had no taste for returning to the terrace. He wanted to get back to his room, to think over all that had been said in peace and quiet . . .

"Very well," Stanton shrugged. "If that's what you want."

Haller advanced with the red leather case in his hands. "It's all in here," he said, "balance sheets, profit and loss statements, and so on." He took a key from his pocket. "Open the box and you become privy to our secrets, Mr. Lambert."

When he returned to his room, he was determined not to look at the statues. He failed. An irresistible force drew his gaze to the sculptured limbs and Melody's beautiful face. Setting the brief-case down on a chair, he escaped onto the balcony. The velvety black sky was studded with stars and a yellow moon cast a soft glow on the water. Navigation lights blinked red and green out at sea. He wondered if they belonged to a boat carrying Roddy and Hugo. But it was only a passing thought, his mind overflowed with the offer from Stanton. His heart thumped. Had he lost Bolton only to regain it as part of a much larger business? Gripped by excitement he wanted to shout. Most of all he wanted to telephone Alec Hargreaves to tell him to hold the team together. Half a dozen had wanted to resign, Alec among them. Now there was no need. They could go on as before . . . even faster because the Brierleys were no longer involved.

He smoked a cigarette to calm down, blessing his extraordinary luck. Half an hour passed before he had his first doubts. Hadn't he decided to strike out on his own?

Okay, I might be in charge of this new set-up, but Stanton will own it. Look what happened with the Brierleys. I'd still be working for somebody else . . .

What fascinated him was the potential. Excel plus Bolton plus Pohl plus Bouvier. It could be enormous. And hadn't Haller mentioned even more business interests? Tom's gaze strayed back to the room and the red case on the chair. Haller's words sprang to his mind—"Open the box and you become privy to our secrets."

Stepping back into the room, he unbuttoned the borrowed dinner jacket. Preferring to work in shirtsleeves, he carried the jacket to the wardrobe and slipped it over a hanger, but even as he did so his gaze strayed back to the statues. He swore aloud. Moving around the table, he arranged the chair so as to work with his back to the figures. Then he sat down and reached for the case.

He lost all sense of time after that. Within half an hour his interest was captured; two hours later he was totally absorbed. A good accountant reads balance sheets the way most people read thrillers. The figures reveal motives and intentions, hopes and ambitions. Tom was spellbound. He applied ratio after ratio. Stanton's business holdings were a dozen times bigger than he had imagined, and diverse without pattern. Someone, Stanton's father presumably, the founder of the fortune, had rampaged through Europe, buying companies as if they were trinkets. Many still bore their original names; in at least a dozen Stanton held only a minority interest, and the variety—electronics, chemicals, shipping, printing, office machinery, food, wine—lacked rhyme or reason. A bigger ragbag of interests couldn't be had in a penny bazaar—except pennies was an insult to the figures involved. The accumulation of assets had been vast. Properly managed they could be turned into a great commercial empire . . .

The balcony windows were still open, and through them came the sound of the sea. From far off echoed faint rumbles of thunder, but by then Tom was quite deaf. Nothing less than an earthquake could have interrupted his concentration. Gripped by a rising excitement, too excited to sleep, he scribbled page after page of calculations. By three in the morning he could see Stanton's "great adventure" staring him in the face. The challenge of turning this motley collection of businesses into an international corporation was the most exciting he could imagine.

It was four-thirty when he stretched out on the bed, intending to rest for ten minutes. His eyes were red-rimmed with tiredness; it had been a long night after the longest, most extraordinary day of his life. For a while the sheer buzz of excitement kept exhaustion at bay, but then his eyes drooped and, still fully clothed, he fell into the kind of deep sleep that comes only to the bone-tired.

The sun was high in the sky when he awoke. It was ten-thirty. He blinked into consciousness, disoriented. Then it all came flooding back, along with the sunshine spilling over the balcony, the red leather case on the table, and the statues still entwined in their lovemaking.

He washed and dressed and hurried downstairs. The odd thing was that never once did he look at the statues in the corridor, nor even at the one at the foot of the stairs. What had seemed important before was forgotten amid the rush of thoughts in his head.

The villa was quiet. The hall was empty. Vases were full of fresh flowers, replaced and arranged by unseen hands. When he stepped out onto the terrace there was no sign of the tables which had stood there at dinner. Nobody had been tempted into the swimming pool's refreshing blue water. For a moment, he thought he was alone. Then a figure sat upright on the far side of the pool. It was Haller. The night before, dressed in a beautifully tailored dinner jacket, the Swiss banker had presented the assured image of a successful man of the world; now, wearing only a pair of black trunks, he looked faintly ridiculous. He rose to his feet, revealing a bulging stomach over white sparrow legs. Self-consciously, he reached for a robe as Tom approached. *"Guten Morgen,"* he said, wrapping himself into folds of white toweling. "You slept well, I hope?"

"Fine, thanks."

Haller indicated the small table and two chairs set under the sunshade. "Help yourself. There is orange juice and croissants, and plenty of coffee." He dabbed his pink face with a hand towel. "Phew. I can only take this Greek sun for an hour every morning. Come, let us sit in the shade."

Tom followed him to the table and poured himself some coffee. Haller sat down, thrusting his skinny legs out in front of him and folding his hands over his stomach. Leaning back, he closed his eyes with a sigh of contentment. "You know," he said, "this is when I like Kariakos best. Everyone is off enjoying themselves and I have time to sit and think. It's a great luxury, Mr. Lambert, to sit and think in the sun."

Tom swallowed some coffee, "So where is everyone?"

"Most of them have gone off on *Aphrodite*. Not Maurice of course, he and Melody have left for an auction in Rome."

"Rome?" Tom echoed.

Mention of Melody brought a pang. Ever since last night, he had tried to put her out of his mind. He had made a deliberate effort. The balance sheets had helped. Absorbed by the figures, total concentration had eclipsed other thoughts.

Haller chuckled without opening his eyes. "Like a couple of kids. Such excitement. Always such excitement with Maurice. Such energy."

Tom sipped his coffee. He felt guilty, he had behaved badly toward Melody, and been unforgivably rude to Jasmine. The truth was Melody had got under his skin. In the afternoon she had seemed so . . . so approachable. He had misread the signs.

Opening his eyes, Haller glanced at his watch. "You're just in time. I have to call Piraeus in fifteen minutes if you're leaving today." He struggled upright in his chair. "Well, Mr. Lambert, what's it to be? You stay or you go?"

Tom hesitated, facing up to the issue. "Look," he said, "I'd better tell you. I made a fool of myself over Melody." He shrugged, searching for the best way to explain. "There's a statue in my room. Her and Stanton. It's really none of my business, but I said things that I shouldn't have said. Uncomplimentary things. And I shot off my mouth at Jasmine. If they tell Stanton . . . well, let's say he might change his mind about me."

Haller's pudgy face showed no expression. "I see," he said. "So what about the papers in the briefcase? Did you examine them?"

"God, yes, I was up all night."

"And?"

Tom's hesitancy vanished. "This thing could be vast. The potential is terrific. Far, far bigger than I thought. But what a hotchpotch! There's no business plan that makes sense. It's too diversified, it needs direction."

Haller held up a hand. "So I don't call Piraeus?"

"Well, no . . . except what about what I just said? About Melody—"

"I shouldn't worry," Haller smiled, shaking his head. "Most people are the same. When they first come to Kariakos they see only the girls and the statues. Yet I'll tell you a strange thing. It soon changes. By their third visit they see only Maurice."

Tom stared, doubtfully, "I dunno, I said some damn fool things—"

"Maurice will have heard them before," Haller said confidently, "put them out of your mind. If you feel you behaved badly, then apologize." He shrugged. "But believe me, not a word will be said."

Tom remained silent. Surprise turned to relief. Even so, a doubt persisted. "Not about the business opportunities," Tom frowned as he tried to explain. "But . . . well, about Stanton. I can't figure him out. All these statues around the place. Don't you think it's a bit odd?"

"Unusual," Haller conceded cheerfully, "but less so when you get to know Maurice."

"Why does he do it?"

Haller laughed. "Why does he make love to beautiful women?"

"No . . . why does he flaunt it?"

The smile remained on Haller's face. "You must ask Maurice. I'll give you my opinion if you like, but first answer a question. Have you ever collected anything? Autographs, records, books, theater programs?"

"Records, I suppose. Not that I've got many. A couple of hundred—"

"There you are," Haller beamed. "The urge to collect is basic. Psychoanalysts give you all sorts of reasons. Some people collect quite humble things—matchboxes, shells from the beach, pebbles." He shrugged. "With Maurice it is art. Over the last twenty-five years he has assembled one of the world's most important private collections. Most of it is in Switzerland, some in the States, only a little is here. Art has been a hugely successful investment. In financial terms the appreciation has been vast—and in terms of esthetic appreciation, Maurice has become an expert. He is friendly with many artists; in some cases he is their patron. He is consulted by museums and galleries—"

"I still don't see what—"

"Please," Haller held up a hand. "I want you to understand the mind of a collector. Maurice collects rare and beautiful things." A gleam lit Haller's eye. "Do you not think Melody is rare and beautiful?"

"I'm not blind."

"And to make love with her would be beautiful?"

Yesterday Tom had harbored hope on his own account. He remained silent.

Haller smiled. "It might be easier if I ask myself the same question. For me it would be simple to answer—"

"Okay, I get the point, but—"

"I'd look back on that for the rest of my life," Haller sighed, "so why not record it? Why not have the best artists in the world—"

"So that you could gloat?" Tom sounded contemptuous.

"Not gloat. Remember with love and affection—"

"Love?" Tom echoed scornfully.

Haller sighed, "Mr. Lambert, you asked for an explanation. I'm trying to give it to you."

"Sorry," Tom was suitably contrite. Lighting a cigarette, he settled back in his chair. "Go on. I won't interrupt."

Haller responded with a wry smile. "I'd have been the same at your age. When I was young, it wasn't that I didn't expect to grow old, simply that I couldn't imagine it. Now I am twice your age and I know how fleeting life is. Nothing lasts forever, not youth, nor physical beauty, and love—being *in* love—is usually the first casualty of the passage of time. Maurice will tell you the same, so I don't say he is in love with Melody or anyone else, but I'm quite sure he loves her. If he didn't there wouldn't be any relationship, not simply for sex. The idea would be repugnant to him."

"He sounds like a monk."

Haller chuckled. "No, he could never be that. He likes people too much. He is—that rarity of all rarities—a spendthrift with himself. He shares himself. He's open and warm and vibrant. He enjoys life and makes sure everyone around him enjoys it too. Come, Mr. Lambert, you have seen it yourself. You must have felt it last night?"

Like a sulky child, Tom shrugged grudging agreement. "Sure, he's got charm, but he's also got money—"

"Nonsense," Haller interrupted, "money has nothing to do with it. What attracts women is his zest for life. Being with him is so exciting that they have to run to keep up. How old do you think he is?"

Tom would have guessed about fifty, except for what Constantin had said in Piraeus, "I don't know."

"Sixty-four."

It was impossible not to be impressed. Tom remembered the muscular back and strong legs on the statues. Even if the artist had flattered, Stanton possessed the body of a man twenty years younger.

Haller smiled, "So you make a great mistake to think it's about money. You also insult Melody, yet she seems to attract you?"

Tom left the implied question unanswered.

Haller said, "If she was motivated by money, don't you think—with her beauty and background—she could marry any rich man of her choosing. Whereas marriage to Maurice isn't even on the agenda."

The explanation was confusing Tom even further.

"I can only tell you this," Haller concluded. "With Maurice, deep friendships endure. A month ago in Florence I met a lady who knew Maurice ten years ago. 'Ah, Maurice,' she said with a fond smile, 'he was my finishing school.' "

The sentiments were so close to something Melody had said that Tom tried to recall her exact words. Failing, he shook his head in bewilderment.

"Let's leave it for now," Haller suggested. "I want to talk business. That's why I'm here." A look of anticipation came into his eyes. "After lunch, I will have a siesta, but until then . . ." He spread his hands, palms uppermost. "I am at your disposal. I want to discover what you thought of those papers."

Almost with relief Tom accepted the suggestion. Much about Stanton puzzled him, but at least he understood business.

"Why not fetch the briefcase from your room?" Haller suggested.

So Tom went back into the villa and again climbed the stairs—sensing that every step took him closer to his "great adventure."

Their discussion lasted the rest of the morning and throughout lunch. It was soon clear that Haller had a razor-sharp mind. His answers to questions were clear and precise. When in doubt, he said so and made a note in a book produced from the folds of his robe. On some issues, such as monies posted to undisclosed reserves, he refused to be drawn, but he was frank and open about everything else.

Agreement on the main issues was quick to emerge. Haller accepted that Stanton's businesses lacked coordinated direction. He agreed opportunities had been lost, and listened intently to Tom's brush-stroke ideas.

"What I can't understand," Tom said at one point, "is why you've waited so long to merge these businesses into one unit."

"History," Haller said with a shrug. "Promises. We are all victims of the past, Mr. Lambert. Besides," he added gently, "sometimes it's for the best for businesses to establish their own markets."

"Markets are international," Tom retorted. "In some areas Pohl and Bouvier compete for the same business. That's crazy. So is the way you conduct research. Each of these companies runs its own R&D sections—"

"All of the companies are profitable," Haller protested.

"I dare say, but think of the future. Big as they are, individually they won't be able to afford enough R&D. They'll be squeezed out by the Americans and the Japanese. Product lines will become dated . . ." Tom's words tumbled out in an excited flow as the potential grew ever more clear in his mind.

Haller listened, nodding occasionally, testing an argument with a question now and then. Meanwhile a maid had brought out a tray of fresh coffee, and the two men repositioned themselves under the canopy as the sun moved across the sky. Haller smoked a cigar. They scarcely stopped talking, absorbed by the subject and the exchange of ideas. Helped by Haller, Tom began to see the structure of the businesses clearly, but what eluded him was an understanding of Stanton. The man owned a veritable empire. So what made him tick? Why did he lead his kind of life? Could he be trusted?

Increasingly Tom's questions strayed from the balance sheets to an examination of Stanton himself, and after a while Haller began to respond. "Of course you want to know about him," he said. "He will be central to your future."

Haller also revealed that they had compiled a thick file on Tom. "So to reciprocate would seem only fair," he admitted with a rueful smile.

Gradually a picture of Stanton began to emerge. Tom listened intently, with hardly one word of interruption.

Maurice Stanton was born in 1905. His father was English and his mother was French. The family owned houses in London, Paris, and Geneva, so the boy had a privileged upbringing. "Not pampered," Haller sought a precise definition. "His father excelled at everything and expected his only son to be equally proficient. The best tutors were engaged. The boy was an excellent pupil; physically strong and bright, he had inherited his father's intelligence and determination. By the age of fourteen he was as well educated as any young man trained for the Sorbonne. He played chess to the standard of a Grand Master. He was fluent in every European language. He shot with the skill of a marksman. And ski . . ." Haller shook his head in wonderment. "He could ski better than anyone of his age in Switzerland."

After university, Stanton went into the family business, first in England, then in Germany. "But his heart wasn't in it," Haller shook his head. "Maurice has one of the shrewdest brains I've ever met, but he wouldn't apply himself. In those days his passions were fast cars and big yachts, ski parties in the Alps, airplanes and horse racing." Haller smiled. "And girls, of course. With Maurice there were always plenty of girls."

Stanton senior died in 1925. Maurice was twenty-one years old. He inherited a host of business interests, controlled by a trust until he was thirty. Haller said, "My father was one of the trustees and our bank was deeply involved. Maurice took the view that the trustees should look after the business while he, as he put it, 'finished his education.' He went to South America and then to the States. He was a wealthy young man and naturally he mixed with the rich and the famous."

Maurice Stanton remained in America until 1935. When he returned to Europe, he went first to London, then to Berlin. "He met Hitler several times. When you get to know Maurice, you must ask him to recount his impressions. And about Mussolini, he met him as well. And of course he knew many British and French politicians."

Within a year, Stanton was forecasting a European war. Haller shrugged. "Maurice was disgusted. He was convinced that war could be averted if London and Paris exerted enough pressure. The truth is they did not."

Tom listened carefully to a description of events which had occurred before he was born. Of course he knew all about the war, but his knowledge had been acquired from history lessons at school and reading the British papers. The version Haller described was not quite the same.

"Hitler received a good deal of private approval," said Haller, "many of the people ruling England and France supported his ideas—especially about Communists and the Jews. So they encouraged him behind the scenes. Naturally, they denied it after the war, but Maurice knew them socially and he has no doubts on the matter."

In the States, Maurice had made many Jewish friends and he knew how they feared for relatives in Germany. He did what he could to help. "That was when he began dealing in art," said Haller. "He bought entire collections from Jews. Always at a fair price. The market had been depressed by then and he could have taken advantage, but he never did. Payment was invariably made in Swiss francs. I know this because we held the money in dozens of accounts in our bank. Sadly, much was unclaimed at the end of the war for the owners had perished in concentration camps."

Stanton's largest commercial interest in Germany was the Pohl Organization, which made printing machinery. "He retained that, as you know, but other businesses, those in the rapidly developing fields of electrical engineering and embryonic electronics, were sold. He disposed of everything that might be directly used in the war. He retained Pohl for one specific reason, which I will come to in a moment."

Haller paused to light a fresh cigar. He made a ritual of it, rolling it between his fingers, smelling it before clipping the end and lighting it with a match. Tom sipped coffee and thought how extraordinary it was to be sitting on a Greek island listening to a Swiss banker describe events which had taken place in Germany before the Second World War—a war that had been over for twenty-four years. Wherever Tom looked, he saw luxury. The swimming pool sparkled in the sunlight. The gardens were beautifully manicured. The villa itself was worth a king's ransom, not to mention the yacht and aircraft. Such vast wealth, owned by a man who became more extraordinary by the minute.

"In the spring of 1939," said Haller, "Maurice applied for Swiss citizenship. It was easily arranged. After all, much of his boyhood had been spent in Switzerland. He owned property in

Geneva and St. Moritz. His bankers were Swiss. The family trust was Swiss-based. He had many Swiss friends—"

"So he's not a British subject?" Tom interrupted, surprised.

"No. He renounced British citizenship in 1939, six months before the outbreak of war."

Tom began to understand why researching Stanton in London had proved so difficult.

"You can imagine," Haller continued, "how unpopular this made Maurice in England. People who were once friends wrote him the most abusive letters. He was called a traitor, a coward, all sorts of things. Maurice was unrepentant. He had taken a view and that was that. He made up his own mind. Everything he owned outside Switzerland became Swiss property. As such it was now protected by international law relating to neutral countries. That included the Pohl factories in Germany."

Haller paused to examine the glowing end of his cigar. He smiled, "You would be surprised at the number of Jews who were employed by Pohl. Over a third of the work force. On some pretext or another, dozens of them were summoned to the Geneva office—not all at once, of course, but in two and threes. Most of them stayed. They owe their lives to Maurice. Naturally, that phase didn't last. The Germans put a stop to it. By 1940 most Jews were in forced labor or concentration camps, but Maurice kept a channel open to the Pohl factories right up until the chaos which marked the last months of the war. He helped hundreds of people; not just Jews but all sorts of people on the run from Hitler's regime."

Stanton's activities did not win favor in his adopted Switzerland. Haller sounded apologetic. "But you must understand that neutral means neutral. If our small country was to avoid being drawn into the bloodbath, it was vital not to be seen to favor one side or the other. And Geneva was a hotbed of spies." He smiled. "So Maurice had his knuckles rapped now and then, but . . . Maurice is Maurice . . . he has wit and charm and he survived."

Just before the war ended, Maurice's wit and charm won him a wife. "A Swiss lady," said Haller, "a cousin of mine, actually, a connection which caused me some embarrassment when their marriage broke down, but"—the driest of smiles touched his lips—"I am a true Swiss so I tried to remain neutral."

A daughter, Kirsten, was born in 1946 and Roddy followed eighteen months later. "Sadly, the marriage was already in difficulties," Haller rubbed his forehead as if perplexed. "I don't know why my cousin *insisted* on marriage. Everyone knew what Maurice was like. Women found him attractive and he could never resist a flirtation. Before the war, when he lived in the States, the papers were forever showing him with this film star or that heiress, always on the edge of a scandal. He was cited in three divorce cases. In America that sort of thing is accepted, but in Switzerland . . ." Haller shook his head and tut-tutted. "It was not done, especially with a lady from a good family. I suppose my cousin thought she could change him. Women do, you know. They fall in love because a man excites them, then try to turn him into some dull old stick who wouldn't look twice at other women. Maybe it worked in the first flush of love, and when the war was on . . . but afterward, when Maurice could travel again . . . the temptations were too strong. Geneva was soon buzzing with stories about Maurice being seen with this lady in Paris or that lady in London."

Other things happened to Maurice in London after the war. A most unpleasant incident occurred in the American bar at the Dorchester. Two men came up to him, friends from before the war, and started shouting. "I was with him at the time," said Haller. "One of the men was related to the British Royal Family, he had a title. He started shouting at Maurice, calling him stupid names—a rat, a skunk, a sniveling coward who had come creeping back now that the danger was past. I had to stop Maurice from hitting him. There was a bit of a scuffle, but other people helped keep them apart. Then we were asked to leave. *We* had to leave, not the man who caused the scene. Afterward Maurice told me that both of those men had been among Hitler's strongest supporters in 1937 and 1938. And I know for a fact that they both made a great deal of money out of the war. Maurice made not a penny, deliberately. Poor Maurice. I felt very sorry for him that day. He's never set foot in the Dorchester since."

Stanton was given the same reception all over London. "I was with him a good deal on that trip, so I saw for myself. People hated him. Perhaps they didn't know about those he had saved, although I'm sure they did because I told them myself in some cases. Maurice wouldn't offer a word in his own defense. We had a terrible couple of weeks."

Haller lapsed into silence, brooding over the memories. Then he said, "It was a bad time for Maurice altogether. He'd asked Louise for a divorce. She was being very difficult. I wouldn't have believed she could be so spiteful. A woman scorned, I suppose. Maurice admitted everything was his fault. He made no pretense. The settlement he offered was generous in the extreme. He confessed that when it comes to women he has an irredeemable liking for the impermanent." Haller smiled and looked Tom in the eye. "He's very honest, you know. About himself and everything else. You will find that if you get to know him."

"You make him sound perfect."

Haller laughed. "No man is perfect. Maurice has his warts, especially about his businesses, but his sins are more of omission than anything else. He's very loyal to the people around him."

The arrival of lunch interrupted the conversation. Two maids wheeled out a trolley, cleared the coffee trays, laid a crisp linen cloth, and set out what proved to be an excellent meal—small fish cooked in wine, a delicious chicken, herb-flavored cheese, and honey and curd *flan*. The wine had the merest trace of resin, much less noticeable than in Constantin's retsina. Watching the maids return to the villa, Tom wondered how many people it took to keep Stanton in style. "Do the staff live in?" he asked.

"Most of them live in the village. You may have seen it from *Helena*. The fishing village in the next cove."

"Yes, I saw it."

"It's tiny. Less than fifty houses. Seven or eight families. They're the only other inhabitants on the island. Some of the men fish, others tend the vines and the olives. They farm a bit, but only enough to make Kariakos self-sufficient in food. Maurice looks after everyone and they worship the ground he walks on." Haller smiled. "So you see, Mr. Lambert, Kariakos is a true paradise."

Tom grinned. He wondered if the villagers referred to Stanton as Constantin did, as a "great English lord." Thinking of Constantin reminded him of the soldiers and the frightening incident in the taverna. "What about this military dictatorship?" he asked, jerking his head in the direction he imagined the mainland to be. "Those Colonels who seized power. Do they interfere?"

"With Maurice?" Haller shook his head. "The Greek economy is a mess. They're desperate for foreign currency. The Colonels vie with each other for the privilege of shaking Maurice by the hand. Not that he lets them often, just enough to make them think he might extend his investments in Greece."

"And will he?"

"That might be your decision," said Haller, "if you join us."

The conversation reverted to business. They discussed Pohl and Bouvier for some time, and then Haller asked, "What did you think of the other businesses? Chemicals and—"

"What a hotchpotch," Tom exclaimed. "I went through those papers with a fine-tooth comb last night. Reading them was like watching someone cover every bet on a roulette table. The spread is too wide. You've got to define what business you're in. I did some calculations. Sixty-eight percent of total profits are generated by the businesses in office and consumer electronics. Sixty-eight percent! That's our core business. The rest I'd sell off, at the right time and for the right price, and reinvest the proceeds in our main business. That would allow us to concentrate our efforts—"

Haller smiled. "Our efforts?"

"Yes, well . . ." Tom flushed. "All I'm saying is what I'd do."

"And I agree with you."

"Then why the hell hasn't it been done?"

To answer the question, Haller went back to describing events at the end of the war. Listening gave Tom another insight into Stanton's character. "Promises were made," said Haller. "Pohl had been kept going by a handful of management people through the war. They were all German. Any one of them could have reported Maurice's activities to the Gestapo, but they kept quiet. More than that, three of four actively helped forge false papers for Jews. Can you imagine the risks? When the war ended, Maurice asked them what they wanted. They all said the same thing: they wanted to raise the Phoenix from the ashes, to build the business again by themselves, with as little help from outside as possible. Old man Pohl was still alive then. He was a patriarchal, autocratic kind of man, but his colleagues loved him."

Haller waved a hand. "It seemed such an easy request to grant, so Maurice agreed. And they did well. Nobody let Maurice down, but in the process they became a proudly autonomous unit, neither wanting to steal other people's ideas nor share their own. They wanted to prove themselves, you see."

"All right, I can understand after the war, even during the Fifties, but not now."

"I agree, but that's how it started. That generation is almost totally gone; retired and so on. The problem is that current management persists with the same attitude. It's a legacy. Old Pohl refused to share his development secrets with Bouvier in Geneva or Excel in England. So in turn they took the same attitude. They still do. Edwards is different. I'll come to him in a minute, but Pohl's son runs the show in Hanover and Amiens runs Geneva and they want to keep it that way."

"You mean they'll oppose integration?"

"They've fought it so far. For the last three or four years Edwards has been pushing for a merger, with himself as top dog. Now he's sick, so he wants his son to take over."

"His son?"

"But yes, didn't you meet Desmond last night?"

Vaguely Tom remembered Desmond Edwards as being tall and dark. "About my age?"

"Two years older. Very bright. A good salesman. His father has trained him in every aspect of the business."

Tom frowned, remembering Edwards' look of stubborn defiance. "Let's get this straight," he said. "Old man Edwards wants his son to take over. You just said he's bright. So why not give him the job?"

Haller sighed. "A number of reasons. He's bright, yes, and a potential asset to the business. But he lacks your experience of general management."

Sensing other reasons, Tom remained silent. Haller tugged the white robe tighter around his body, as if suddenly cold. An anxious, unhappy look came into his eyes. "The truth is," he said, "the others wouldn't accept him. Carl Pohl detests Desmond. If Desmond got the top job, Carl Pohl would resign."

"Would that be such a loss?"

Haller's expression turned to surprise. "You don't understand. Carl is an electronics genius. The ideas he's developing will transform people's lives. He runs the best research team in Europe. Believe me, Mr. Lambert, Carl Pohl is one of our most valuable assets; if he goes, his team will go with him. He could write his own ticket with Phillips, or Siemens, or IBM—"

"But he's not a manager?"

"At business he's hopeless. The Pohl Organization makes money because the products are technically ahead of anything else, and Carl keeps them ahead. But if we were to lose him . . ." Haller raised a hand, with the thumb turned down.

"And Amiens? What's he like?"

"French, very able; smart enough to marry the boss's daughter." Haller smiled. "Yvonne was Pierre Bouvier's heir and only child. Yvonne also happens to be Maurice's goddaughter."

Sensing a reservation, Tom frowned. "You don't like him?"

"I didn't say that," Haller shook his head. "Andre is very capable. What is that American expression? A whiz kid? A production whiz kid, brilliant at organizing the factory. By the time old Pierre Bouvier died, Andre had risen to general manager. He accomplished that on merit."

"But he wouldn't have gone higher, is that what you're saying?"

Haller chewed his bottom lip and fell into a thoughtful silence. Eventually he said, "Pierre was against the marriage. I don't know why. Yvonne is older than Andre. Perhaps that was the reason. Women age, lose their looks, a six-year gap might become a burden." He shrugged. "Anyway they married after Pierre's death and Maurice became involved. He was Yvonne's godfather, Pierre's oldest friend, and, of course, the biggest shareholder in the Bouvier business. Yvonne wanted Andre to become the chief executive so she went to Maurice and said so."

"And he said no?"

"Not exactly. He felt pressured. And, of course, he knew old Pierre's views on the marriage. So he made Andre wait. He made him sweat. I think it was a mistake, Maurice regrets it now, but there you are. Eventually he recognized that Amiens was exactly right for the job and he gave in. But Yvonne became quite bitter about it." Haller paused, then added, "Old history now, but that's the story."

"Bouvier has an excellent reputation. Amiens must have made a go of things."

"Certainly."

"So what's the problem? Why not let Amiens run the whole show?"

Haller shrugged. "The personalities, I suppose. Amiens and Yvonne can be very arrogant at times. Desmond is always complaining that Andre treats him like shit. Pohl heard him one day. Pohl laughed. 'Why complain?' he asked. 'You are shit.' "

"I bet Edwards loved that," Tom said drily.

Haller responded with a rueful smile. "The fact is that Pohl, Bouvier, and Excel are three different empires, run by men who'd cut each other's throats. Not one of them would accept either of the others in the top job."

Tom knew he had reached the heart of the problem. He sat quietly assimilating the information, gauging the difficulties, thinking back over his brief contact with the people concerned.

The rueful smile remained on Haller's face. "You've had hostile colleagues before," he pointed out gently.

"Some difference," Tom retorted. "I fired Hunter in the first week. Thornton went the week after. You're telling me that even if I wanted to, I couldn't get rid of Amiens because of Yvonne Bouvier?"

"It would be difficult," Haller admitted.

"And I can't fire Pohl?"

"You'd lose a genius."

"Or Desmond Edwards?"

"He might become your strongest supporter."

Tom doubted it. Excel was run very differently from the way he had run Bolton. "So your theory is they won't accept each other, but they'll have to accept an outsider?"

Haller smiled. "You do yourself an injustice, but I suppose it could be put that way."

Tom squinted up into the sun. "There's another side to the penny."

"Oh?"

"I'm the one thing that might unite them. They could join forces against me."

Haller smiled, but remained silent.

Tom's eyes lit with a look of grudging admiration. "Very clever. Was this your idea, Herr Haller?"

The banker twitched a quizzical eyebrow.

"You want this merger, right?"

Haller nodded.

"If I do it, and hold the team together, you get your merger."

"Exactly," Haller agreed.

"And if they join forces against me, you'll get your merger anyway."

The smile on Haller's face widened to a grin. "In that case, Mr. Lambert," he said, "it would be heads I win and tails you lose."

The odd thing, Tom reflected afterward, was that he liked Haller. Perhaps it wasn't so odd; after all, Haller was a pro and Tom always worked well with professionals. The amateurs were the ones to avoid, always acting unpredictably in ways which led to disaster. Professionals knew the rules. Haller was as tough as old boots but he put his cards on the table. "Give me the right return on Maurice's investments," he had said, "and I'll give you every support." When Tom had pointed out that reorganization might create short-term disruption, Haller answered severely, "I wouldn't like disruption in profits, Mr. Lambert. We Swiss believe in the short term. After all, in the long term, we die."

Haller had spelled out the offer by then: a generous package of salary, expenses, bonuses, stock options, and a job contract which ran for five years. "Getting rid of me will be expensive," Tom pointed out with a grin. Haller shrugged. "We are not the Brierleys, Mr. Lambert. We accept that after one bad experience you might be chary of another, so we have geared our offer accordingly. And, remember, we know what we are buying; we vetted you thoroughly. You were right to say you are the catalyst to make this merger work one way or the other. But I hope you will run Stanton Industries for the rest of your life."

Tom believed him. After spending all morning talking business, Haller's sincerity rang clear as a bell.

"It's good of you to say so," said Tom.

"Not really. I have Maurice's interests at heart. I believe you will be good for him. I also think," Haller said as a speculative gleam lit his eye, "that Maurice will be good for you in ways you cannot yet even imagine."

After which, and with lunch over, Haller went off for his siesta, leaving Tom on the terrace. The wine, the hot sun, and the very late night would ordinarily have made him similarly drowsy, but under the circumstances, sleep was out of the question. He knew it was pointless to go to his room. His mind was hyperactive, buzzing with thoughts. He might have remained on the terrace except for the heat which grew increasingly intense. Eventually, when even the canopy failed to provide sufficient protection, he remembered the clearing on the cliff, with the bench and the telescope under the trees. Leaving the terrace, he followed the path around the villa and into the pines, pausing now and then to look with unseeing eyes at the view, his mind too full to absorb more than the pathway before him. After a while he came to the clearing, where he sat down on the bench to smoke a cigarette while pondering his decision. Not that there was much doubt in his mind. Whatever the difficulties, and he anticipated many, he could think of no more exciting challenge than to run Stanton Industries.

He sat there for over an hour. The soft breeze rustled the pines, the sea lapped the rocks at the foot of the cliff. He thought about Carl Pohl and Andre Amiens and Desmond Edwards. He wondered how they would react to his appointment. Would they accept him or fight him?

Eventually he stirred himself, which was when he remembered the red briefcase. He had left it under the table on the terrace. Guilty about overlooking something placed in his charge, he hurried from the clearing, down the path to the villa, cursing his forgetfulness as he went. Passing the gap in the trees which afforded a view of the sea, he skirted the villa and emerged onto the terrace, walking at a pace just short of a run. His gaze went immediately to where he had been sitting. The cloth had been removed from the table, the remains of lunch had been cleared, but—thankfully—the red case was exactly where it had been left.

Breathing a sigh of relief, he began to cross the terrace when he became aware of a movement in the pool. A figure was swimming under water. A female figure. Nude, wearing only a white swimming cap. As she surfaced she turned on her back, revealing plump, pink-tipped breasts and limbs bronzed by the sun. For a fleeting second, as the girl twisted and swam to the edge of the pool, Tom thought she was Melody. Only when she reached the steps did he recognize Jasmine. She saw him at the same moment, by which time she had hauled herself out of the water. She remained motionless, hands clasping the chromium hand rails, her startled gaze fixed on his face. Feeling like a Peeping Tom caught in the act, he turned away, his embarrassment eased by the sight of a towel on a chair. Quickly he reached for it and took it to her, making a conscious effort to look at her face and not her body. Two steps brought her out of the water and a third carried her to within reach of the towel. Twirling, she wrapped it sarong fashion around her body. "Thank you," she said in a cool-sounding voice as she turned to go.

"No, wait," he exclaimed. "Jasmine. Please."

Hesitating, she looked back over her shoulder.

"Sorry about last night. I was a bit . . . um, confused, I suppose. I shouldn't have spoken like that. I really am sorry."

Her dark eyes searched his face.

"I am sorry," he repeated lamely.

Gradually her look of hostility faded. A softness, even a glint of amusement came into her eyes. "I forgive you," she said and walked over to the chairs. As she sat down she was careful to draw the towel tightly around her. "There's a jug of lemonade on the tray. Pour me a glass, would you. Have some yourself, or do you have another meeting with Herr Haller?"

"No, he's having a siesta." When he poured the lemonade, ice cubes clinked against the rim of the jug. He filled the glasses and passed one to her, catching the inquisitive gleam in her eyes.

"Tell me," she said, "I'm curious. Something provoked you last night. What was it?"

The question took him off guard. "Oh, I dunno," he shrugged, "this place, I suppose. It takes some getting used to."

"I got used to it very easily," she said lightly, her amused eyes watching him over the rim of her glass. "I don't think it was this place," she said, removing her white bathing cap and shaking lustrous black hair into place. "I think it was Melody."

"Oh? What makes you say that?"

She gave him a knowing smile. "The way you were looking at her."

He began to feel vaguely discomfited. He had enough sense not to ask for an explanation, but his silence on that subject left him with nothing to say.

"Don't look so shamefaced," Jasmine laughed. "It's not a crime to be smitten by a beautiful girl. I think you were shocked," she said lightly, tugging the knotted towel more tightly around her as if determined not to shock him again. "Come now, aren't I right?"

"Perhaps," he answered, sitting down in the other chair. "You must admit it's a bloody odd set-up. I mean you and Melody and Velvet—"

"And Maurice?" she interrupted, teasing him with a look. "Stop being so conventional. Monogamy isn't universal, you know. Arabs take half a dozen wives—"

"Is that how you see yourself? As Maurice's wife?"

She laughed, a joyous, bubbly sound from deep in her throat. "Don't be absurd," she said, shaking her head. "Maurice neither wants nor needs a wife. He's a most delightful companion, experienced, charming, generous—"

"And lecherous," Tom interrupted sarcastically.

Her eyes widened in surprise. "Do you imagine he forces himself on us? Sexual desire is not a one-way street, you know. What about us? Don't you think we get as much out of it as Maurice? He's a marvelous lover—"

"To *all* of you?"

Her eyebrows arched upward. "Should I be jealous? Why? I don't own him. He doesn't own me. Besides, Melody and Velvet are my friends. Would it please you if I scratched their eyes out?"

Recognizing the absurdity, he began to feel foolish and out of his depth. She was looking at him with a mixture of bewilderment and amusement. "I'm not sure I know how to explain, but can't you understand, Maurice has given us this golden gift . . . a perfect summer. By the end of it, the magic will fade. That's where he's so clever; that's why he sends us away." A far-away look came into her eyes. "Meanwhile . . ." she sighed, turning in the chair to smile up at the sky.

"Meanwhile?"

"Meanwhile everything," she answered dreamily, shaking her head before bringing her gaze back to him. "Meanwhile I've learned so much. I shall always look back on this summer. Maurice has taught me more than a dozen younger men could teach me. And without the heartache and disappointments, thank you very much, or the clumsiness men display when they're inexperienced."

Tom frowned in silence.

Her dark eyes watched him. "I think you are rather a serious man, Mr. Lambert?"

A wry grin tugged at his lips. "I'm paid to be serious."

"In your private life too?" she asked gently.

He had precious little *private* life. Bolton had been his life. The business had absorbed him twenty-four hours a day, seven days a week, month after month and year after year. Jasmine's question reminded him of the old adage about all work and no play. He made an effort to brighten the conversation. "You're right," he smiled. "I'm dull and conventional. Tell me about you. How did you meet Maurice Stanton?"

"Why do you ask?"

Her quick question took him off guard. "Just friendly interest," he said defensively.

"But you are not interested in me," she admonished with mock severity. "You're interested in Melody. Anyone who saw your face last night would know that. I'm not offended, but why pretend?"

"I'm not pretending anything."

Her eyes disbelieved him. With an enigmatic little smile, she tucked her legs under her and snuggled deeper into the towel. "Funny," she said, "everyone talks of Swinging London and the sexual revolution, but most men don't understand it. They think it's all about the pill and girls in mini skirts who hop into bed. But that's not the half of it."

"So what's the other half?"

"Women doing their own thing, the way men do. You'll never understand Melody unless you understand that. Melody is one of a new breed; a new breed of female tycoons."

He grinned. Anyone less like a tycoon was hard to imagine, and he said so, only for Jasmine to contradict him. "You're blinded by her beauty. There's more to Melody than mere looks."

He had sensed that himself; even the short time he had spent with her had been enough for her intelligence and strong will to shine through. And a moment later, as Jasmine plunged into the story, his first impressions were confirmed. Melody had grown up in Oslo, the only child of a government official. The family were comfortably off and Melody had lacked for nothing. Doted on by her parents and a score of uncles and relatives, her nursery had overflowed with playthings. When she was eight, her father was promoted to the Norwegian embassy in Paris and the family moved home. Melody was allowed to take with her a collection of Scandinavian dolls. In Paris she acquired French dolls, usually from her parents but occasionally by swapping a Norwegian doll for a doll owned by a school friend. After Paris, the family had moved to Tokyo, where again Melody added to her collection. And after Tokyo they went to Rome, and after Rome came Madrid. Wherever she went, Melody added to her collection, and by the time they moved to Washington, she owned fifteen hundred dolls. A special room was set aside in the new family home to house her collection. Visitors admired them, journalists wrote about them, and a wealthy American collector offered to buy them. By this time Melody was eighteen. Her interest in dolls had faded. Accepting the offer from the American collector gave her a sizable sum of money, her *own* money, nothing to do with her parents. Affluent beyond her wildest dreams, she invested in paintings, restricting her purchases to one small segment of the art market. Specialization paid off, for when the family moved to London five years later, she sold her paintings for a considerable profit.

"She had enough money to open her own gallery," said Jasmine, "which was what she was planning to do, when she met Maurice."

"I see." Tom was intrigued in spite of himself. He had misunderstood the situation yesterday and ever since done his best to put Melody out of his mind.

Jasmine smiled, "So Melody will make her own fortune. She won't play second fiddle to the men in her life."

"Not even to Maurice?"

"It doesn't arise," Jasmine demurred, shaking her head. "I tried to explain. Maurice is a force of nature, a teacher, a lover too when the mood takes; their friendship will generate lasting affection, but that will be all."

"You sound very sure."

"Of course. I love him in the same way. To be with Maurice is always exciting. He has enriched my life, but he is not my life."

Tom grinned. "I know, he's a great adventure."

"Aha!" she laughed. "I do you an injustice, you *do* understand."

He didn't, not completely; he pretended for fear of appearing naive, but real understanding continued to elude him.

Jasmine smiled. "So now you understand, you don't have to glare at poor Melody when you meet her again."

"You mean tonight?"

"Not just tonight. Aren't you seeing her in London?"

"She told you?"

"Why not? Was it a secret?"

"Well, no, but—"

"You've changed your mind?"

"That was before . . ." He stopped himself from saying: before he had recognized Melody as one of the statues. Instead, he said, "I shall be working for Maurice—"

"And that makes a difference?" Her eyebrows arched and her voice sounded mildly scornful.

"I'll be very busy," he tried to avoid the issue. "I'll have a great deal to do."

Jasmine gathered the towel about her and rose from the chair. "Forgive me, I misunderstood you. I thought that having apologized to me you would be even more anxious to make your peace with Melody. Perhaps I was wrong."

In the event, he did make his peace with Melody, although not in the way Jasmine meant. No arrangements were made for further meetings in London. Attracted though he was, he was determined to put Melody off-limits—a resolve which was helped by the events of the evening.

By seven o'clock, the villa was again filling with people. From his room, he heard sounds of doors opening and closing, and of baths being run as other guests returned from their day on *Aphrodite.* He had been sitting on the balcony, the red briefcase open at his side, leafing through the papers, listing further thoughts and ideas until the noises from other rooms reminded him it was time to get ready. Bathed and shaved and dressed in the fresh clothes that had been laid out for him, he was just stepping into his shoes when a knock sounded at the door.

It was Haller, and behind him was Stanton, beaming his megawatt smile. Haller grinned, "I told Maurice I think we've reached an agreement. He insisted on coming—"

"Of course I insisted," Stanton interrupted, advancing into the room. "Well, Mr. Lambert, are you with us?"

Surprised, Tom nodded, "Yes, I think—"

"Splendid!" Stanton's hands had been behind his back; now he revealed them, shaking hands with his right while flourishing a bottle of champagne with his left. "Get some glasses, Gunther. Let's celebrate." As Haller walked over to the cabinet, Stanton began to pace up and down. "Well I *am* pleased," he grinned. "It's Maurice and Tom from now on, right? None of this Stanton and Lambert stuff. And I tell you, Tom, your talent and my businesses will make a formidable combination. A great adventure, eh? You'll work your balls off, but that's what you like, isn't it? And by God we'll have some fun. *You* should pay *me* for the privilege!"

Maurice Stanton was at his most ebullient that night. His day in Rome had gone exceedingly well—"Melody bought a dozen lots that will quadruple in value. I tell you, that girl's got a sensational eye."

They met *that girl* at the top of the stairs. Melody was dressed in a white off-the-shoulder gown which bestowed an extra sheen to the flawless bronzed skin. Tom was beset by conflicting emotions, his excitement at seeing her clashing with determination to avoid her in the future.

"Tom's going to run my businesses," said Stanton, as a radiant Melody took his arm.

Her eyes betrayed a flicker of uncertainty as she turned to face Tom. He managed a small grin. "Hello. I hear you had a good day in Rome."

A smile bloomed on her lips. "We had a wonderful day, didn't we, Maurice?" Squeezing Stanton's arm, she tilted her face up to him, and was still smiling when she looked back at Tom. "I am glad for you both," she said with the careful correctness of someone conferring a blessing. "I am sure you will be successful, yes?"

Stanton laughed. "Successful? We'll conquer the bloody world! Come on, let's tell the others."

Jasmine was waiting at the foot of the stairs. Stanton swept her up in a bear hug, swinging her off the ground, around and around, before setting her down and kissing her full on the lips. "Come on," he laughed, linking a girl on each arm, "I've an announcement to make."

It was easy to understand what Jasmine meant by describing Stanton as a force of nature. The man generated excitement. Haller was right—the girls *did* have to rush to keep pace. So did everyone else, Tom and Haller included. Scarcely had they hurried through the Moorish arch when Stanton was scooping Velvet into his arms. She squealed and kicked in mock protest, while he carried her across the terrace, laughing uproariously, as he threatened to throw her into the pool. She clung to him, lips seeking his, her hands in his hair. He kissed her hungrily before setting her down.

Meanwhile all activity on the terrace had stopped. Those who had been dancing stood and watched, others looked on from where they sat at their tables, musicians ceased playing, servants stood motionless. Such an entrance was bound to create an air of expectation, and Stanton was not about to disappoint his guests.

"Be seated, everyone," he called, advancing to the clearing amid the tables. "I have something to tell you."

Tom followed Haller to a table. A moment later Melody sat down beside him, so near that he could smell her perfume and admire the length of her eyelashes. She smiled briefly before looking to where Stanton stood accepting a glass of wine from one of the servants.

"This goes back a long way," Stanton began, "but when we talk of the future, it is right to remember the past . . ."

A silence descended. Not immediately—during the opening moments the listeners settled deeper into their chairs, sipped their drinks, lit cigars, puffed cigarettes, fingered napkins and fidgeted in numerous ways—but gradually they became so still that the only sounds beyond Stanton's voice were the chirping of the cicadas and the faint swish of the sea on the beach far below.

Stanton used the setting with the skills of an actor. Immaculate in a white tuxedo, he prowled up and down the terrace under a fat yellow moon with the flares as a backcloth. When he paused, he held the silence, creating an expectant thrill in the audience; people sat transfixed, caught up in a story about the dark days of the war against Hitler.

Tom had expected a short statement about the formation of Stanton Industries. But what was emerging was a picture of the past. Stanton's warm and resonant voice crackled with excitement as he talked of one incident in particular—when Hans Pohl was almost caught smuggling refugees across the German and Swiss frontiers.

"Imagine the danger." Stanton's eyes gleamed. "Hans arriving in Ravensburg with the Gestapo waiting on every street corner. Someone had talked. If Hans was arrested he would have been tortured and killed. A lesser man would have thought only of his own safety. And Hans *could* have been safe. He had authorized papers. He was permitted to travel. He could have left the three men to fend for themselves. Instead he spent the entire day searching for a hiding place. Finally he hid them in a sewage works and told them to stay there. Then he crossed into Switzerland to tell us what had happened."

Savoring the memory, Stanton paused until his eyes found Yvonne Amiens in the audience. "We got them out two days later. Your father and I went in together."

The story of the escape was spine-chilling, but what made it more remarkable was the way Stanton gave Bouvier all the credit. It was a story told to illustrate the courage of Pierre Bouvier, not to bolster Stanton's own ego.

Tom began to wonder about the purpose of such recollections. Why, and why now? What had they to do with the announcement? And why was Stanton so keen to pay tribute to Yvonne's father? Tom found himself watching Yvonne. There was no mistaking her pride, it shone from her eyes. He guessed her to be about forty, fair-haired, with a strong nose too large for her face. From time to time she slid satisfied glances at her husband beside her, who responded with smiles of his own.

Not that Stanton talked exclusively about Bouvier. A few moments later, he directed his attention to Carl Pohl.

"Your father worked under the noses of the Gestapo. He risked his life every day . . ."

The German was very different from Andre Amiens. Whereas the Frenchman had a certain style, Pohl seemingly cared little about his appearance. His dinner jacket was unbuttoned, and his bow tie inelegantly loose. He sat with his chin cupped in his hands, elbows on the table, pale eyes myopic behind thick spectacles, his face expressionless as he listened.

It dawned on Tom what Stanton was doing. By harking back to the past, he was reminding Yvonne Bouvier and Carl Pohl of his long links with their families. By paying homage to their fathers, he was underlining the fact that their fathers had paid homage to him. He went on to include Edwards—still talking in that seductive voice, he stepped out of the circle of light and walked to where Desmond Edwards sat with his father.

"And this man," said Stanton, placing a hand on Sir Bernard's shoulder, "stood by me when I was friendless in England. He gave me his trust and, I hope, has never had cause to regret it."

The effect on Edwards was surprising. He had been truculent the previous evening; but as Stanton talked of friendship, Edwards was visibly moved. His eyes glistened. He coughed to clear a lump in his throat, and he reached up to grip Stanton's hand in a gesture of reciprocal affection.

But if Sir Bernard was moved, no such emotions were shared by his son. Desmond Edwards sat stony-faced, staring directly ahead, and when he felt Stanton's hand on his own shoulder, he flinched. His eyes fastened on Tom with obvious hostility, causing Tom to flinch in return.

". . . But time marches on," Stanton was saying as he walked back into the light cast by the flares, "each generation hands onto the next . . ."

Tom was reminded that Stanton had sired his own next generation. It seemed odd that Edwards and Pohl had followed their fathers into the businesses, yet apparently Stanton's own son had no interest.

". . . Merging together," Stanton was saying, "to become a united force, not just in Switzerland and France, Britain and Germany, but beyond Europe, and throughout the world . . ."

Watching the faces, Tom wondered who would be friend and who would be foe. Catching Amiens' eye, he was met by a look of studied indifference. Desmond Edwards scowled, while Pohl looked up at the night sky as if wishing Stanton would finish—a wish Tom shared a moment later. . . .

"Tom Lambert," Stanton was saying, "is a young man of quite exceptional application and ability—"

Tom felt every eye turn to him.

"—who will become the chief executive officer."

Too late to back out now, Tom thought. Not that he wanted to back out. The scope and opportunities were clear from the balance sheets. The challenge was irresistible. There were bound to be problems.

". . . I know you will give him every support . . ."

The speech became recognizable for what it was—a plea for unity, cleverly constructed with enough references to bygone days to remind them of Stanton's past magnanimity. Tom wondered whether it would be enough. Stanton was winding up with a flourish as servants circulated with trays of champagne.

"A toast," Stanton cried, collecting a glass. "I give you Stanton Industries."

With an answering murmur everyone rose, pushing chairs back from the tables, raising their glasses.

"To Stanton Industries," Amiens echoed with a sneer.

"To Stanton Industries," Desmond Edwards muttered with unconcealed disgust.

"Stanton Industries," Pohl barked, meeting Tom's eye with a challenging look.

Feeling a hand on his arm, Tom turned in response to Melody's touch. Moving closer, she brushed his cheek with her lips. "To your great adventure," she said softly, green eyes bright with excitement.

BOOK THREE

1978

"An exciting few hours," Constantin mused thoughtfully, "even if you faced enemies from the outset."

"Yes," Tom admitted drily, "it was quite an evening." When he smiled he felt the tension ease in his face. Remembering back down the years was more demanding than he had expected.

"A *consigliori*? Isn't that what Roddy called you? I suppose Edwards and Pohl and Amiens saw you in the same light?"

"They weren't pleased," Tom conceded, "but merging those companies made such enormous sense that I thought they'd come to accept it—"

"Always the optimist."

"Maybe," Tom grinned ruefully. "On the other hand it was a huge opportunity for me. My chance to break into the big-time. I was damn near broke, remember. I'd just walked out of Bolton and here I was being offered this tremendous challenge—"

"I understand," Constantin nodded. His glass was empty and he began to pull himself up from the chair.

"I'll get it." Tom rose and collected Constantin's glass on his way to the sideboard. Glancing out at the terrace, he was surprised to realize that darkness had fallen. The flares had been dispensed with long ago. Now underwater lights came on in the pool and electric lanterns shone from the balustrades.

"And Melody?" Constantin cocked his head. "Your friendship blossomed?"

Tom laughed, "As a matter of fact she left the island a week later. Not that I knew at the time. But within the month she had set up her gallery in Paris and embarked upon her great adventure as she called it."

"What did Maurice say about that?"

Tom paused in the act of pouring the brandies. "Do you know, I never asked him. The subject never came up. Not that I saw him for a couple of months . . ." The words tailed off as Tom remembered. For a moment he stared into space. Then he finished pouring the brandies and handed Constantin his glass. "I hardly slept in the next couple of months," he said, returning to his chair, "Alec and I . . ."—he broke off—"where the hell *is* Alec? He should have been here by now—"

"He'll arrive in a minute. Go on. Maurice had just announced this merger—"

"It was all a bluff," Tom interrupted.

Constantin stared at him. "What do you mean? A bluff?"

"He would have backed down if they'd stood firm."

"No?" Constantin sat back, astonished. "But you just told me—"

"He was bluffing."

"Maurice was? But he had appointed you—"

"What he gave with one hand he took away with the other." Tom's face darkened, "We had a terrible row the next day . . ."

Not that there was even a hint of an argument to begin with. They met early the next morning, in fact so early that Tom wondered if he had misunderstood. Had Stanton *really* suggested they meet at seven? He shaved and dressed and went downstairs, half expecting to have got it all wrong, but Stanton was already there—dressed in yellow cotton trousers, white shirt and white sweater, drinking coffee and smoking a cigarette. "First cup of the day," he grinned, "tastes like nectar. Get some inside you, then we'll be off."

"Off?"

"To a high place," Stanton joked, "where we can sit undisturbed and ponder the meaning of life."

Nobody else was about. The terrace was deserted when Stanton led them away from the villa, along the path and through the gap in the pines. He walked like an athlete, covering the ground with springy strides which suggested he could run if he liked. Tom guessed where they were going. To the clearing at the top of the cliff, with the bench and the telescope.

"This is where the thinking gets done," Stanton announced

as they emerged into the clearing. "If everything works out, this will be our office, away from the madding crowd, just you and me, plotting and pondering the meaning of life."

It was the second time he had used those words, and although he spoke lightly his dark eyes glimmered in a way which suggested he was partly serious. He certainly wanted to talk, mostly about the past, as if discussing what had gone before would help explain the present. And Tom was ready to talk. He wanted to get to know the man. Years later he was to recall Haller saying—*People are all the same when thay come to Kariakos. At first they see only the girls and the statues. After a while they see only Maurice.* The full truth of Haller's words began to register that morning. The night before Tom had seen Maurice Stanton at his most flamboyant, holding center stage, dominating an audience by sheer force of personality. He already knew Stanton had charisma, he had seen it at work. He had watched Stanton make people warm toward him with almost magical skill—but that morning he met a more reflective man, a man who talked of his life with such candor that afterwards Tom was annoyed for not seeing where it was leading. In fairness, it was some time before Stanton got to the point.

They sat on the bench, next to the telescope, and gazed out to sea as they talked. The early morning sky was a pearly white and the sea more gunmetal than blue. Gulls circled overhead, dipping past them from time to time, screaming and squawking on their way down to the water. The pine trees cast long shadows and the air was fresh and cool, full of the scent of the sea which splashed onto the rocks at the foot of the cliff.

Stanton talked of the war, and his friendship with Hans Pohl and Pierre Bouvier. Their fight against Hitler had bound them together, a fight against fascism more than against Germans, as Stanton made clear. "What happened in Germany could happen anywhere," he said, "I had to fight that. I'll always fight that."

Sharing from Tom's packet they smoked cigarettes, mildly surprised to find they smoked the same brand. "Did it change you," Tom asked, "the war and all that?"

Stanton thought for a moment. "I suppose so. I hadn't taken anything seriously until then." A rueful smile touched his lips,

"People said I was making a career out of sowing wild oats. They were probably right. But then I came back to Europe and saw what a mess the politicians were making of things. . . ." He shrugged. "That was enough to sober anyone up."

After the war he had made decisions about the rest of his life. "Nothing very profound," he laughed, "I wanted to cultivate things of beauty, and to look after my friends. That was all. I knew I'd be happy if I could do that."

He had remained in Switzerland for some years, "based in Geneva, but I was able to travel again. Part business, part pleasure."

Tom speculated on the pleasure. Haller's story about women prompted thoughts which may have shown on his face, because Stanton continued with a wry smile, "I had been stupid enough to marry during the war. Quite the wrong thing for me, totally senseless looking back. I'm not cut out for marriage, never was, never will be." A thoughtful look came into his eyes. "Don't get me wrong. I'm not against it. It suits some people. You're a young man, I daresay you'll try it one day. It's just that I can't come to terms with the idea of locking people up in pairs. It stifles individuality and I think that's appalling."

Few men, Tom thought, were as individualistic in their approach to life as Maurice Stanton.

"The divorce was a bad business," Stanton admitted. "The Swiss get bloody stuffy about divorce. It's better these days of course, but just after the war . . ." He shook his head, "You'd have thought I committed murder. The truth was that Louise felt humiliated and was bent on revenge. She took it too. I didn't mind the money, I gave her a fortune, but I resented not seeing my kids."

Tom was surprised. Stanton hardly lived the life of a family man.

"I disliked being treated as an ogre. I was forbidden to see them until they were eighteen." Stanton's hands clenched into fists. "For God's sake!" he exclaimed. "The most formative years of their lives and I couldn't get near them!"

Every Christmas and on their birthdays he had sent his children a gift, setting great store on the day he would see them again. "Damn stupid really," he admitted, "after all, they were mere babies at the time of the divorce."

On his daughter's eighteenth birthday he had sent her a diamond necklace and an invitation to visit Kariakos.

"She returned it with a note saying she never wanted to see me. I'm a monster in her eyes," he said with obvious sadness. "Louise has poisoned her against me. I've tried to make contact several times since, but been rebuffed every time." He fell silent, staring out to sea until his face brightened. "I've seen her though, this year, quite by chance, at the theater in London. She was there with her mother and a party of friends. She's a beautiful girl. Twenty-five now. Good God! Twenty-five . . ."

He sat shaking his head, lost in thought, his smile fading. "She works for the Red Cross, you know." Dry amusement came into his voice. "Mind you, socially that's very acceptable in Geneva. It's the Swiss heritage. The Red Cross and cuckoo clocks. Still, rumor has it that she takes her work seriously."

"But you see your son."

"Roddy? Oh sure," Stanton laughed. "Roddy's a different kettle of fish. He was a bit of a rebel, always in trouble, thrown out of school, that sort of thing. Louise ran herself ragged trying to control him. Serves the spiteful bitch right! Roddy was out here like a shot within a week of his eighteenth birthday."

"Does he spend a lot of time here?"

"He comes and goes." Stanton cocked a quizzical eyebrow. "Some people say he's a genius, you know. Him and Hugo. They're inseparable. They met at university, doing amateur dramatics. Mostly they're into films now; producing and directing, that sort of thing. Some critic in Paris reckons they'll become the most important filmmakers the world's ever seen. I hope he's right." Stanton laughed. "I've seen some of their stuff. Couldn't make sense of it. No proper story. Still, that's what they want to do, so good luck to them."

Something jarred as Tom listened. Stanton sounded more wistful than proud, as if disappointed, perhaps wondering what he might have made of Roddy had the boy come to him sooner. The impression was strengthened when Stanton continued, "Of course, Yvonne more or less grew up here. She was always out here on holiday. Desmond too, and Carl. They're like family to me. Family bequeathed, you might say, by Hans and Pierre. And poor old Bernard's on his last legs. His one wish is to go to his grave knowing that Desmond is all right." Stanton's eyes darkened. "You can understand that, can't you?"

Tom nodded.

"I owe Bernard that," Stanton said softly, "just as I owed Hans and Pierre."

Even then Tom had no idea where the conversation was leading. Stanton fidgeted, picking a pine cone up from the ground and tossing it idly from hand to hand. Suddenly he turned to look Tom straight in the face. "I curse this merger at times," he said. "Oh, don't get me wrong, it makes sense, I know that, Gunther has been saying so for years, and I agree, but . . ." He shook his head. "The world was a hell of a sight easier when it was smaller. You could make promises then. Now everything is shrinking . . . a decision here affects something there. Sometimes when I look back . . ." He sighed and fell silent for a moment. Then, very softly, he said, "I was bluffing last night."

Tom started with surprise. "Bluffing? About what?"

Gazing out to sea, Stanton avoided his eye. "I wanted them to believe this merger was a fait accompli . . . that there was no point in their arguing—"

"I thought it *was* a fait accompli." Tom's surprise changed to alarm.

"We must persuade them," Stanton said, an edge of determination in his voice. "If push comes to shove, I don't think I can force them. I can't. My conscience won't let me. I owe their fathers too much—"

"What the hell? I thought we had a deal. Haller and I spent all afternoon—"

"Gunther told me, your contract and the rest of it, that's fine—"

"So what are you saying?"

Stanton hesitated. "If they'd stood together last night, I suppose I'd have backed down. I'm not sure how I would have played it." Hope crept into his eyes. "But I think I got away with it, don't you?"

Staring at him, Tom tried to control his temper. And his disappointment. He was re-assessing the deal . . . wondering if he even had a deal. Last night it had been cut and dried. He said, "My brief from Haller was to put this merger together and keep your people on the team—"

"Exactly."

"But you're saying if they don't want to play there's no game?"

The accusation stung. A flush came to Stanton's cheeks. "That's not quite fair," he retorted. "The worst you can accuse me of is trying to make an omelette without breaking eggs. I *want* this merger, but I'm trapped by my promises to Hans and Pierre—"

"What about your promise to me?" Tom jumped up from the bench. "For Christ's sake! Last night we had a deal—"

"We still have if you'll listen."

Afterwards Tom was to look back on that conversation a hundred times and always with a sense of wonder at Stanton's ability to persuade. Tom had been blazing mad. And bitterly disappointed. The whole concept of Bouvier plus Pohl plus Excel plus Bolton had grabbed him from the first minute. Now it was being snatched away. And somehow Stanton emerged with honor. That was the most incredible part. Somehow Stanton's point of view had seemed understandable. Stanton was trying to behave with integrity; to honor past promises while recognizing the future. Changes had to be made.

"But I *am* obligated to Yvonne and Andre, to Carl and Desmond. I do want them to accept it . . ."

Tom argued vehemently. "It was never going to be easy. I knew that. I told Haller he wanted the impossible. Now you're asking for a miracle. Bloody hell! It's not on. It's damn well not on . . ."

But Stanton persisted, "You wouldn't be here if I could solve this myself, but I can't. I admit I can't. That's why I picked you—"

"Thanks for nothing!"

The warm smile returned to Stanton's face. "You know," he said, "there's a word in Greek. *Polymichanos.* It's hard to translate. Resourceful. Fertile in devices. Someone who can always devise a new plan. That's you, Tom. It sums you up. I'm in a hell of a jam. I know it, but I believe, somehow, God knows how, you'll find a way to persuade them. Succeed in that and you'll run Stanton Industries for the rest of your life, I promise—"

"Promise! You promised last night—"

"I haven't reneged. There were some details—"

"Details!"

"There's more."

And there was. One more detail. The bonus. Two hundred thousand pounds if the merger went through with universal agreement. Two hundred thousand pounds!

Tom had less than three thousand in the bank. His car was four years old. His apartment was mortgaged. Resigning in temper from Bolton had been expensive—no severance pay, no compensation, simply the cessation of a monthly salary. Meanwhile bills had to be paid . . .

"They'll fight you all the way," Alec said bluntly. "You'll never get it off the ground—"

"But Stanton *wants* them to merge. He's backing me. I've got his full support," Tom protested.

They were at his flat the next morning. He would have arranged the meeting for the night before but it was past ten when he arrived home, so he had settled for a long telephone call giving Alec the bare bones. Now, fleshing out his account of an incredible seventy-two hours, he was struggling. He was meeting unexpected resistance. Part of the bond between them was that wherever Tom went, Alec would follow—but Alec was expressing some doubts. "Let's get this straight," he said. "The plan is to sell everything off except Pohl, Bouvier, Excel and Bolton. Then we merge them into a new outfit to be called Stanton Industries and build it into one of the biggest electronics groups in the business."

"That sums it up," Tom grinned, "as easy as that."

Alec scowled.

Few people were impressed when they met Alec for the first

time, but then he never set out to impress. "Making impressions is Tom's job," he would say. "Mine is to make sure we make profits." It was claimed by some that even as an idea formed in Tom's mind, Alec could work out what it would cost. Almost as tall as Tom, he was more slightly built, with unruly sandy hair which, deceptively, gave him the look of a young college professor. His eyes were his best feature: large, gray, well-spaced and bright with intelligence. With Excel's takeover and Tom's resignation, Alec had been left in joint charge at Bolton, cooperating with someone named Sedgemore who had been sent down from Excel.

Alec shook his head, "If the people running these businesses say no, Stanton will back off. Is that right?"

Taking a deep breath, Tom launched into an account of the promises Stanton had made to Pierre Bouvier and Hans Pohl.

"Okay." Alec raised his hands. "I understand all that. My question remains. What will Stanton do if they say no?"

"They didn't say no on Kariakos—"

"But Stanton was bluffing—"

"They don't know that. He did it that way to give us the best possible start—"

"But the fight is still to come," Alec insisted. "As soon as you get them round a table they'll wreck every plan you put up."

"Unless I persuade them of the benefits—"

"What benefits? They run their own shows. Put them together and they become cogs in a wheel—"

"But just think about it! This can be enormous. Can you imagine Pohl plus Bouvier plus—"

"They won't let you do it. They'll fight every move."

For a moment they sat staring at each other—Tom desperate to convince, Alec resisting every word. Finally Alec shrugged. "Okay, just suppose you pull if off—"

"And we become rich," Tom grinned.

The *we* had been another concession from Stanton. Tom had insisted on being allowed to recruit Alec as soon as he returned to London. As Tom's assistant, Alec would also receive a bonus if the merger went through. Fifty thousand pounds would be paid into Alec's account.

"We've got more chance of breaking the bank at Monte Carlo," Alec sneered. "Is that why you're doing this? Come on, Tom, act your age. You're behaving like some crazy mining prospector chasing off after a gold mine. Think of your reputation, for God's sake! Eric Marcus was on the phone while you were away. He wants you to run Europe for him. Other offers will come, believe me. Your track record is fantastic. But take this and fail . . ." Alec shook his head miserably, "your market value will plummet to zero."

Tom gnawed his lip. It was reassuring to have another offer; comforting, good for the ego . . . but nothing could equal the excitement of merging Pohl with Bouvier with Excel with Bolton . . .

"We've met other high flyers!" Alec exclaimed. "Until their wings caught on fire. Remember Sammy Lee? Harry Bradford? Golden boys five years ago. Now they can't get a job—"

"But this could be enormous," Tom protested. "If we pull this off—"

Alec groaned. "Okay," he conceded, "just suppose. Just suppose you convince them to go ahead. Who will be on the board of this Stanton Industries?"

"Stanton will be chairman. I'll be CEO, then Pohl, Amiens and Desmond Edwards. Oh, and Haller will be a non-executive director."

"What about Sir Bernard?"

"He's a sick man, Alec. I doubt he's got long to live. He's agreed to retire."

"Okay, so that makes six directors. Presumably Stanton won't play an active role?"

"No, he'll chair board meetings, that's all."

"So the full-time directors are you, Pohl, Amiens, and Edwards?"

Tom nodded.

Alec pulled a face. "That's not a board of directors. That's a lynch mob. Even if Stanton and Haller vote with you, it's three against three. Stanton will have to use his casting vote . . . and if ever he votes against you . . ." Alec drew his finger across his throat.

"Give it a chance, Alec—"

"Why? Nobody else will. Stanton and Haller are shrewd cookies. Stanton could push this through if he wanted to. But he hasn't. Why? Because he wants this merger without blood on his hands."

Without answering, Tom rose from his chair and walked to the window. Mentally he began to replay the events of the previous three days. So much had happened, so quickly. Had he allowed the excitement, the sunshine, the wine, perhaps even Melody to color his judgment? Hands in pockets, he stared down at the street while listening to Alec do what Alec did best—analyze a business problem in the bleakest light possible.

"They've set you up," said Alec. "They want this merger, but can't agree on the top man. So what do they do? Bring you in and deal you an impossible hand. Pohl, Amiens, and Edwards will wreck every plan you put up. What happens? Three or four meetings go by and it's stalemate. Battle after battle, until eventually Pohl or one of the others says, 'We think Lambert's ideas are crap, here's what *we* want to do.' Once he says that, you're dead. Stanton or Haller will say, 'That's a good plan, let's adopt that, Pohl you'd better be chief executive from now on.' Then he turns to you and says—'Thanks very much, Mr. Lambert, we no longer need you.' "

In silence, Tom continued to stare down into the street. It was raining outside. He watched a girl in a red coat daintily circumvent puddles.

"You're in a no-win situation," Alec said bluntly.

Tom remembered Haller saying—*In that case, Mr. Lambert, it would be heads I win and tails you lose.* Dismissing the thought, Tom concentrated on the argument. "Stanton will have to pay us our bonus—"

"Not necessarily. You could have endless meetings trying to put this together and fail. What might emerge is a formula acceptable to the others if we are removed. So we exit *before* the merger takes place. Result? Stanton gets what he wants and we get shafted. Bloody marvelous!"

Doubt grew in Tom's mind. He argued against it—*No, no, Stanton won't try a trick like that . . . this is a great opportunity.*

Aloud he said, "You could be wrong about Pohl and the others. They could get over it. Sure, they feel sore now. They've been passed over for the top job. Hell, I'd be pissed off—"

"Pissed off! You'd explode. You'd tell Stanton to fuck himself, then belt him the way you belted Tim Brierley."

Grinning ruefully, Tom turned from the window.

"None of them have resigned," Alec pointed out, "they're waiting to see what happens, sweating it out, betting they'll beat you one way or the other."

"And how would you bet?"

Alec reached for his cigarettes. Lighting one, he exhaled a long stream of smoke while considering his answer. Finally he said, "Individually it would be no contest. I'd bet on you every time. But Stanton has given them a power of veto—"

"They don't know that. When everyone was together, Stanton said I'll run the whole show. It was only in private that he—"

"What's he told *them* in private?" Alec sneered.

At noon they went out, for a breath of air and to lunch at a local restaurant. Afterwards, still deep in conversation, they returned to the flat. "Okay," Tom conceded, "the odds are against us, but what about the odds at Bolton? Admit it, Alec. Everyone said we'd go bust—"

"At Bolton you had executive control—"

"So? Different ball game, different rules, but consider the *size* of this game!"

The thought had become a fixation—Pohl plus Bouvier plus Excel plus Bolton. Together, properly organized, the new outfit could become a giant. And although Alec resisted, he too was intrigued. He argued with Tom because that was their way; every problem they encountered they argued about, stripping it bare to examine every possible pitfall. And there were plenty of pitfalls. "If these guys detest each other," Alec said, "how will you get them to work together? At the first meeting you'll have a bloody great row—"

"So don't have a meeting." Tom shrugged. "It was your idea. You said you'd bet on me if I took them on one at a time. Why don't I do it that way?"

"To achieve what?"

Tom frowned. "I'm not sure. I need to get to know them, find out what makes them tick. A big merger creates big jobs. If these guys are any good—"

"They won't be satisfied to be cogs in a wheel."

The discussion droned on into the afternoon. The air in the apartment became stale with tobacco smoke. They drank endless cups of coffee while examining the balance sheets Tom had brought back from Kariakos. And gradually, as he sifted the evidence, Alec shifted his ground. Not that there was an obvious change in his manner. He continued to point out the impossibility of the task . . . but the sheer scale of the project captured his imagination. By four o'clock he could see the possibilities as clearly as Tom. "Jesus," he muttered, "wouldn't it be fantastic to put this together?"

"Come on, Alec," Tom encouraged, eyes shining.

Alec still hesitated. "Suppose Stanton turns out to be another Tim Brierley?"

"No," shaking his head, Tom sounded positive. He had forgotten the erotic displays at the villa, forgotten Stanton's eccentric lifestyle, forgotten the girls and the statues. It was all as Haller had forecast—*After a while, people see only Maurice.* And at that moment Tom could see Maurice Stanton on the bench in the clearing, he could hear him saying—*I want this merger, but I'm trapped by my promises to Hans and Pierre . . .*

"You sound bloody sure," said Alec.

"He sets great store on keeping his word. That's why he's in this mess. He tries to keep his promises. And he promised if I put this together, I'd run Stanton Industries for the rest of my life."

A sudden gleam lit Alec's eyes. "Okay, if he's so hot on promises, what did he promise about our bonus?"

Tom stared. He had already explained about the bonus. Stanton had promised to give irrevocable instructions to his lawyers in London. The bonus monies were to be held by the lawyer in escrow, payable the day the merger went through.

Alec said, "He promised to do it *immediately.* That's the point. His lawyer should have the money by now. Why not make this the test? Call the lawyer, if the money's there, we do it. If not, forget the whole deal."

Hairs rose on the back of Tom's neck. He swallowed hard. "You mean . . . gamble the whole deal on one phone call?"

"It's not a gamble if Stanton has kept his word."

Tom licked his lips. "Be fair. He would have to put these instructions in writing. Perhaps his letter hasn't arrived?"

"He said immediately, didn't he? He sent you home *immediately.* He could have sent instructions on the same plane."

Tom felt cornered.

Alec said, "We've gambled on your instincts before. It's paid off. You've got a gut feeling about Stanton. Fine." He pointed to the telephone. "Convince me."

Tom glanced at his watch. It was ten to five. "Suppose the lawyer's not there?"

"It's a big firm." Alec rummaged through the documents which Tom had obtained in Kariakos. "Here it is. They've got . . . eight, ten, twelve partners. A circle has been drawn round one of the names. Ackroyd. Presumably he deals with Stanton's affairs."

Tom's mouth was bone-dry. "If the money's there we do it?"

Alec nodded. "And if it's not, we don't."

They stared at each other. Tom said, "You're a hard sod, Alec. Did I ever tell you—"

"Come on. Call Ackroyd. I want to know if I'll ever get rich."

Taking the sheet of paper, Tom dialed the number. His shirt collar felt tight. "Give me a cigarette."

Handing him a cigarette, Alec went over to the sideboard. "I need a Scotch."

Secretly, Tom knew Alec was right. They were doing what they had done a hundred times before. Argue everything through until a decision emerged. And if a decision remained unclear, force the issue, make it happen. The telephone felt sticky in his hand. Maybe Stanton Industries was not meant to be? God, he hoped so. This was the biggest challenge of his life.

"Oh, hello. Yes, I'd like to speak to Mr. Ackroyd."

"Who shall I say is calling?"

"My name's Lambert. Tom Lambert."

Swallowing a mouthful of Scotch, Alec groaned, "This is worse than Russian roulette. I dunno, Tom, I think I was hasty, perhaps—"

"Oh no," Tom covered the mouthpiece with his hand. "You called the bet. You can't chicken out now."

Their eyes met. They both wanted the same answer. Alec had also become trapped by the challenge . . . Pohl plus Bouvier plus Excel plus Bolton . . .

A cordial voice boomed in Tom's ear. "Mr. Lambert? Good afternoon, Peter Ackroyd here. I've just signed a letter to you. Confirming Mr. Stanton's instructions . . ."

Next morning they went to find the suite of offices in Jermyn Street which Stanton had suggested they use as a temporary base. They found them via a discreet doorway sandwiched between a gentleman's outfitters and a firm which made custom footwear. A simple brass plate announced: *Maurice Stanton—First Floor.*

"Hardly the hub of an empire," Alec commented dryly.

Tom hadn't known what to expect. He led the way up the staircase, sinking into carpet which appeared not to have been walked on since the day it was laid. There was a hushed atmosphere to the place. No distant typewriters clattered, no telephones rang. Alec grunted, "I've heard noisier morgues."

The door facing them across the landing was half-glazed and the name Maurice Stanton had been painted on the glass panel in black script. The silence within led Tom to suspect the door might be locked. He was relieved when the handle turned in his grip. They stepped across the threshold into a well-furnished reception area. A brunette looked up from behind a mahogany desk. "Mr. Lambert?" She rose and came around to greet them. "Good morning, I'm Barbara Howard. Mr. Stanton wrote to say to expect you."

She was in her early forties, elegantly dressed in a woollen suit of moss green, with a pleasant voice and a warm smile.

"Would you like me to show you around?" she asked after Tom had introduced Alec.

The small suite of offices seemed deserted. "I'm Mr. Stanton's sole employee in London," Barbara Howard confessed as she led the way. "Mr. Stanton only uses the office for the odd day now and then. Mostly I book his theater tickets, but they could do that for him at Claridge's."

Behind the reception office was a well-proportioned room overlooking Jermyn Street, and beyond that an oak-paneled conference room. A highly polished table stood surrounded by ten leather chairs. On the far side of the reception office were four smaller rooms, and beyond them a lavatory and a kitchen. The kitchen came complete with a cat, a fat tabby curled up in a wicker basket.

"Mr. Stanton knows about Marmaduke," Barbara Howard explained hastily, "I'm allowed to bring him in for company."

Crouching over the basket, Tom stroked the cat. "If you rely on this feller for company," he said, glancing up, "how do you fill your time?"

"I knit," she confessed frankly. "During the past six months I've knitted fifteen sweaters for Oxfam. And I read a good deal. I've just finished Trollope; everything he ever wrote."

Tom wondered about her history. She was attractive. He wondered if she'd had an affair with Stanton? Years ago probably. Stanton seemed to pick women in their twenties and thirties.

She glanced anxiously around the kitchen, making sure everything was in place. Seeing a saucer of milk on the floor, she took it to the sink to tidy away. As she passed, Tom noticed that she limped slightly, and the light from the window caught the side of her face, revealing a fine scar beneath her makeup. The thin line traveled down her neck to lose itself in the silk scarf at her throat.

"Mr. Stanton wrote to say you'd be arriving," she said, repeating herself. She seemed hesitant, unsure of what was expected of her.

Straightening up, Tom smiled, "I'm afraid this office won't be so peaceful in future—"

"Offices should be busy, not peaceful," she interrupted. "Some days I go potty for something to do." Facing him, she took a deep breath and plunged on. "Oh dear, you must be wondering about me. I'd better explain. I had an accident two years ago. Mr. Stanton helped me get through it. He was very kind. He *is* a very kind man. When I was able to get out and about, he offered me this job. I was told to find an office and equip it. It was fun to begin with; looking at different premises, negotiating the lease on this place, buying the furnishings and so on. But . . . well . . . that was nine months ago. I've hardly seen him since, and whenever I do he says not to worry about having so little to do, something will happen . . ." She swallowed nervously. "I really am an excellent secretary. I was once employed by . . . well, never mind that, but I do assure you that I'd much rather be busy—"

"Steady on," Tom laughed and put a reassuring hand on her arm. "How about making some coffee? Then we'll have a chat."

Leaving her in the kitchen, they returned to the large room on the far side of the reception office. Alec went across to the window and stared down into the street. Tom sat behind the desk and tested the chair. Each knew what the other was thinking. *Stanton had planted a spy in the office.* Tom drummed his fingers on the desktop, considering the situation.

When Barbara Howard arrived with coffee, he asked her to bring a cup for herself. Then he ushered her into a chair. "This is a bit awkward," he began, "but it has to be said. I've been appointed to reorganize Mr. Stanton's business affairs. I run things my way, which means the only reports Mr. Stanton will receive from this office will be from me. In other words, my secretary will report to me and only to me—"

"Mr. Lambert," she interrupted, placing her cup on the table, and rising to her feet, "naturally I would expect . . . confidentiality would be part of the job, but may I show you something? It . . . er . . . might save time and embarrassment."

Pink-faced, she hurried from the room, quickly returning, clutching an envelope which she handed to Tom. "Mr. Stanton has been very generous," she said. "I assumed you'd know about this."

Opening the letter, Tom spread it on his desk. It was from Stanton.

DEAR BARBARA,

Mr. Lambert will be arriving within the next couple of

days and I'd be grateful if you'd show him around. No doubt he will want to engage his own staff, therefore I think it best if you do what I suspect you wanted to do last time we spoke—which, of course, is to resign. Knowing how bored you've been, I'm sure you'll be glad to see the back of the place; though for my part I can't thank you enough for all you've done. Enclosed is a check for six months' salary, and I know all will go well for you in the future.

With every good wish,
MAURICE

When Tom looked up, Barbara Howard handed him another sheet of paper. "My resignation," she said pleasantly, "and I quite understand about you wanting your own staff."

He was taken by surprise. "I see," he murmured, handing Stanton's letter to Alec. Curiosity got the better of him. "May I ask how you came to know Mr. Stanton?"

"I hardly *know* him," Barbara Howard shook her head. "Know of him, yes, but that's not the same, is it? My brother was his pilot for six years. Then we had an accident . . . a motor accident, nothing to do with flying . . ." She studied her hands in her lap. "I was driving; my brother died, I survived." She looked up as if expecting to see accusation in his eyes. Tom kept a blank expression. Her scar was invisible full face. She had deep violet eyes and full sensual lips. After a moment she continued, "Mr. Stanton arranged a private hospital, convalescent home, everything, and afterwards gave me this job. It was really only a temporary thing, to help me get going. To be honest, these last six months have been rather awkward. I would have preferred to leave and find something worthwhile . . . more demanding, I mean . . . but that would have seemed ungrateful." She finished with a smile, "So now you're here, I can hand over with a clear conscience, if you understand what I mean."

His understanding had as much to do with Stanton at that moment. Barbara Howard's story was a further example of Stanton's loyalty to people. Another thought occurred . . . that by writing as he had, Stanton was leaving the decision open, making it easy for him.

Looking at her, he liked what he saw. Her embarrassment had been temporary, caused by a misunderstanding which she had quickly corrected. Fully recovered, she looked calm, assured, elegant and efficient. Suddenly Tom remembered a remark made on the terrace in Kariakos. That boy Hugo had made it. Tom had disliked him; he had seemed supercilious and sneering, but he might have been right when he told Roddy—"Your father is famous for choosing wisely in people."

"Do you have another job lined up?"

"No," she shook her head. "Mr. Stanton's letter only arrived yesterday."

He made up his mind. "Why don't we give each other a month's trial?" he suggested, opening a drawer and holding the resignation above it. "Find out if we suit each other?"

Her face brightened. "That would be splendid, my apartment is just round the corner. Thank you, I'd like to, but . . ." Her eyes clouded with doubt. "I really am looking for a *proper* job, I do want to work—"

"Don't worry, you'll work all right," he grinned as the letter slipped from his fingers.

Her smile widened until a thought occurred. She hesitated, "Er . . . just one other thing. Would it be acceptable if Marmaduke—"

"Why not? We'll need some luck. He'll be our mascot."

And that was how they started. Tom, Alec, Barbara Howard and Marmaduke the cat. They *were* Stanton Industries to begin with.

Tom's hunch paid off better than he had dared hope. Barbara Howard was quick, shrewd, intelligent . . . and a woman with a void in her life. There had been a man, not Stanton, but a man with a wife and a family. Barbara's affair with him had consumed ten years of her life. Finally, when she ended it, she cut herself off from one set of friends, intent upon finding another. Her brother had helped until his tragic death. By the time Tom met her, Barbara was desperate to throw herself into some kind of activity . . . and he and Alec gave her the chance. They worked all hours and Barbara toiled along with them, doing everything asked of her, determined to master every detail. Facts and figures about Stanton's businesses flowed into Jermyn Street. And while Barbara collated and Alec recruited accountants, Tom began to list priorities. The scale of the operation kept him in perpetual excitement. "I feel like a tugboat captain taking command of the *Queen Mary.*"

"Aye," Alec sniffed, "maybe, but no skipper of the *Queen Mary* had other men fighting to get their hands on the wheel."

There was truth in that. Other men *were* fighting to get their hands on the wheel. Amiens telephoned from Geneva, Desmond Edwards called from Coventry, even Sir Bernard made contact from his sick bed . . . all asking when the first meeting would be held. Tom was friendly, polite, pleased to hear from them, but completely unyielding. "I'll let you know when I'm ready."

It was an answer which satisfied no one. Eventually Gunther Haller called from his office atop the First National Bank in Geneva. "Amiens keeps pestering me. He wants a meeting."

"He wants a bloodbath," Tom answered sharply.

Haller sighed. A certain perplexity sounded in his voice. "You were aware of potential antagonism—"

"Which I will deal with—"

"But we must call the first board meeting."

"I'll call a board meeting when we amalgamate."

"We must decide *how* to amalgamate."

"No!" Tom was quite definite. They had reached the crunch—the first test of his authority. Win this and he had a chance; be stampeded into an early meeting and he lost everything.

Haller fell into a long silence, gauging Tom's determination. Finally he said, "I must warn you, Sir Bernard has complained to Maurice. Maurice is somewhat concerned. So am I, for that matter."

"Gunther, you asked me to put this together and I will, but my way. If anyone comes crying to you, I expect you to refer him to me."

Afterwards Tom told Alec, "We bought some time. Haller

knows we won't be stampeded. He'll help hold them at bay for a while."

Meanwhile they made every day count. They worked evenings, weekends and right through a Public Holiday—demanding and receiving a torrent of information on Stanton's businesses. Every balance sheet was analyzed. Tom came to know every profit statement well enough to recite them. He knew the values of sites, buildings, plant and machinery, inventories . . .

By the end of three weeks they had gleaned all that was possible from the figures. It was time to meet people. Alec grinned, "We know more about their businesses than they do."

They divided the businesses. Alec was to visit those companies earmarked to be sold, starting with the bottling plant in Belgium and proceeding to the shipping line which operated out of Rotterdam. Meanwhile Tom was to visit Excel in Coventry, Bouvier in Geneva and the Pohl Organization in Hanover.

Alec waxed hot and cold: more enthusiastic than ever about the potential, but still apprehensive about the outcome. "It still boils down to the same thing. If they refuse to merge, and Stanton won't force them—"

"I know," Tom grinned, "I'll just have to persuade them."

His arrival at Excel found the workforce on the verge of a strike. With Sir Bernard on his sick bed, Desmond was finding the old man's shoes several sizes too big, especially when it came to dealing with the unions. "Bloody people," he fumed in the boardroom. "Give 'em an inch and they take a mile."

Tom made non-committal noises. His priority was to discuss the merger; about everything else he was prepared to listen first and act later. His good intentions were soon put to the test. Touring the Excel factory was like entering a time warp. The products were excellent, but working conditions verged on Victorian. So did attitudes, epitomized by three separate dining rooms—one for directors, one for office staff, and a canteen for workers from the shop floor.

"Not that many of them use it," Desmond grumbled, "most of them bring sandwiches and a thermos of tea."

Tom would have done the same. The canteen looked like the kitchen of a nineteenth century workhouse.

Desmond was taller than Tom, and bulkier, with the beginnings of a beer drinker's gut. His wide humorous mouth suggested he might be good company in different surroundings; but in the factory his expression was stern, bordering on grim. His manner toward Tom was resentful: the attitude of a young man whose inheritance is threatened. He answered questions with reluctance, and his grudging cooperation fostered a similar attitude in his managers. Tom was made to feel out of place and unwelcome.

That evening, from his hotel, he telephoned Alec in Bruges. "The daft thing," he complained, "is that Desmond tries to ape his old man. Sir Bernard's a disciplinarian, so Desmond tries to be one too. Maybe that style of management worked once, but it's a recipe for disaster now."

"What's his attitude about the merger?"

"We haven't even discussed it. He's been embroiled with the unions all day, but his attitude is abundantly clear. I was greeted like a dose of the clap."

"That bad?"

"The only useful thing I did was look over the factory."

"And?"

"It's worse than we thought. The whole place is like something out of Dickens."

Alec fell into a thoughtful silence. Then he said, "Those figures become all the more amazing, don't they?"

Tom knew what he meant. He had been asking himself about the figures all day. One of the surprises provided by the data analyzed at Jermyn Street was the strength of Excel's export performance. It was excellent, particularly to the States. Which made for a contradictory situation—poor production methods, yet good products, backward management but high exports.

He set out to discover the reasons the next day. Arriving at the factory early, he was determined to make progress, but for that he needed Desmond's cooperation.

"Oh, it's you," Desmond said, looking up as Tom entered his office. "I've no time for you today. I've got these bloody shop stewards again this morning, then I'm lunching in Birmingham, so I won't be back until late afternoon—"

"That's okay," Tom said agreeably. "I'll just sit in today as an observer."

"Oh, will you?" Desmond scowled, sounding doubtful. "I'm not sure about that."

Tom closed the door to the secretary's office, and sat down by Desmond's desk. "Naturally you must deal with day to day problems, but we need to discuss the future. How about dinner tonight?"

"I'm busy tonight . . ." Desmond stopped in mid-sentence as Tom's earlier words registered. "What do you mean—sit in as an observer? Are you suggesting you come to my lunch?"

"Is it business?"

"I'll say it is. Important business. Ken Stacey, our Australian distributor is in Birmingham, just for the day—"

"I'd very much like to meet him."

Sir Bernard would have said "Go to hell." Desmond wanted to, it was in his eyes, but he couldn't quite bring himself to utter the words. Tom was there backed by Maurice Stanton's authority, which was enough to make Desmond hesitate, and as his mind searched for the right words, the door opened and his secretary came in. "The men are outside, Mr. Edwards," she said with a reproachful look at Tom.

The rest of the morning was spent dealing with the unions. Badly, in Tom's opinion, but true to his promise he remained silent; and at eleven-forty they set off for Birmingham, with Desmond at the wheel of his Jaguar.

"I don't like this," Desmond grumbled darkly. "How do I explain you to Ken? He's going to think it's bloody odd—"

"Say I'm a colleague from London. Don't elaborate. . . ."

Lunch was a revelation. Tom was reminded of Jeykll and Hyde. During the drive to Birmingham, Desmond had been truculent, argumentative and downright bad-tempered, but when he parked the car, he seemed to change. "Just don't interfere," he warned, "let me get on with my job." And he did, in some style. With Ken Stacey, Desmond was charming, persuasive, knowledgeable and convincing. For the first time, Tom began to understand how long was the shadow cast by Sir Bernard. In the factory Desmond felt obliged to follow in his father's footsteps, enforcing Sir Bernard's out of date methods. Outside the factory, there were no such restraints. Beyond an environment dominated by his father, Desmond was a changed man.

The atmosphere during the drive back to Coventry was quite different. With a successful meeting, and a good lunch under his belt, Desmond was far more amenable. His mood was relaxed. At times he actually smiled, and Tom, choosing his words with tact and care, began to draw him out. Desmond's story was not so remarkable when it was unraveled. He had joined Excel straight from school. "The old man thinks universities are a waste of time," he grumbled with wry acceptance. Working in the factory had been more of a chore than a challenge. Sir Bernard ran the place as he saw fit, discouraging innovations, so Desmond had turned his energies elsewhere. "Harry Chambers was sales manager then," he recalled. "Harry took me under his wing. We didn't do much export in those days, so I persuaded Harry and the old man to let me try my luck in the States. I got lucky, that's all."

Luck had nothing to do with it. Desmond had a natural aptitude for selling. Tom had seen it first-hand, and the export figures were added proof.

"Tell me about the States," said Tom. "Why do you do so well over there?"

"It's the biggest market there is. I love it. Just to land at Kennedy gives me a buzz. I'm due over there again in a couple of weeks." There was no mistaking his enthusiasm. "Oh, selling's easy," he said cheerfully, "I enjoy that part of the business."

But back at the factory he reverted to a scowling, snarling imitation of his father. He was in the same mood when he joined Tom later at the hotel. It was as if he wore one face in Coventry and an entirely different face elsewhere. He spent most of the meal complaining about the unions and the difficulties of running the factory. "And if that's not bad enough," he added, "I've got you to contend with, and this bloody stupid idea of a merger." His face flushed and his lips set in a determined line. His fists clenched on the table.

Tom hesitated, deciding on the best way to respond. "The merger was agreed on Kariakos—"

"Oh no!" Desmond interrupted. "*Nothing* was agreed on Kariakos. Haller got his own way for once. He's wanted this merger for years. We humored Maurice, that's all. Kariakos wasn't the time or place to argue, but you'll have to call this blasted board meeting sooner or later. This little game is all over then. So don't get your head full of fancy ideas."

"But the merger makes so much sense—"

"It makes sense to *you,*" Desmond interrupted, leaning across the table. "Without this so-called amalgamation, you're out of work. But I'm not. I've worked bloody hard and my father worked hard before me. And don't think he made things easy for me, because he didn't. Not that I blame him . . ." Desmond paused, aware that his voice had carried to the next table. People were casting curious glances. Pushing his cup aside, he leaned forward. "This is a bloody charade," he hissed. "Haller's tried to fly this kite before. It won't fly and I'll tell you why. Maurice Stanton is a randy old goat, but he's rock-solid on promises. He never goes back on his word. Pohl was promised the Pohl Organization, Yvonne wangled Bouvier for Amiens, and Excel was promised to me. Christ, Maurice even promised our *fathers*! Years ago. We're shareholders in these businesses, don't forget. You and Haller can make all the plans you like. They won't do you any good. Not unless we go along with them. And we won't, take it from me. Come this board meeting, whenever you call it, I shall say no, Amiens will say no, and Pohl will say no. Believe me, you're wasting your time."

Sitting on the train, gazing gloomily at the wet English countryside, Tom's thoughts returned to that sun drenched Greek island and Maurice Stanton shaking his head—*If push comes to shove, I won't force them. I can't. My conscience won't let me. I owe their fathers too much . . .*

Perversely Tom continued to admire Stanton's loyalty. Promises had landed the man in a mess from which he wanted to be extricated, but if that proved impossible, he would live with it rather than renege on his word. It augered well for the future . . . if Tom could engineer a future.

Another setback awaited him at the office. Scarcely had he settled behind his desk when Alec telephoned from the offices of Van Kirst, the shipping line in Rotterdam. "We have a small problem," he began, breaking the news gently.

Small problem was an understatement. A massive marine claim had been lodged against the shipping line. "I've seen the lawyers," Alec reported, "and things could be worse. Styvessen, the senior partner, gives us a fair chance of winning. Trouble is it will take eight or nine months to get into court. Meanwhile we're stymied. Nobody will buy this outfit with a potential liability of three million outstanding."

Alec had also visited the French vineyards. "That's not so good either." The vineyards had suffered an unusually wet autumn, followed by a hard winter and a late spring. "They'll be lucky to break even this year. If we want top dollar for the business, we'll have to nurse it along for a while."

Tom groaned. "Any more good news?"

Alec chuckled, "They make a decent drop of plonk. I put a case in the car. We'll get pissed when I get back and everything will look better."

Barbara came in with her notebook as Tom replaced the telephone. "Captain Masters called while you were away."

It took a minute to place Masters.

"Mr. Stanton's pilot."

"Of course."

"Apparently the Learjet is at your disposal for the rest of the month."

He frowned. A private jet to dash around Europe. What was the point? Fly to the Pohl plant in Hanover, drag around on another grudging inspection, only for Pohl to refuse to cooperate?

"May as well use it," he shrugged. "See if you can get Carl Pohl on the phone. And after that, try Andre Amiens at Bouvier."

Ten minutes later Barbara buzzed through to say that Carl

Pohl was out of his office—"but I have Monsieur Amiens on the line."

Tom picked up the handset, "Andre?"

"Tom! How are you?"

The warmth of the greeting took Tom by surprise. On Kariakos, Amiens had been brittle and sharp, a week before he had been complaining to Haller . . .

"I was hoping to come over to see you—"

"Tres bien! Excellent. When can you come? How long will you stay with us? Tell me how I can prepare for your visit?"

The questions were so unexpected that Tom was lost for a reply. This was far different from Edwards. Edwards had agreed to a visit with sulky reluctance.

"Er . . . when would suit you, Andre?"

"The sooner the better."

"Shall we say Monday? For a couple of days?"

"Monday is perfect. You must stay with us. We will . . . ah . . . a moment please, I am consulting my calendar. I have some people coming Tuesday lunchtime. My paint suppliers. We meet twice a year. Usually we work through until about six . . ." Amiens hesitated, sounding doubtful, "Would you like me to cancel their visit?"

Tom's eyebrows rose to his hairline. This was *indeed* a different Amiens. "No, we'll have a day and a half. That should do for an initial visit—"

"Please don't rush off. Spend the full day with us on Tuesday. Even if I am engaged in the afternoon, there are many people here who wish to meet you."

The tone of the conversation was extraordinary. Where Tom had expected resistance, he was meeting a willingness to cooperate. Instead of reluctance, he was showered with good will.

Afterwards he asked Barbara to call Pohl again, only to learn that Pohl was still away from the office. "Leave a message," he said, "say I'll be there on Wednesday morning."

He gave the instructions without thought, his mind still occupied by the amazing change of attitude shown by Andre Amiens. His hopes rose . . .

The aircraft dipped, revealing a patchwork of vineyards and fields, and a moment later, the shimmering blue of the great lake itself.

Gregg Richards emerged from the pilot's cabin. "Geneva in five minutes, Mr. Lambert."

"Very good."

He watched a white cruiser steam majestically across variegated blue water. Surrounding the lake, amid the trees, could be seen the rooftops of large houses, discreet and hidden behind high walls. Hidden residences, hidden wealth . . . hidden motives, he thought, pondering on Amiens. Why the sudden change? On Kariakos, Amiens had been cool and aloof . . .

They touched down exactly on time. Nine A.M. European time. Tom adjusted his watch.

Within a few minutes the steps were lowered and he was walking the short distance to VIP Reception, with Richards walking alongside. "They've sent a limousine for you, so I'll leave you here if that's okay, Mr. Lambert."

"Fine."

Richards handed Tom his bag. "See you tomorrow evening then."

"Six o'clock sharp." Smiling at his own needless reminder, Tom turned away to offer his passport to the Swiss official at the door. The man flicked through the pages, leaving Tom to stare into space, which was when he caught sight of a blonde beyond the glass partition. Catching his eye, she waved.

The official returned the passport. "Merci, monsieur. Have a good stay in our country."

"Thank you," said Tom, advancing through the doorway.

"Tom!" cried the woman. "Bonjour! Welcome to Geneva. How lovely to see you again." Smiling, she proffered her cheek.

His first thought was that he had been mistaken for somebody else. She was a plain faced woman whose larger than average sized nose was in part compensated for by good eyes; brown, with a teasing gleam to them. Recognizing a vague familiarity, suddenly he realized who she was. "Madame Amiens—"

"Yvonne!"

Stifling surprise, he dutifully kissed her. "I hadn't expected you to meet me—"

"Who else," she laughed, "except Andre, and he's busy organizing your reception at the plant. Come, we have a car waiting."

As she led the way, he had a chance to recover. The brief meeting on Kariakos, with so much happening, had left him with only the sketchiest of memories. Looking at her he saw a good figure, clad in a lemon wool suit, the skirt of which stopped short of her knees. Forty years old but wearing clothes designed for someone much younger. Not beautiful, not even pretty, but surprisingly sexy. Good legs, a gracious walk. Unconsciously he was admiring her bottom when she glanced over her shoulder, catching him with a look of amusement.

The car was a large black BMW, complete with a chauffeur who hurried forward to relieve Tom of his case. Yvonne shimmied over the back seat and beckoned him to follow. "Is this your first time in Geneva?"

"It is," he admitted, averting his gaze from her cleavage. Most women would have worn a shirt or a sweater beneath the yellow suit jacket. Yvonne Amiens wore not even a bra.

"It's a nice enough town," she said airily, "we're hoping you'll like it."

The significance of the remark did not become apparent until later. He had no time to think about it then for the journey developed into a guided tour, commencing as soon as they left the airport. "See over there?" Yvonne asked, pointing, "See? Mont Blanc." In the distance rose the great mountain, familiar from a hundred photographs.

"I think that was the peak I saw from the plane."

"You would have had a good view today," she smiled. "Isn't it gorgeous?"

The morning belonged on a picture postcard. Primary colors shone crisp and bright in the clear air.

A moment later Yvonne was pointing out another landmark and very soon they were driving parallel to Lake Geneva itself. He admired all that was shown to him, while inwardly speculating on the change in her attitude. On Kariakos she had been as cool as her husband. Yet here she was, sitting closer than need be, with her hand on his arm as if she had known him for years. . . .

"Over here," she was saying, "we have the Château Rothschild. And over there . . ." reaching past him, her cheek brushed his as she pointed across the lake, "Is the great Château Stanton. Two powerful barons confronting each other over the water."

Sunlight on the lake was dazzling. Squinting in the direction of her outstretched arm, he managed to identify three conical turrets rising as spires from the trees. She laughed, "Not that Rothschild lives in his castle or Maurice in his, but they used to." She shrugged, dismissing the subject as her eye caught something else. "Ah, look, there is where we live. You can just see. Down from the Château Stanton, see?"

Very little of the Amiens residence was visible, but Tom did his best to be polite. "It looks marvelous—"

"We have a view right across the lake. You will see tonight."

The car slowed, caught in traffic. They crawled past some hotels on the right, with balcony restaurants looking down upon the striped awnings of pavement cafés. Across the lake the famous fountain lifted a frothy white plume of water four hundred feet in the air.

"The banking district is in front," Yvonne said, adding with a look of innocent enquiry, "Will you see your friend Gunther Haller on this trip?"

He noted she said *your* friend and not *our* friend. Did she dislike Haller? Did her husband dislike Haller? "I doubt if I'll meet with him on this trip."

She seemed pleased. "It's not so far to go now. The Bouvier plant is in Carouge." Her sideways glance stiffened to a look of mock severity. "I have told Andre to bring you home no later than seven—"

"It's very good of you. I could have stayed at an hotel—"

"Nonsense. We wouldn't dream of it. Besides we have so much to talk about, and tomorrow . . ." her face brightened, "I have a surprise for you."

He was already surprised; baffled, but he listened and looked attentively as she pointed to landmarks, and moments later the

BMW swept through the main gates of the Bouvier plant. A curved driveway led up to a central building. "Ah!" Yvonne exclaimed. "There is Andre."

Amiens was waiting at the top of the steps. Smiling broadly, he trotted down to open the door as the car rolled to a halt.

"Tom! Welcome!"

Shaking hands was a forceful reminder of the differences between Amiens and Desmond Edwards. Edwards was still emerging from the shadow of a dominant father. Amiens suffered no such disadvantage. He had long since acquired the assured air of the rich and successful. In his mid-thirties, he was younger than his wife, who showed to disadvantage in the strong sunlight. Amiens was tanned and fit looking, whereas Yvonne's face was colored only by cosmetics. His features were clean-cut and regular, where her large nose looked even larger.

The meeting on Kariakos might not have happened. Throughout the day, Amiens did everything possible to make a fresh start. Following coffee in the board room, he led the way on a grand tour of the Bouvier plant—an inspection so thorough that even the lavatories were included. The reasons for Bouvier's good reputation soon became obvious. The factory was run with superb precision. Production techniques, especially the use of robotics, were ahead of anything Tom had ever seen, including his best efforts at Bolton.

Lunch in the board room was attended by Bouvier's senior managers, and in the afternoon each of them made a presentation on the workings of his department. Nothing was held back. Every fact and figure was laid out on the table. It was an impressive demonstration, made even more so because it was so unexpected.

Tom began to doubt his own memory. He wondered if the malevolent looks cast his way on Kariakos were figments of his imagination. But he knew they were not. There had been real opposition on Kariakos. . . .

Amiens admitted as much as his chauffeur drove them home in the evening. "I read this situation the wrong way at the outset," he said. "I suppose I was disappointed. After all, Maurice is Yvonne's godfather. Naturally we hoped . . ." He shrugged and raised his hands in a characteristically Gallic expression, "but Maurice was in a difficult position. He had to consider Pohl and Edwards. What else could he do but appoint an outsider?"

Tom's spirits rose. "I'm glad you see it that way," he said as the car turned off the road to pass through high gates of wrought iron.

Amiens smiled. "Thank Yvonne. She convinced me."

She was waiting on the steps of her home, much as her husband had waited on the steps of his factory. The yellow suit had been replaced by a turquoise silk dress with a scalloped neckline and bare arms. Like the previous outfit, the dress was too young for her, but she wore it with such style that it suited her.

The time was exactly seven o'clock, a fact which Tom commented upon as he kissed her cheek.

She smiled. "Ah! Andre is not always so reliable," she said, casting a look at her husband. "Sometimes I have to prise him out of that factory."

After being installed in a sumptuous guest suite, Tom was shown aspects of the house in much the same way as he had been conducted over the Bouvier plant. Everything was displayed for his inspection, including the grounds, three manicured acres overlooking the lake, with a tennis court, a swimming pool, and specimen trees set in rolling green lawns.

What had already been a remarkable day extended into a remarkable evening. They dined on the terrace. The hostess was charming and the host was agreeable. Even when the talk turned to business it remained uncontentious. At one point Amiens said, "The Japanese are hitting their stride in electronics. Give them a few years and they'll catch the Americans. This merger *must* go through. Without it, Bouvier will be lost. Elsewhere in Europe, Philips may survive, and Siemens perhaps, but not Bouvier." He turned his thumb downwards. "Pohl and Excel will go the same way, but together . . ." his face brightened, "we'll be big enough to fight back, eh?" He laughed. "You agree? Of course. Only fools like young Edwards and that idiot Pohl would argue . . ."

Tom began to tingle with excitement. If Amiens agreed, surely they could persuade Edwards? And perhaps Pohl would see sense . . .

As the meal progressed, he relaxed. He felt a great sense of relief. And then Yvonne announced her surprise. "Tomorrow," she said, "I have arranged a little lunch party for you. Only for twenty, but all the right people. It is important to introduce you into the right circle."

"Oh?"

"But naturellement," she smiled, her hands fluttering upwards. "If you are to live here, we must help get you settled."

"Live here?"

"Where else?" Yvonne asked, her eyes rounding in surprise, and while her husband beamed approval, she continued, "Wait until you meet Pepi. She's our real estate tycoon. Already she has marked out a wonderful villa for you."

Tom listened in amazement. They had worked everything out. He was expected to live in Geneva. They saw him establishing the head office at the Bouvier plant, and running Stanton Industries from Switzerland. It was all perfectly logical . . . Maurice Stanton was a Swiss citizen with homes in Geneva and St. Moritz, with Swiss bankers . . . where else would Stanton Industries have its head office?

"I'm not sure," Tom confessed. "For the time being . . . I thought—"

"Not Excel?" Amiens betrayed alarm for the first time. "You're not thinking of making Excel the head office?"

"In Coventry? No, Excel will absorb Bolton, but that's all—"

"So where is the head office?"

"I can manage in Jermyn Street for the time being—"

"Non," Amiens shook his head, "surely the whole point is to merge everything. To run things from under one roof. Centralize decision making, accounting, everything. Besides, I have been to Jermyn Street. There is no prestige . . ."

Prestige was important to Amiens. His lifestyle reeked of it. A head office in Geneva would enhance that prestige and put him one up on Edwards and Pohl.

Seeing the trap, Tom was non-committal and played for time.

Amiens had been flying the flag of an ally until then. It made no sense to antagonize him.

"I suppose," Tom said cautiously, "we might consider the idea . . ."

But the idea had been considered, as became apparent the next morning when Amiens unveiled another surprise. "We have some people coming at ten o'clock," he said as they arrived at the Bouvier plant.

The "people" were architects, commissioned by Amiens to develop plans for the new head office of Stanton Industries. Unprepared and wrong-footed, Tom was compelled to examine sketches and elevations of three massive buildings which would rise high in the sky above the Bouvier plant.

Amiens was delighted. "Magnifique! We will dazzle all of Geneva."

Tom did his best to remain calm. He contained his exasperation until they were alone. "Andre, I haven't agreed to any of this—"

"Of course not, but I want us to be ready. Imagine how impressed Maurice will be when you unveil these plans at the first board meeting . . ."

They argued for the rest of the morning. Amiens was adamant. "Stanton Industries will be a Swiss corporation," he said. "*Of course* we must have the head office in Geneva."

"Apart from anything else," Tom protested, "the others will never agree."

Amiens merely smiled. "Then you must persuade them," he said.

Tom was glad to retreat to his lunch with Yvonne, leaving Amiens to meet his suppliers. But to retreat was not to escape. When he was delivered to the residence overlooking the lake, Tom found Yvonne waiting with plans of her own.

"Chèri," she greeted him, nuzzling her face against his before steering him through the hall and out onto the terrace, "everyone is dying to meet you."

Everyone included Pepi Scrimgeour, a middle-aged American with a blue rinse and "the most desirable properties in the world on my books." The British consul was there—"Hello, old boy, they tell me you're coming to live here." Tom met an Italian count, an American novelist, a French movie star with his Swedish girlfriend, the local chief of police, two internationally known musicians and countless people who were writ large in *Who's Who*. Different people with different accents from different backgrounds, with one thing in common—a firm belief that he planned to live in Geneva.

Tom knew he had been ambushed. He survived on such phrases as "nothing's settled yet . . . naturally I'll spend a good deal of time here . . . yes, I'm sure we'll meet again soon . . ." Through it all, he maintained a good-natured smile, while inwardly seething. And Yvonne Amiens knew it. Her dark eyes met his often enough for him to realize that she sensed his anger and, infuriatingly, was rather pleased, as if it was all part of a game she was playing, a game she was steering toward some sort of conclusion, because as people began to drift away after lunch, she caught Tom's arm. "Another few minutes and we'll have the place to ourselves. Time for us to talk I think, don't you?"

"Definitely," he agreed darkly.

He wondered if Amiens had rid himself of his paint suppliers and was about to join them. But Amiens remained absent, leaving Tom to pace the terrace while his hostess escorted her guests to the door.

It was a good fifteen minutes before she returned, laughing, "*Mon Dieu!* I thought they would never go." Flopping into a chair, she smiled her approval. "You made *la grande impression*. Everyone wants you to dinner. All of Geneva lies at your feet. Do you realize—"

"I realize you are taking a lot for granted," he said sharply.

Her smile faded to a mere pout, but she seemed neither alarmed not offended. Instead she watched him with interest, waiting for him to continue. He drew a chair out from the dining table. "Did you know," he asked, positioning the chair opposite her, "that Andre had some preposterous plans to build a grandiose head office—"

"Of course. It was my idea."

"*Your* idea?"

She smiled up at him, "Before you sit down, pour me an Armagnac, would you?"

She might have been talking to her husband. Her voice flowed with the same easy assurance, conveying an identical expectation of being obeyed. Disconcerted, he turned to the drinks trolley.

"I don't think it's grandiose," she said, "I think it's imposing. Oh chèri, *do* help yourself, I hate drinking alone."

He passed her the brandy and sat down. "Edwards and Pohl will scream blue murder—"

"Let them scream," she said contemptuously.

"You can't force my hand by telling people I'm coming to live here—".

"You came here for a deal," she interrupted coolly. "Don't you understand? I'm offering you one."

He stared at her.

"Would it be so bad?" She cocked her head appealingly. "I could help you have a good life in Geneva—"

"Why be so insistent?"

"Because I want it for Andre." Her shoulders rose in the tiniest shrug. "Is that so unreasonable? You want something, and I want something in return. What's wrong with that?" A knowing look came into her eyes, "You do *want* this merger, don't you?"

"Of course—"

"Then let us stop fencing," she said, rising and walking to the edge of the terrace. Leaning against the balustrade, she turned to face him. "I accept you have ability. Maurice wouldn't have plucked you from oblivion if you were a fool. But Andre had ability too. Great ability. Tell me honestly. Have you ever seen a more efficient factory than the Bouvier plant?"

He considered. "No, I don't think I have—"

"Exactly! But Maurice has never liked Andre. God knows why. In the early years, Andre worked like a dog to please him. Then, when recognition was withheld . . ." She shrugged. "Andre needs a bigger challenge. He has the vision and energy for a big job. You heard him last night—"

"He will face a bigger challenge—"

"Non!" She shook her head. "It will be the same as before.

Andre will run Bouvier. Edwards will *try* to run Excel, and Pohl will fool about with his inventions as usual. The only difference is they will all answer to you."

He remained silent. His own ideas about the merger were still too vague to articulate.

She turned away to face out over the lake. "This is my city," she said, "I grew up here. I am Bouvier. My husband runs the plant which still bears my name. I will *not* suffer this humiliation. Neither will Andre. We do not deserve this. Maurice is behaving very badly . . ." Words failed her as she struggled to control her temper. Tension showed in her face as she turned round. "So," she said, tossing her head, "you and Maurice can have your merger, but on certain conditions."

"That I live in Geneva?"

Her smile was strained. "That is the first one."

He waited.

"Condition two is that the head office of Stanton Industries is based here."

"I see—"

"And there's one more," she interrupted crisply. "That Andre is seen as your equal. I want him appointed *joint* chief executive of Stanton Industries. Pohl and Edwards will answer to him as well as to you." She smiled, but not enough to melt the ice in her eyes. "Those are my terms, Mr. Lambert. Take them or leave them."

As the Learjet flew north to Germany, the impossibility of his task weighed heavy in his mind. Now three people had said he was wasting his time—first Alec, then Edwards, and now Yvonne Amiens. He had been unable to dissuade her. "Those are my terms," she had insisted, "take them or leave them."

Bitch!

Stubbing out one cigarette, he reached for another.

Richards came through to tidy the cabin, removing Tom's glass and the bottle of Scotch. "We land in five minutes, Mr. Lambert. Are you being met at the airport?"

Tom shook his head. "No, they're not expecting me until the morning."

"Shall I arrange a cab to the hotel?"

"Please." Tom looked at his watch. "Is the airport far from the city center?"

"Half an hour. You'll be checked in by eight-thirty."

Richards was wrong by ten minutes. It was twenty to nine by the time Tom was shown into his room at the hotel. A message awaited him; to call Alec in London.

Jean answered the phone. Alec's wife was always a bit wary of Tom, resentful of the demands he made on Alec's time. Tom liked her without being blind to her reservations about him. She was the only woman he knew with strawberry hair, not tinted or dyed, an exuberant glossy head of natural hair which was neither red nor blonde but a curious combination of both. "Jean's crowning glory" according to Alec.

"Is he in?"

"Halfway through dinner. You do pick your times."

Alec was still chewing his food when he came on the line. "Bad news, I'm afraid."

Tom groaned. "My cup runneth over."

"We had a call from a guy called Hollenberg. Walter Hollenberg."

"Never heard of him."

"He used to work for old man Pohl. He still works for the Pohl Organization as some sort of consultant. Well . . . it seems Carl Pohl is very upset about this merger plan—"

"Surprise, surprise," Tom said drily. "I suppose he's ready to make ridiculous demands when I see him tomorrow."

"That's just it. You won't see him. When Pohl heard that you were coming, he walked out. He refuses to meet you."

Carl Pohl had always been different. He had grown up in the Pohl factories. His mother had died in childbirth and his father was dedicated to the business, so a normal upbringing had been out of the question. Young Carl had faced a dilemma, either stay home with a fractious housekeeper, or go to the factory in search of his father. Carl had chosen the latter, only to find that even at the factory his father was busy. Tender-hearted secretaries had taken the boy by the hand. "Your papa is in conference. Come, let's have some strudel in the canteen."

Carl met other people in the canteen—foremen and charge hands and men from the shop floor. Soon he knew most of the employees. He was a quiet, serious boy who wore his loneliness like a badge on his sleeve. An ordinary boy, with no airs and graces. People liked him for that; and although his constant questions were exhausting, one thing was said in his favor—"He never needs twice telling. He soaks it up like a sponge."

By the age of eight, Carl had graduated to the shop floor. His presence there was quite out of order. The shop floor was off-limits to unauthorized personnel. Yet what could the foremen do? "He's the boss's son. We can't send him packing with a clip round his ear. Besides, he's no trouble."

Once accepted, Carl spent every Saturday and every day of his holidays on the shop floor. His father was secretly pleased. "Carl will soon be running the place," he chuckled, oblivious of future disappointments.

At school, Carl was neither a dunce nor a genius. "Could do better" was the constant cry of his teachers. The truth was that school never captured his interest. Theories chalked on a blackboard were no substitute for the real products he saw at the factory.

At the age of twelve he took an electric kettle to pieces. "Always he does this," said the foremen, "everything we make, he takes apart. He asks how does it work? Could it work better?"

Carl certainly improved on the kettle.

Pohl technicians compared Carl's kettle to their best model, the kettle at the top of the range. Carl's kettle boiled twelve seconds faster. They compared it with every kettle they could find. None boiled as fast as Carl's kettle.

Kettles were only the beginning.

When he was fifteen, Carl quit school and went to work full-time in the factory. Over the next ten years he improved the efficiency of every product in the Pohl range, even the famous printing machines. His father was proud, yet at the same time anxious to expand his son's training. "Carl, developing products is only part of our business. Everything we make, we must sell. I want you to spend time as a salesman."

Pohl sales managers took turns trying to teach Carl the techniques of salesmanship. After six months, they gave up. They explained to Hans Pohl, "Every product has good features and poor features. Our job is to accentuate the positive. Herr Carl does the opposite. If a customer finds fault, Herr Carl won't list the benefits. Instead he strips it down and begins over again."

Realizing that Carl would never make a salesman, his father took him aside—"Carl, we run a big business. I want you to learn all about cash flow, profit statements, balance sheets and finance." Three months later, the Pohl Organization's chief accountant reported—"Herr Carl's interest in finance stops at what a product will cost. He shows no desire to learn beyond that."

Hans Pohl was forced to accept what was obvious to everyone else—that Carl was a brilliant development engineer who would never be capable of running the business.

By now, the legendary Hans Pohl was a shadow of his former self. He had only a short time to live. He summoned his six senior managers, the men who had helped rebuild the business after the war. "You all know your jobs," he told them, "you can run things between you. I ask only that you give Carl a free hand to develop his inventions. Believe me, that boy will deliver the future."

A month later Hans Pohl was dying. His closest friend, Walter Hollenberg, general manager of the Pohl Organization, was called to his bedside. Hollenberg was comforted by the calm way in which Hans Pohl prepared to meet death. *Why should I expect otherwise?* Hollenberg thought, remembering how Hans had stood up to the Gestapo. Yet something more than courage accounted for Pohl's manner. Extending an enfeebled hand, his weak smile was triumphant. "Walter," he said softly, "Maurice has been to see me. He made me a solemn promise. My name will remain over the door. The name Pohl will always be part of our business."

It was the faithful Hollenberg who had been pressed into service by the time Tom arrived at the factory. Tom had taken a cab from the hotel. At the main factory gates he announced himself to the two gatekeepers whose command of English put his schoolboy German to shame. Even so, "Herr Lambert from London" elicited only shrugs of disinterest, whereas "representing Herr Stanton" captured heel-clicking attention. The men rushed to their telephones to report down the line, "It is *that* Herr Lambert." After which a good deal of confusion ensued. Escorted from the main gates, Tom was handed over to a flustered receptionist who, in turn, ushered him up to the top floor before passing him over to a pink-faced secretary. Acute embarrassment was the order of the day. Asked to wait in a board room dominated by a portrait of Hans Pohl, Tom was fed coffee and cakes, and coffee and strudel by a succession of girls who came and went amid a flurry of apologies—"Herr Muller will be here in a moment"—"Herr Leiber is on his way from the paint shop"—"Herr Bertels is just finishing a meeting."

Eventually they all arrived together—Muller, Bertels, Leiber, Siegrist, Zaisser and Herrnstadt; the men who ran the Pohl organization—with the bent, elderly figure of Walter Hollenberg leading the way.

"On behalf of us all," Hollenberg began, speaking English with hardly an accent, "I welcome you as the honored representative of our much respected patron, Herr Stanton, to whom we all owe so much . . ."

Tom interrupted as soon as he decently could. "Please," he said, indicating the long board room table, "shall we sit down?"

They did so, looking askance at Hollenberg who had been elected their spokesman.

As the old man took his seat, he explained that although retired, he lived locally and his colleagues were—"kind enough to consult an old man whose life has been devoted to Hans Pohl and this business. . . ."

It had been to Hollenberg they had turned when Carl walked out.

"I've known him since he was child," said the old man with a sad shake of his head. "Naturally my colleagues hoped he would listen to me." Hollenberg reproached Tom with rheumy blue eyes. "Carl was very upset about Herr Stanton's recent decision. We thought Pohl would always be Pohl . . ."

Tom assessed the others while Hollenberg talked. They were all younger, in their forties, competent-looking men whose faces at that moment betrayed their anxiety.

"Without disrespect to you, Herr Lambert," Hollenberg said cautiously, "we were wondering if I should visit Herr Stanton—"

"Perhaps you could tell me exactly what happened."

After looking at his colleagues for approval, Hollenberg fidgeted with his tie before clearing his throat. "Carl hasn't been himself since his last meeting with Herr Stanton, when these new arrangements were announced . . ."

Apparently Pohl had returned to Hanover from Kariakos and shut himself away.

"He lives by himself. He's always been a loner, even when his father was alive . . ."

After a week's absence, Carl Pohl had reappeared at the office.

"He was a bit distant, preoccupied, but he's often like that. Usually it's a sign that he's working on some new development . . ."

So Pohl's brooding went largely unnoticed.

"Until he learned you were coming. Yesterday he called my colleagues together . . ." Hollenberg indicated the men around the table, "and told them he was going. I'm afraid he said some very bitter things."

"Such as?"

Bertels answered; a short, squat figure at the end of the table. "Carl said Herr Stanton has gone back on the promise he made to his father. Then he walked out. He just went."

"You mean resigned?"

Bertels shrugged. "It is hard to say. When I called Walter he asked the same thing—"

"As soon as I heard," Hollenberg interrupted, "I hurried round to Carl's home. He was packing a bag. He was very upset. He says to me, 'Walter, I will not set foot in the factory while Herr Lambert is there. If he goes, I come back. If he stays, don't expect me to be there.' "

Hiding his dismay, Tom remembered Haller saying *Carl is a genius. He could go anywhere—Phillips, Siemens, IBM . . .*

"Where's he gone?"

The old man's lined face twitched into a smile. "For a walk. To think things over. He has gone hiking in the Black Forest."

An hour later, Tom concluded the meeting. From the privacy of an office hastily allocated to him, he telephoned Alec in London. Alec was incredulous. "Hiking? What is he, some kind of nut? Can't you contact him?"

Alec was all for Tom returning to London. "You can't stay. A snub like that undermines your authority. He's made you look a prize prick. Christ, Tom, get back over here. Call Stanton and get him to fire off a rocket . . ."

Tom was tempted. He was as angry as Alec. But he was reluctant to call Stanton, reluctant to admit failure. "I dunno. Maybe I can have a good look round with Pohl out of the way. It gives me a chance to get to know Bertels and the others." He edged toward a decision. "That's what I'll do, Alec, stay here for a few days."

Those few days were to stretch. In the end he stayed nine days in Hanover, nine days and nine nights without sight or sound of Carl Pohl.

For a week he toured the factory. It was huge, with a daunting diversification of products. Before the war the business had made only printing machines. After the conflict, with the German economy in ruins, the Allied Powers had decreed that Pohl should also make badly needed radio components. Making components had encouraged Hans Pohl to assemble radio sets, and in turn they had led him to produce tape recorders, after which had come televisions and domestic appliances such as steam irons, toasters, electric kettles, coffee perculators . . . and all this was in addition to the office products division.

Tom could not fail to be impressed. Spread across seventy acres, the Pohl plant was modern and well managed. Labor relations were good; employees were well paid and took pride in their work. Yet the actual organization owed not a jot to Carl Pohl. Leiber, Bertels and Muller made the decisions, aided by Siegrist, Zaisser and Herrnstadt.

By the end of the week, Tom was beginning to see weaknesses as well as strengths. There were too many products. The business had become *too* diversified. Lines were added because Pohl had an idea, not because of a gap in the market. Nobody ever said to Pohl—"If we expand into this we lose the resources to do that." The business needed to be streamlined.

Tom mentioned as much to Leiber one day. The German looked aghast. "Herr Carl would never agree. The Pohl Organization is famous for innovation."

Tom wanted to say, "Yes, but there's no point in re-inventing the wheel."

Every night he took work back to the hotel. Dining alone, he pored over production schedules, cost centers and profit forecasts. But one thing eluded him. A real understanding of Carl Pohl. He kept telling himself that to know the man was to solve the problem—but the man remained infuriatingly absent.

Eventually he sought out the world's expert on Carl Pohl—Walter Hollenberg, who had known Pohl every day of his life. On the Sunday he invited Hollenberg to join him for lunch at the hotel. "Tell me," he said as they sat down, "can you list all of Carl's inventions?"

It was exactly the right opening. Hollenberg was delighted. Recounting stories one after another, he talked through the soup, the main course, the pudding and the cheese. His eyes shone with pride when he talked of Carl Pohl.

Tom was impressed. And he warmed to Hollenberg. Despite his years, the old man was as sharp as a knife. And shrewd. No wonder Hans Pohl had relied on his judgment, and no wonder young Carl did the same.

Hollenberg brushed such compliments aside. "I help where I can," he said modestly. "With some things, Carl is so smart he can see around corners. Yet sometimes, ordinary little problems, things you and I wouldn't think twice about, land him flat on his back."

Tom smiled. "Perhaps he should find a good wife?"

"Ha!" Hollenberg's laugh was dry as a cough, "Don't even think it. Carl and a woman? When the Rhine flows red with wine."

Tom was as persuasive as he knew how. "The need for change won't go away," he said. "If I fail to reorganize these businesses, Stanton will find someone who will. Carl can't hide forever. He has a choice. Either resign or make the best of things. Naturally the future will be different, but different needn't mean worse. With goodwill on both sides, it could even mean better."

Hollenberg listened, eyes narrowed in concentration. He sipped his coffee, accepted a cigarette, and said nothing.

Frustrated, Tom let his gaze roam around the dining room. Earlier, most of the tables had been occupied; now, with lunch over, waiters were spreading clean tablecloths and setting places for dinner. Only one other table remained in use; a young man and a young woman sat together and lingered over their coffee. The sight of them added to Tom's feelings of loneliness. Here he was in a strange town, in a strange country, going nowhere. . . .

His fingers drummed on the table. "Does Carl *want* to resign?"

The old man sighed and shook his head. "I don't think so. Carl is too proud to want to leave the Pohl Organization. He will if he is forced to, but no, I don't think he wants to."

"So what does he want?"

Frowning, Hollenberg fell silent for a moment. Then he said, "Carl's is a sad story in some ways. He and his father were never close. Hans was always so busy and Carl was . . . well, Carl was just Carl . . . but always he idolized his father." A reflective look came into Hollenberg's eyes. "It was easy to idolize Hans, he was a great man. And Carl grew up in his shadow. Indirectly he competes with his father. Not in the same way, you understand, Hans was a leader of men, an organizer, an administrator. Carl is none of those things, but he has his own potential and he knows it. Hans changed people's lives by giving them employment . . . but one day, with his inventions, Carl could change people's lives all over the world." Hollenberg smiled his sad smile. "If that happens, Herr Lambert, for the first time in Carl's life, he will feel a worthy son to his father."

Tom sat back in his chair. For the first time he felt he was making some progress. "Suppose . . ." he said slowly, edging his way toward an idea, "suppose I could help bring that about? Would you help me?"

"I would do anything to help Carl."

Tom smiled. "It amounts to the same thing."

Hollenberg hesitated. "Does it?" He looked thoughtful, even troubled. "Let me be honest with you, Herr Lambert. Always I have had a great respect for Herr Stanton. I would like to please him and to please you, but . . . you must understand, Hans was like a brother to me. I cherished his friendship, and Carl looks upon me as an uncle—"

"I understand that."

Hollenberg fidgeted in his chair, "What I am trying to say is, I will certainly help you to help Carl in any way I can, but, I must be honest, Carl's interests will be paramount, even above those of Herr Stanton's and yours."

Tom beamed. "Does Carl know this? Does he know you would always side with him, no matter what?"

"Yes, I am sure—"

"Herr Hollenberg," Tom leaned across the table and gripped the old man by the hand, "I think you're the answer to one of my problems."

"Let's go through this again," said Alec. "Edwards will fight you to the death—"

"He's still sore," Tom admitted.

"Amiens wants an impossible deal."

"It's Yvonne. She's ambitious for him—"

"And Pohl won't even talk to you!" Alec threw up his hands. "When will you admit we're wasting our time?"

"Pohl will listen to Walter Hollenberg. We could be in business if I get him on my side—"

"If," Alec said darkly. "And what about Amiens?"

"Yvonne holds the key. I've been thinking about her. She's old money, Swiss establishment, all that stuff. Amiens is a bloody good production engineer, but she's the brains when it comes to wheeling and dealing. Yvonne is the Bouvier in the family, as she pointed out. I've just got to give her something she wants."

"We know what she wants."

Tom shrugged, "Then I have to find something else."

Alec sighed, "And Edwards? I can't see him backing off."

"He might," Tom said hopefully, "after I've bent his ear for a couple of weeks. I'm going to the States with him. I called him this morning."

Alec raised his eyebrows, "Oh, boy. That sounds like a wild goose chase if ever there was one."

"Quarreling won't help," Barbara sniffed reprovingly as she passed Alec his coffee.

Tom grinned. Barbara became ever more protective. Devotedly loyal herself, she sometimes mistook Alec's criticisms for lack of commitment. Nothing could be further from the truth. Doubts which Alec expressed in private were never vented in public. He had visited all eight of the businesses to be sold, and already opened negotiations on two. His program was well under way, as was Barbara's; the clatter of typewriters could be heard down the hall as the recently engaged secretaries worked on reports.

Studying the calendar on his desk, Tom considered his schedule: two weeks in the States with Edwards, and a few days afterwards to get everything ready. He drummed his fingers on the desktop. "I want to see Hollenberg again, privately, at his home, not the Pohl plant. And another chat with Yvonne wouldn't go amiss." Frowning, he ticked off the days. "If I finish by the twenty-eighth, we could hold the meeting on the thirtieth."

Barbara looked up from the pad on her knee. "Will you hold it here?"

The frown remained on Tom's face. He had not considered the venue, but the moment Barbara spoke he knew London was wrong. Amiens would resent coming to London. So would his wife. They would see it as a summons.

"No," he said slowly, "Kariakos would be better."

It took over an hour to get through to the island. Maurice Stanton's voice boomed down the line. "How are you? I've been worried . . ."

They talked for a long time, at least forty minutes, with Tom doing most of the talking. Stanton grunted "Uh huh" at regular intervals. There was no mistaking his anxiety. "Do you think you can pull it off, Tom? Do you?"

Tom was slow to answer. The odds were still against, even if the ideas half formed in his mind came to fruition. "What was the word you told me about? That Greek word?"

"Polymichanos," Stanton laughed. "It's what I call you. Mister Polymichanos."

"Yeah? If I pull this off I deserve a Knighthood. You can call me *Sir* Polymichanos."

Lulled by the steady drone of the aircraft's engines, he let his mind drift back over the preceding weeks. America already seemed a lifetime away. He and Edwards had crammed a seemingly impossible number of meetings into fifteen days . . .

Praise had been heaped on Edwards wherever they went. Deservedly so, in Tom's opinion. In five years Edward had carved out a valuable niche in the market. He had appointed the best distributors, backed them with advertising, and created an after-sales service second to none. Tom's earlier impressions had been confirmed. Edwards was a different man away from the factory. His marketing expertise was applauded even in America, a country which prided itself on inventing the word.

That was the good news; the bad was that every effort to break down the barriers had failed. Edwards had been the picture of geniality with distributors, introducing Tom as "my colleague from London," but in private his opposition to the merger was cast-iron.

Tom sighed. He glanced at his watch. Twenty-four hours to go. In twenty-four hours the board meeting would begin. In twenty-four hours, if persuasion failed, Maurice Stanton would have to come down from the fence. But would he?

A scowl settled over Tom's face. American competitors were spending vast sums on research and development. Bouvier and Pohl and Excel and Bolton could only compete by pooling resources. And that wasn't all. Pohl, manufacturers of the best printing machines in the world, were almost invisible. He had asked Edwards about that. Edwards had shrugged. "Pohl's distributors are asleep." And Bouvier had been little better. The biggest market in the world and Pohl and Bouvier weren't even there!

The door from the pilot's cabin opened and Gregg Richards emerged. "Athens in fifteen minutes, Mr. Lambert. Can I get you more coffee?"

Declining, Tom was mildly amused to remember that eight weeks before he had been contemptuous of the Learjet, regarding it as a rich man's toy. Now it had become a tool of his trade. Five days earlier it had taken him to meet Hollenberg in Hanover, before flying him on to Geneva for a private meeting with Yvonne Amiens.

Hollenberg had been flattered. "Come to Kariakos? But why?" he asked in surprise.

"Carl may need your advice, and Herr Stanton will be pleased to see you again."

Yvonne had been openly suspicious. "What's your game? Why should you want me there?"

"Desmond will be bringing his father, and Carl will have an advisor. Why should Andre be at a disadvantage? He trusts your judgment, he talks everything over with you; whatever the outcome, you will be part of it."

"We gave you our terms. They are not negotiable."

The memory brought a wry smile to his face. Yvonne would come. She was too intrigued to stay away. They would all come—Desmond and Sir Bernard, Carl Pohl and Hollenberg, and Yvonne and Andre.

He bit his lip. Tonight he would dine at the villa privately with Maurice and Gunther Haller. Tonight they would hear his plan for the first time. . . .

"Good luck," Alec had said, shaking hands. "If anyone can do it, you can."

"You *will*!" Barbara had exclaimed, unexpectedly giving him a hug, "and we'll be waiting when you get back."

He smiled. Thinking of Barbara reminded him of the medallion. He looked down at his belt. It had been Barbara's idea to have the medallion made into a buckle. He had forgotten it until he had sent his lightweight suit to be cleaned. The medallion had been in the pocket. The scene in the taverna had exploded again in his mind: the men escaping over the balcony, soldiers rushing in, fear on the girl's face, and Constantin's brave defiance. Tom had taken the medallion into the office. Hefting it in his hand, feeling the weight of it, had made him feel guilty. "I should never have accepted it. I hope it's not valuable . . ."

But it was. Barbara had taken it to the jeweler along the road. "It's gold," she said when she returned, "the jeweler wanted to know if you would sell it?"

He could never sell it. It was a gift, from a brave and generous man. "But I can't wear it. Medallions aren't really my style."

And Barbara had taken it to the jeweler to fashion into a buckle.

He patted his pocket, reassured to feel the outline of the oblong box. He had bought a watch as a present. It eased his conscience to give a gift in return.

He patted his pocket again later, when he was bouncing along in the jeep on the way out of Hellenikon Airport. Gregg drove with his usual nonchalance, one hand on the wheel while gesturing and pointing with the other. More than before, Tom was struck by the contrasts. Dazzling white buildings drew the eye. Flower stalls blazed with color on street corners. The white marble Parthenon rose gloriously atop the Acropolis, and spires of water arched up from the fountains in Constitution Square. The parks were lined with tables shaded by blue awnings, beneath which people sat drinking coffee. The city looked peaceful, at ease with itself . . . and yet . . . in the shadows of a doorway, glinted a steel helmet. An armored troop carrier lumbered out from a side street. A movement beneath the trees betrayed a soldier transferring his carbine from one shoulder to the other. . . .

Tom thought—*maybe it's my mood. I'm all tensed up about meeting Stanton*—but the more he looked, the more he saw beyond the superficial to what had become everyday life in the city—a city in the grip of a military fist. And Piraeus, when they reached it, was worse. More soldiers than stevedores populated the docks. Dun-colored troop carriers outnumbered farm lorries, and from every street corner came the threat of military force.

Anxious-faced people cast their eyes neither left nor right as they scurried along.

In eight weeks, he had seen a dozen cities. None had the same nervous atmosphere as Athens and Piraeus. Even in the jeep it was easy to feel intimidated, and as he met the hard-eyed scrutiny of soldiers patroling the streets, he felt strangely anxious for the big Greek who ran the taverna, the innkeeper who had once been a lawyer.

"How's Constantin?"

"Indestructible," Gregg answered cheerfully.

Moments later they pulled into the narrow street, with its ancient pockmarked walls of white stone. Gesturing at the taverna, Gregg said, "I'll be about an hour. Do you want me to come and introduce you again?"

"No, I'll be fine. See you later."

Parting the bead curtains at the entrance, Tom blinked as his eyes adjusted to the cool shade of the interior. He saw Constantin at the bar. The big man looked up and stared, his eyes widening in recognition. A huge grin engulfed his face as he hurried forward. "Eh!" he exclaimed, reaching for Tom's hand. "Didn't I say you'd be back?" The warmth of the greeting was unmistakable. Gripping Tom's hand, he dragged him in the direction of the kitchen. "Melina!" he shouted. "Look! The Kyrios Lambert is here. Didn't I say he'd be back?"

The pretty girl Tom remembered from his first visit emerged from the kitchen, her eyes lighting with pleasure. Constantin drew her toward him.

"This is Melina, my wife," he said as they stood before Tom, grinning and smiling. But Constantin's smile faded as they led the way up to the balcony. A severe look came into his eyes. "Eh? Where's the medallion I gave you? You don't wear it?"

Opening his jacket, Tom displayed his belt. "I hope you don't mind. I had it made into a buckle. It's . . . more English somehow."

"Eh!" The huge grin returned. "How about that! That makes us blood brothers!"

Strong arms encircled Tom in a bear hug while Melina drew a chair out from the table.

Before sitting down, Tom reached into his pocket. "I've a small gift in return."

"For me?" The big man looked astonished. Opening the box, his eyes rounded as he inspected the watch. Holding it by the strap, he lifted it up to the sun, admiring it with delight. "A small gift," he echoed. "It's magnificent . . ." Lapsing into voluble Greek, he drew his wife to the edge of the balcony, beyond the shade, for her to strap the watch onto his wrist and admire the way it glinted in the sun.

They returned to the table, laughing and talking, throwing warm looks of gratitude at Tom. He felt awkward, pleased at their excitement but regretting his lack of a gift for Constantin's wife. "I should have realized. Next time I will bring something for Melina—"

"No, no," Constantin protested, translating to Melina and interpreting her rapid response. "She says she's had a wonderful gift. She never thought to see you again."

After that it was like a reunion. Constantin hurried down to the bar to collect a jug of retsina while a radiant Melina brought dishes up from the kitchen. They were so pleased to see him.

"Remember last time?" Constantin grinned. "You sitting here when those soldiers rushed in? Eh, that was close."

The incident, beginning to fade in Tom's memory, was as fresh as paint to them. Constantin acted it out, playing all the parts, while Melina looked on with dark frightened eyes. Afterward she insisted that he tell the full story. Two of the men who escaped were Melina's brothers. The third one, the older man, was Constantin's uncle. "Now they are living with friends up in the hills," said Constantin, raising his glass. "We miss them, but they are safe, thanks to you."

They hovered over Tom while he ate, plying him with questions about the world beyond Greece. Trying to answer gave him an insight into their lives, especially as each question echoed the last—"What are the British saying about the Junta ruling Greece?"

He had no idea. The intensity of their enquiries made him uncomfortable. He had his own problems. In a few hours he would be seeing Stanton and Haller. Tomorrow he faced the most important meeting of his life. He had been desperately busy. . . .

But listening to Constantin made him feel awkward. He experienced the same apprehension that he had felt in the jeep. They were giving him a welcome as warm as the sun, but beneath the surface lurked a terrible tension. In truth, he hadn't the faintest idea what the British were saying about the Junta. He doubted they were saying much at all. Busy with their own lives, few people had time for the problems of others.

He did his best. "I think there's been stuff in the papers."

They were disappointed.

He tried to reassure them. "I'm sure a lot's going on, but I've been rushing around. I haven't had time to keep up with the news."

Their dismay was profound. Seeing his embarrassment they tried to hide their disappointment behind a veil of politeness. They changed the subject, but even when Constantin launched into a funny story, the laughter which shook his huge frame stopped short of his eyes.

Tom felt he had let them down. Liking them, he experienced a pang of concern when he left. Waving goodbye from the jeep, he wondered what it was that he saw in Constantin's expression. Envy perhaps? Envy that he was free to come and go—Britain, America, Switzerland—whereas Constantin was not free at all, not even free to practice his profession.

"Come again soon." Constantin called.

"Sure." And Tom meant it. He liked these people. Something about them reached out and touched him. But he knew that seeing them again, coming to Piraeus again, rested with others. Everything depended upon the board meeting tomorrow.

They were assembled in Stanton's study, around a large table, with Tom at one end and Stanton the other. Yvonne and Andre Amiens sat on Tom's left, with Gunther Haller beyond them. Bernard and Desmond Edwards were on his right, down the table from Hollenberg and Carl Pohl. Behind him were three large easels, upon which were the sheets of white card he had brought with him from London.

He spent little time in his chair. For an hour Tom paced up and down, recounting thoughts and impressions. No word of criticism passed his lips. He said nothing of Desmond's truculence, or Yvonne's demands, or Pohl's absence. Instead he talked of Excel's successes in the American market. He described the smooth efficiency of the Bouvier plant. He listed the number of inventions developed by Pohl. Where praise was due, he laid it on with a trowel. Then he began to change tack. Gradually, imperceptibly. He talked of the industry, the quickening pace of change and the need for investment. He talked well, fluently, without notes, with the confidence of an expert, so that for long periods he spoke uninterrupted, with his audience attentive and quiet. It was only when he began to insert mentions of Stanton Industries that people began to fidget. Pohl scratched his nose as he stared down the table, his eyes myopic behind pebble-thick glasses. The legs on Sir Bernard's chair creaked as he tilted it backward. Andre Amiens ceased to doodle and started to bite the end of his pencil. Yvonne toyed with the rings on her fingers.

Having led his horses to water, the moment had come to persuade them to drink. "Obviously," he said smoothly, "all expansion must be sales-led, and I propose we appoint the best marketing man in the business to run the Stanton sales organization—"

"Another outsider?" Sir Bernard interrupted, his bushy eyebrows rising as a sarcastic edge came to his voice. "Or are you describing yourself?"

Tom smiled, "I'm simply repeating what I heard all over the States. We have the best man for the job in this room. I mean Desmond, of course."

Heads swiveled. Desmond's eyes widened in surprise. A slight flush came to his cheeks. Next to him his father started in surprise. He looked at his son as if seeing him through new eyes.

Pohl was the first to find voice. "Do you mean," he sounded outraged, "Edwards will sell Pohl equipment in the States?"

"Not just the States," Tom answered in the same calm voice he had used throughout, "Desmond will sell Pohl equipment worldwide. Even in Germany. SISM will market all of our products—"

"SISM?" Pohl interrupted. "What is this SISM?"

Walking across to the first of the easels, Tom turned over the white card on the top. The words STANTON INDUSTRIES SALES & MARKETING were printed in large black letters. Below, a size smaller, were the words—*Chief Executive Officer—Desmond Edwards.*

Everyone started talking at once. Pohl was on his feet shouting *"Nein, nein!"* with Hollenberg doing his best to restrain him, while Stanton began beating the table with the flat of his hand.

When order was restored Haller asked his question, exactly on cue as had been rehearsed the previous evening. "This SISM," he asked innocently, "if Desmond is chief executive, who will be the other directors?"

"That's up to Desmond," Tom replied. "I reserve a place for myself, and naturally the entire board of SISM will be answerable to the parent company, Stanton Industries itself, but it will be Desmond's board—"

"Wait a minute," Amiens went red in the face. "You mean it will sell Bouvier products—"

"Oh yes," Tom nodded, "it will sell everything we make—"

"And I'm not guaranteed a place on the board!" Amiens flushed crimson.

"Ridiculous!" Yvonne agreed, shaking her head, eyes blazing with temper.

"Trust the British to stick together," Pohl sneered.

Sir Bernard jerked upright, "I resent that. We didn't know a bloody thing about this proposal—"

"Hah!" Pohl snorted. "You think I'm a fool. The whole thing stinks." Swinging back to face Tom, he demanded, "Give me one reason why—"

"I'll give you plenty of reasons," Tom retorted crisply, "if you'll sit down and listen."

Pohl opened his mouth, thought better of it, and sat down.

Tom began, "This will make the Pohl name famous—"

"It already is," Pohl barked.

"Perhaps," Tom nodded agreeably, "in fact, you're right in a way. People *do* know the name, but I went from coast to coast in the States and saw very little Pohl equipment—"

"So we'll change our agent," Pohl countered.

"You've had long enough to do that." Tom picked up a folder from the table in front of him. "This is a report compiled by a top market research organization and completed only last week. They questioned six hundred business executives. Most of them knew the name Pohl, some went so far as to say Pohl equipment was the best in the world. So we asked why they weren't using it. Half of them thought it wasn't available in the States—"

"I said," Pohl interrupted icily, "we will change our agent."

Instead of responding, Tom looked at Hollenberg. The old man sighed, "America has never been easy for us—"

"Has Australia? Or Canada. Or India? Or even Britain or France?"

Hollenberg looked wretched. "Exports have been difficult—"

"Walter," Tom interrupted gently, "isn't it true that the strength of the Pohl Organization is not the sales organization but the unique inventive genius of Carl Pohl?"

A look of relief came into the old man's eyes. "But of course, there is no one like Carl—"

"Or Andre," Yvonne said sharply. "How can you even consider forming this . . . this . . ." She pointed at the easel, "This SISM or whatever you call it, without having Andre on the board? How can you—"

"He won't have the time," Tom smiled. "Honestly, Yvonne, Andre simply won't have enough time—"

"Time? What do you mean, won't have enough time?"

"We're talking about a twenty percent increase in sales," Tom explained calmly. "That means a hell of a jump in production. Andre will have to perform miracles—"

"Andre will?"

"Can you suggest anyone better? I want to merge all manufacturing output into one organization."

Turning away, Tom turned the top card over on the second easel. The words STANTON MANUFACTURING leapt out in black letters. Below, slightly smaller, was printed—*Andre Amiens—Chief Executive.*

Tom returned to the table. "Every factory in the group will be answerable to Andre—"

"Mine won't," Sir Bernard grunted. He glared down the table. "That's bloody daft. You can't run my factory from Geneva."

"Run locally," Tom explained patiently, "but manufacturing policy will be laid down in Geneva. All production managers will be answerable to Andre—"

"You mean he can hire them and fire them?" Sir Bernard went red in the face.

"Of course—"

"Bloody rubbish! What the hell does Amiens know about making typewriters in Coventry?"

"He might not even make them there. He might centralize typewriter production in Germany and use Coventry to make copiers." Tom shrugged. "That will be up to Andre, but my guess is that he will rationalize production—"

"You mean?" Sir Bernard turned to put a hand on Desmond's shoulder. "You mean my son . . . *my* son will be chasing about all over the world, selling Excel typewriters which are famous for being Coventry-made, and they won't be made in Coventry at all?"

"Which is more important," Tom smiled, "where a product is made, or how competitive it is in the market place? I think Desmond should tell us that, after all, worldwide sales will be his responsibility."

But Desmond remained silent. He kept looking at the easel. Enthusiasm for the idea showed on his face; excitement shone in his eyes. Absorbed by the big picture, he had scant interest in the petty detail raised by his father.

Disgusted by such lack of support, Sir Bernard looked elsewhere. "Maurice? You don't go along with this rubbish—"

"In a minute, Bernard," Stanton said calmly. "Tom hasn't quite finished."

Neither, it seemed, had Yvonne. "Who else will be on the board of this Stanton Manufacturing?"

"Me," said Tom, "just as I shall be on Desmond's board, as an aid to coordination, but with that exception Andre will have a free hand." Turning away, he returned to the second easel and removed the top sheet. Revealed was an architect's sketched elevation. "World Headquarters of Stanton Manufacturing will be in Geneva. Naturally the increased personnel will require more space . . ."

But Yvonne was no longer listening. She was staring at the sketch, pink-faced with excitement. True the drawing had been amended from the original; only two towers and not three rose into the sky, but the effect was enough to make Yvonne's eyes sparkle with pride.

It also brought Pohl back to his feet. "So much for your promises," he sneered at Stanton. "My father gave his life to this business. The Pohl name will live forever. That's what you promised. And now—"

"The Pohl name," Tom repeated, "will become even more famous."

Pohl swung around to face him. "Yeah? Edwards runs sales, Amiens runs production. What the fuck do I do?"

"What none of us has the talent to do," Tom answered calmly. He had been on his feet for well over an hour, facing a barrage of questions, but he remained completely composed. "Why not sit down? It will take me a few minutes to explain."

Hating to lose face, Pohl hesitated.

Hollenberg helped. "Carl, let's listen to Herr Lambert's proposals. I'm sure it won't take long. We agree to nothing by listening."

The scowl remained, but Pohl seized the excuse. "That's right. We agree to nothing," he said, resuming his seat.

Before Tom continued, he snatched a look at Yvonne. Her eyes were still fixed upon the architect's sketch, the faintest of smiles touching her lips. His surge of excitement doubled when he glanced at Desmond who sat staring at the easels, a look of fascination on his face.

Encouraged, Tom continued, "One of the things I did in the States was analyze how much our competitors spend on research—"

"I could have saved you the trouble," Pohl grumbled. "We're not even in the same league."

"Exactly. For instance, Xerox is assembling a team of scientists out on the West Coast that would blow your mind—"

"Not my mind."

"No, because you would have loved the whole project. You'd have understood the objectives . . ." Tom allowed his attention to stray to the others. "The Xerox place out at Palo Alto is a center for pure scientific research, a haven of Ph.D. scientists and technologists, all probing away at the frontiers of artificial intelligence. A cross between a university campus and a laboratory. More than a hundred of the world's leading technologists are there, dreaming up the future. . . ."

Launched into his theme, he seemed to direct his attention to the whole table. In reality he remained watchful of Pohl. Gradually, grudgingly, Pohl began to respond. Instead of interrupting he doodled on his pad, feigning indifference until Tom turned to the third easel and began to flick over the pages. Photograph after photograph appeared, all depicting the lush surroundings of the Xerox Research Center. Pohl's face became a study in concentration.

"For the next couple of years," Tom said, "our existing products will allow us to compete, but we can forget the future unless we embark upon a similar program of research—"

Amiens cleared his throat, "A set-up like that would cost millions of dollars—"

"Three million," Tom nodded. "And six percent of group sales to sustain it."

"Group sales!" Amiens' chiseled face betrayed his alarm. "That's a hell of a burden—"

"Not a burden, an investment. Carl must buy the best brains in the world. He should recruit in Europe, the States, Japan—"

"Carl?" Sir Bernard interjected. "You mean you'll entrust these huge sums to Pohl? He couldn't run a bath!"

"You don't run ideas," Tom countered, "you foster them, you nurture them. Even a failed experiment illustrates—"

"How to go bust!" Sir Bernard interrupted. "So now we have a third subsidiary. One for sales, one for production, now some great bottomless pit—"

"Not a subsidiary." Tom returned to the flip chart. "Not a

corporation or a company in the normal sense, but a foundation with sufficient funds to bestow generous research grants." Pausing to make sure Pohl was watching, he lifted the sheet on the easel to reveal the final page.

The words were set out in block letters. THE CARL POHL INTERNATIONAL INSTITUTE FOR SCIENTIFIC RESEARCH. Below, slightly smaller, was printed—*Principal—Carl Pohl.*

The color drained from Pohl's face.

Tom said, "Naturally Carl will have a seat on the main board, but in his case I propose . . ."

Pohl's eyes remained fixed on the easel. He was beginning to recover. Some of the color returned to his face.

"I propose," Tom continued, "that Carl be allowed to nominate Walter Hollenberg as his alternate for main board meetings, simply because business matters might distract him from R&D—"

"Carl," Hollenberg was whispering anxiously, "are you unwell?"

Pohl was taking deep breaths. He removed his spectacles, making his face more moon-shaped than ever. Polishing his glasses on his shirt, he turned in his seat. He spoke in a hushed whisper, shaking his head. "Walter, what do you think?"

Tom felt a huge wave of exultation. He sensed victory. He walked to one side, leaving the three easels in clear view.

Carl and Hollenberg were whispering together.

Yvonne had seized Andre's hand and was gazing into his face.

Desmond's eyes were half closed, visualizing himself in faraway places, with Pohl and Bouvier equipment to sell, as well as Excel's and Bolton's. They could all see a more valuable prize than they had now. They were exchanging one empire for another.

Now it was Stanton's turn. He rose from his chair and advanced down the room, to stand shoulder to shoulder with Tom. Taking a deep breath, he began, "Honor thy fathers," he said. "That's what we've been trying to do, yet with the best of intentions, we all got it wrong. It took this remarkable young man . . ." he placed a hand on Tom's shoulder, "to open my eyes. Bernard, Desmond, I owe you an apology. Bernard, I promised you that Desmond would run Excel as long as he wanted. Did we ask Desmond? No. We just assumed he'd get as much satisfaction running the factory as you did, never realizing we were restricting a remarkable talent . . ."

He went around the table. "Carl," he said, "I should have listened harder to your father. He didn't mean to leave you in the business to emulate him. How could anyone emulate Hans? He meant to give you your chance to do *your* thing, to stamp your own name on the world . . .

"Yvonne, the whole of Geneva knows Andre is a production genius. Isn't it time we told the whole world . . ."

His summing up was soon over. He was satisfied. His conscience was clear. Tom had found a remarkable way to honor the past while creating the future.

"I will now take a vote," he said. "I propose that Tom Lambert's plans be adopted immediately in every respect."

"Seconded," said Haller raising his hand.

Desmond was the first. With a sideways glance at his father, pausing to receive a nod of forgiveness, he raised his hand.

Amiens was next, raising his left hand because Yvonne still clung to his right.

And then Pohl.

"Carried unanimously," Maurice Stanton pronounced with a huge smile.

BOOK FOUR

1978

Tom's enthusiasm had returned when telling his story. Lines had softened in his face. Hate had gone from his eyes. When the room had grown cold he had set light to the kindling in the hearth and fed the flames with pine logs. The pungent smell would have reminded Constantin of his boyhood if his attention had strayed, but he had remained vigilant, driving Tom on with a series of questions in the hope that talk might somehow disperse the poison, would stop him talking of murder. He dared not let up. "What was it Maurice called you? Sir Polymichanos. I was here once when he said that. I wondered what it was about—"

"A standing joke," Tom smiled. "Those were the good years," he said, "building the business, making Stanton Industries a force to be reckoned with."

Good years for you, Constantin thought, *but bad years for me.* He laughed. "Eh! Do you know what Melina used to say whenever you came into the taverna? 'That man' she would say, 'grows taller every month. Soon he will be a Colossus.' "

Tom smiled. It had felt like that. Everything he touched had turned to gold. Forming Stanton Industries had been the turning point. The huge bonus had helped. He had become financially secure for the first time in his life. And the share options in his contract had added to his wealth. Not that money was the sole object; money was a measuring stick; a score card to record how well the game was played. And he had played well . . .

His thoughts were interrupted by the sound of the wind. Glancing out to the terrace he was surprised to see the lanterns shudder on the balustrade. The wind was gusting, blowing up for a gale. He was even more surprised when he looked at his watch. "My God! Do you know the time?"

Constantin was well aware of the time. It was midnight. His mutilated leg had been aching for hours, but he had remained still and stiff in his chair for fear of interrupting Tom's memories.

But now Tom *was* interrupted. The door opened behind them. "Ah!" Tom exclaimed looking around, "Alec! Where the devil have you been?"

Alec looked windswept. He smoothed his hair back into place. "There's a storm blowing up," he said. Oddly enough the years had been harder on Alec than on Tom. His hair, once sandy and vibrant, was now pepper-and-salt and well back from his forehead. His shoulders had rounded from years at a desk. But the eyes were the same—gray, well spaced and bright with intelligence. "That's a good idea," he said, seeing the glass in Tom's hand, "I could use a stiff drink."

Regretting the interruption, Constantin sounded reproachful, "I thought you were upstairs—"

"I was earlier."

"How is she?"

"Worried to death. Worse than we are—"

"I'll go up to her," said Tom.

"No." Alec shook his head. "I gave her a pill." Advancing to the sideboard, he glanced at his watch, "She's been asleep a good hour."

"So where have you been?"

"Talking to Mavros," he replied, pouring a brandy. "He wants to see you."

"To see me?" asked Constantin.

"No. Tom."

Constantin frowned. "Where is Mavros? I haven't seen him all day."

Alec glanced at Tom, as if expecting him to reply. But Tom remained silent.

Constantin's eyes narrowed. "Mavros. Where is he?"

Ignoring Alec's look, Tom swallowed some brandy.

Creases in Constantin's forehead crept upwards to his bald pate. "Alec, what's going on?"

"Mavros has been working up on the cliff. He was going back up there when I saw him."

"Up on the cliff?" Constantin sounded incredulous.

"There's a clearing up there. Just an opening in the pines really, with a seat and a telescope looking out to sea."

"But it's pitch dark outside."

Alec turned with a glass in his hand. He shrugged, looking at Tom with silent accusal.

Concern sounded in Constantin's voice. "Are his men with him?"

"They were still up there," Alec answered.

"So what are they doing?"

Stung by Alec's look, Tom reacted angrily, "You don't have to know. They're building something, that's all."

Constantin's concern grew. "They are good men, Tom. Decent, honorable—"

"Who will keep quiet!" Tom interrupted. "Four reliable men who can be trusted—"

"You can't involve them in killing—"

"They won't kill anyone. I'll do the killing when the time comes."

Alec fidgeted at the sideboard. Like Constantin, he had hoped to persuade Tom to abandon this madness, but like Constantin he was beginning to wonder if it was possible. "Anyway," he shrugged, "Mavros asked would you go up to see him."

"Right. I'll go now. You two stay here—"

"No." Constantin's contradiction was forthright and final. Setting his glass down, he began to pull himself up from the chair, "I will come with you."

Watching the battle of wills, Alec knew neither would give way.

"It won't do your leg much good," Tom said harshly, "it's a long walk."

A grim smile touched Constantin's lips. "My leg aches when I worry, not when I walk."

Alec finished his drink. "It's pointless arguing. We'll all go." Glancing at their open-necked shirts and thin cotton trousers, he warned, "There's a wind blowing up—"

"Don't worry," Constantin joked. "I'll run all the way."

The joke seemed wishful thinking when they emerged onto the terrace. A strong breeze was buffeting in from the sea, hurrying clouds across the night sky, creating dark moving shadows against the face of the moon. The three men trudged around the villa and took the path up into the trees. Wind whistled through the branches and rattled the pine cones. Constantin shuffled along, aware that the others could have walked faster without him, but determined to see for himself what Mavros had been set to build. He scowled. The interruption had come at a bad time. He had been making progress until Alec arrived. Tom had been talking easily, the story had been flowing.

The path narrowed. Tom forged ahead, sure of his way. Alec slid a sideways glance at Constantin and lowered his voice. "Any luck?"

"Some," Constantin whispered. "I got him talking about the old days, hoping to find some sort of clue."

Alec walked on. He knew about the old days. He had lived them first-hand. Clues were there by the dozen, but no certainties. Just suspicion and doubt. Meanwhile time was running out. Come tomorrow, Tom's guests would arrive. Come nightfall, at least one would be murdered.

Constantin muttered, "He was watching that film again."

Alec cursed. *Damn that film. Tom was driven by it. It consumed him. It fed his anger. It could reduce him to tears and send him into a towering rage.* Aloud he said, "That bloody film is why we're all here."

"I know," Constantin answered breathlessly. The girl was dead. The man in the black mask might also be dead. Did it matter who he was? Constantin swore long and hard. Yes, it mattered. It would matter to him if the girl had been Melina. Suddenly his damaged left leg buckled. He stumbled. Alec threw out a hand, catching his shoulder, breaking, but not preventing the fall. Hands outstretched, Constantin staggered, swearing and cursing as he hit the ground. Alec was at his side in a moment, helping him up, brushing him down, while with rasping breath, Constantin panted, "I'm all right. Just give me a minute."

Huddled in the darkness, with the wind howling through the pines, Alec felt a moment's despair. Tom had gone on without waiting. True, the shriek of the wind may have muffled Constantin's fall, but in days gone by Tom would have waited. In days gone by, Tom had been different.

Testing his leg, Constantin winced, "Is it far?"

Alec tried to remember. He had been up to the clearing once before, on a spring afternoon when the breeze had been gentle and the path was dappled in sunshine. Not as now, in pitch darkness with the wind crashing though the trees like a wild animal.

"Not far, but you go back and—"

"No!" Shifting his weight, Constantin put a hand on Alec's shoulder. "I want to see Mavros."

They progressed like a couple of drunks, Constantin clinging to Alec whose most fervent wish was for a torch in his hand. The uneven path threatened disaster at every step. From the right came sounds of a sea whipped up by the wind gusting in bursts, bowling them sideways when they rounded a bend. Catching his breath, Alec realized where he was. He remembered it as the break in the trees where he had caught a glimpse of the sea. Placing their whereabouts helped him calculate distance. "Not far now," he shouted over the wind, pulling Constantin after him as he staggered on up the incline.

The next hundred yards were a test of Constantin's strength. Falling had hurt more than he cared to admit. But equal to his physical pain was the pain of frustration; frustration with Tom—Tom, the rational man, always ready to listen, totally logical—until he had fallen victim to this obsession. Constantin's anxiety deepened to bitterness. He swore. He had seen enough killing. "Killing won't bring her back," he panted into the wind.

The trees thinned and the path widened, until finally half a dozen steps brought them into the final bend. As he emerged into the clearing, Constantin stopped dead in his tracks. He caught his breath, this time from shock not exertion. The sight which met his eyes made him shudder. Even in that gray light, with the moon half hidden behind scurrying clouds, the gallows stood stark on the skyline. His grip tightened on Alec's shoulder. He heard Alec gasp. Mavros was there, with his men, surrounding Tom as he struggled with a rope. Constantin's blood ran cold as he realized what Tom was doing—looping a noose over a man's head—a naked man wearing a black mask.

"No!" Constantin cried. He pushed Alec aside to stumble blindly past the bench and the telescope. A yard from the scaffold realization brought him to a halt. The naked figure was not real—it was a plastic man, a shop window dummy. Only the mask was real, black, falling to the neck with slits for the eyes and a gash for the mouth, an exact replica of the mask worn by the man in the film.

Tom turned, waving an arm and shouting in the wind, "Get back!"

Constantin felt Alec's hands restrain him from behind. He watched the dummy on the rope rise from the ground. Simultaneously Mavros started to turn a wheel at the base of the scaffold. Cogs meshed into cogs. Above them the gallows began to swing out toward the sea, like a derrick carrying cargo to the bowels of a ship—except on the end of the rope was no ordinary cargo but the effigy of a man—naked save for a black hood.

Constantin prayed, "Dear God!"

The gallows rotated until the long arm reached over the cliff. Buffeted by the wind the effigy twisted round and round on the rope. Constantin saw what he had missed before. Instead of hanging from the neck, the dummy was fastened around the chest. A man on that rope would still be alive! Constantin imagined him kicking and screaming as he hovered above the sea-lashed rocks below.

This rehearsal was for no ordinary hanging. The victim would die as *she* had died . . . with the cruel rocks racing up to meet her.

Even as Constantin watched, Tom pulled a lever on the scaffold. The wind screamed in the trees. Rope raced over pulleys. The dummy dropped . . . falling through space . . . falling, falling . . .

Constantin felt sick. Overcome by nausea, he stumbled to the bench and sat down. He put his head in his hands, closing his eyes against nightmares he yearned to forget . . .

1967

Constantin's nightmare had begun in the early hours of April 21, 1967. A noise disturbed him. Yawning, rubbing sleep from his eyes, he rose from his bed and went naked to the window, where he stood scratching his hairy stomach while staring down into the street. Moments passed while his eyes adjusted to the gloom. Dimly lit and mostly in shadow, the narrow street looked normal enough, cars parked at the curb side were all familiar . . . yet something had disturbed him. Listening intently, he detected a distant rumbling which he took to be thunder until realizing that the sounds were continuous. Pressing his face sideways onto the window pane, he squinted towards the end of the street, but even then he saw nothing unusual. The noise persisted. Finally it dawned on him that he was listening to the wheels of heavy vehicles. He relaxed. Perhaps the lorries going to market had been more fully laden than normal? Or perhaps a convoy of trucks was bringing goods into the city from the port at Piraeus? Either way he cursed those responsible for disturbing his sleep, for by now he was fully awake, there was no point in returning to bed, even though it was only four-thirty.

Moving quietly to avoid disturbing Melina, he collected his dressing gown from the back of a chair. On the bedside table, the Socrates medallion glinted in the gray light. Wrapping himself in the robe, he picked up the medallion, careful not to let the chain clink as he looped it over his head. He smiled, remembering his wedding night six months before; the first time he had removed the medallion from his neck in twenty-three years. Melina had clung to him all the way home from the wedding party. She was in his arms immediately after he closed the front door. He had undressed her in the sitting room and carried her naked to the bedroom. Lowering her to the bed, he had kissed every inch of her body, letting his tongue explore every secret place, until her hushed cries of pleasure had deepened to soft groans of desire. Hurriedly he stripped off his shirt, throwing it to the floor. He kicked off his shoes and pulled down his trousers, and was turning for the bed when her voice stopped him. "Please, just my husband. Not Socrates too."

In the kitchen, he made coffee which he placed on a tray and carried to his study. Switching on a desk lamp, he settled into his chair. To start work early was not unusual. If Constantin had not been disturbed, he would in any case have started at six. He had worked hard all his life . . . and work had brought its rewards, for nobody in Greece was as happy and contented as Constantin Peponis.

At thirty, he had all that he wanted. His own practice as a lawyer, an elegant apartment in the best part of Athens, and the loveliest, best-tempered wife in the world. It mattered not that along with her beauty and sweet disposition Melina had brought an army of relatives to the marriage. It was a joke among their friends—"Two days a week Constantin works to support Melina; four days a week he works to support her mother and father, her three younger brothers, her Uncle Anastassis, her cousin Orestis, her aunt Anna, her grandmother, her . . ." The list was endless. Constantin genuinely did not mind. He saw himself as big and oafish, whereas Melina was so slim that he could encircle her waist with his hands. He was plain, whereas she was beautiful. He would have died for her; so helping her family was nothing. Besides, they amused him. He had no one of his own except Uncle Mikis. Constantin's father had been executed by the Gestapo during the German occupation. Constantin scarcely remembered him. He knew his father had been brave because his mother had said so, but Constantin's only enduring link was the medallion. "Wear it always," his mother had said when she placed it around his neck. And Constantin had worn it like a medal of honor.

At the end of the war, Uncle Mikis had come down from the hills. By then he had become a legend. When the Germans had invaded, Uncle Mikis had gone underground—which young Constantin imagined meant living like a rabbit in a warren. Later he was told that Uncle Mikis was a guerilla, which conjured up visions of him beating his chest like an ape. It was quite a disappointment to meet such an ordinary-looking man, even if his coat *was* covered with medals. Uncle Mikis had moved into their home, and throughout Constantin's school days, it was Uncle Mikis as well as Constantin's mother who provided stability.

They lived well, not luxuriously but comfortably. Uncle Mikis had a pension, and when Constantin was not studying he earned extra money by working as a porter in the meat market. Big and strong at the outset, he had grown even bigger. His mother died a month after he had obtained his law degree. "She lived long enough to set you off on the right road," said Uncle Mikis by way of consolation. The "right road" for Uncle Mikis meant only one thing—first the law, then politics. But for Constantin, the law was enough. The only times he expressed an interest in politics was when the telephone company went on strike, or the cost of living rose by a point, or something else happened to impinge on his life. "The government should do something about it," he would grumble. Uncle Mikis would exclaim, "Why don't *you* do something about it? We live in a democracy. Government *of* the people, *by* the people, *for* the people. If you won't involve yourself, you can't blame the government. Lazy people get the government they deserve."

Yet to call Constantin lazy was unfair. He was busy, not lazy, busier than ever when Melina came into his life. Within six months he had given the house to Uncle Mikis and moved into an apartment which he furnished to the highest standards, higher than he could really afford, but he could do no less for Melina. And she loved the apartment. So did her family. When Constantin returned home from his office, it was usually to find at least one of Melina's relatives there on a visit from Piraeus. He really did not mind, he was pleased. Melina's entire family looked up to him. They treated him with respect. "Melina has married well," they said, awed by the apartment and Constantin's status as a lawyer. Meanwhile Melina kept the place spotless, cooked like a gourmet chef, always looked beautiful, was perpetually sweet-natured, and behaved like a wild thing in bed. At thirty years old, Constantin Peponis had everything he wanted from life.

That morning, the morning of April 21, 1967, after being awakened so early, he worked at his desk for an hour. Outside the sun brightened the sky. After preparing for his day, he put his papers away and went to the bathroom. He shaved and showered. In the dressing room which he shared with Melina, he put on a clean shirt and the trousers of a gray suit. Leaving his tie and jacket in the wardrobe, he padded on stockinged feet to the kitchen to prepare breakfast. By now time had caught up with him. Most mornings found him in the kitchen just after six. As usual he set up a breakfast tray for Melina—fresh orange juice, croissants and coffee—and, as usual, he switched on the radio.

What happened next however, was not usual. Instead of an announcer reading the news, Constantin heard music. He fiddled with the dial. The music continued. He gave the radio his full attention, turning the dial this way and that. Just music. He gave up. Leaving the radio playing, he returned to the coffee percolator. The fresh coffee needed another few minutes. He went to the telephone, intending to remind his assistant of their eight o'clock meeting. The telephone was dead. He rattled the instrument with the ferocity of a cat shaking a rat. Still dead. "Oh boy," he muttered darkly, "today looks like being one of those days."

His spirits revived in the bedroom. One look at his wife was enough. Putting the tray on the table, he bent over to nuzzle her neck. His hand slid under the covers. Melina moaned softly and reached for him. He moved his head down, tracing his tongue over the contours of her breasts and beyond the flat stomach to the bush of pubic hair. Purring, Melina arched upward and obligingly parted her legs—only for Constantin to bite deep into her thigh. "Bastard!" she screamed, throwing the covers aside and leaping naked towards him. Laughing, he avoided her and went to the window to draw back the curtains. When he looked around, she was sitting cross-legged, black hair tumbling over her face as she inspected the bite mark. He went over and kissed the impressions of his teeth on her thigh, while she ran her hands through his hair and nibbled his ear.

"The phone's out of order," he said. "I'll report it from the office."

With a parting kiss, he returned to the kitchen. The radio was still playing. Suddenly the music ceased. Abruptly, a man began talking.

". . . because of an abnormal situation that developed after midnight, endangering the internal security of the country, the Army has been asked to take over the government of the country."

Constantin stood frozen, coffee cup in one hand.

The voice on the radio continued *". . . manifest internal threat to public order . . . the Minister of the Interior will publish and implement this decree. Given in Athens this day, twenty-first of April, 1967."*

Constantin sat down on a kitchen stool. He wondered what "*abnormal situation.*" Yesterday had been a day like any other. He had neither heard nor seen anything unusual.

Having proclaimed a state of martial law, the voice stopped and the music resumed. Constantin stared at the radio. He wondered why the announcement was not followed by a news commentary. Why were politicians not airing their views? What the devil was going on?

Swallowing his coffee, he hurried to the dressing room, put on his jacket and knotted his tie. Stepping into his shoes, he collected his briefcase from the study, and returned to the bedroom. "Something has happened," he said, explaining what he had heard. "I'll be back at midday. It might be best if you stay in the apartment."

Three minutes later he was out on the street, almost colliding with a neighbor. Out of breath, the man pointed behind him. "Tanks," he gasped, "there are tanks at the crossroads."

Constantin hurried down to the corner to see for himself. His eyes rounded with disbelief—facing him were two huge tanks with guns as long as pine trees. The tanks stood motionless and menacing. Now he knew what had woken him—the rumbling of tanks on the streets. Looking about him, he saw very few cars. Usually the rush hour had started. Normally there was a rising hum of traffic noise—but the streets were quiet and only a handful of pedestrians populated the pavement.

"Hey you!" A soldier emerged from a doorway, followed by a policeman.

Constantin watched them approach. The soldier, an officer, held out his hand. "Identification," he demanded imperiously.

Constantin was not easily intimidated. Ever since boyhood, size had endowed him with an air of authority. Besides he was a lawyer, accustomed to making his presence felt in court. Ignoring the officer, he glanced at the policeman, whom he recognized. "He knows who I am."

"*He* is not asking," the officer sneered.

More politely the policeman explained, "This is the lawyer, Constantin Peponis."

Resenting the interruption, the officer glared until the policeman lowered his eyes and shuffled his feet. A tense moment passed before the officer turned back to Constantin. "Very well," he said sharply. "Where are you going, Lawyer Peponis?"

"About my lawful business."

"I will decide what is lawful," the officer retorted.

Nothing was likely to infuriate Constantin more. By nature he was easy-going, the mildest mannered of men, but his reverence for the law was total. People joked that although Melina was his wife, the law was his mistress. He loved them both with a fierce passion, some of which showed at that moment.

"You're in the wrong place," he snapped. "Law is

administered in the courts, not on the streets." Inwardly seething, he turned away and set off for his office.

"Stop!" The officer pulled his revolver from the holster at his belt. "I will ask you once more. Where are you going?"

Unable to believe his eyes, Constantin stared down the barrel of a gun for the first time in his life. He felt outrage, not fear. In a voice cold with fury, he said, "I am going to my office. Later I'll be in court, where I shall report you—"

"All courts are suspended. The country is under martial law."

Constantin froze. It simply hadn't occurred to him that the courts would be shut down. What would happen to the law? Who would administer justice? He glanced at the policeman. The man looked shaken and shamefaced. Without fear for himself, Constantin felt a moment's worry for Melina. *Thank God I told her to stay in the apartment.* Mustering what dignity he could, he answered, "In that case, I am going to my office—"

"Why?" sneered the officer. "You won't be able to work. We have disconnected all telephones."

"Disconnected?" Constantin echoed, shocked.

"The only phones working are those needed for national security."

"What the devil has happened? Has there been an invasion?"

A contemptuous gleam lit the officer's eye. Turning to the policeman he asked, "Do you know the location of this man's office?"

"Yes."

"Is he political?"

The policeman swallowed nervously and looked increasingly anxious. Silently he shook his head.

"Very well," said the officer, jerking his revolver at Constantin, "go to your office."

Constantin moved off feeling dazed and uncertain. He had half a mind to return to the apartment to satisfy himself that Melina was safe. But of course she was safe—she was obedient, she would remain indoors until he returned at midday. Pulling himself together, he set out to walk the three blocks to his office. Without the usual rising hum of traffic, the streets seemed eerily silent. The few people who were about looked grim-faced and frightened. Doubting the evidence of his own eyes, Constantin reminded himself that this was 1967, this was Athens, a city of almost two million people, a city he had known all his life . . .

Two hours later, seated behind his office desk, he was still struggling to absorb the full impact of events. Only two members of his small staff had turned up: Helen Seferis, his secretary, and his assistant, who had brought a transistor radio to the office. They listened intently, drinking thick black coffee and smoking cigarettes as an unidentified radio voice announced the suspension of the Constitution. The new Emergency Government had assumed sweeping powers—authorizing arrest and detention—abolishing trade unions—declaring strikes illegal—authorizing searches in private houses by day or by night. . . .

Unable to reach him by telephone, several of Constantin's friends braved intimidation in the street and made their way to his office. By ten o'clock the small suite of rooms overflowed. Every new caller had a fresh tale to tell. Rumors were rife. The King was under house arrest at the palace. Politicians had been dragged from their beds and thrown into prison. Trigger-happy soldiers had shot a young girl and two boys only three streets away . . .

Constantin's nightmare had started.

For a few weeks he nursed the hope that the situation would revert to normal. After all, the Junta had promised to restore democracy as soon as possible. Yet some disturbing things were happening. A decree was published dissolving all political parties. Some politicians were deported to detention camps on the remote islands of Leros and Gyaros. Army officers slow to pledge allegiance to the Junta were prematurely retired. A ruthless purge of civil servants was carried out.

Even when weeks extended to months, Constantin found it hard to accept the situation as permanent. "Greece is part of NATO," he argued, "we're members of the Council of Europe. Our Allies will come to our aid. Countries like America and Britain will exert pressure to restore democracy."

But countries like the United States and Britain sat on their hands. Even worse, it was rumored that America's CIA had helped the Colonels seize power.

Meanwhile the Colonels tightened their grip. Trade unions were dissolved and their assets confiscated. Young people were ordered to cut their hair, to dress in an approved manner, and to go to the church now controlled by the Junta. Offenses against martial law were rigorously punished. Censorship of the press was total. It was forbidden to read the works of Shakespeare, Sophocles, Aristophanes and over two hundred Greek and foreign writers.

In December, the King attempted a coup of his own, but he failed and fled to exile in Rome. And at the start of the new year came further bad news—the United States gave official recognition to the government of the Junta. Two days later the British government did the same . . . and within weeks most other countries followed suit.

The oppressed people of Greece stood alone.

Eight months had passed since the Junta seized power; Greece was much changed and Constantin too began to change. He found it harder to refute his uncle's arguments. "Now you see what happens," said Uncle Mikis, "when you take democracy for granted. Freedom is a delicate flower, to survive it must be nurtured. Otherwise it will perish."

Constantin was only too aware of how freedom had perished. He faced the death of it every day. The courts were a sham, concerned only with enforcing the rule of the Junta, never with justice. When a client of Constantin's was sent to prison, Constantin made a point of visiting him. The tales he heard, of brutality and torture, made his blood run cold.

Meanwhile he did what he could to look after his wife and her family—and Melina's family were quick to include all their friends, so that sometimes it seemed that the whole of Piraeus had assembled in Constantin's apartment; all asking for advice, all wanting to know what to do.

By April 1968, the Junta had been in power for a year. Democracy was a fading dream. Constantin faced the dilemma which ultimately confronts all honorable men. His belief in the rule of law was as passionate as ever; but what does a man do when the law is unjust? His spirited displays in court had already made him a marked man. Judges appointed by the Junta had long since reported his resistance to their masters. Friends warned him that he was being investigated by the secret police.

Constantin sensed his own danger. He knew his mail was being opened. He guessed his telephone was tapped. He suspected he was followed. None of which he confided to Melina. He was a proud man; proud of the protection he gave her. And Melina was proud of him in return; pleased at the way everyone asked his advice. But she was neither blind nor deaf, and with each passing month she took note of the changes. One day a whisper reached her that the ESA, the military police, were taking an interest in her husband. Constantin came home that evening to find the apartment empty save for Melina. Having barred her relatives for twenty-four hours, she met him with a flurry of questions. Gradually the truth emerged. After supper they talked long into the night. "Why didn't you tell me?" Melina demanded, angry and tearful.

"I didn't want you to worry—"

"Am I a child? Not to be trusted—"

"Of course not, but—"

"I'm too stupid to understand? Without brains—"

"No, no! Nothing like that, but—"

"Always you must be the big dominant male. The macho Greek protecting his little girl."

Never had Melina been so scornful; nor so honest, because when she calmed down, she admitted how much she enjoyed being cosseted. "You are a good husband. The best in the world. My family are always telling me how lucky I am. Do they think I don't know? Of course I know you love me. I'm not blind, it's in your face whenever you look at me. I know you protect me, but you must understand that it works in reverse. I love you too. I worry about you, and I'll worry all the more if I don't know what's happening. You must let me be your *wife*. Not just make love to me. I'll give you my body whenever you want, but you must *tell* me these things. A wife must be a partner. . . ."

Constantin listened in amazement. It had not occurred to him that Melina wanted to be treated as his equal. She had never spoken in such language before.

They went to bed and clung to each other with the soft light of dawn streaming through the windows. The next day Constantin knew the relationship had changed in a way almost too subtle to define. But from then on, he told Melina everything. He had no choice. Every evening, Melina quizzed him about events in the courts, and every day the regime of the Junta became more repressive.

Late one May evening a friend of Constantin's came to see him at the apartment. Alexandros Dedas was a lawyer himself. He had grown up with Constantin. They had studied at law school together. Usually Alexandros arrived with a smile on his face, but that evening was different. He looked harried and tired to the point of exhaustion. "I can't go on any longer," he confessed. "More lawyers are arrested every day. The Junta aren't even bothering to bring them to trial. They just hold them in detention. Constantin, it gets more dangerous all the time. I'm getting out. I've invented an excuse to go to London on business. I've got permission. I'm going with my wife and not coming back."

Alexandros scarcely gave them time to absorb his announcement before he went on. "Come with me," he pleaded, "both of you. We can make a new life in London. Perhaps we can open a law office together. Think how many of our friends have gone already. They're in England, France, America, Australia—the day has come when a man can do more for Greece in London than in Athens."

For the next few days, Constantin and Melina discussed nothing else. Should they go with Alexandros? He had set a date a month ahead, so time was short. Constantin's heart hesitated but his head told him to go. Lawyers who still struggled for justice ran an ever-increasing risk of arrest. The prospect of a free life in London was gloriously tempting. . . .

A week later, they told Melina's family. Her mother wept and her father's face crumpled into lines of dismay. Only her brothers responded bravely, especially seventeen-year-old Elias, who was the first to speak out. "Of course they must go. Constantin can tell the British people what is happening. He will rally them to the cause. He can fly to America and petition Congress . . ." Elias idolized Constantin. He believed that his big brother-in-law could do anything. Starting law school himself, Elias modeled his every act on Constantin. The boy's devotion was touching. Sometimes the family teased him about it, but in their hearts they shared his admiration for Melina's husband.

One emotionally charged evening led to another, for the next night Melina's aunts and uncles arrived. So did Constantin's Uncle Mikis. "Go," said Uncle Mikis, "do as I did in the war against Hitler. Retreat now, return later in truimph."

Melina's relatives disagreed. "Stay," they implored, "we shall perish without Constantin's help. Besides, Melina's father is sick. She may never see him again. Melina would never forgive herself . . ."

Melina was desperately torn. Her family meant much to her, especially her father. The thought of never seeing him again broke her heart. If it actually came to saying goodbye, she wondered whether she could go through with it . . .

"London is awful," said her aunts, "cold and wet. At least here you'll have the sun. Here you are surrounded by friends and family, people who love you . . ."

Constantin weighed the alternatives. He knew how much Melina's family meant to her. They were a vital part of her life. She would pine for them. London might become a hell-hole of recriminations where they would be free but desperately unhappy. The mere possibility of Melina being miserable filled him with dread. He lived for her smile and drew strength from her gaiety. Destroy Melina's vitality and what would be left?

"Go," said Uncle Mikis, "link up with the British. They helped us against Hitler . . ."

Constantin knew his uncle was brave and wise. He had learned much from him. Yet, in a corner of Constantin's heart, burned a small glow of resentment. His father could also have taken to the hills in the war; instead he had chosen to remain in Athens. "How can I desert these people?" his father had said. "I'm the mayor. I must stay and help protect them from any suffering the Germans might inflict."

Confirming his worst fears, the Germans inflicted terrible suffering. Many Greeks came to curse Constantin's father, not knowing then of the countless times when his quick thinking averted further atrocities. He remained mayor for two years, apparently working hand-in-glove with the Gestapo but in reality thwarting them a hundred times over. Finally his secret was discovered. He was hanged in the square on a meat hook. Yes, Uncle Mikis was a brave man, but he had retreated, while Constantin's father had remained to help those in need.

"I don't know what to do," Constantin confessed to Melina in private. "If we go, your brothers may get into trouble with the Junta. You know how wild they can be. Your father is too frail to keep them in check—"

"But you can't continue as you are," Melina said miserably. "It's too risky. I won't let you. We must go . . ."

A week later, Alexandros called for their answer. "Have you reached a decision?"

Constantin nodded, "I wish you every success in London, you know that. But I think you exaggerate the state of things here. Conditions will get better soon. Why, only in this morning's paper—"

"The papers tell lies," Alexandros exploded. "What's up with you? They print what the Junta tells them to print. You know that as well as I do!"

They argued for two hours before Alexandros left in a temper.

Melina had remained silent. She would not argue with her husband in front of his friend. Even in private she doubted she could change Constantin's mind. She knew perfectly well why he had reached his decision. He was doing it for her and her family. Gratitude did not even begin to express her emotions. Never had she felt so proud. Her heart was bursting with love. But she had been doing her own thinking, making her own plans, and as soon as Alexandros left, she laid down her conditions.

"*If* we stay," she began, emphasizing the *if*, "you must give up the law—"

Constantin was still agitated from arguing with Alexandros. Melina's words were the last straw. "What?" he exploded, "don't be stupid. How will we live—"

"Please," she begged, "listen to me." She made him sit down. She poured him a glass of Ouzo. Then she sat on his lap and stroked his hair as she talked. Her voice was husky with love, and pride, and gratitude for his decision. "But if anything should happen to you," she said, "your decision would be pointless. Who can you help from a prison?"

Constantin tried to make light of her worries, but he had confided too much; Melina *knew* the risks and would no longer allow him to take them.

"But how will we live?" he protested. "I'm not so rich that we don't need an income."

Melina explained: they would leave the apartment and move to Piraeus. She smiled, "Most of Piraeus already seek your advice. You will be surrounded by admirers if we live there."

"But live on *what*?"

When she talked about opening a taverna the disbelief in Constantin's eyes was almost comical. But his laughter faded when he saw how serious she was. He became angry. The prospect of his beautiful wife waiting on tables filled him with outrage. "No!" he said, "no, no, no! The idea is out of the question."

"Oh?" Melina exclaimed with a toss of her head. "Do you object when I serve our friends here in the apartment?"

"Of course not—"

"So who do you think will patronize the taverna?"

"That's different. When we give dinner here, we don't charge—"

"Ha!" Melina exclaimed, jumping up from his lap. "You're too proud," she snorted, "*you* can be generous, but your friends can't reciprocate. You can love us, but we can't love you. We all know you're doing this for us. Don't you think people will want to show their gratitude? Don't you think . . ."

Constantin reeled under Melina's attack. Never before had she been so adamant, or so articulate. He did his best to counter her arguments, but his every protest drew a scorching reply. And when he said a taverna would need a trained chef, Melina went up like a sheet of flame. "What's wrong with my food? Have you ever tasted better mousaka? Doesn't Alexandros say my psari plake are the best in the world? And what about my stifatho?"

Nothing Constantin said could dissuade her. Yet his heart ached at the picture of her serving in a taverna, wearing drab work-a-day clothes. Ever since they had married, he had dressed her in the latest fashions. Her wardrobe bulged with Italian silk dresses, French lingerie, and smart English suits. "I like you to look beautiful."

"Oh? Are you saying I only look good when I wear expensive things?"

"No, but—"

"Ha! You flatter me. What kind of beauty depends on a label? Do I only please you when I wear elegant clothes?"

With a rueful smile, Constantin confessed that she pleased him most when she wore no clothes at all.

Melina had left her most persuasive argument until last. "A lawyer who doesn't practice law is no lawyer at all," she pointed out. "But you're not practicing law now, the Junta won't allow it. So you lose nothing by helping me run a taverna. And think of the free time you will have? You can put that to good use. How often have I heard you complain about the lack of good textbooks? Twenty times, fifty times, a hundred times? So here is your chance. Part of each day you can write new textbooks for the next generation. . . ."

Constantin's eyes gleamed. He was thrilled by the idea, but he continued to argue—"I've never tried to write. I might not be able to—"

"Of course you can write! The great Constantin Peponis—"

"The Junta wouldn't let anyone publish—"

"Ha! You couldn't do it just now. Suddenly it's finished already. Think, Constantin—do you imagine you'll write a great textbook in five minutes? Of course not. To write will take time. And these pigs can't retain power forever . . ."

With the matter undecided they went to bed, and that night Melina took charge of their lovemaking with a passion that drained even Constantin's great strength. Yet the following morning, he still could not bring himself to agree. "Please," he said, "let's wait a while longer to see how things go."

Things went disastrously wrong within a few hours.

Alexandros's partner was arrested. When Alexandros heard the news, he abandoned his carefully made plans and took his wife directly to the airport. They flew out to London just in time; ninety minutes later a warrant was issued for his arrest.

Constantin was in shock when he arrived home, where he received a shock of even greater magnitude, the biggest shock of his life. Melina had left him. On the table was a note: "I don't think I can live without you, but neither can I live with this desperate fear of you being arrested. Forgive me for being so weak. I will love you always."

An hour later, with a pounding heart and anxiety etched into every line of his face, Constantin arrived in Piraeus. Melina met him at the door of her father's house. Throwing herself into his arms, sobbing uncontrollably, she clung to him with every ounce of strength.

And so it was settled. Within a week Constantin had closed his law office, and within a month they had bought the taverna.

Constantin Peponis was received as a hero by the people of Piraeus. He was amazed, because he saw nothing heroic in his behavior. But other people said differently. "Here is a man," they said, "whom the Junta can't buy. Rather than do their dirty work, he has given up his fine apartment in Athens to live among us. He will help us, he's educated, he's strong . . ."

Strong was a word Constantin began to associate more with his wife. Melina's strength amazed him. It was Melina who took charge of the taverna. Melina bought the vegetables, the fruit, the fish and the meat. Melina cooked and waited on tables, Melina organized everything. At times Constantin's heart ached to see her in the clothes of a simple peasant girl, working barefoot when expensive shoes were stored in her wardrobe. He had always wanted so much for her. "Nonsense," Melina retorted when he remonstrated, "I have the finest husband in the world, I have my family, my friends, my sunshine, my wine and good food. I'm idyllically happy."

Certainly she seemed happy. Every morning she set Constantin to work in their rooms above the taverna. "From lunchtime onwards you can be patron in the taverna," she told him. "Until then you're a professor of law, writing the best textbook the world's ever known."

Having organized Constantin, she went downstairs to organize the taverna.

Twice a week, usually on Wednesdays and Saturdays, Melina's family took over the tasks of cooking and serving at tables. On these evenings; after soaking in a bath, and powdering and primping and splashing on perfume, Melina donned her prettiest clothes; Constantin wore a good suit, and they dined in the taverna surrounded by friends—much as they once did in their smart Athens apartment.

Of course there were differences, some of them huge. In Athens, Constantin had entertained lawyers, journalists, bankers—many of whom had fled the country or now languished in prison. The people of Piraeus were rather more humble—they were fishermen, or tradesmen, or stevedores. As such they were less articulate and considered more controllable by the Junta. Individually they escaped persecution though collectively they felt the iron fist of injustice. Without the protection of trade unions, working conditions worsened. Rates of pay fell. Prices in the shops rose. Shortages became prevalent. Protest was impossible because strikes were illegal . . .

Despite which, and although often bone-tired, Melina was content. Compared to the rich life she had enjoyed in Athens, she was poor. The people of Piraeus could not afford fancy meals. They supported the taverna because they wanted Constantin's advice, and because Melina gave such good value that it was as cheap to eat there as in their own homes. Melina earned only the slimmest of profits, but she cared little about money. What was important in these troubled times was to be close to her family. What was important was that her precious Constantin was safe.

Yet how safe was safe? While Constantin spent his mornings writing about justice, he spent every day listening to talk of injustice. People came in droves to buy his advice for the price of a coffee. He felt frustrated not to do more. Sometimes he talked of becoming a lawyer again, only for his friends to close ranks against him. "No, no," they cried. "The Junta will arrest you in five minutes. We need you here to advise us." Which, increasingly, was what Constantin found himself doing. As the regime's laws became ever more repressive, Constantin became adept at finding loopholes for his friends to exploit. No single loophole was vast, but each was a handhold on the slippery slope of survival.

Conditions worsened all the time. Corrupt government breeds a corrupt society. Soon graft became a way of life among policemen and all echelons of officials. Some leeched on the population by demanding payment for so-called protection; others turned a blind eye to petty infringements for the right sum of money. Either way, extra money had to be found, and the only way to find it was to steal. In the docks, stevedores pilfered from every cargo unloaded. If they stole food, they shared it. If they stole goods, they sold them on the black market. At first there were arguments about dividing the proceeds; until someone said, "Let Constantin share out the money. We all trust him."

And so Constantin became the banker. Although disliking the job, he accepted it—just as he accepted that he was best able to drive a hard bargain with the leeches, for apart from his skills as a lawyer, he was even bigger and stronger than most of the stevedores. His soaring reputation brought other responsibilities. The taverna became the courtroom of Piraeus. Quarreling neighbors brought their disputes to Constantin so often that eventually he set Tuesday afternoons aside for that business and no other. His judgments were always accepted, for even though they could not be enforced, it was enough for Constantin to pronounce on the matter. Credited with the wisdom of Solomon, he became an unofficial ruler—an unofficial mayor. The parallels between him and his father became more obvious. "Phaidon Peponis sired a worthy son," people said proudly, carefully forgetting that Phaidon Peponis had died at the end of a meat hook.

One person did not forget. Melina. Little escaped her when it came to her husband, but one thought consoled her—that surrounded by family and friends in Piraeus, Constantin was safer than in the law courts of Athens.

Constantin struggled to reconcile the contradictions in his life.

He wrote of the need for law in the mornings, and actively flouted it the rest of the day. He once confessed such worries to young Elias. Elias was outraged. "How can you even think such a thing. The Junta are the law breakers. *They* suspended the Constitution, *they* deny people their basic rights, *they* have turned Greece into a police state . . ."

By now it was 1969; Constantin and Melina had been running the taverna for twelve months. The Junta had been in power for two years. "Where are our Allies?" Constatin demanded. "Why do the Americans and the British not come to our aid?" He gleaned little from the Greek media which was heavily censored, but foreign newspapers were still allowed into the country and Constantin read all he could find. Not that he derived much comfort; content that Greece remained a member of NATO, the governments of the United States and Britain turned a blind eye. He ached for news from his friends outside in the world. "People like Alex must be doing *something* in London!"

But with mail censored and telephones tapped, no word of encouragement reached Piraeus.

And then, one day, Maurice Stanton appeared on the scene.

Constantin had just come downstairs. A few of the tables were occupied with friends in for lunch. Melina was taking their orders when a stranger stepped through the entrance, a short man wearing a blue uniform. Few strangers patronized the taverna, and even fewer wore uniforms.

Constantin approached him at once. The man addressed him in English. "Are you Constantin Peponis?"

Constantin answered in surprise, "Yes, I am." As he spoke the bead curtain parted and three other people entered—a man in a superbly tailored suit and two women. Even Constantin, besotted with Melina, could not restrain his admiration. Until then he would have doubted that such beauty existed. He tried in vain not to stare, and while he did so the man in the well-cut suit surprised everyone by speaking in Greek—"I am the Kyrios Stanton," he said. "We'd like some lunch, please."

"For three," said the man in the uniform. "I have an aircraft to attend to."

Constantin guessed that the aircraft was the seaplane moored at Passalimani. Automatically he was suspicious. Invariably rich foreigners were friends of the Junta. The Colonels were always boasting about the foreign investments they were attracting into the country. Why should these people choose to lunch here? The taverna served good food, but the dishes were simple and unsophisticated, not fitting fare for such people. Wrenching his gaze away from the women, Constantin answered the man, "I'm not sure," he stumbled over his words. "Our menu is limited—"

"Your menu is famous," said the man, turning his smile on Melina. "Your mousaka is talked about the world over."

Melina felt blood rush to her face. She told herself she was blushing in response to the extravagant compliment, but she knew she was lying. That look from those dark brown eyes made her feel weak at the knees. The wave of raw emotion left her shocked and ashamed. She expected to feel such things for Constantin; a wife should lust for her husband . . . but to feel such things for a stranger—a foreigner, a man older than Constantin, big yes, but not *so* big; handsome yes, but since when had looks been so important? For the first time in a year Melina missed her fine clothes. She glared at the women. Instinct told her that they belonged to the stranger. He had them both. He *fucked* them both. Melina refused to believe she was thinking such things, but she was, and all the time a voice inside her was crying *I can look better than this, I'm beautiful too, wait until I go upstairs and change . . .*

The uniformed pilot departed, leaving Constantin no choice but to usher his unexpected customers up to the balcony. Melina fled to her kitchen. Clutching the sink to steady herself, she heard the women's excited voices praising the view. Melina knew very few English words, but "Ooohs" and "Aahs" are universal. *Whores,* she snorted, throwing crockery into the sink.

Arriving with the order, Constantin was met by an inexplicably truculent wife. Glaring at him, Melina erupted, "So? Our menu is limited, is it? My food is not good enough for such beautiful mouths?"

Constantin served the meal that day. Even when the Kyrios Stanton wanted to compliment the cook at the end of the meal, Melina refused to emerge from the kitchen. Constantin was bewildered. Melina had never behaved in such a manner before.

When the pilot returned an hour later, the meal was over and the Kyrios Stanton and his ladies were ready to depart. After paying the bill and leaving an extraordinarily generous tip, Stanton stood up and made his way to the door. At the bead curtain he paused, fixing Constantin with a penetrating look. "The food was excellent," he said, speaking in English for the first time, perhaps to confound eavesdroppers, "but something was wrong with my chair. You should look at it." With which he swept out.

Frowning, Constantin hurried back up to the balcony to inspect the chair for himself. The first thing he saw was an envelope left on the seat. Surprised, he picked it up and was turning to dash after his departing customers when he saw his own name. *To Constantin Peponis.* Constantin stared in astonishment. Then his startled gaze went to the bead curtain. Fighting his curiosity, he stifled his impulse to tear the envelope open, fearful of the watchful eyes around him. Luckily most were directed elsewhere; men had left their tables to crowd the entrance for a last glimpse of the two magnificent women. Stuffing the envelope into his pocket, Constantin collected the dirty coffee cups and hurried into the kitchen, where Melina was still in her unfathomable rage. "Listen to them," she sneered scornfully, "you'd think they'd never seen a woman before."

Constantin was too preoccupied to concern himself with such things. Lowering his voice, he told her about the envelope. Melina took it from his hands and inspected it with eyes full of wonder. Constantin said, "I'll open it upstairs. Come up as soon as you can."

The letter was from Alexandros Dedos in London. He wrote, "*. . . my cousin Costa arrived here last month and told me of your changed circumstances. The man who brings this to you is to be trusted; though you must never mention his name in connection with helping us . . .*"

It was the strangest, most exciting letter Constantin had ever received. Alexandros told of how Greeks in London and elsewhere were trying to rally world opinion. "*. . . It is not easy because most governments are more interested in arms contracts* *than in human rights. The Americans, the British and the French continue to pour tanks and guns into Greece. The Junta make very good customers. However, the Scandinavian governments have presented evidence of torture in Greek prisons to the European Commission of Human Rights . . ."*

Elsewhere in the letter, Alexandros wrote, ". . . *The Junta continue to fool the rest of the world with talk of introducing free elections. Prove it, we say, fix a date. Of course the Junta refuse. Our allies advise us to be patient, diplomacy takes time they tell us—meanwhile blood-curdling stories are reaching us. Did you know that a concentration camp had been established on the island of Leros? Hundreds of so-called political prisoners are exiled there, in barbaric conditions. And countless other camps have been set up in villages remote in the mountains. We have proof, but of course never enough. Some of the stories reaching us are heartbreaking. How much of this is known there—in Athens and Piraeus? What can you tell us? Can you list specific acts of repression* . . ."

Constantin saw examples of repression every day. His fingers itched to write a long report. But with all mail opened by the Junta, how would he get it to London? Anticipating the question, Alexandros wrote, ". . . *Send anything useful via this courier. Do not talk to him or discuss anything, simply slip him what you have when nobody is watching. He will come to your taverna about once a month* . . ."

When Melina read the letter, her eyes rounded with surprise. Constantin wondered why a wealthy Englishman should concern himself with poor Greeks. Melina shook her head in bewilderment, but even as she did a blush warmed her cheeks.

From that day onwards, Constantin produced a regular report, detailing every act of repression, and since there were many, his reports ran to dozens of pages. Knowing full well that what he saw was only the tip of the iceberg, he went further. Soon he was following up rumors and buying information from corrupt officials.

One night he went too far. One such official told him bluntly, "Your questions make me suspicious. Helping the local people is one thing. After all, I myself am from Piraeus. If I tell you a few odds and ends which help keep the peace, that's good for both of us. I don't want the top brass swarming in any more than you do, but these questions are off-limits. Why do you want to know about the prison at Leros, or what goes on in ESA Headquarters at Bouboulinas Street? Take a tip from me, you *don't* want to know. And if you ask me again, I'll report you. Understood?"

The warning was clear—Constantin was playing a dangerous game. After such blunt words, he became more subtle. Questions were cloaked behind a laugh and joke. But he still asked his questions. He still wrote his reports, and whenever the Kyrios Stanton passed through on his way to Kariakos, his table napkin concealed a neat little packet.

The man puzzled Constantin. Although always polite, Stanton managed to preserve his distance. Frequently a warning look lit his eye, as if to remind Constantin of the dangers of the game they were playing. Not that Constantin was likely to forget. Neither was Melina, who continued to give the Kyrios Stanton a wide berth. She still refused to serve him meals. Constantin imagined she disliked him, never suspecting more complex emotions.

Far from disliking the Kyrios Stanton, Melina found him attractive, but memories of her feelings when she first met him no longer filled her with shame. He was a very handsome man, and she was a healthy and sensual woman. If she had reacted physically it was because she had not met his like before. Now that she had, she had regained control of herself. She was even mildly amused, though wise enough to restrict further contact. Her curiosity was satisfied by surreptitiously watching him from her kitchen—him and his female companions—for the Kyrios Stanton rarely traveled alone. Melina examined their clothes and speculated on their lifestyle, content in the knowledge that no man could suit her as well as her husband. And it was her husband about whom she worried, for although she was grateful for the news Stanton brought, she fretted that he brought danger as well.

"Don't worry," Constantin reassured her. "I won't take chances."

He was becoming adept at the game. He even disguised the

reasons for Stanton's visits by inventing a tale about Gregg, the Australian pilot. "I keep him sweet with a few drachma," Constantin told his regulars with a shrug and a wink. "Gregg says bad things about the other tavernas, so they always come here."

It was the perfect reason for the poor people of Piraeus. It was what they would do to keep a good customer. "Ah," they nodded, approving yet again of the wisdom of Constantin Peponis.

So skillful did Constantin become at covering his tracks, that it was a shock when trouble arose—even though danger came not through any action of his, but because of Melina's brothers Demetrios and Theo.

In many countries the offense committed by Demetrios and Theo would have been laughable. In Greece it meant torture, possibly death. They were guilty of daubing anti-government slogans on walls. Seen and chased by the police, they hid in the house of Uncle Mikis, thereby involving him as a collaborator. After a while, believing the coast was clear, Uncle Mikis had brought them to the taverna—on the day that Gregg Richards arrived, bringing with him not the Kyrios Stanton, but an unknown Englishman called Tom Lambert.

BOOK FIVE

Constantin paused, the brandy decanter in his misshapen hands, a smile on his face. "What a day that was. When you saved Theo and Demetrios and Uncle Mikis."

Tom shrugged, uncomfortable to be thought of as a hero. His reaction that day had been quite automatic. He had acted without considering the consequences.

Constantin stood at the sideboard, his gaze fixed on Tom's face. He could deal with Tom in this mood. A reflective mood. Earlier Tom had been out of control, ranting and raving, demented by this obsessive search for revenge. It had taken half an hour to persuade him down from that accursed scaffold on the clifftop.

Turning back to the sideboard, Constantin poured the three brandies. "I liked the reunion better though," he smiled, "and the meetings afterwards. Every visit from you counted as a holiday for us."

That summer had marked the start of their friendship. They had seen each other every four or five weeks when Tom had passed through on his way to Kariakos.

"Melina fell in love with you," Constantin grinned as he passed Tom his glass. "I told her you would steal her away from me."

Alec laughed, "I can't believe that. Nobody could steal Melina from you."

With a good-natured smile, Constantin returned to his chair. He and Melina had teased each other about Tom. Liking him and wanting to be liked in return, Melina had used all of the ways of a woman to win his approval. She remained in the kitchen when the Kyrios Stanton lunched at the taverna, but when Tom Lambert arrived she actually joined him at his table. Not that she went there straight from the kitchen. First she hurried upstairs to change her dress, to brush her hair and powder her face, and *then* she joined Tom Lambert for lunch. Constantin had grumbled, "I can see you running off with that man." And Melina had teased, "You were the one who made him your blood brother. Don't blood brothers share everything, even their wives?"

Language was a problem, but Melina had bought a Greek/English phrase book and Constantin threw in the odd bit of coaching. And Tom had helped by learning some Greek words—*kallymera, kallyspera, psomee, parakalo,* and a few dozen others. He was never as industrious as Melina, but she had been pleased with his modest attempts.

"We could never decide how much you knew," said Constantin, "Melina was forever asking me, 'Do you think he knows about the Kyrios Stanton bringing us messages from Alexandros?' "

Tom looked at him, "You know I didn't."

"I do now," Constantin nodded. "I suspected he hadn't told you even then, but I couldn't be sure."

Whenever he met the Kyrios Stanton, Constantin had tried to read the man's mind. He had never succeeded. Stanton's eyes, so often full of amusement, could become dark and unfathonable at the blink of an eyelid.

Constantin said, "I used to tell Melina that I doubted anyone knew, not even the pilot. I'd say to her, 'The Kyrios Stanton is clever. I think he runs his life in water-tight compartments, nothing overflows from one to the other. We must never say a word. Not even to the Kyrios Lambert.' "

Tom smiled as he remembered those early meetings. The friendship had blossomed that summer. It could hardly fail. He was as responsive as the next man to the charm of a pretty woman, and he and Constantin had liked each other from their first meeting. Without sharing confidences, each had gleaned an insight into the other's character and had liked what he saw. Tom thought it ironic that Constantin admired him for his courage. Constantin was lion-hearted. Many a time Tom had wondered what he would do in similar circumstances. Would he have stayed, given up a profession to become involved in God knows what? For even without knowing details he had seen the looks of respect directed at Constantin by those who frequented the taverna, and it had not been hard to imagine what lay behind them. "I used to feel guilty at times," he said, sipping his brandy. "I guessed you were having a rough time, but you were always so welcoming—"

"Why not? You always came bearing gifts," Constantin joked.

Tom smiled, remembering the presents he had acquired at duty-free shops in the course of his travels. "The thing is, life was going so well for me that summer. What with the business, and Melody and everything."

Melody had returned to his life with the force of an explosion. "The Golden Tycoon," as Alec had dubbed her. She had called Tom at the office one day—"I'm in London. What about that dinner you promised?" One dinner had led to two. Three dinners had led to bed. And bed was marvellous. Fantastic. *Melody* was fantastic. When she was there. Usually she was in Paris, Sydney, Hong Kong or anywhere but London. Having opened her gallery, she was selling paintings to wealthy clients all over the world. She spent more time than Tom on a plane. But it suited them. They both thrived on work. Invigorated by the pace of their lives, finding time to meet every month was a challenge they took in their stride. Syncronizing schedules added even more spice to their meetings.

Constantin was curious. He cocked an eyebrow. "And your employer? Did he know about Melody?"

"Sure. I told him."

"Asked his permission?"

"No," Tom shook his head. "Nothing like that."

Melody was a free spirit, the freest spirit he had ever encountered. Maurice had smiled at the news. "I knew she liked you," he had said. "Enjoy your time with her. She will be good for you."

"So you see," Tom grinned, "I had everything I wanted from life, which was why I felt guilty about you—"

"You were the best thing to happen to us," Constantin interrupted. "You know that."

Few good things happened to Constantin that summer. The Junta's grip upon Greece had grown ever tighter. He had tried to believe that conditions would improve, but even his resilience had started to fade. It died completely at the end of the summer. A new figure burst upon the world stage. Across the Mediterranean, Colonel Qaddafi seized power in Libya. Within days he ordered the U.S. Air Force to close its base at Wheelers Field. The Americans were instructed to cease all flights and evacuate the base as soon as possible. And a day or so later Qaddafi ordered the British to close their naval station at Tobruk.

Constantin had been quick to see the implications. NATO would need a new base in the Mediterranean. Constantin had groaned at the news, fearing what was to come.

Then another blow, this time much closer to home. The Kyrios Stanton had passed through on his way to Kariakos. Once again there was a note from Alexandros—this time containing disastrous news. *Our courier does not use this route in winter. I'll try to find an alternative, but communication may have to cease until spring . . .*

Spring! Constantin had been appalled. The flow of letters and money had served as a lifeline. He had felt useful, he had felt that he was doing something.

Spring had seemed a lifetime away.

1970

On 8 January 1970, the U.S. Air Force began to evacuate its base in Libya. Two days later, President Richard Nixon appointed a new ambassador to Greece. Arriving in Athens, Ambassador Henry Tasca set about securing U.S. bases on any terms possible. The Colonels were waiting. "You support us," said the Colonels, "and we will grant you the bases you need."

Constantin groaned. "God forgive the Americans, for they know not what they do."

He came close to despair that winter. His beliefs were put to the sword. The fact that Greece was part of NATO, a member of the Council of Europe, with powerful allies, all counted for nothing. The world's politicians ignored the plight of the Greeks.

Constantin clung on, sustained by responsibilities and glimmers of hope. One such glimmer was the International Committee of the Red Cross. For two years the ICRC had nagged away at the Junta, and the Junta had made some grudging concessions. ICRC delegates from Geneva were permitted to open an office in Athens. They were allowed access to prisons . . . relatives of men in detention were permitted to call at the ICRC office.

"See," the Junta trumpeted. "There is no torture in our prisons. This is a lie spread by our enemies. We have proved it. The Red Cross has found no evidence of torture . . ."

Greeks were dumbfounded. They *knew* prisoners were tortured. "The Red Cross has been duped," they said. "Of course men in prison won't talk. They have wives and families on the outside . . . wives who could be on the *inside* if the Junta so orders."

One day Constantin took the bus into Athens. He went to see the ICRC for himself. "I am Constantin Peponis," he said to the girl on the desk. "I would like to talk to a delegate from Geneva."

They were all Swiss. Later he found out that membership of the ICRC was restricted to Swiss nationals. Few of them spoke Greek, so the meeting was conducted in English. It did not go as well as Constantin had hoped. They knew who he was. Copies of reports he had written for Alexandros had found their way to Geneva. Yet there was no welcome. The delegates conducted the meeting formally, with little warmth or even a hint of common interest. They showed no sign of being on Constantin's side.

"We cannot take sides," said one of the delegates. "Our function is to be impartial."

Constantin went red in the face, "How can you be impartial between right and wrong, between good and evil?"

"Forget you are Greek. You are also a lawyer. Concentrate on that and you will understand our position."

Gradually he came to realize what they meant. Their agreement with the Junta was hopelessly one-sided. The scales were weighted against them. The Junta represented the sovereign state of Greece. The ICRC was a private institution, with no right to be in the country. The Junta had already thrown Amnesty International out of Greece. The ICRC was there on sufferance. They knew the Colonels would try to use them for propaganda, but it was a risk they took in order to help. Every day they walked on glass.

Constantin was reminded of his father. His father had walked on glass. Many Greeks had despised him, calling him a tool of the Nazi regime.

That night Constantin pleaded the ICRC's case in the taverna. "They do what they can," he argued. "At least they do *something.*"

And they did. The ICRC obtained access to a few of the prisons, negotiated the release of some prisoners, distributed aid to dependants—but it was never enough. The regime of terror continued. People were arrested at dead of night, dragged from their beds to be taken off God only knew where.

It was a testing time for Constantin. So many people depended upon him. He bought all the protection he could from corrupt officials, despising them and himself at the same time—but what else could he do? He was determined to care for Melina and her family, and their many friends. He watched over them, listened to them, worried about them—and nobody worried him more than young Elias.

With Demetrios and Theo still in hiding, Elias was the only one of Melina's brothers still living at home. Everyone in the family was proud of him, sometimes it seemed, everyone in Piraeus. Now in his second year at the Law School in Athens, Elias was developing into an exceptional student. Constantin was forever boasting, "When I return to the law, Elias and I will become partners."

He was a serious young man, with dark brooding eyes, as slim and quick as his sister. Unfortunately he lacked Melina's light touch. "Too solemn by half" had been said of him for as long as people could remember. Even so, he was well liked by his fellow students, some of whom even held him in awe. "A brilliant boy can't always be laughing and joking," his mother would say, though at times a wistful note could be heard through her pride.

Ever since his entry into the Law School, Elias had spent Saturday mornings at the taverna, receiving extra tutoring from Constantin. It was the high spot of Constantin's week. They worked upstairs in the apartment, while Melina filleted fish in the kitchen below. Increasingly Elias talked to Constantin as man to man, or as lawyer to lawyer, for by now Elias could argue with sharpening skill. Sometimes their debates flashed and crackled with the force of a duel, a development which prompted Constantin to forecast, "Elias will graduate with the highest honors the Law School can bestow."

Ironically the Law School became a bone of contention. Constantin loved the Law School. Mere mention of it was enough to revive some of his happiest memories. Yet the Law School of which he was so proud was vastly different from the Law School inherited by Elias. Elias attended a school from which the principal professors had been expelled, a school where the new textbooks extolled the virtues of a police state, where totalitarianism was praised as a model of good government. Laws which Constantin had been taught to cherish were things of the past. Knowing how radical ideas can set a campus afire, the Junta held the universities in an iron fist. Students were spied upon by their tutors. Student Unions were kept in check. Students who protested were conscripted into the Army . . .

All of which Constantin knew, but what could he do except encourage Elias to continue his studies? "Pass your examinations, become qualified. Think of the future . . . all this will pass."

But increasingly Elias began to question, "*When* will it pass?"

Constantin could only talk about "the pressure of world opinion." He could only hope that "freedom will come *soon.*"

Soon, especially an unquantifiable *soon,* was a long time for a young man. Elias was growing restless. With political debate stifled within the university, he began to seek it outside. Accompanied by a few fellow students, he had taken to attending secret meetings. Behind locked doors they talked of freedoms taken for granted elsewhere in Europe, but which were labeled treason in Greece.

Over the weeks a tension began to creep into the Saturday mornings. Knowing the boy's mind, Constantin encouraged him to talk, hoping to dissuade him from rash action, but Elias had learned to argue well and the discussions became heated. A divide began to open between them; a divide which widened to a rift when Elias revealed that he had forged links with men outside the university, men who talked of guns and armed insurrection.

Constantin was appalled, "No, no, that's not the way. Violence only begets violence—"

"Tell that to Papadopoulos. Look at the way he seized power . . ."

So bitterly did they quarrel that after a while Elias ceased to mention his *friends,* though Constantin guessed that he continued to see them.

Constantin worried himself sick. He loved Elias. He was proud of the boy. Elias possessed a good brain, he could have an excellent future . . . but if he was discovered with such people, he would have no future at all.

The Junta would kill him.

At long last came the first signs of spring. The cold damp Athenian winter gave way to warmer days. The sun turned from pale lemon to orange, quickening the almond trees into bloom on the hillsides. On the balcony at the taverna, the bougainvillea began to blaze purple and gold, and the first geraniums burst from their buds.

Somehow, by what at times he thought a miracle, Constantin had survived and secured the safety of his friends. Everyone knew of people who had been arrested, but none under Constantin's protection had perished. Even Elias—darkly brooding and restless as ever—had remained unscathed, although the Saturday morning tutorials often erupted. By mutual agreement, they said nothing to Melina of their arguments. One of the joys of Melina's life was Constantin's friendship with her brother. It gave her real pleasure to see them together. So on Saturday morning, she was happy to leave them to talk while she descended to her kitchen below.

Like a shepherd guarding his flock, Constantin was constantly vigilant. Listening to gossip in the taverna, he weighed every rumor. His spies verified this and double-checked that. Little happened locally to take him by surprise. But he ached for news from further afield. What of Alexandros in London?

Then came the day when the Kyrios Stanton returned. As

always his visit was unheralded. Early one lunchtime the bead curtains parted to admit Richards the pilot, followed a moment later by Stanton himself.

The Kyrios Stanton fascinated Constantin. The man possessed everything. Wealth and power, charm and energy. And women. This time there were two; an Indian girl in a silver sari, and a blonde; different from the green-eyed blonde of last year but almost as beautiful. They praised the view from the balcony with breathless cries. The scenes, the taverna, the food, were all new experiences. Their eyes rounded with delight and excitement, while the Kyrios Stanton beamed his approval. "All part of your great adventure," he purred as Constantin poured the wine.

And afterwards a large envelope was left on the chair.

Constantin rushed upstairs like a lover receiving news from a mistress. But when he opened the letter, the news was bad. Worse than bad. Disastrous. Greek exiles and sympathizers were fighting a losing battle. Especially in Washington. Alexandros wrote: *Nixon is determined to secure a home port for his sixth fleet in Greece. He will do anything for the Junta if they give him his bases . . .*

In London, Paris and Rome—*The Americans are twisting arms to stop Allied governments from protesting. They insist that the value of securing new bases outweighs the misery of a few Greeks.*

A *few* Greeks! Constantin was outraged. How could anyone say a *few* Greeks, when the whole country lived in terror?

Elsewhere in the letter, Alexandros wrote: *You must encourage more people to speak out about torture, particularly to the ICRC. We hear countless rumors, but the ICRC is hampered by lack of evidence . . .*

Constantin became angry. He felt betrayed. He expected better from Alexandros. It was easy to be critical from London. Alexandros should try living in Athens. He would soon change his tune. Lack of freedom erodes the spirit. It creates a dull acceptance of injustice for fear of even greater repression. Not for Alexandros the terrifying knock on the door at two in the morning.

The bad news sent Constantin into the blackest of depressions. It lasted for weeks. Melina was at her wit's end. She cooked his favorite meals. She served him the taverna's best wine. She was a seductress in bed; all to no avail. No sooner had Constantin eaten, emptied the bottle, made love—than his depression returned.

The truth was he could see no end to the repression. The Junta grew ever stronger. A series of show trials were in progress. The court, of which Constantin had once been so proud, had deteriorated to a lynch mob. On trial were thirty-four members of the Democratic Party, including General Iordanidis, former Greek representative at NATO Headquarters, and various prominent lawyers, several of whom were Constantin's friends. All were charged with conspiracy and possession of explosives. One by one they revoked admissions extracted under torture. Not that it mattered. All were judged guilty.

"Eighteen years," Constantin groaned at the sentences. "They will rot and die in those prisons." Melina wept. She recalled entertaining the men in her smart Athens apartment. A lifetime ago. A different world. A world which no longer existed. And in the world which now did exist, all hope was dying.

Then a miracle occurred. Constantin could think of no other word. At the very moment when the misery seemed unendurable, when deprivations sapped human spirits to their lowest ebb, occurred an event which brought a smile to people's lips and hope to their hearts.

Nine men escaped from the Averoff prison. The ESA, the dreaded military police, traced them to Piraeus. The port was searched from end to end. At three in the morning people were roused from their beds and forced to shiver in the street while armed troops rummaged through rooms and attics. Every possible hiding place was examined. By dawn the search had extended to the docks. Every ship, every tanker, every rust-stained bucket afloat was boarded and searched. All day and all that night the hunt continued . . . until, finally, more than fifty hours after the men had escaped, the ESA had to accept what had become obvious to everyone else . . . that somehow, miraculously, wonderfully, the men had vanished into thin air.

Constantin celebrated that night. All of Piraeus celebrated. The taverna was packed with people laughing and joking.

In the days which followed, speculation ran rife. Everyone had a pet theory about the escape. Graffiti appeared on walls, taunting the Junta. *Long live freedom. Long live the Averoff Nine.* The escaped prisoners became symbols of hope. Folk heroes. The ESA swooped here, the ESA swooped there, but the Averoff Nine were never recaptured.

As mystified as everyone else, Constantin refused to speculate. "They are free, that's all that matters," he said. "Who cares how they escaped." He never expected to find out, but one night he became one of a handful of men to learn what had happened to the Averoff Nine.

It was late, past two in the morning. Melina had gone to bed. Constantin had bolted the front door. After emptying the ashtrays and sweeping the floor, he was carrying the shutters out to the balcony when a pebble arced upwards from the alley. It flew over the balustrade to land on the floor. He went to the balustrade and peered over. The narrow alley was hidden in shadow. Squinting into the darkness, he searched for a movement. Nothing stirred. For a moment he blamed his imagination—he was tired, it had been a long day, he'd had a few drinks. Then a hoarse whisper called his name. He leaned out as far as he dared. The whisper came again, "Constantin, help me." He stared down into the shadows. Even with the voice to guide him several moments passed before he saw the figure of a man, flat on his back, covered with so much dirt that he could be seen only by the whites of his eyes. Constantin called, "Who is it?" Silence. He was about to raise his voice to call again, when the barest croak came in response. "Roufus . . . Panos Roufus." Frowning, Constantin tried to put a face to the name. Then it came to him. Roufus was a fisherman. He and his brother had two boats. By reputation they were honest and hard working; Constantin knew them both, but not well.

"Help me," came another whisper from the ground.

Quickly, quietly, he went to the door and slid back the bolt. Outside the street was cloaked in the pitch-black of a moonless night. Leaving the door ajar, he hurried around the corner and into the alley. Roufus had rolled over and was trying to push himself up onto his knees. His breathing was labored. Reaching him, Constantin dropped to one knee. "Panos?" When Roufus turned his head, Constantin gasped. What he had thought was dirt was not dirt at all. It was blood. Roufus was covered with blood. His face was misshapen with bruises. For a moment he looked up with eyes full of pain, then he collapsed forward.

Gently, Constantin turned him onto his back. Then, with both arms under the body, he lifted. Roufus was not a small man, of medium height and strongly built, but Constantin carried him with ease. Roufus groaned and whimpered every step of the way.

Inside the taverna, Constantin lowered him into a chair before turning back to close the front door. By now his own shirt was wet with blood, and he was taking it off when Melina came down the stairs. She cried out when she saw him. Her face emptied of color, and she was halfway across the taverna before seeing Roufus. Quieting her with hurried words, Constantin bent over the injured man. Under electric light, Roufus looked even worse. Hurriedly, Constantin sent Melina for hot water. Then he pushed two tables together and lifted Roufus onto them. The man groaned and opened his eyes. He tried to speak but gagged on a mouthful of blood. Turning his head, he spat onto the floor, drawing bruised lips back over broken teeth. His left arm was fractured, as Constantin had guessed when carrying him in from the alley.

"Lie still," Constantin ordered as Melina returned with the water. Tearing a tablecloth into strips, she began to bathe Roufus's face. "We must get a doctor—"

"No," Roufus protested weakly. "No doctor. Constantin—"

"Ssh," Constantin hushed. Unbuttoning Roufus's shirt, he winced at the blood. "Dear God! Who did this—"

Roufus groaned and pushed Melina aside to struggle upright. "You must go . . ." he began, but the effort defeated him. His face contorted with pain.

"Brandy," Constantin muttered to Melina, while restraining Roufus, pushing him back on the table. The blood on the man's chest came from a jagged cut in his shoulder. His ribs and stomach were black with bruises. He had taken a terrible beating.

He coughed on the brandy, which trickled out of his mouth and ran down his chin. Clearing his throat, he again tried to speak. Constantin bent over him.

Roufus' speech was distorted. Every word was an effort. A feverish look lit his eyes. "You know Ritsos . . . Inspector Ritsos? You know him?"

Constantin frowned, trying to place the name. Finally he pictured the man. Ritsos ran the police station south of the docks. "Yes, I know him."

"Find him," Roufus begged. "Give him a message. In secret. Tell him Mercouris found out about Kariakos."

Constantin caught his breath. *Kariakos?* Home of the Kyrios Stanton? Kariakos was such a small island; one of hundreds scattered across the Aegean, so tiny that few people had heard of it. "Kariakos? You mean the island? What about it?"

Roufus sank back. His eyes glittered. His voice was very weak. "Ritsos will know . . . just say Mercouris found out. Go now . . . at once."

"No!" Melina interrupted fearfully, gripping Constantin's arm.

Suddenly the street door opened. Constantin whirled around, realizing he had forgotten to secure the bolts.

Four men entered. One carried a shotgun. Constantin started forward in alarm until he recognized Roufus' brother. They came directly to the table, crowding around the injured man. Hope shone from Roufus' feverish eyes. "Mercouris," he croaked. "God forgive me but I told him—"

"Mercouris is dead," said his brother. "He told no one."

Roufus responded by closing his eyes and taking a deep breath. He coughed. Next moment his chest heaved as he began to weep. Struggling for control, he compressed his lips, but awful animal sounds were torn from his throat; mucus ran from his broken nose. The brother tried to provide comfort. "Panos, you did well. You held out. You got Kazantzaki and we killed Mercouris. It's all over . . ."

One of the men turned to Melina. "May I suggest that the Kyrenia Peponis retires to her bed. We will not be long here."

Overcoming her fear, Melina drew her nightgown tighter around her. "That man needs a doctor—"

"I am a doctor," said the man on her right. Already he was exploring Roufus' ribs with deft fingers, searching for damage. Taking the bowl of water from Melina's hands, he regarded her with solemn eyes. "Thank you for your help, but my friend is right. It would be best if you went to your bed."

Melina turned fearful eyes to Constantin, seeking advice. Intercepting the look, the doctor sought to reassure her. "Please! We are in your debt, but we must hurry!"

Melina waited for a reaction from Constantin. Behind her, Roufus whimpered piteously while his brother stroked his hair. Constantin nodded. "It will be all right. Go upstairs."

Melina hesitated "Are you sure?"

"Please!" Insisted the man with the gun.

With a final look at Constantin, Melina retreated and began to climb the stairs. The doctor immediately set to work on Roufus, who groaned and writhed on the table.

Unable to help and not caring to watch, Constantin walked over to the bar and poured a large brandy. The man with the shotgun followed. Sliding another glass over the counter, Constantin poured out a good measure. The man took it and drank. Wiping his mouth with the back of his hand, he looked hard at Constantin. "What did he tell you?"

Despite the shotgun, Constantin kept his nerve. He shook his head, "You tell me something. Roufus has been beaten half to death, and by the sound of it two men have been killed. What's this about?"

The man was smaller than Constantin, but so were most men. In his mid-thirties, he had a weather-beaten face and the level-eyed look of a man no more easily intimidated than Constantin himself. The man swallowed some more brandy before answering. "Tonight could cost you your life, my friend. Those ESA bastards would kill you to find out what you know. And I would kill you if I thought you would tell them."

Without flinching, Constantin drank from his glass. His apparent calm was deceptive, his mind was in turmoil. *Kariakos!* Was the Kyrios Stanton something more than a courier? What about their friend, the Kyrios Lambert? But Ritsos was police. These men weren't police. Why had Roufus wanted to get a message to Ritsos?

The man watched him. "Don't be a fool. You have a good reputation with us. We're on the same side. Tell me what happened."

"Tell me about Ritsos."

Surprised, the man glanced over to the table, seeking instructions. Constantin felt a tingle of fear. Had he condemned himself to death? And condemned the man on the table? But Roufus was being tended by his own brother. They were fishermen, not police. But they were killers. Roufus' brother had said *We killed Mercouris.* Recovered, stifling alarm, Constantin was in two minds. Half of him wanted them all out of the taverna, now, immediately. He wanted no dealings with killers. The other half said find out about Kariakos. Was the Kyrios Stanton involved? In danger? Did he do more than carry letters from London?

Leaving the bar, the man went to the table. Constantin heard him mutter something about Ritsos. Still tending Roufus, the doctor grunted. His eyes gleamed with approval. "Clever," he muttered. "I wouldn't have thought of getting a message to Ritsos in his state."

The man with the gun jerked his head at Constantin. "But he knows now."

The doctor nodded. "I think we can trust him."

Looking doubtful, the man returned to the bar.

"This Mercouris," asked Constantin. "Who is, who *was* he?"

The man looked back at the doctor.

"Tell him," said the doctor.

The man shrugged. "Very well," he said turning to Constantin. "Mercouris and Kazantzaki were ESA. They boarded one of the boats and took Panos by surprise. You've seen what they did. I can only guess what happened. Perhaps Panos pretended to pass out, I don't know, somehow he got his gun from the locker. He killed Kazantzaki and wounded Mercouris, but Mercouris got away. We were only a few minutes behind. They had a car but we found the keys in Kazantzaki's pockets. That meant Mercouris left on foot. Panos followed him. He must have collapsed, no surprise considering what they did to him. Where did you find him?"

"In the alley."

The man's eyes lit with understanding. "That makes sense," he said. "We caught up with Mercouris near here. We saw your lights on the balcony . . ." He broke off, alarmed. "Spyros, get those shutters up. We don't want anyone blundering in here."

Watching the man Spyros attend to the shutters, Constantin was still confused. *Why Ritsos? Why did Roufus want me to get a message to Ritsos?*

The man read Constantin's mind. He turned to the doctor, "Shall I tell him?"

The doctor was fastening the shredded tablecloth around Roufus's chest. "He already knows about Ritsos. You'll have to."

The man leaned across the bar, his gleaming eyes proud and triumphant. "We sprang the Averoff Nine. It was Ritsos who helped us."

Constantin stared. The words took a moment to register. Then everything fell into place. Ritsos must have directed his police elsewhere while the men made their escape. *Ritsos!* Who would have thought? No word had reached Constantin. Not a hint had been picked up by his spies. His spirits rose. All of his bouts of depression, believing the situation was hopeless . . . and now this. Who would have guessed? A police inspector working against the Junta. One man, hidden in the enemy camp. Constantin remembered his father . . . plotting against the Gestapo . . .

Across the room, Panos Roufus had been helped upright, supported by his brother and the doctor. Gray-faced, his chest bound tight and one arm in a sling, he lowered his feet tentatively to the floor.

"Try a few steps," the doctor encouraged. Roufus managed to shuffle to a chair before sinking down with a groan of relief.

Constantin crossed the room, glasses in one hand, brandy in the other. First they helped the injured man. The doctor held the glass and dribbled a few drops between Panos' bruised lips. Then they all had a drink. The doctor's severe, beak-nosed face eased into a thin smile. He held out a hand to Constantin. "Thank you, my friend. We won't forget. But if ever you see me again, you don't know me. If I come into your taverna, you'll greet me as a stranger. The same for the others. Understand?"

Constantin was about to ask a question when a muffled knock sounded at the door. The doctor went rigid with tension. Spyros crossed the room with less noise than a cat, followed by the man with the gun. Spyros tapped twice on the door. Four knocks sounded immediately in return. The man with the gun grinned his relief, while Spyros smiled at the doctor, "It's okay. They're here—"

"We go," the doctor interrupted abruptly. His gaze swept the taverna, lighting on the bowl of bloodied water and the torn tablecloth. "Get rid of that as soon as we've gone," he commanded as he turned to help Roufus up from the chair.

Constantin remembered his question. "Why was I to tell Ritsos about Kariakos?" he asked.

The doctor's eyes narrowed. "The island? Have you been there?"

"No."

The doctor smiled his grim smile. "It's tiny. My cousin lives in the village, if you can call it a village. He's a fisherman." Wry amusement came into the doctor's eyes. "When boats meet at dead of night, who knows what passes between them?"

There was no time for more questions. No time even for goodbyes. Spyros had opened the door, just wide enough for one man to slip through. The man with the gun had already left; then Spyros, followed by the Roufus brothers and the doctor. "Bolt the door immediately," he instructed. "Don't look into the street."

The man's natural authority drew obedience even from Constantin. Closing the door without looking out, he was surprised by his automatic response. But something about the man, in his face, his eyes . . . "He's no more a doctor than I am," Constantin muttered under his breath. A soldier? He had that look about him. An Army officer? Could it be? A police inspector ***and*** an Army officer?

Sliding the bolt quietly into place, he put his ear to the door, listening to the rumble of heavy wheels as a vehicle coasted down to the corner. A goods vehicle? Or . . . something more . . . a truck belonging to the Army?

It was a long time before Constantin saw "the doctor" again. He fancied he saw Spyros once, and he *did* see the Roufus brothers, but they passed by in the street without even a glance. He accepted the lack of acknowledgment without resentment. It was enough to know that such men existed, that resistance to the Junta had spread to include even a high-ranking policeman . . . and maybe many more.

As for the Kyrios Stanton, he remained an enigma. He called in at the tavern again a month later. To the world at large he was simply breaking his journey—a wealthy man, accompanied by two lovely women, apparently without a care in the world. And Constantin played the attentive patron to perfection, so that the scene would have fooled even the sharpest observer. Yet the courier service continued. There was always a letter from London. Alexandros sent money and news, and in return Constantin sent lists of detainees, addresses and dates of arrests.

Constantin wondered if the Kyrios Stanton even knew about the Averoff Nine. Sometimes he doubted it. Some days he was convinced that Stanton was simply an aging playboy, without interest in Greece or anything except women. Conversations at the table were all about pleasure; parties on yachts, the best restaurants in Rome, a new play in London . . .

The relationship was different with the Kyrios Lambert. He became one of the family. He met Elias on one visit and Melina's mother on the next. Melina's nature compelled her to share her friends, and she seized every opportunity to introduce one to the other. Constantin worried that the Englishman might take offense, but when Tom Lambert greeted everyone with a good-natured grin, all such concerns were forgotten.

"He has matured," Melina said in private. "He has developed into a very confident man."

There had been no lack of confidence in the first place, but Constantin knew what she meant. Tom Lambert exuded the air of a man in charge of his life. Clearly his business with the Kyrios

Stanton had gone well. Constantin was pleased, yet unable to stifle a slight twinge of envy; envy for a man who could pursue a career all over the world. Privately he mourned his own lost career. Sometimes he wondered if he would spend the rest of his days in the taverna.

"This time will pass," Melina encouraged. "We should be content to survive, all of us, you, me and the family."

That was Constantin's task—to ensure they survived.

But then Petros Kappos was arrested and everything changed.

Petros was arrested at three in the morning. Word reached Constantin an hour later. By dawn he had gleaned the full story. Sickened by what he heard, he caught the early morning bus into Athens. He was already at the ICRC offices by the time the delegates arrived. Still shaken and shocked, he was shown into a conference room, and shortly afterwards interviewed by two of the delegates. Speaking in English, he told them the details. He had expected them to share his outrage, but their reaction was almost clinical. As a lawyer himself he respected the need to avoid hasty judgments, but their caution made him angry. He thought of Alexandros writing complacent letters from London: *Tell the ICRC . . . give them hard facts.*

"These are the facts. This is what happened."

"But you weren't present," one of the delegates demurred. "Your story is second-hand. Where are your witnesses?"

Constantin's hands clenched into fists. Biting back his temper, he said, "Everyone knows the ESA watch this office. People are afraid to come here. Don't you know that? Anna is terrified—"

"Anna?"

"Petros' wife."

He had hoped that the ICRC might contact the ESA and demand to be told Petros' whereabouts and the reasons for his arrest.

"We can't do that," said one of the delegates shaking his head. "It would be beyond the scope of our agreement with the government. We can only ask permission to interview *convicted* prisoners. So, until your friend is convicted in court—"

"They may never bring him to court," Constantin interrupted, his heart sinking.

He sat there in a fever of frustration. He knew the delegates were not fools. They were experienced men who had negotiated with the most hated despots in the world. In Peru, Angola, El Salvador; wherever dictators ruled, the ICRC pitted their wits against them. The delegates were honorable men; but winning concessions from the Junta was like walking on quicksand.

He told them about the rumors on the streets. That it was in the police stations, not the prisons, where torture was most common. "That's where the ESA extort their trumped-up confessions. Men in enough pain will confess to anything. The police stations—"

"The Colonels do not allow us to inspect police stations."

Constantin tried not to blame the delegates. They were negotiating with treacherous men, men who agreed to something one day and reneged the next. But he wanted help *now*. Petros had been arrested. He was probably being tortured even as they sat there. Where else could Constantin go? Who else might help? He knew the answer. Nobody. The ICRC was his only hope. Restraining anxiety and impatience, he began to plead his case, using all the skills learned in the courtroom. "Anna will give you a statement," he said. "Petros' mother will give you a statement. Petros' young brother will give you a statement. Hasn't that been your problem? That people are afraid to speak out? People won't give you statements. These people *will*, if you see them today. You can use such statements in your talks with the Colonels. As levers. 'Here is proof,' you can say. You can threaten to publish the statements. You can send them to the world's press. You can hold a press conference in Geneva . . ."

Desperation led him to say more than he intended. Would Anna sign a statement? He would have to persuade her.

"But where are these witnesses?"

"They won't come here. They are too frightened. But if you come back to Piraeus with me . . ."

Constantin left the ICRC offices some thirty minutes later. Alone. The delegates would not come to Piraeus at once, but they had agreed to be at the taverna at four o'clock.

First he went to Anna's house, to persuade her to sign a statement, "There are no guarantees," he confessed, "but it might help."

Then he went to find Elias before going home to Melina. More people than usual were at the taverna that lunchtime, all asking about Petros, all looking to Constantin for a lead. He said as little as possible, nothing about his meeting with the ICRC for fear of raising false hopes. Anna and her mother-in-law had not agreed to sign statements. He had left them thinking about it. Not that poor Anna was in a fit state to think.

At three o'clock, he bolted the front door and told Melina of the arrangements. "It would be best," he said, "if you stayed upstairs—"

"I can't do that." Melina was appalled. "It will be bad enough for Anna as it is, she'll need the support of a woman—"

"Petros' mother is coming—"

"A mother-in-law isn't enough," Melina said scornfully.

"And Elias is bringing Andreas later—"

"Oh no! Andreas is what? Thirteen? Fourteen? You can't—"

"He was a witness. He might give a statement." Constantin straightened a chair and emptied an ashtray. "They'll be gentle with him."

"They? How many will there be?"

"God knows."

Melina sighed unhappily. It was right to help Anna, she *wanted* to help, but she had fears of her own. Constantin took so many risks. The reports he wrote, the questions he asked . . . now, to bring the Red Cross into the taverna, when everyone knew they were followed wherever they went.

Constantin was equally worried. Holding the meeting at the taverna had been his idea. He had not been able to think of an alternative. Anna would need all her courage. He would be there to support her. The plan had made sense. Except for the risks. He worried about Melina constantly. Worry was all he could do He had tried to reason with her; a hundred times he had said, "What you don't know can't hurt you." He was afraid to say what he really meant, "They'll hurt you to find out what you *do* know." Unknown to her, he had made what arrangements he could. If anything happened to him, Elias was to smuggle her out of Piraeus to Uncle Mikis up in the hills . . .

Scarcely had they cleared up when a knock sounded at the door. The knock came again. Constantin hurried to the door and slid back the bolt.

Even with a bruise on her temple, Anna Kappos was a good-looking woman. Dressed in black, with a shawl on her head, she stood in the bright sunlight, too embarrassed to meet Constantin's eyes. Instead she stared directly ahead. Her skin was the color of honey and her eyes a shade or so darker. Next to her stood her mother-in-law, fifty years old but looking much older, a woman whose face bore the signs of an unsuccessful battle with life.

"Come," said Constantin gently, drawing them over the threshold.

The sight of Anna was enough for Melina to forget her earlier fears. She hurried forward to embrace her.

Anna gazed around the taverna with wide, frightened eyes.

"Please," Constantin murmured, drawing chairs back from the table.

Removing her shawl, Anna revealed more fully the purple-black bruise on her temple. She folded the shawl over her lap, examined it, then folded it again, and over once more. Not once had she met Constantin's eye. Her body was rigid with tension.

The mother-in-law broke the silence, "Where are the men from the Red Cross?"

Constantin glanced at his watch. He frowned. The ICRC were ten minutes late. "They'll be here soon," he placated.

"We are ready to sign a statement," said the mother-in-law.

Constantin breathed a small sigh of relief, "Are you ready, Anna?"

The woman nodded wordlessly, her gaze fixed on her lap.

Melina opened her mouth to speak, but Constantin silenced her with a glance. He wanted no false encouragement. Signing a statement was a serious matter. To set their names to paper put people at risk.

Sensing his tension, Anna looked up to meet Constantin's eye for the first time. "I am ready," she said quietly.

He wondered. He explained that although the Red Cross could do nothing for her, they might help to trace Petros. Even as he spoke, questions loomed in his mind. *Where are the delegates? Why are they late? Will they actually come?* He tried to hide his anxiety.

For a big man his voice had surprising range. In court he could boom, attacking opponents with the roar of a cannon; but to Anna he spoke slowly and softly. "The Red Cross will take one statement," he said. "And I'll take another. Nobody here will see the statement you give me. A friend will take it to London, where other friends will show it to people in foreign governments who are trying to help us. Is that all right, Anna?"

She nodded.

"You will tell me about last night. I will write it down, then you will sign it as a true record. Do you agree?"

Anna's face mirrored her misery. She flicked a sideways glance at her mother-in-law before returning her gaze to her lap. Her hands dry-washed each other in a fidget of worry. "I thought . . . we hoped . . ." She swallowed and cleared her throat. "They've got him somewhere . . . if he's still alive . . . we thought you'd help find him—"

"I'll do all I can, I promise, but the Red Cross—"

A knock sounded at the door. Constantin leapt up, relieved and irritated at the same time. The Swiss were supposed to be punctual. Didn't they realize what delays did to stretched nerves? He would tell them a thing or two . . .

But when he opened the door, a girl stood framed in the entrance. Under her arm was a document case bearing the Red Cross emblem. Constantin stared. She had chestnut shoulder-length hair and tanned healthy skin. Her dove-gray shirt was tucked into a charcoal-gray skirt. A small enamel Red Cross badge decorated one lapel. He looked over her shoulder, expecting to see the delegates behind her. But the street was empty. He found himself acknowledging his identity and was so surprised that he missed her name. Astonishment was turning to anger. The Red Cross had sent a girl! A secretary or someone. She could only be about twenty-six. Suddenly he realized she was speaking Greek and asking, "May I come in?"

"I expected a delegate," he said, stepping aside.

"You mean you expected a man." Her dark-brown eyes glimmered with wry amusement. "Don't worry, I know my job, and I speak Greek. Your witness is a woman, I believe. She will talk more easily to me." Her tone was pleasantly matter-of-fact, and the accompanying smile so genuine that Constantin faltered. She had charm, he had to admit. And a dazzling smile. A sly look at her bare legs confirmed his impression of an attractive young woman. Competent too, he imagined, watching her absorb the scene at a glance.

"Just you?" he managed at last. "Nobody else?"

"Just me," she smiled.

He would have protested in other circumstances, but with Anna verging on tears he dared not worsen her ordeal. So he led the way to the table. "This is the delegate from the Red Cross," he began, trying to remember her name. "The Kyrenia—"

"Kirsten," she said. "Kirsten Moutier."

She went around the table shaking hands before sitting down. Unzipping her document case, she extracted a writing pad and placed it on the table. Her manner was neither brisk enough to be businesslike, nor effusive enough to be friendly. It fell somewhere between. Like a doctor, he thought as he watched her accept some coffee from Melina. Her attention had already focused on Anna.

Anna sat biting her lip, feeling her courage drain away. She dreaded the ordeal of telling her story. Especially in front of a man, even a man like the Lawyer Peponis. She had debated with her mother-in-law for an hour before concluding, "I'll only do it to help Petros." Poor Petros. Where was he? Was he still alive? Could she see him? Would he want to see *her*? The last question tore at her heart. Stifling a sob, she tugged at the shawl in her hands.

The Red Cross woman began to ask questions in such a quiet, sympathetic voice that Constantin took a moment to recognize more than casual conversation. The interrogation had started. Hurriedly he went to the kitchen where he kept a pen and paper. When he returned, he heard Anna say, "It was last night. We were in bed. Petros gets up at five every morning . . ."

Constantin began to write, using the tiny script he had developed for his reports for Alexandros.

". . . it was very late, about three o'clock. We woke to this crash at the front door. I heard boots running upstairs. There wasn't time to do anything . . . it all happened so fast . . . Petros was getting into his trousers. I was still in bed when the door crashed back on its hinges and men ran into the room, four or five of them, pulling him to the door . . ." Anna swallowed and raised her eyes to look the Red Cross delegate full in the face. "He hadn't even got his shoes on his feet or a shirt on his back. They were dragging him down the stairs, hitting him with their rifles, kicking him . . ." Her voice broke and she shook her head in despair. "It was horrible," she whispered, casting her eyes down to her fingers in her lap.

Gently, the Red Cross delegate asked, "Were these men in uniform?"

"Some were," Anna began to nod then changed her mind. "They weren't all the same. Some were soldiers, but one, no, two I think, wore ordinary clothes."

Constantin's pen raced over the paper.

"It was dark, you see," Anna struggled to explain. "There wasn't time to switch on the light. They didn't put it on, they weren't there long enough. Suddenly there was all this noise, shouting and bellowing, then they were down the stairs, dragging Petros. I was screaming at them not to hurt him. By now I was on the landing, Mother-in-Law was coming from her room, Andreas was at his door . . . then I was running downstairs, calling for Petros . . ."

Writing furiously, Constantin flicked a sideways glance at the delegate. Her attentive expression again reminded him of a doctor.

". . . I stumbled into the street, blinded by lights from a truck facing the house. Another one was next to it, parked the other way. I couldn't see at first, the lights were dazzling, more than just headlights, two big beams shone from the top of the cab. . . ."

Anna's appearance provoked a gale of whistles. Rising naked from bed, she had grabbed the first item of clothing to come to hand. Mindlessly, intent on reaching Petros, she had run after him dressed in only her slip.

"I didn't hear the men's whistles. Mother-in-Law told me afterwards, but . . . I didn't think, I mean I was screaming for Petros at the top of my voice . . ."

Petros was being dragged into the second truck, up over the tailboard. Soldiers were beating him.

". . . I'd seen him by then. I'd seen the second truck, everything. It's a narrow street. The trucks were taking up all the room, almost on the pavement. I got to the second truck, so close I could almost reach it, when this man grabbed me and threw me against the wall . . ."

Anna's only thought was that he was preventing her from reaching Petros. But then . . .

". . . I was dazed. My head hit the wall. All the breath was knocked out of me. I lost my strength. I was gasping and crying and . . . then he got a hand between my legs. I was screaming, trying to fight him off, struggling . . . my shoulder straps broke or he tore them, I don't know . . . my slip was up round my waist . . . he kept trying to kiss me, I kept turning away . . ."

She was raped, up against the wall.

". . . Petros was like a wild thing in the truck. I could see him . . . over the man's shoulder . . . he could see me, see what was happening . . ."

Barefoot, wearing only a pair of trousers, already battered and bruised, Petros fought free of the soldiers. He threw himself down from the truck and hurled himself at Anna's attacker.

"After that . . ." Anna gulped. She shook her head, resisting the memories, closing her eyes. A shudder shook her body. Tears coursed down her cheeks. Bending forward she cradled her head in her hands, and began to weep uncontrollably. The mother-in-law turned to embrace her. Anna's shoulders heaved. A primeval wail escaped her lips. Pushing her chair back, Melina knelt next to her, encircling her with her arm, colliding with the mother-in-law. The two women rocked back and forth with the girl; faces contorted, hands searching for Anna's hands, squeezing fingers, bodies pressed to her body as if to share their strength.

The tan seemed to have faded from the Red Cross girl's face.

Now there was pain in her eyes, but she remained in her place, writing on her pad.

Lighting a cigarette, Constantin went to the bar and returned with brandy and glasses. The Red Cross delegate declined with a shake of her head. As Constantin sat down, the mother-in-law looked up, her gnarled face stricken. "Don't do this to her. I can tell you what happened. I was there—"

Hating himself, Constantin shook his head. "It must be Anna's own statement. I'll take one from you afterwards." He was already flouting the rules of evidence. The two statements should be taken independently, but Anna could not have coped on her own. He consoled himself with thoughts of Andreas. The boy had seen everything. . . .

Ten minutes passed before Anna could continue. The Red Cross Delegate was still making notes, so Constantin took up the questioning. He was as gentle as he knew how, but no amount of gentleness could diminish the brutality of that story.

The soldiers had clubbed Petros to his knees. Anna was knocked down; her slip torn from her body. Spreadeagled, held down, half in and half out of the gutter, she was raped within three yards of her husband.

". . . Petros saw . . . he kept trying to reach me . . . blood was pouring down his face . . . they kept kicking him, beating him with rifle butts . . . he was screaming my name . . ."

Anna said four soldiers raped her while she was on the ground. Afterwards her mother-in-law said she counted six. Raped in the gutter, outside her own home, in the glare of the lights from the truck, while her husband looked on. Anna passed out when she thought Petros was dead.

"He's *not* dead," the mother-in-law insisted. "I saw . . . when they threw him into the truck . . . when it drove off, he pulled himself up, I saw his face above the tailboard." Turning, she clasped Anna's hands. "Petros is alive. I know, I swear, believe me, our Petros is *alive*."

Anna responded with a look blank with incomprehension. Her eyes were swollen. Her face was no longer the color of honey. Instead it was blotchy and gray.

The soldiers had tried to keep the mother-in-law in the house, but she had struggled and squirmed her way to the broken front door. "They couldn't shut it, you see, they smashed it when they came in . . ."

Andreas too had witnessed the scene. Fighting and screaming, he had fought his way outside, only to be caught by other soldiers at the edge of the crowd.

"How many soldiers were there?" Constantin asked.

The mother-in-law said eighteen. Anna couldn't even hazard a guess.

"What about your neighbors? Did they try to help?"

The mother-in-law sneered, "Lights came on, shutters flew open, people stuck their heads out. Then the soldiers shouted at them, pointing their guns . . ." She shrugged. "Nobody came until the soldiers had gone."

When the trucks drove off, Anna was left naked and unconscious at the side of the road, with her mother-in-law kneeling over her, keening and wailing hysterically. It had been left to fourteen-year-old Andreas to take charge. He had been badly beaten himself. Several teeth had been dislodged and one leg was covered with bruises. Limping into the house, he had returned with a blanket to cover his sister-in-law before calling on the neighbors to help.

"They came then," said the mother-in-law with withering contempt. "When it was safe, they crept out like thieves in the night."

Leaving his mother and Anna in the care of their neighbors, Andreas hobbled as fast as he could to a doctor's house a dozen streets away. When the doctor learned that troops were involved he slammed the door in the boy's face. Andreas was in tears, utterly desperate. He knew only that one doctor. He hammered on the door for many minutes, but the doctor refused to answer. Finally Andreas remembered his cousin Vassilis Plytas, a second-year medical student. By now Andreas's left leg was swollen. Every step was agony. Limping, hobbling, running, he reached the Plytas home almost incoherent with pain and worry and shock. Vassilis left at once, racing through the darkened streets, leaving his parents to tend to Andreas.

Even two years at medical school had not prepared Vassilis for the sight of Anna's abused body. She was conscious by the time he arrived. With gentle hands he bathed her bruised limbs, cleansing her of dried semen and blood. He dared not do more. He was not a qualified doctor. But he knew doctors, and thirty minutes later he returned with a lecturer from the medical school. One hour later, Vassilis rendered one last favor. He roused his friend Elias from his bed and together they went to tell Constantin what had happened.

Inwardly Constantin was in a rage of despair. Justice, the law, his ability to haul these butchers into court, had vanished.

The Red Cross delegate looked at the mother-in-law. "Where do you think they have taken your son?"

The mother-in-law raised her hands in a gesture of hopelessness. She and Andreas had already been to the police station. They were not alone. Every police station in the country was besieged by anxious-faced people enquiring about relatives. In the case of Petros Kappos, police officials even refused to admit that Petros Kappos was in custody.

In his tiny handwriting, Constantin took it all down, covering both sides of his paper. So much for the Red Cross, he thought bitterly. Ask for their help and what happens? They send a girl . . . a slip of a girl. The Colonels will laugh themselves sick.

While Melina cleared the dishes, Constantin sat hunched and despondent. "She should have waited to see Andreas," he complained.

"Why?" Melina wiped the table with a damp cloth. "He can't help Petros. Why do *you* have to see him? The poor kid's suffered enough."

It was a lawyer's way to obtain statements. To build evidence. To present an overwhelming case. "It's been arranged," Constantin said heavily. "Elias is bringing him. They should be here any minute."

"Why put the boy through another ordeal?"

"It gives me another signed statement for Alexandros. We need every scrap of evidence we can get—" He broke off, interrupted by a knock at the door. "I'll get it," he said, hurrying across to slide back the bolt.

Young Andreas stood framed in the entrance, with Elias beside him.

The sight of Andreas brought a lump to Melina's throat. Such a small boy. Only fourteen. Little more than a child with a tousled head of black hair. To think of him seeing poor Anna raped . . . to take over as he had . . . to cover Anna with a blanket before running for help. Seeing the bruises on his face, her heart went out to him. "Andreas!" she cried, sobbing his name as she went to embrace him.

"Melina!" Constantin said sharply, reproving her with a look.

She stopped in her tracks.

Constantin's expression was grave. "The Kyrios Kappos has stopped by to share a glass of wine with me," he said sternly, turning back to the boy, his voice respectful as he stepped to one side. "Please, won't you come in."

Andreas seemed to grow taller. Squaring his shoulders he lifted his chin. He limped badly, but it was a dignified limp, the limp of the new head of the family Kappos.

Constantin showed more deference to this small boy than he had ever shown anyone. Melina watched him usher his guests to a table. She knew his instincts were right. Her way would have reduced the boy to tears. Constantin's way gave the boy courage.

She took her cue. Even to have smiled at Elias would have devalued Constantin's gesture. Quickly she brought wine and glasses to the table. She made no attempt to sit down with them. Instead, at her most subservient, she smiled her own small smile of respect. "I think I should leave you men to yourselves."

Constantin nodded approval. "The Kyrios Kappos and I have much to discuss."

So she withdrew, climbing the stairs to the apartment, with a backward glance at the small boy who so bravely was becoming a man.

There was a tremendous argument afterwards. Elias had controlled his temper in front of Andreas, not wanting to distress the boy further, but when Andreas left, Elias erupted. With Melina beyond earshot upstairs, he gave vent to his temper. "So you won't countenance violence," he sneered. "How will you stop it? By talking to some girl from the Red Cross? Men like Petros are beaten half to death, Anna is raped, and all you do is write it down? It's not enough. By Christ, it's nowhere near enough . . ."

Nothing could placate Elias. Anna was his friend. So was Petros. He had known them all his life. He stormed out of the taverna. "Some men do more than write letters," he snarled, "and I know where to find them." Constantin rushed after him, catching him in the street, trying to persuade him to return to the taverna, but Elias shrugged free and hurried away.

The following days tested Constantin's nerves to the limit. Petros had vanished from the face of the earth. The police were admitting nothing, and when Kirsten Moutier, the Red Cross delegate, returned to the taverna two days later, she brought with her no comfort. The Junta had told the ICRC to mind their own business. "We'll keep trying," she promised. "But at present there's not much we can do." Constantin and Melina listened to a catalogue of explanations. The ICRC were permitted to visit only *political* prisoners; men interned because their political beliefs did not coincide with those held by the Colonels. The ICRC had no access to other prisoners—criminals or men held pending trial. "If Petros was charged and convicted of a *political* offense we could reach him, otherwise . . ." her unfinished sentence expressed the hopelessness of the situation.

Afterwards, Melina said, "She is trying to help. She has taken a doctor to see Anna, she has given Anna some money, she *cares,* Constantin. It shows on her face—"

"We all *care,*" Constantin interrupted angrily. "The question is what can we do?"

He wondered what Elias would do. Elias had not been near the taverna since the argument. Constantin began to worry that the boy would not come for his Saturday morning tutorial and they would not have a chance to repair the friendship. Meanwhile, to make matters worse, everyone was talking about Petros and Anna. A delegation of Petros' friends went to the police station to enquire. "Petros who?" the police sneered. Defeated, the men came to the taverna to complain to Constantin, "We must do *something.* We don't know if he's dead or alive."

"We can do nothing," Constantin said. Inwardly he seethed. He was as angry as any man there, but he chose his words carefully. Piraeus was like a tinder box. The air crackled with tension when troops passed on the street. One inflammatory word could stir a mob to frenzy. Against armed troops protest would lead to a massacre—and Constantin knew it. So he took refuge behind pious hopes and mealy-mouthed platitudes. "Only bad news travels fast," he said. "No news about Petros might be good news disguised."

Such words brought little comfort to Anna. Poor Anna had further reason to grieve. When Melina visited the girl, Anna broke down and wept. The inevitable had happened: she had not started her period. The thought of conceiving a rapist's child was too much to endure. Wringing her hands, she sobbed uncontrollably.

"It broke my heart," Melina told Constantin later. "She even talked of doing away with herself."

Constantin ground his teeth in helpless frustration.

By Saturday morning the strain was showing. Another sleepless night had left him raw-eyed. Taking his law books from the shelf he set them out on the table, going through the motions, while all the time wondering if Elias would come for his tutorial.

"Elias is late," said Melina on her way down to the kitchen.

Elias *was* late. Normally he was there by eight o'clock. Constantin fidgeted and waited. Nine o'clock came, and then ten. He tried to concentrate but every sound from the street was a distraction. Pushing his books aside, he went to the open window to gaze down at the sun-drenched pavement below. Then, to his huge relief, he saw Elias. The boy was hurrying up from the corner, clearly agitated. Seeing Constantin at the window, he waved and broke into a trot. Returning the wave, Constantin wondered about the cause of the excitement. Next moment Elias ran into the taverna below. Constantin turned from the window, hearing the boy's feet on the stairs. When the door opened, Elias almost threw himself over the threshold.

"Steady on—"

"Andreas saw two of them," Elias gasped, catching his breath. "Two of the soldiers who raped Anna. We've got them—"

"Got them?"

"We know who they are, where they are! They're in the Averoff barracks. Don't you see? We can bring them to trial."

Constantin sucked in a deep breath. A trial was out of the question. The police would not issue a warrant. It was nonsense to talk of a trial. "You know better than that," he said, gruff-voiced as he led Elias to a chair.

The boy was too agitated to sit down. "We'll put them on trial. We'll convene our own court—"

"We?" Constantin echoed in amazement. "What do you mean—"

"My friends and—"

"Nonsense—"

"We'll need your help. Constantin, please, you can't let us down."

Constantin walked to the other side of the table. "What madness is this?"

"Is it madness to want justice? Is it—"

"These friends of yours," Constantin interrupted, "they must be mad—"

"No, listen. We've worked it all out . . ."

Constantin could scarcely believe what he was hearing. Elias talked of arresting the men and conducting a trial. "In *our* court. The People's Court—"

"You damn fool. You really imagine you can arrest armed soldiers—"

"We have weapons of our own."

Constantin's big hands closed into fists. A mad scenario whirled in his head. He pictured Elias on the street in a pool of blood, Melina running to the inert figure, kneeling next to the body, cradling the boy's head in her arms . . .

Elias continued to plead. "Please, Constantin, we need your help. We want you to preside at the trial."

That was too much. Constantin went red in the face. "I can't believe what I'm hearing. You don't know what you are saying—"

"Why not? You do it downstairs. You act the Judge often enough—"

"For God's sake! These people come to me as their friend. I arbitrate. They're friends themselves most of the time. It's one thing to resolve some trifling squabble, it's another to start handing down judgments."

Elias was white with defiance. "It amounts to the same thing—"

Constantin struggled to demonstrate the absurdity, to illustrate the sheer stupidity of the idea. "Suppose I do as you ask? Suppose I act as a Judge? If these men are guilty, I'll give them twenty years. What happens then? Do you march them off to the nearest prison—"

"We execute them."

"Kill them?" Constantin blanched. "Murder them—"

"It's martial law—"

"It's no bloody law. It's anarchy—"

"We live in anarchy."

"Dear God!" Constantin buried his face in his hands. He tried another argument. "What happens if I find them not guilty? What happens then? I set them free and they're back an hour later with a truck full of troops—"

"They *are* guilty. One of them was boasting about Anna, what a good fuck she was . . ." Elias colored. "Andreas heard them. The poor kid was terrified, he *is* terrified, he says they talked about going back to the house . . ."

But Constantin had ceased to listen, terrified, terrified that this madness would lead Elias to his death. Fear sparked his temper; the next moment they sounded like mortal enemies as pent-up frustrations burst forth on both sides.

"You're all talk," Elias shouted, white-faced and tearful. "You talk as if the law still existed. It's vanished. Can't you get that into your thick head—"

"Justice will survive—"

"Like hell! Every judge worthy of the name has been sacked. Half of them rot in prison—"

"Your way won't help—"

"And your way will?" Elias sneered. "Running to the Red Cross? Don't make me laugh. There's not a decent lawyer left. Those who aren't in some stinking cell have either fled or daren't practice. Look at you, for God's sake! The great Constantin Peponis! You can't even earn your own living. My sister keeps you—"

Constantin's face darkened with fury. On his feet, he gripped the back of the chair to stop himself from striking the boy. His voice came strangulated from his throat, "Get out! Get out!"

But as Elias moved towards the door, it burst open and Melina rushed in, breathless from running up stairs. "What's going on? I heard shouting—"

"Ask him!" shouted Elias, pushing past her and out to the landing. "Ask that famous husband of yours."

"Elias!" She reached out her hand, but he broke free and ran down the stairs.

Melina turned to Constantin. She never thought to see him and Elias quarrel so bitterly. A few days before the sight of them with young Andreas had brought a lump to her throat. They were so gentle. They were the greatest of friends. For them to argue in this way was unthinkable.

"Why have you quarreled? What did he say?"

"Too much!" Constantin slumped into his chair. "That's his trouble. His mouth runs away with him."

Melina turned and hurried downstairs. Grabbing a shawl from the kitchen, she walked the mile to her father's house and confronted Elias. "What happened between you?"

Her brother shrugged. Tense and white-faced, he refused to discuss the matter.

Melina's father, frail and ailing, questioned the boy. Biting his lip, Elias remained obdurately silent.

Melina's mother begged the boy to explain. No explanation was forthcoming.

Over the next few days, Melina's aunts and uncles, cousins and friends, joined forces in a quest for the truth. Their questions yielded no answers. Neither Constantin nor Elias would reveal what had passed between them.

"As if I haven't enough to worry about," cried Melina, throwing her hands in the air. Of late her smiles had become strained. The brutality inflicted on Petros and Anna had shaken her badly. The Junta was striking closer to home . . .

The only explanation from Constantin was that he and Elias had argued over "a matter of principle."

Melina went up like a sheet of flame. "And for this we all suffer? My whole family is divided. Elias is no longer welcome here. My father ignores him because he has offended you. My mother says you should set him a better example. And all this is for some legal quibble—"

"It's more than that—"

"So tell me!"

Constantin remained stubbornly silent. The wound had cut deep. Elias' sneering insult rang in his ears. But another reason made Constantin hold his tongue. Even to hint of the cause of the argument would make things worse for Elias; perhaps even endanger his life, for if Melina was told, and she told her parents and they told her friends, all of Piraeus would know that Elias was involved with subversives.

Meanwhile Elias gave the taverna a wide berth, remaining absent even on Saturday mornings.

Constantin faced each day as it came; outwardly phlegmatic, inwardly churning with worry. Every morning he expected to hear of a clash between soldiers and students; and every afternoon he sent Melina to her father's house to spy out the latest on Elias.

"Why should I go?" she complained. "You should go. See Elias. Put an end to this stupid quarrel."

Constantin refused with a shake of his head. But as the days slipped by and no soldiers came under attack, he began to hope that the danger had passed. He began to think Elias had come to his senses. That nothing would happen. . . .

Then tragedy struck. Most of the heated exchange with Elias was imprinted on Constantin's memory. He could recite some word for word. What was forgotten, indeed overlooked at the time, was Elias's warning about the soldiers—*Andreas heard them . . . he's terrified . . . he says they talked about going back to the house.*

Three weeks later, the soldiers *did* go back to the house.

Young Andreas had used the interval well. With Petros still absent, Andreas had assumed the role of head of the household. He attended to his responsibilities with great care. The broken front door had been replaced. Windows were shuttered and barred. At night the house was a veritable fortress. But in the sticky heat of the day, when a breath of air was as precious as gold, the Kappos house was like all others in Piraeus. Shutters were opened and doors left ajar, all to catch even a hint of a breeze.

The two soldiers had been drinking that Saturday lunchtime, and drinking led to boasting, especially to boasting about women; most especially of all to boasting about Anna. The desire grew to see her again, to *have* her again.

"Why not? Who's to stop us? There's only that kid and the old crone of a mother."

Wine and bravado got the better of them. Each egged the other on. "This time I'll screw her in comfort. I'll have her in her own bed."

The other soldier laughed, "It's five weeks since we took her old man. Her tongue will be hanging out for a good fuck."

They even obtained gifts; one purchased a bottle of wine at the bar, the other bought some flowers from a street vendor. It was a great lark. They couldn't look at each other without laughing. What a story it would make in the barracks.

Staggering slightly from the effects of drink, they reeled down Pythagoras Street and on past the harbor to climb the narrow road on which Anna had her home. Every door was ajar. An elderly woman sat outside one, darning old clothes. The soldiers flourished their gifts. "Look Mother, this is how good we are to our women."

The Kappos house stood at the top of the rise. The soldiers became wary as they approached. "We daren't have any screaming," said one. The other agreed. He touched his army knife in his belt. "Grab the old woman and put your blade to her throat. Keep her downstairs with the kid. I'll do the same for you . . ." he laughed. "When I finish enjoying myself."

His companion grinned. "You never know, the kid might be out."

But the kid was not out. Andreas was in the kitchen with his mother. Anna was upstairs, washing her hair as a favor to her mother-in-law. Weighed down by worry and grief, Anna had neglected her appearance for weeks. "To please me," the mother-in-law had begged. "Just wash your hair. You will feel better."

When the soldiers pushed open the door, Anna was halfway down the stairs, a towel in one hand, her glossy hair still damp. She wore only a loose robe which gaped as she descended, revealing bare legs up to the thigh. Distracted by the flowers which the man thrust towards her, her scream caught in her throat. In that split-second, the soldier mounted the bottom two stairs. Turning, Anna tried to retreat, but his hand caught her ankle, bringing her down with a thump.

Startled by the noise, Andreas emerged from the kitchen. His eyes widened in sheer disbelief. Blocking the passage was a soldier! The boy gasped. He had fortified the little house for a siege, but a siege by night, never by day. He opened his mouth to cry out, but too late; the soldier was onto him, driving him back into the kitchen as Anna's muffled cries came from the stairs. Behind Andreas, his mother was knocked backward, her eyes widening with horror.

"Sssh," the soldier hushed. "Keep quiet and no one gets hurt."

But his warning was wasted. Even as he went for his belt, Andreas scooped up a kitchen knife. He plunged it deep into the man's thigh. Blood spurted everywhere. Roaring with pain, the soldier grabbed for Andreas. Quick as a fish, the boy squirmed away. His mother swung a pot from the stove, aiming at the man's head, catching his shoulder. He lashed out with a huge backhand swipe, knocking her breathless against the wall. Screaming, Andreas hurled himself forward, just as the soldier's knife came free of his belt. The boy's own momentum carried him onto the blade. Piercing his throat, it went through his neck. A froth of pink blood vomited from his mouth. A gurgling scream choked up from his lungs. Knees crumpling, he began to slump to the floor, hands clawing at his throat. The embedded knife was torn from the soldier's grasp by the weight of the boy's falling body.

The mother screamed a terrible wail. Stunned by her fall, she crawled to her son.

Staggering into the table, the soldier clutched at his thigh. Blood oozed between his fingers. His drink-fuddled brain reacted first to pain, then to the carnage around him.

The boy writhed in a pool of blood which grew wider and wider.

Turning, the soldier hobbled out to the hall, shouting up the stairs with a voice hoarse with panic.

On the landing, Anna clawed the face above her. She bit deep into the hand held over her mouth. With failing strength, twisting and writhing, she denied her attacker. She sensed more than saw him open his trousers. Suddenly they heard the shouts from below. The man swore. Cursing violently, he turned his head, hearing terror in the voice of his companion.

Moments later, both men were in the kitchen. They kicked the sobbing woman away from her son. Andreas no longer moved in the blood now smeared over the floor.

"You fucking idiot!" screamed the soldier from the landing. Stooping, he pulled the knife from the boy's throat. It emerged with a sucking sound and a spurt of blood.

They ran from the house, the wounded man hobbling, his left leg soaked in blood. The other soldier was still buttoning his trousers.

Behind them, Anna pulled herself up from the floor. She moaned through bruised lips. In the kitchen below, the mother slithered in the blood of her son. She sobbed his name again and again. But there was no response.

Andreas Kappos was dead.

Anna's screams raised the alarm. Anna's screams and the awful wailing and keening of her mother-in-law. Neighbors converged on the Kappos house. Peponis was the first name to spring to people's lips. A boy was sent racing to fetch him, while others spread the news through the warren of streets.

Constantin ran all the way, heaving his big frame along in the heat, arriving gasping for breath. A knot of people fell back from the door to allow him admittance. He blanched at the sight of so much blood. He shuddered. His stomach heaved. The mother howled like an animal over her son. Anna sat on a stool, staring at the wall with unseeing eyes.

He took charge. He did what he could. He sent for the police, a doctor, an ambulance. He pulled Anna out of the kitchen, shaking her until her teeth rattled, making her blurt out the story. He spoke to an elderly woman who reported seeing the two soldiers running away. He found some neighbors who promised that Anna and her mother-in-law could move in with them. He did what he could until the police arrived. . . .

And all the time a terrible guilt grew in his mind. Gazing at the carnage he thought *I could have stopped it. This is my fault.* Elias's warning ran around and around in his head: *The poor kid is terrified—the soldiers talked of going back to the house.* He choked with remorse at the sight of Andreas's body. Poor, brave, dignified little Andreas, who had deserved better from life.

Overcome, he felt giddy and faint. He had to have air. Pushing his way down the passage he went out into the street. Outside he leaned on the wall, eyes closed, struggling against nausea. Emotions conflicted within him—guilt, disgust, hopelessness, anger. And when he opened his eyes tears distorted his vision.

By now the police had been on the scene for half an hour. An ambulance stood at the door; a police car next to it, and beyond that two motorcycles. Inside the house, a doctor had pronounced death. A priest was trying to comfort the boy's mother. Outside, the policemen were holding neighbors back from the doorway . . .

Constantin's misery knew no bounds. He felt wretched and useless. Above all, he felt guilty. Responsible. In shock and confusion his brain failed to function. He tried to concentrate, to think of how to help . . . he told himself to do *something.*

Stretcher bearers appeared in the doorway. The boy's body was borne from the house, drawing murmurs of horror and sympathy from the onlookers. Women crossed themselves. An old man removed his hat. A respectful silence fell as the corpse was transferred to the ambulance.

A moment later the Police Captain emerged from the house. He paused in the doorway.

Constantin pulled himself together. He made his brain function. Stepping forward, he asked, "Is there anything I can do?"

Cool and unfriendly, the Captain's lips twitched. "Yes," he said, "try not to teach us our business. Go back to your taverna, *lawyer* Peponis. You'll have customers waiting."

Constantin flushed at the insult. "Have you ordered a search for the soldiers? They can't have got far. One was wounded—"

"What soldiers? This squalid little domestic tragedy had nothing to do with soldiers."

Constantin was so bewildered that he began to stutter. "What . . . what do you mean? Domestic tragedy. I don't understand . . . didn't Anna tell you—"

"She heard them quarreling. She fell down the stairs in her rush to get to the kitchen." The Captain shrugged. "Too late, I'm afraid, the boy was killed before—"

"She was being raped!"

"Rubbish. The doctor examined her. There were no soldiers. This was a family quarrel which got out of hand."

"No!" Constantin shouted. Disbelief and outrage welled up inside him. "That's not true." He swung around, seeking the elderly woman among the onlookers.

The old woman had gone.

"We have the weapon," said the Captain, "a kitchen knife covered in blood—"

"No!" Shaking his head, stamping a foot, Constantin lost control. "I can't believe this. I *refuse* to believe this. Two soldiers came to this house—"

"Peponis!" the Captain said sharply. Stepping forward, he thrust a finger into Constantin's face. "I warn you. Don't start trouble. One more false accusation and I will arrest you. One more word."

Constantin wanted to smash the man's face; to pick him up and throw him to the ground. He wanted to jump on his body. Shaking with rage, he fought for control. A red haze marred his vision. A vein throbbed in his neck. Angry black blotches showed beneath his eyes. Clenching his hands into fists, he might have failed to restrain himself had a small woman not darted forward.

It was Melina's mother. Gripping Constantin's arm, she clung like a leech. "Melina needs you. *Please,* Constantin, Melina needs you at once."

He wrenched his gaze away from the policeman.

"Please, Constantin. Melina *needs* you."

She might have been a stranger from the baffled look in his eyes. But suddenly, over her shoulder, he recognized someone who was far from a stranger. Elias was running up the hill. Even in his fury, Constantin sensed danger. Elias would go beserk. Elias would explode with uncontrollable temper . . .

Breaking away, Constantin began to hurry down the hill.

Behind him, sobbing piteously, Andreas' mother was led out from the house. Small voices of protest rose as she was ushered into the police car. The voices faded and died as policemen moved among the onlookers, taking names.

Constantin hurried on down the hill. The murderous look on Elias' face was visible from ten yards away. As the gap narrowed, he veered to one side. "Get away from me," he shouted.

Thrusting out his hand, Constantin caught his shoulder. "Wait!"

Intent on shaking himself free, Elias missed the next muttered words. Then he realized what Constantin had said. He stared into the big man's face. "What did you say?"

"You heard. Find me a gun."

The two soldiers were crossing the road when it happened. One still walked with a slight limp and the other's face bore scratch marks which had turned into scabs. They both counted themselves lucky. A limp and a scratched face were small prices to pay for what that day might have cost. Quick thinking had saved them; quick thinking and the ability to lie through their teeth, helped by a Police Captain who had no wish to antagonize the Army.

The death of Andreas Kappos counted little with them. Intent on saving their own skins, they had invented a tale on their way back to barracks. Breathless and distressed, they went straight to the guard room. "We were playing cards in a bar. The game got out of hand and turned into a brawl."

The Guard Commander had believed them. After all, few of his men laid themselves open to be punished. Gambling with civilians was strictly forbidden. So they were punished, but fourteen days confinement to barracks for a petty crime of which they were innocent, was much preferred to being charged for a major crime of which they were guilty.

It was mid-afternoon. After being cooped up for fourteen days, they sniffed the air appreciatively. As usual their talk turned to girls—where to find them, how to pick them up, what they might cost. They eyed the women they passed, mentally stripping them, calling lewd invitations. Not once did they glance over their shoulders, or look at the traffic which trundled along in the afternoon sun.

Few people would have looked twice at the old Fiat van. Nothing about it caught the eye. Once upon a time it had been gray; it still was in places, but the nearside wing had made contact with blue paint and various scratches had been daubed with rust colored primer. No insignia marked its sides to denote a proud owner. It looked in a poor state of repair, like many of the vehicles on the highways and byways of Greece.

At that time of day, traffic in Piraeus is moderately light. Congestion occurs in the morning and sometimes at night, but rarely in mid-afternoon. With room on the road, traffic moved freely enough for the soldiers to take care as they stepped from the curb. A truck lumbered past. Then came the gray Fiat van. Concentrating on the gap in its wake, neither soldier noticed the driver was masked. Instead, when it had passed, they stepped into the road, their gaze fixed on the next oncoming car. Suddenly the Fiat's back doors burst open. Inside, prone on his stomach lay a masked man with a gun. His first shot caught one soldier in the back of the head, scattering hair and bone in every direction. The second shot missed. So did the third. Down the road the oncoming car skidded and mounted the pavement. The other soldier looked with horror at his fallen companion. Then a bullet grazed his temple. He staggered, clutching his head, before a fifth bullet tore into his chest to send him spinning into the gutter.

The Fiat engine screamed. Leaping forward in low gear, the van scraped past the truck to speed on to the next turning. By now one door was shut; a figure could be seen closing the other—a big man, balancing precariously on his knees, wearing an ill-fitting black hood—gripping the swinging door with one hand.

Behind in the road, one soldier lay dead and the other was dying.

As the van cornered, Constantin lost his balance. Sprawling, he slid from one side of the van to the other. The door sprang from his grip. The mask slipped, marring his vision. As the van cornered again, the swinging door smashed back. He caught the handle. Slamming the door shut with one hand, he tore at the black mask with the other. "Your mask!"

The warning was needless. Behind the wheel, Elias had already discarded his hood and tossed it aside. "Did you get them?" he shouted, swinging the van into another back street.

"Yes," Constantin sucked his skinned knuckles. "Slow down."

Again the instruction was needless. Elias was already reducing speed. From far away came the wail of police sirens.

"Both of them?" Elias persisted.

Constantin was trying to wrap an Afghan rug around the rifle. Working on his knees was awkward; twice he bumped his head on the side of the van.

"Did you get them both?" Elias repeated.

Constantin grunted "Yes." Taking string from his pocket, he fastened the rug with a series of loops, drawing them tight. Sweat ran down his face. His hands, steady before, began to tremble.

Elias drove carefully, checking his wing mirrors.

Ten minutes later the van drew up outside a modest house in a suburb of Athens. Alighting from the passenger side, Constantin went to the rear of the van and opened a door. Withdrawing the rug, he hoisted it on to one shoulder. Then he slammed the door and banged goodbye on the roof. His movements seemed casual, yet he reached the front door surprisingly quickly. He took a key from his pocket. Opening the door, he crossed the threshold, while behind him the van moved off and was soon out of sight.

He had grown up in this house. It was the family home which he had given to Uncle Mikis. He knew every inch of it. Shafts of sunlight squeezed through cracks in the shutters to paint tramlines on the tiled floor. The living room was musty and damp. Dust lay thick on every ledge, for the house had been unoccupied since Uncle Mikis had fled to the hills with Theo and Demetrios.

Dropping the rug, Constantin flopped into a chair. His hands had stopped shaking. Killing had been surprisingly easy; easier than he had imagined, but then it had been totally unimaginable only a few weeks before. Was that how it was with killers? Did they agonize more over the thought than the act? The act was simple, the decision was hard. It triggered so many others. It led to a new life. There would be no going back. If he survived, if he lived to see freedom restored, he would never again practice law. He would feel unworthy, like an unfrocked priest . . .

Slumped in the chair, collecting himself, he was surprised at how little it mattered. The law had been everything once. But there was no law in the jungle. The weak went to the wall. Animals killed to protect their young. Constantin had killed for the same reasons, to protect Elias, to keep him from joining the hotheads. Elias would have got himself killed in a week, or worse, got himself captured and tortured. Which would have brought Demetrios and Theo down from the hills, thirsting for vengeance. The whole family would have been imperiled. With Elias in line, Melina was safe . . . the family was safe . . .

Not since the days of the Gestapo was there such a manhunt. Soldiers and police went from street to street and house to house. Thousands of people were questioned. Informers were promised a bonus. "We'll make you rich if you find out who did this." The military presence in Piraeus grew to overwhelming proportions.

For a few weeks, Constantin believed he would escape suspicion. His main worry was Elias. He lectured the boy constantly.

"One careless word," he said, wagging a finger, "that's all it will take. There are spies everywhere."

"I know."

"Stay in line at the Law School. No protests, no arguments with the professors, no disputes, no nothing."

"Okay."

"And stay away from the hotheads."

Elias nodded agreement. The truth was the scale of the manhunt terrified him. Having seen the Junta's brutality, he feared it first hand. He was determined to keep a still tongue. It was enough to have extracted vengeance for Andreas; the next step in the battle could wait.

Constantin considered his options. He would have liked to send the boy to join his brothers and Uncle Mikis, but that would lead to questions at the Law School; neighbors would wonder, and the family would ask questions. For the time being, it was best to sit tight.

At least Melina was happy. Ignorant of their role in the killings, she was delighted with the reconciliation. Seeing them together again warmed Melina's heart. She breathed a sigh of relief. God keep us all safe, she prayed, let us survive.

Who had killed the soldiers remained a mystery. To begin with, nobody connected the slayings with the death of Andreas. But when photographs of the dead men appeared in the newspapers, Anna and her elderly neighbor recognized them. Soon, like a leaf on the wind, the word spread far and wide. Speculation mounted. Grim smiles of satisfaction appeared on people's lips; although Andreas was gone forever, *someone* had struck back.

Compared to the excitement generated by the escape of the Averoff Nine, the celebrations were muted. The great escape had been a total victory. Killing the two soldiers was not seen in the same light, but their deaths counted as a kind of rough justice.

Constantin poured scorn on the idea. "Rubbish. What can the killings have to do with Andreas? Men like that would have had enemies by the dozen."

But despite his efforts to lay a false scent, the speculation continued. Police spies carried the theory to their masters and, lacking other clues, the ESA began to take an interest. So did other people. One night the Roufus brothers came into the taverna.

Melina was alarmed. In the kitchen she whispered, "They've never used this place before. What can they want?"

Apparently nothing. The Roufus brothers ordered a simple meal and afterwards went on their way without a word of recognition. They might have been strangers, setting foot in the place for the first time.

But the next night the man called Spyros stopped by for a drink.

And the evening after brought another visitor to the taverna—this time the man who had carried the shotgun.

None of them stayed long. They treated Constantin as a stranger . . . and yet . . . they *knew*. It was in their eyes. Warning looks. Looks which said as clearly as words—"You're one of us now. Be careful. We are here if you want us."

Constantin needed his strong nerves. He wondered how they had pieced the clues together. And he asked himself: If the Roufus brothers had worked it out, would the ESA be far behind? The ESA *knew* he had brought the Red Cross to the taverna to meet Anna. The ESA *knew* Constantin had rushed to Anna's house when Andreas was killed . . .

Fate seemed to be working against him. The Red Cross delegate, Kirsten Moutier, had taken to making regular visits to see Anna, and since Anna now lived with neighbors instead of alone in her house, it had become more convenient for them to meet at the taverna.

Melina approved of the visits. "Anna needs all the help we can give her." A friendship developed among the three women, surprising in some ways, yet less so in others. Melina, Anna and Kirsten Moutier were of a similar age. All three were attractive, yet not one gave much thought to her looks. And each had a sympathy for the other's predicament. "It's not easy for the Kyrenia Kirsten," Melina told Constantin one night. "She tries not to take sides, but it's becoming a strain. It shows in her face. She'll get into trouble if she's not careful. Her heart is with us."

"We need more than hearts," Constantin said gruffly. He almost confessed everything. It was on the tip of his tongue. He wanted to tell her. Perhaps she would go away to Uncle Mikis, take Elias; hide out until the danger was past. But the thought of confessing murder defeated him. He could picture the pain in her eyes. Her image of him would be shattered. He just couldn't do it . . .

So he remained silent and stayed where he was, hoping against hope.

But even as Constantin hoped, the ESA was on the verge of a breakthrough. In all logic, a breakthrough was inevitable. Too much was at stake. Soldiers kept the Junta in power. If soldiers were shot in broad daylight, people might nurture thoughts of open rebellion. The Colonels had decreed: "*Find the murderer.*"

One man led the manhunt. Major Zagora. Torturer-in-Chief. They told jokes about Zagora. An archeologist finds a statue and is baffled—"What period are you from," he cries in exasperation. And the archeologist's assistant says, "Professor, take it to Zagora. He'll make it talk." And so Zagora's reputation grew, as the torturer who could make even statues talk.

His men had found the stolen Fiat van within days. It had been abandoned on the outskirts of Athens. Wiped clean of fingerprints, the van yielded no clues, but its very location meant it had been driven through Athens—driven *from* Piraeus to Athens.

"Search every possible route," Zagora ordered. "Question every household. Someone must have seen it."

And somebody had. An old man who had intended to remain silent, who *would* have remained silent, but who became muddled and frightened by so many questions. Something in his manner, fear in his eyes, gave him away.

"He knows something," the Captain told his soldiers. "Take him back to the Major."

One old man who had known Constantin as a boy. One old man who had wondered why Constantin should return to the family home with an Afghan rug on his shoulder. . . .

They came at three in the morning. Roused from a fitful sleep, Constantin heard the clatter of boots as the troops leapt from their trucks. He was out of bed before the first crash at the door, into his trousers as the hammering started. There could be no escape, he knew that as he stepped into his shoes. . . .

"Constantin!" Melina screamed from the bed.

He swung around. "Stay here until they've gone—"

"But—"

"Do as I say!" Snatching the key from the lock, he ran out to the landing, slamming the door behind him. Locking it, he wondered what to do with the key. Dropping to his knees, he was about to push it under the door when he stopped. Melina would come after him. She was already beating on the other side of the door. "Constantin—"

"No! Stay there. Elias will come for you." Thrusting the key into his pocket, Constantin ran down the stairs, shouting above the sounds at the street door. "Coming, I'm coming!" For a split second he considered the balcony. Should he leap over, down into the alley? Draw them off? Away from Melina. But unless they saw him they would rush upstairs. . . .

"Coming, I'm coming," he shouted, running to the door which was splintering under the onslaught.

"Coming," he screamed as drew back the bolt. "Coming."

The door burst open with the force of an explosion. Soldiers charged in, sending him backwards. Desperation kept him upright. He threw himself at them, knocking them sideways. Bulk and strength carried him forward. He plunged over the threshold into the street. His one idea was to reach the corner, ***around*** the corner to draw them away from Melina. Twenty meters. Running the gauntlet. A sea of uniforms engulfed him. Blows came from every angle, hands dragged him back, boots kicked and tripped, rifle butts swung viciously. Ten meters. He was blinded by blood, swallowing blood, spitting blood. His knees began to buckle. He felt himself falling. He was down, crawling through a hail of kicks, being beaten by truncheons and rifles . . . crawling, sprawling, reaching the corner, rolling . . .

He collapsed face down in the gutter. The soldiers towered over him, pulling each other aside, each wanting to deliver a kick of his own. Clutching himself, Constantin curled into a ball.

Boots smashed into his head and his body. The coppery taste of blood filled his mouth . . .

"Enough!" A voice rang out, full of authority, rising above the grunts and panted exertions. "That's enough!"

Dragged to the wall, Constantin was propped upright. He opened his eyes. Dazzled by headlights, blinded by blood, he struggled to focus, seeing double, triple—a blurred collage of uniforms and faces merging one into the other. His vision cleared as the uniforms parted. A pair of highly polished boots approached. He raised his head, but the face above was too far away. Obligingly the man squatted in front of him. Constantin saw a pockmarked face beneath a military cap. The man's face had been disfigured by smallpox or some other infection. He had black, staring eyes . . . cold eyes . . . the eyes of a snake. He was smoking a cigarette. His thin lips extended into a satisfied smirk. He blew smoke into Constantin's face.

"So? At last. The ringleader."

Painfully, Constantin shifted his position.

Suddenly the man began to shout. "Where are the others? Who are they? Give me their names?" He drew back his left hand and struck Constantin viciously across the face. "Talk, murderer, talk, or I'll tear you to pieces." He struck again and again, shouting all the time, "Talk, talk, talk."

The heavy blows knocked Constantin's head from side to side. His ears began to bleed. Suddenly he felt an unbearable burning. A stab of pain seared through his body. The cigarette was being ground into his neck. The man was twisting it round and round. Constantin bit his tongue to stop screaming. He knocked the man's hand away, but the cigarette stuck to his flesh. . . .

They dragged him feet first across the road, bouncing his head on the stones. For a moment he blacked out. When he came around he was in the back of a large limousine, arms pinioned by men either side. His hands were handcuffed behind him. The pockfaced man was on a jump seat opposite. "You'll talk," he sneered, kicking Constantin's shins. "Do you know who I am?" he shouted. Leaning forward, he slapped Constantin's face. "Do you? Do you? Do you?"

The car was moving. Racked with pain, Constantin glimpsed the tail lights of a truck in front, a truck with soldiers aboard.

"Do you?"

One thought gave Constantin hope. They had left the taverna. Word would reach Elias. . . .

"Do you?" screamed the man, hitting Constantin in the face.

In his mind, Constantin saw Melina with Elias. *Go! Run! Uncle Mikis will hide you.* He gathered his courage. Thrusting aside fear and pain, he harnessed his willpower, his pride. *This man will not break me . . . nothing will break me . . . even if I die, Melina will live . . .*

"Tell me my name!" roared the man.

Melina will escape. Melina will live . . .

"Tell me my name!"

Constantin spat, but his mouth was too dry. Blood-speckled spittle fell short of the man's face.

The ugly, pockmarked features twisted into a mirthless smile. The black eyes glittered. "So? You dare spit upon Major Zagora. You will be sorry. You will sing my name before this day is out. Not long now, Peponis, not long now . . ."

But Constantin had ceased to listen. He had retreated into his mind, husbanding his strength. *Say nothing. Tell them nothing. Remain silent . . .*

Dawn was streaking the pale sky as they joined the thin traffic on the outskirts of Athens. The automobile stopped at an intersection, next to a lorry laden for market. The lorry driver looked down, his casual expression stiffening as he saw inside the limousine. His eyes met Constantin's. Constantin wanted to cry out. "Help me! Help set me free!" Instead he remained mute as he saw the man's eyes light with fear.

The limousine sped onward, past the Olympic Stadium and the Hilton Hotel. The best section of Athens: tree-lined green avenues, little white villas, exclusive apartments. Constantin himself had once lived here. He guessed where they were going. He knew the district well, with its consulates and embassies, its well-tended gardens and well-polished brass. Every second house had a cook and a butler. Were they blind, the people who now lived here? Did they not *see* what was happening? Were they deaf?

Did they not *hear* the screams? Or did they shut their eyes and cover their ears? Reaching the American embassy, the limousine turned right. Beyond the acacias he saw what he was dreading: the Special Investigation Center. Headquarters of the ESA. The torture center.

Sentries snapped to attention as the car swept into the courtyard. Soldiers encircled the vehicle, submachine guns at the ready. Zagora sat forward on the jump seat, drooling his satisfaction. "Welcome to my home, Peponis."

They pushed him from the car, knocking him to the ground before hoisting him back onto his feet and frogmarching him up the steps. Zagora followed, laughing at Constantin's efforts to remain upright. "Dance, lawyer, dance!"

In a small office, soldiers pushed him into a chair. Zagora issued jeering orders. "This man is a famous lawyer. We must do it by the book. Let's have the doctor."

And in came a doctor, or at least a man wearing a white coat. He shammed surprise at Constantin's injuries. "Who did this?" he asked, examining the cigarette burn. "Did someone mistake you for an ashtray?"

Soldiers sniggered and Zagora grinned gleefully in the background.

"Does this hurt?" asked the doctor, probing at a bruise on Constantin's temple. "Does it hurt here? Or here. . . ."

Constantin remained mute. *Say nothing . . . tell them nothing . . . remain silent.* He winced as his face was sponged with cold water. Zagora shouted, "That's right. Clean him up. The newspapers want a good picture."

Constantin blinked as a light flashed in his eyes, realizing too late that the doctor had moved aside. A man with a camera had stepped forward. The light flashed again, then it was gone.

Zagora showed his impatience. "Well, Doctor. Is he fit to face questions?"

The doctor hesitated, and Constantin's hopes rose.

The doctor shook his head, seemingly doubtful. "I'm not sure. He doesn't answer me—"

"He's playing dumb!" Zagora shouted.

"Perhaps, but I'd like to examine him further—"

"We will examine him. Thank you, doctor. That will be all." Zagora pushed the doctor unceremoniously to the door.

Constantin watched in dismay. He wanted to go too. He wanted to clutch the doctor's sleeve. *Take me with you. Find an excuse. Take me away!*

Too late, the man had gone. The door slammed behind him. Pulled to his feet, Constantin was turned sideways, seeing for the first time a door to his left. He was pushed into a room, larger than the office, twice the size, with a table and chairs beneath the barred window. Against the far wall was an iron cot flanked by two men. Big men, as big as Constantin, with chevrons on their sleeves and wooden clubs in their fists. They leapt forward, grabbing his shoulders and turning him around. They threw him backwards onto the cot. Broken springs tore into his shoulders. The cot lacked a mattress. Steel prongs cut his lacerated flesh like barbed wire. He gagged on a scream as they held him down. Fear and panic welled up within him. Suddenly, above his rasping breath, he heard a shout, "Wait a minute! Goddamn it, will you hold that man still!"

Constantin gasped with relief. Twisting awkwardly, he used his manacled hands behind his back to raise himself slightly from the broken springs. Looking towards the door, he expected to see Zagora. Instead he saw a tall man in a gray suit, followed by a squat, fleshy-faced man dressed in the same fashion. Carrying clipboards and files; they looked like a couple of clerks. The fleshy-faced man shut the door before following his companion to the table.

"Let him sit up," said the tall man, pulling a chair out from the table.

Constantin raised himself painfully. His neck throbbed from the cigarette burn. Slowly he swung his legs to the floor and gingerly eased himself onto the edge of the cot.

The tall man announced, "I am Inspector Zakras of the anti-Communist section of the Central Police Bureau."

"And I am Inspector Sefaris of the same section," said the fleshy-faced man.

"And you," said Zakras, "are a dangerous criminal."

"An enemy of the State," said Sefaris.

"A traitor." Zakras nodded.

"A terrorist."

"A killer."

"Whom we have been watching for ages."

"More than three years."

"Nearly five years."

Their voices were surprisingly similar—lacking expression, monotone, matter-of-fact. Voices of officialdom. They spoke in sequence but without interrupting each other. Like actors reading lines. Bored actors who knew the script by heart. Actors who cared nothing for their audience. Why should they care? The audience could not leave. The audience had no choice but to stay and listen.

"We know a good deal about you," said Zakras.

"We know about the soldiers."

"That you murdered them."

"Shot them down in cold blood."

"We know that others were involved."

"You had at least one accomplice."

Constantin braced himself, fearing to hear the name Elias. *Dear God, not that. Please God, don't let them know that. Let Elias escape with Melina. . . .*

"But that's only the tip of the iceberg," said Zakras.

"Scarcely significant," Sefaris nodded.

"You are guilty of much greater crimes."

Constantin tried to imagine a crime greater than murder. What crime outweighed the killing of two human beings?

"For instance," Sefaris continued, "we know you run a Communist network."

"The most important in Greece."

"Easily the biggest."

"The most powerful."

"We know you send reports to Moscow."

Constantin wanted to laugh. Him a communist? Reports to Moscow? It was absurd. A joke, a sick joke. A stupid joke. Except these men were not joking. They looked incapable of joking. They lacked the facility for laughter; they were in deadly earnest. Suddenly Constantin forgot his physical pain. Instincts developed in a hundred courtroom battles took over. What were they saying? Why were they making such claims? Then it came to him.

His lawyer's mind grasped what lay in store. He saw into the minds of his enemies. Twisted minds. Evil minds. He felt shock, then fear. Of course. Where was the glory for Zagora in bringing Constantin Peponis to trial? With what would they charge him? The killing of two soldiers who had raped poor Anna and murdered a young boy. In the hearts and minds of the people, justice would have been served better by Constantin Peponis than the men who brought him to trial. That would never do. That would not serve the interests of the Junta. So other crimes would have to be invented. And what better than to portray the man in the dock as the engineer of a communist plot . . . to show him as an enemy of the people . . . a traitor in the pay of a foreign power. Much better for Zagora. Much, much better. Major Zagora would no doubt become Colonel Zagora, promoted by a grateful Junta for defending the freedom of Greece.

Zakras and Sefaris droned on relentlessly, talking of Communist cells and clandestine meetings with Albanians and Czechs. "All of which we know about," said Sefaris.

"We have written it down," said Zakras, "as a true and factual account."

"Which you will sign as a confession."

There would be no witnesses. No proper evidence. The mythical Albanians and Czechs, of course, had returned to their countries. Their embassies would deny all knowledge. . . .

The sergeant to Constantin's right began to pace up and down. Holding a truncheon in his right hand, he smacked it into the palm of his left, his small piggish eyes watching Constantin with undisguised anticipation.

Even then Zakras and Sefaris had not finished. The case they were building was monumental. The trial of Constantin Peponis was destined to be the biggest show trial of the Junta's regime. Seconds later, Sefaris was unveiling another strand.

"And of course," he said, "we know about the Averoff Nine."

"We know you organized the escape."

"With the help of a member of the police force."

"And someone from here."

"Someone employed within ESA headquarters."

"Another traitor who conspired with you."

"Fellow terrorists who plot against Greece."

Names ran amok in Constantin's mind. Names he wished he had never heard. Men he wished he had never met. Not because he despised them. On the contrary. But he feared he might betray them. The Roufus brothers. The man called Spyros. Inspector Ritsos. And the one he knew simply as the doctor.

"All of which you will tell us about," said Zakras.

"Oh yes," Sefaris nodded agreement. "You will tell us everything."

"The names of your fellow conspirators."

"All of whom are dedicated communists."

"Oh yes." It was Zakras' turn to agree. "Communists to the last man."

"And we will write it all down."

"Your confession."

"Which you will sign."

"Then we shall put you on trial."

Constantin remembered past trials staged by the Junta. He remembered thirty men in court with General Iordanidis. Lawyers among them. Friends. Found guilty of subversive activities. Portrayed as enemies of the state. Men like Professor Vouros and Doctor Stavrou. Mild-mannered men, found guilty of possessing explosives. The nearest Stavrou ever came to causing an explosion was to strike a match for his pipe. Yet all had confessed. At the trial, all had claimed that they had confessed under torture . . . but such claims were dismissed.

"We have standard procedures," said Zakras.

"A long list of questions."

"Which you will answer."

"But you must answer correctly."

"That's very important," Zakras nodded gravely. "Wrong answers waste our time."

"And we get very angry."

"So you must answer correctly."

"Not to answer counts as a wrong answer."

"Which wastes our time even more."

"And makes us angrier still."

The duet had turned into a game. A spiteful, sadistic game, interrupted at that moment by the door opening. Zagora entered, followed by another sergeant, as tall and as broad as his colleagues, both of whom now paced up and down, swishing their clubs like athletes limbering up.

"Well?" Zagora looked at Zakras. "Have you read him the charges?"

Zakras shrugged as he rose to his feet. "There are so many. We gave him thc outline."

"And has he confessed?"

"Not uttered a word," said Sefaris, picking up his clipboard and making for the door.

Eyes gleaming, Zagora turned towards the cot. "Oh, that will change," he said with a satisfied look at Constantin. "Give us a few hours and he will answer all of your questions."

Constantin rose awkwardly to his feet. His hands fastened behind his back made him feel like a cripple. Defenseless. Vulnerable. He knew all about Zagora. The tales of brutality were endless; as many stories were told of Zagora as of ESA headquarters itself, with its special interrogation rooms where motors were turned on to drown the sound of the screams. Is that where they would take him? To the interrogation rooms? The torture chambers. He tasted fear in his mouth. And desperation. *God give me strength.*

"I'm off for a decent breakfast," Sefaris said casually from the door. "What time do you want us back here?"

Zagora half-turned. "Give us a few hours," he replied over his shoulder. "Come back at noon."

Beyond him, across the room, the door stood open. The door was big and made of steel, painted battleship gray, scratched and scuffed at the edges. Zakras had already passed through into the outer office. Sefaris stood on the threshold, looking at Zagora. Zagora was returning the look, his back to Constantin. For a split-second Constantin had ceased to be the object of attention. In that moment, he made his decision. Protest was out of the question. All that was possible was an act of defiance. Lowering his head, he charged for the door. Taken by surprise, Zagora swung around on the balls of his feet. He sidestepped to block Constantin's path. Like a sprinter leaving his blocks, Constantin's body was angled forward. His lowered skull caught Zagora full in the face. A tremendous head butt, every ounce of Constantin's weight and strength lay behind it. He felt Zagora's nose break on impact, *heard* the bone crack, heard Zagora's scream of pain. Deflected, Constantin staggered and stumbled in a desperate effort to regain his balance. Then the sergeant nearest the door unleashed a murderous blow. The club arced through the air to crack the side of Constantin's head. Simultaneously a club caught him from behind; scorching down his spine to smash his manacled wrists. He staggered and fell. Seemingly a thousand blows hit him at once. Boots kicked him from every angle. The clubs rained down. Then blackness.

When he regained consciousness, he was back on the cot. They had locked his left wrist to the cot with the handcuffs. His right wrist was bound to the bedpost above his head. Spreadeagled on his back, with steel prongs gouging holes in his flesh, pain racked his whole body. He realized that his left foot had been secured to the far end of the bed. His eyelids were puffy and sticky with blood. Unable to see properly, he squinted through matted eyelashes. A moment passed before he identified the blurred, shadowy figures around him. One shadow was stooped over the end of the cot, a length of cord in his hands as he prepared to tie Constantin's right foot to the bedpost. Gritting his teeth, Constantin bent his right knee, bringing his thigh right back onto his chest. Then he kicked. He kicked with all the strength he could muster. The heel of his shoe caught the sergeant full in the mouth. Roaring with pain, the man dropped the cord. His hands flew to his face. Suddenly other shadows loomed into Constantin's vision. Two other shadows, two other sergeants, both swinging clubs. Constantin's rib cage threatened to collapse under the force of the blows.

Through his buzzing ears, he could hear the men shouting, "You bastard! We'll break every bone in your body!" He felt his shoes ripped from his feet. His right foot was secured. Then a club struck the soles of his feet. Once, twice . . . and again and again. "Take that! Bastard! Take that! Fucking bastard! Take that. And that!" On and on.

Constantin had never felt such pain. Like a red-hot needle pushed through his feet to his brain. Worse, like electric shocks applied to his ears, his stomach, his guts. He began to pray—*God, let me faint. Please let me faint. Don't let me scream.* But his prayers went unanswered. He opened his mouth, his jaws gaped wide. He screamed. He screamed and he screamed. His body arched up from the cot as he screamed.

Then the unthinkable. They did something worse. One of the sergeants began to punch Constantin's face. He landed blow after blow. Suddenly his hand ceased to be a fist. It was the flat of his hand. The palm of his hand, the fingers of his hand, pressing down on Constantin's nose and covering his mouth. He couldn't breathe. He was being suffocated. *God, I can't stand it! Dear God! God, let me breathe! Let me breathe!* The blows to his feet continued. "Take that, you bastard! And that! And that!" The felange. Suffocation. *God, give me air. Please God, give me air.* Strength began to drain from his body. Twisting his head, he forced his jaws open. Slowly. Wider. Wider. Then he bit. He sank his teeth into the man's finger. He bit as hard as he could, concentrating every ounce of fading strength into his jaws. The finger cracked. A scream of pain. The man leapt away, his hand dripping blood, his finger broken in two. After that they lost all control. They screamed. They shouted. All three attacked him at once. One slammed his head against the cot, again and again. Another seemed intent on breaking his kneecaps. The third battered the soles of his feet. "Take that! Bastard! Take that! Take that!" The steel springs gouged his flesh. *Oh God, let me faint. Please, God, I can't stand it. Please, God. . . .*

Finally came a roaring in his ears . . . then darkness and silence. Nothing. An empty void.

The nightmare began all over when he regained consciousness. When his congealed eyelids opened, they were all there . . . waiting. Zagora. The two inspectors. The three sergeants. But something was different. They looked different. Constantin concentrated. His fuddled brain was slow to respond. His eyes moved painfully. Everything was painful. Breathing hurt. His ears buzzed. His temples were bursting. He focused on the blurred shadows around the cot. Then the unbelievable happened. He giggled, he couldn't help himself. It was difficult to breathe, let alone laugh. His ribs ached as though clamped in a vise. But he laughed. Zagora's nose was encased in plaster! A narrow bandage held it in place, bisecting his skull, with his angry black eyes above and lips twisting in fury below. Next to him stood a man with the balloon lips of someone kicked in the mouth by a mule. And beyond that was another plaster cast, this time on the index finger of a sergeant. The scene struck Constantin as screamingly funny. For a man bound hand and foot to have inflicted such damage seemed the funniest thing in the world. His split, misshapen lips parted and he giggled hysterically.

Zagora heard defiance in that laughter, and lost control. Nobody laughed at Zagora. Snatching a club from a sergeant, he leaned over the cot. "An eye for an eye," he roared. Stepping back to give himself room, he raised the club high above his head . . . and smashed it down with all the force he could muster. The blow was badly aimed. It caught Constantin full in the mouth, dislocating his jaw and breaking his teeth. The second blow worsened the damage. It was the third blow which broke his nose . . . but he had lost consciousness by then.

And so it began. The interrogation of Constantin Peponis. Constantin lost all sense of time. When he was conscious every minute lasted an hour, an hour was as long as a day. *God, let me faint. I can't go on. Please God, make me faint. . . .*

They broke his fingers one by one. That was the sergeant's idea, the sergeant whose own finger had been broken. "An eye for an eye. A tooth for a tooth. Eight fingers and both thumbs for my finger, you bastard."

The doctor who had examined Constantin visited every day. Or was it twice a day? Or three times? Constantin wondered if the man came to see if he was still alive. Mostly the doctor cleaned him up. Bones were reset, loose teeth gouged out . . . all without anaesthetic.

He was moved into one of the special interrogation rooms. Not that he knew it at the time—he was unconscious.

And always the questions. "Who helped kill the soldiers? Who stole the van? Who was with you in the van? Who got the gun? Where from . . ."

He knew he would tell them. Eventually. Soon. But not yet. Elias and Melina had to have time to escape. To flee to the hills. To reach Uncle Mikis. Uncle Mikis would protect them. Perhaps they were already there? How long had it been? Two days? Three days? A week? A month? A year? The only meaningful units of time were periods of consciousness. Each brought its own pain. Excruciating pain. Agonizing pain. Unbearable pain. And each time he promised God that he would tell them next time if allowed to faint now. Each time he broke his promise. Each time his cry to God was the same—*I'll tell them next time, sweet Jesus, make me faint. Make me faint* NOW!

Then he would slip away into that dark world where Zagora could not follow.

His laughter about Zagora's nose taught him a valuable lesson. Zagora lost control when provoked. A calm Zagora was more deadly. A calm Zagora could measure out pain. He would know to the minute how many hours a man could be hung by his wrists. "Cut him down now," he would sneer with a glance at his watch. And Constantin would fall like a sack; arms, wrists and shoulders horribly distorted, every tendon and muscle searing with pain. A calm Zagora could scorch Constantin's bare flesh with cigarettes and laugh while he did it . . . could order the felange and press a blanket over Constantin's face until he squeezed the last puff of air from his lungs. But an enraged Zagora lost control and hit with enough force to render Constantin unconscious. And to lose consciousness was to win a valuable respite. More. Much more. In Constantin's mind, to lose consciousness was to survive one more round. And if he survived that round, he could survive another. . . .

So Constantin tormented his tormentor. He called him names. He insulted his manhood. He put his tongue to every gutter word ever invented. He devised crude jokes. He sang ribald songs. Until the sky fell in . . . and he escaped again into blessed oblivion.

"We've got your wife," Zagora gloated.

For a moment the words failed to register. Constantin's mind wandered, seeking a refuge from his mutilated body.

"We've arrested your precious Melina."

His heart missed a beat. His eyes remained closed from exhaustion. Lacking the energy to open them made him oddly grateful. Zagora was denied the chance to read his expression.

"She's interned in the Averoff barracks."

The groan escaped before Constantin could close his bruised lips. His pulse quickened. He had been fighting the battle of his life. Or his death. He suspected the latter. Death would be welcome. Death was an ally. Death was his trump card and he was ready to play it. Death would cheat Zagora of his show trial and trumped-up confessions.

"We have Melina."

Was it true? Could it be? After all this time? How long had it been? Was it a trick? Some kind of trap? If it was true, everything changed. He had to go on. Endure. Slowly he opened his eyes and stared up at that hated pockmarked face. He knew exactly where to look. He had heard Zagora enter the cell, listened to the conversation with the guard, winced at the sound of Zagora drawing up a chair. But the expected blow had not come. Instead he had felt Zagora's breath on his face as the man leaned over the cot.

Their eyes locked. The battle of wills began all over again. The plaster had been removed from Zagora's nose. Now only a livid scar testified to the single blow struck in a one-sided battle.

Staring up from the cot, Constantin rallied his frail strength. He struggled against the nausea and dizziness brought on by his physical condition. He had refused food from the outset. Not that Zagora would let him starve. "We must keep up your strength," Zagora had pronounced. And they had stuck a tube down his throat and forcibly fed him; six times by Constantin's calculations, or it might have been seven. Maybe eight. He had lost count. The first time was so brutal that he knew he couldn't endure it again. He would eat what they gave him. But he hadn't. When they released his hands, he had thrown the tin plate of food all over the sergeant. Since then it had been the tube. Every time. But agonizing though that was, the sexual tortures were worse. The first time he had not known what to expect. He had been stripped naked and tied to the cot. He had not understood what the sergeant was doing. The man had groped Constantin's testicles, stroking his penis into an involuntary erection. Then they had pushed an iron needle into the urethra, holding it there, while they heated it with a cigarette lighter. . . .

"Half the barracks have fucked her already," Zagora told him. "We shall use her as the camp whore."

So faint was the sigh of relief that the air above Constantin's lips scarcely moved. He closed his eyes. Zagora was lying. If Melina had been arrested, she would have been brought here, to this cell. They would torture her in front of him, knowing the effect it would have.

"I screwed your wife, Peponis. And you know what? She begged me for more."

The chuckle sounded like a death rattle. Constantin's whisper was hoarse. "You're a faggot, Zagora. You wouldn't know what to do with a woman."

Zagora's face darkened. His open hand slapped Constantin across the face. Then again. And again. Blood began to trickle from Constantin's nose and his mouth and his ears . . .

"Major Zagora."

The blows stopped. Zagora stepped back from the cot and glanced over his shoulder. A uniformed figure stood in the doorway. Zagora joined him.

Constantin's head swam. Coughing to clear the blood from his throat, he drew it into his mouth and spat onto his chest. The buzzing in his ears died away. Something about the voice at the door was familiar. Twisting on the cot, he tried to see the man. Zagora was blocking his view. And the man had lowered his voice. Zagora, too, was talking softly. But there was an urgency in Zagora's voice. Constantin strained his ears. "Forty-eight hours," he heard Zagora say. "Give me another forty-eight hours."

There was an answering murmur from the man.

They were discussing, not arguing. Which was odd in itself.

Zagora did not discuss. He shouted. He gave orders. He ranted and raved. Yet with this man he lowered his voice, his tone was respectful.

Constantin peered desperately, through bloodshot eyes, catching the glint of gold braid on the man's peaked hat. The man had turned away, but as he spoke to Zagora, Constantin glimpsed him in profile. A beaked nose. A strong face. The man turned again, his back to the cot.

But Constantin knew. He had seen him before. In the taverna, late at night, long ago. It was the man known as the doctor.

BOOK SIX

1978

Tiny beads of sweat stood out on Constantin's face. His voice had fallen to a whisper. He stared down into his lap, directing his words less to Tom than to his broken hands which clenched and unclenched as if pulled by the strings of a puppetmaster.

Tom crouched over the hearth and placed another log on the fire. The horror of reliving Constantin's story had driven every other thought from his mind. For a moment the film projector, the hated reel of film, even the newly erected gibbet on the skyline were forgotten.

Alec returned from the kitchen, bearing a tray on which stood a coffee pot so large that little room was left for the cups and the saucers.

Constantin whispered, "He was incredibly brave, you know, that doctor."

"He was a hero," said Tom, "so were you."

Setting the tray on the sideboard, Alec poured the coffee. From outside came the sound of the wind as it gusted across the terrace and slapped against the face of the villa. Tom rose from the hearth and returned to his chair. He felt an urge to say something, a word of comfort, some sort of encouragement, but a glance at Constantin's face stifled the intention. Instead, in silence, he accepted the cup of coffee from Alec. Looking down into the black liquid, his mind drifted to the black past. . . .

Greece, Athens, Piraeus had become interludes in Tom's life. Pleasant interludes, for his coming and going was unrestricted by the Junta. Athens and Piraeus were gateways to Kariakos, gateways to sun-drenched weekends with Maurice Stanton. He and Maurice had become friends, firm friends, and if the friendship owed much to the success of Stanton Industries, Tom saw that as a credit, not a debit. He took for granted that he was expected to do a good job. Maurice and Gunther Haller had learned to trust his judgment, and he made sure they had no regrets. In truth he had learned much in return, especially from Maurice, whose range of interests was a constant source of amazement. If Tom was an expert on business, Maurice was an expert on life. So to land at Hellikon Airport was always a pleasure . . . and to be driven to Piraeus was never a chore . . . especially with the prospect of lunch with Melina and Constantin before him.

Which was how it was that day. He came bearing gifts, perfume for Melina and a book for her husband.

"How is the big ape?" he asked in the jeep, grinning sideways at Gregg.

The pilot shrugged, "I haven't seen him since your last visit. Mr. Stanton has stayed on Kariakos all month."

"Ah," Tom nodded. He looked around at the passing scene, enjoying the view. He had been in the States. Three weeks of nonstop wheeling and dealing in company with Desmond Edwards. Successful, stimulating, exciting, but exhausting. Two days on Kariakos would recharge the batteries.

A column of soldiers filed along the road, sweltering in the midday sun. Tom grimaced, "This place gets more like an army camp every month."

"And how," Gregg nodded. He slowed to a crawl, to give the troops a wide berth.

Leaving the coast road, they cut through the familiar back streets, past the church and on up the hill. "I may be a bit longer today," Gregg said. "I want to check the oil filters. Will two hours be okay?"

"Fine. I'll unwind with a jug of retsina and sleep all the way to Kariakos."

Gregg grinned, "Why not? Cabin service on *Helena* is lousy."

As the jeep rolled to a halt, Tom grabbed his bag from the back seat and leapt out. "See you later."

Raising a hand in cheerful farewell, Gregg let in the clutch and moved off.

"Like coming home," Tom grunted to himself as he parted the bead curtain. Sniffing the aroma of cooking, he expected to see Constantin at the bar. Not seeing him, not even seeing him with the three men who sat near the kitchen, came as a surprise. He knew the men, familiar faces from previous visits. Their expressions brightened when they saw him. He grinned hello, expecting to see Constantin in the kitchen with Melina, but when he looked through the archway he met another surprise. The woman at the stove was a stranger. An unexpected voice called from the balcony. "Kyrios Lambert." He turned as Melina's father hurried to greet him. Beyond him, on the balcony, he saw Melina's mother. She was weeping. A young woman was trying to comfort her. Seeing Tom, Melina's mother broke away and followed her husband with outstretched arms, to arrive sobbing in Tom's arms. His bewilderment gave way to concern. She hugged him hard before clutching his hand and tugging him toward the balcony. Her husband kept pace alongside. Both of them were pouring their hearts out in incomprehensible Greek. Their grief was blindingly obvious. The old woman was almost tearing her hair. As soon as they reached the balcony the old man turned to the girl, his voice rising, waving his arms, and pointing at Tom. Nodding her understanding, the girl was making placating signs with her hands, trying to calm him. She kept saying something, but they insisted on interrupting, so several moments passed before she turned to Tom. "You are a friend of the family?" she asked, speaking English.

"Sure? What's happened?"

"You had better sit down. I have some bad news."

Tom could scarcely comprehend what he was hearing.

"Murder?" He shook his head in disbelief. "Constantin's been arrested for *murder*? For Christ's sake! I don't believe it."

Falling into a chair, he listened to her story. When she finished, he needed a stiff drink. He asked for a whisky, which even the old man understood.

Tom looked at the girl. "When did this happen?"

"He was arrested a week ago."

He groaned, thinking first of Constantin, then Melina. "Where is she? Upstairs?"

The girl hesitated, choosing her words carefully. "She's not here. They are afraid she will also be arrested—"

"Melina? Arrested? For what? Has everyone gone crazy?"

When the girl looked at him, he noticed her eyes. Dark brown, almost black, framed by long eyelashes. Little about her had registered until then. Now he noticed her white teeth, her tanned complexion and chestnut hair. An enamel Red Cross badge was pinned to her shirt. He detected a faint French accent when she spoke. She said, "Some men will confess to anything if their wives are in danger."

Would they threaten Melina? Shit! It would certainly work. Constantin *would* confess to anything. . . .

The old man returned from the bar with a tumbler of whisky. Tom swallowed some, coughed, and added water. The girl was explaining the Red Cross situation. She was a delegate, whatever that meant. He was only half-listening, his brain stalling as he came to terms with the news. She said, "I've been trying to explain. There's nothing we can do. Murder is a criminal charge, quite beyond our mandate . . ." She broke off as the old man pushed a crumpled newspaper across the table.

A haggard Constantin was on the front page. "They say he is a Communist," said the girl.

Tom no more believed that than he could believe Constantin had been arrested. He was about to reply when the old man began talking more volubly than ever. Next to him, his wife trembled, clutching her handkerchief while beseeching Tom through swollen eyes.

The girl said, "They want to take you to Melina."

"Sure," Tom nodded absently, still staring at the newspaper, trying to take it all in. "Christ, this is terrible."

The girl added, "They've been waiting for you. Melina has sent them here every day."

Hearing his daughter's name, the old man nodded eagerly and rose from the table. He clutched Tom by the arm. Tom knew he would help. Of course he would help. He wondered how. With money? Certainly. And perhaps he could find a good lawyer. Maurice might know a top man in Athens. *Christ, what's up with me. Constantin IS a lawyer!*

Recovering from the shock, he concentrated on what he could do. "Wait a minute," he said, holding the old man at bay. "Where are we going? Is it far?" He turned to the girl and explained about Gregg, "He'll be back in couple of hours. He could take us."

But when the girl translated, Melina's parents became agitated, both talking at once. Even without understanding, Tom recognized panic. They were terrified. It took the girl several minutes to calm them. "They want you to go now," she said urgently. "They'll bring you back to meet your friend later."

He nodded his acceptance.

Melina's mother rose from the table and began to hurry down the steps. The old man tugged insistently on Tom's arm. But Tom hesitated, thinking ahead. "Hold on. Will Elias be there? He can speak English."

When the girl relayed the question, the old man's expression changed. A furtive look came into his eyes. He muttered to his wife, who became more agitated then ever.

"Now what?" Tom demanded.

The girl shook her head. "They say they don't know about Elias. He might be there, he might not."

Tom groaned. Communicating with Melina's parents was hopeless. And even when he reached Melina, there might be problems. She did speak some English, but not much. Not enough to explain anything complicated. Suppose he couldn't understand what she wanted? Looking at the girl, he had a sudden idea. "Will you come? I might not understand everything they tell me. It could be important."

A doubtful look came into her eyes. She hesitated. "I shouldn't . . . I shouldn't even be here. This isn't ICRC business. We can't get involved—"

"Please. Melina must be worried to death. There may be things I can do, I won't know until I see her, but I don't want to risk a misunderstanding."

The girl wanted to help, he could see it in her face, but something was troubling her. He tried again. "Please. These are good people. Decent people—"

"I know, I know . . . I'd like to help, but—"

"It won't take long. If you could interpret, that's all, make sure I get everything straight—"

"I'm not supposed to be here. Officially I'm not here. Today is my day off—"

"Please," he repeated.

She hesitated for a long moment, her dark eyes full of doubt and indecision. Finally she took a deep breath. "All right, but just to interpret. I can't get involved beyond that. You must understand—"

"Thank you." He breathed a sigh of relief. "Thanks very—"

The old man started to argue. Pointing at the girl as she rose to her feet. It was clear that he wanted her to remain at the taverna. Melina's mother supported him from the foot of the steps, waving her arms and shaking her head.

But Tom was determined. "If they want me, you come too," Taking the girl's arm he propelled her down the steps, pointing at the old man. "Explain to him that Melina might want some quick decisions. I can only make them if I understand what's going on."

The girl did as she was told, raising her voice above a barrage of interruptions before finally admitting, "They don't want me to come."

"You must come," Tom retorted, glaring at the old man.

Melina's father held Tom's stern gaze, then looked away. Reluctantly, he began to move to the door. His wife followed, still muttering and shaking her head.

Turning to the girl, Tom apologized, "Sorry, I've no right to insist," I don't even know your name."

"Kirsten. Kirsten Moutier."

"Tom Lambert." He held out his hand, "And thanks. I really am grateful."

Responding with the sketchiest of smiles, she allowed him to steer her toward the bead curtain.

The three men watched anxiously from the table next to the kitchen. One of them put Tom's bag behind the bar for safe keeping. Tom nodded his thanks with a worried smile. Seeing the bag reminded him of the perfume it contained for Melina. *What a useless irrelevancy at a time like this!*

"How is Melina?" he asked. "Have you seen her since—"

"No. It's been very difficult. Officially we can do nothing. I have been told to stay out of it, but hordes of Constantin's friends descend on the office every day. I came to ask Melina to stop them. It won't do any good . . ." She shook her head in frustration. "I wish I knew what would."

There was no mistaking her sincerity. He found himself liking her.

Outside they blinked in the strong sunlight. Melina's parents had turned left and were already ten yards away.

Setting off in pursuit, Tom said, "They seem scared to death."

Even as he spoke, he saw the reason. Two uniformed policemen emerged from a doorway opposite. They had been watching the taverna. Their hard-eyed scrutiny sent an unexpected chill through his bones. Glancing sideways, he saw Kirsten's face stiffen with tension. She muttered, "I daren't come any further if they follow us."

"Why? We're not doing anything illegal."

"You don't understand. The ICRC is under constant surveillance. The Junta will expel us from Greece at the first opportunity. . . ." She broke off as Melina's parents stopped as a door opened down the street. Stepping inside, the old man beckoned to them to hurry. Reaching the doorway, Tom glanced over his shoulder. The two policemen had started after them. The old man pulled him across the threshold, with Kirsten behind him. The door closed immediately. A stranger, a middle-aged woman, pointed to the staircase. Steps descended. Melina's mother was already lost from sight and her husband was hurrying after her. Fearing Kirsten might argue, Tom grabbed her hand. "Come on." He led the way down the steps to emerge into a garage. A door was open, leading to a street at the rear. Melina's father was already crossing the road to an open door on the other side.

Hurrying after him, they crossed the street and entered the house. The door closed behind them. They went down a passage and out of another door—and that became the pattern—in one door and out of another—all opened and closed by unsmiling men and women. Melina's father scurried ahead. At some point Melina's mother had ceased to be part of the procession. Tom lost all sense of direction. The maze of alleys and narrow streets which made up Piraeus confused him at the best of times. The farther they went, the more Kirsten protested. Twice she stopped and he had to plead with her to continue.

But he too had his doubts. Less about the distance than the *purpose* of the journey. What was he getting into? There was no mistaking the fear on the faces of the people who opened their doors to him. Fear mingled with something else. He recognized defiance. The look of a people who had spent their whole lives running away but who were now determined to stand firm.

Yet firm against what?

"Oh no," Kirsten groaned as a passageway opened up into a kitchen. "I can't go down there."

The kitchen table had been pushed to one side. Melina's father and another man were rolling up a rug on the floor revealing a trapdoor. The other man bent over and grasped a brass ring. Grunting with exertion, he heaved the trap open and stood back from the opening.

Melina's father said something to Kirsten in Greek.

"What did he say?"

Kirsten stared at the opening. "Melina is down there. She's been down there for a week."

Melina's father went first. Descending the flight of open steps backwards, the old man clambered down as if he were descending a ladder. Encouraging Kirsten with a glance, Tom followed, with the girl close behind him.

There was light in the cellar, not good light but adequate. Two bare bulbs hung from the ceiling, casting wide pools of yellow into the gray shadows. Before he reached the bottom step, Tom saw Melina. She was on a cot in the corner, dressed all in black like a widow. Nearby was a table bearing the remains of a meal: cups and plates had been pushed to one side, and a wine bottle, half-empty, stood next to some grapes. Across the cellar an open door revealed a lavatory and a hand basin.

Face crumpling and eyes spilling forth tears, Melina came into his arms. He embraced her, encircling her with both arms. He kept saying how sorry he was, while cursing himself for his lack of the right words. Hugging her, he let her lead him back to the cot. Suddenly angry voices erupted behind him. Swinging around, he saw the men with the guns. Two of them. They had been sitting on an old sofa beneath the stairs. The sight of Kirsten brought them to their feet. One of them was berating the old man, who was arguing back, giving as good as he got. The other man grabbed Kirsten by the wrist, and began pulling her to the table.

"Hey!" Tom started towards Kirsten, when another shout came from above. Elias was peering down from the hatch. He cried out again when he saw Tom. Next moment he swung through the opening and clattered down the stairs. "Thank God," he exclaimed, seizing Tom's hand. "We thought you'd never get here."

Tom shook his hand with a sense of relief. Elias looked ill, but at least he could explain what was happening.

Melina's father was still arguing with the armed men.

Kirsten stood to one side, her expression one of alarm.

Melina sank down onto the cot. Reaching up, she caught Kirsten's hand and drew her down beside her. The two women embraced. The movement caught Elias' eye. Until then he had seen only Tom. He gaped at Kirsten, before reacting with anger.

"What's she doing here?"

"I asked her to come," Tom said. "I needed an interpreter—"

"Oh no," Elias groaned, "no, no, no. This is bad. This is bad for us and bad for her."

Waiting for an explanation, Tom pulled a chair out from the table and sat down. Elias seemed ready to collapse. Not so the men with the guns. They were angry, furious with Melina's father. They kept shouting at him while pointing at Kirsten. The old man shouted back. Kirsten now watched from the cot, dismay written across her face. Earlier her tanned complexion had shone with youthful good health. Now, under the light cast by the bare bulbs, she looked ashen.

Tom banged the table. "For Christ's sake!" he shouted, pulling Elias down into a chair. "What's going on?"

His outburst quelled the others. The men with the guns fell silent, glaring at the old man.

Tom stood up, taking a pack of cigarettes from his pocket. He offered them around, first to Elias, then the men with the guns, then the old man. They accepted without so much as a smile of thanks. One of the armed men returned to the sofa. The other hesitated before walking to the stairs, where he slouched down on the bottom step, his shotgun over his knees. Elias said something to his father in Greek. The old man replied.

"Speak English," Tom commanded sharply. He glared at Elias, "Now then—"

"You shouldn't have brought her—"

"She came to help—"

"But she's *seen* us. She could identify us—"

"So what?"

"You don't understand," muttered Elias, shaking his head.

"So make me," Tom retorted, grim-faced.

The boy drew deeply on his cigarette. Casting an anxious look at Melina, he lowered his voice. "Constantin can't last much longer. The things they are doing to him . . ." Swallowing his words, he coughed, clearing his throat. His hands trembled as he made a determined effort to bring his nerves under control. With eyes full of misery he looked at Tom. "They will kill him unless we get him out. . . ."

For the past half hour Tom had been trying to absorb the news of Constantin's arrest. But to hear tales of torture! He could hardly believe what Elias was saying. Torture didn't happen, not these days. Torture was medieval. . . .

Elias sat with his back to Melina, talking in a low voice, not wanting his words to carry. But Melina understood. Pain and anguish contorted her face. And Elias sweated with desperation as he talked.

Tom felt fear. For the first time in his life he was afraid. He lived the life of modern man, a high-powered executive facing a hundred problems a day. But not problems like this! The terror in that cellar reached out and embraced him. Taking the wine bottle, he half-filled a used cup and gulped it down. "Are you sure?" he kept asking. "How do you know these things?"

Elias jerked his head toward the man on the stairs. "Panos has a friend on the inside. Someone we trust."

Tom rubbed the palm of one hand. It was hot in the cellar. Stuffy. But that wasn't why he was sweating. He looked over at Kirsten. "Did you hear any of that?"

"Most of it."

He stood up and drew another chair out from the table. "Come and join us."

Frowning slightly, Kirsten rose and walked to the table. It wasn't far, twelve feet, maybe fifteen. Fifteen feet from where Melina dry-washed her hands in a fever of worry. Melina's gaze raked Tom's face, seeking his intentions, begging for help. He turned away, unable to respond, ignoring her while he seached for the truth. With elaborate courtesy, he helped Kirsten into the chair. His face brushed her cheek, as he murmured, "Do you believe this? About Constantin?"

Sitting down, she threw him a glance, "We need *proof.* We can never get proof—"

Elias hissed, "If she had his corpse she wouldn't believe it. The Red Cross was a waste of time."

Tom was staring at Kirsten. She did believe it. He could see the torment in her eyes. *Christ! It's true. Now what? What the hell do I do?* He looked across the table at Elias. "What were you saying? About getting him out?"

Anger contorted the boy's face. "Are you mad?" He pushed his chair away from the table. "To talk in front of her—"

"She's here now! We can't change—"

"She'll identify us—"

"Why should she?"

"What choice will she have?" Elias jumped to his feet. Before Kirsten could move, he reached across the ripped the badge from her shirt. "You think that will save her?" Sneering, he flung the Red Cross emblem onto the table. "Don't make me laugh! They'll tear her to pieces to find out what she knows."

Tom flinched. Kirsten was his responsibility. She had not wanted to come. He had insisted. Now she was in danger . . . and it was his fault.

Melina cried out from the cot. She was close to tears. Rising hurriedly, she came to the table to stand behind Kirsten. She looked from Elias to Tom. "This is my friend," she said, gripping Kirsten's shoulder. "This is a good person. My Constantin also say this."

Kirsten reached up to hold Melina's hand.

"Don't shout at her," Melina scolded, her lower lip trembling.

Kirsten was pale. Strain lingered in her eyes, even after her tight little smile to Melina. Squeezing Melina's hand, she released it to turn back to Tom. Unexpectedly she reached for his cigarettes on the table. She took one, her hand shaking slightly as he leaned across with his lighter. She coughed on the smoke, then shook her head. He was surprised to see a rueful smile on her lips.

"I was warned." She said, "They told me in Geneva. They even gave me lectures. Don't get involved. Remain impartial. It's the only way to cope." Her mouth drooped until the wry smile became a look of defeat. "This is the first time I've worked in the field. The first and the last. I'm totally compromised now. Not that I mind much, but I can't let it affect the others. The entire ICRC mission could be jeopardized . . ."

Tom found himself admiring her. She had heart. And courage. She was more concerned about the Red Cross than her personal safety.

"I couldn't have gone on much longer, in any case," she shrugged. "It's been getting to me for weeks. You can't remain impartial and stay human. At least I can't. I was thinking of resigning . . . and now this . . ." She gestured around the cellar before looking at Tom. Seeing his concern, she said, "Don't blame yourself. That's all I'm saying. I broke the rules by going to the taverna. I put myself in the wrong place at the wrong time. You weren't responsible for that."

He was about to respond when she continued, "I go home next week on leave." Turning, she grasped Melina's hand and looked up into her face.

Melina could guess what was coming, and tears filled her eyes. "You won't come back," she choked, as Kirsten rose to take her in her arms.

"Oh Melina," Kirsten's own voice trembled. "I'm not doing any good here. I can't help you. I wish I could—"

But Melina had ceased to listen. She lived on hope. Hope kept her going. One reason for hope was Kirsten. Now Kirsten was abandoning her. Melina broke down and wept. She tried not to, which made it worse. Her shoulders heaved and tears sprang from her eyes. She choked, putting clenched hands to her mouth, biting her knuckles. Kirsten hugged her tight before leading her back to the cot.

Tom watched in helpless frustration. He felt desperate, needing to do something without knowing what. He looked at Elias. "This escape. Is it possible?"

The boy nodded. "We think so . . . with your help."

He knew he would help. He couldn't not help. "Go on."

Elias cleared his throat nervously, "Constantin is in very bad shape. Our friend on the inside might be able to transfer him to hospital—"

"Might? You're not sure?"

"We will try tonight. Now you are here."

"Why have you waited for me?"

On the cot, still sniffling, Melina was regaining control. Her father moved to stand behind Elias, obviously anxious about Tom's reaction. Elias began to explain. "If we can get him transferred to the hospital, we can waylay the ambulance en route. We won't have long . . . twenty minutes, half an hour, then all hell will break loose. Troops will be all over the place. Roadblocks will go up on every street corner. . . ." He shook his head, frowning with worry. "Constantin is too weak to travel far.

A long journey is out of the question." He hesitated, fixing Tom with a look of desperation. "We want you to airlift him out in the seaplane."

Seconds before, Tom had been sweating. It was hot in the cellar. Now it was as if a current of cold air was blowing up his spine, to lift the hairs on the nape of his neck.

The man on the sofa rose and joined them at to the table. He stared at Tom, watching his reactions. When Tom glanced at him, the man shrugged, "I have a little English to help, not much . . . but a little."

Panos too rose, from his place at the foot of the stairs, and advanced to the table. With his father behind him and the two armed men either side, Elias fell silent, waiting for Tom's reply.

Tom tried to clear his mind. He wondered what Maurice would say. *Helena* belonged to Maurice. Maurice lived on Greek soil. Suppose Maurice was dragged into this? "I'm not sure," he began, "I mean, I don't even know how far *Helena* can fly. Where would we go?"

Amazingly, Elias actually smiled. "The same place as always," he said, "to Kariakos."

A nightmarish picture leapt into Tom's mind. He saw armed troops scaling the cliffs to the villa. Would helping one friend endanger another?

Elias leaned forward, talking urgently. "Panos and his people have used Kariakos before. More than twenty people have escaped there."

Tom's first reaction was disbelief, then he remembered the fishing village. Was it possible? He had visited Kariakos many times, but still not been to the village.

Unexpectedly, Kirsten leapt up from the cot, and joined the men at the table. "You mean Kariakos, the island?" She sounded incredulous.

They ignored her. Elias was concentrating on Tom. "There is something more," he said. "The Kyrios Stanton brought Constantin messages. Secret messages. And he carried reports back to London. I knew about the reports. Constantin was always writing them, but the courier was a mystery until Melina told me."

Melina squeezed between her father and Panos to complete the ring of figures.

Tom gaped up at them.

Seeing his incredulity, Melina slapped the table. "It is true. My Constantin does this. I say the truth, I swear."

Her tear-stained face dispelled any suspicion of a lie. She was telling the truth, but not about Maurice. Surely not Maurice? Tom began to shake his head. "This courier must be someone else—"

"No!" Melina cried. "The Kyrios Stanton. *Your* Kyrios Stanton."

He had to believe her. But why hadn't Maurice said anything? Not a word. Not a single bloody word. Ever. Except . . . Maurice was consistently contemptuous of the Colonels. The only restriction on Tom's business dealing was that no investment would be made in Greece while the Junta held power. Maurice had declared bluntly, "*I won't help Fascists,*"

Melina reached across to grasp Tom's hand. "We say the truth. The Kyrios Stanton brought us much money from London—"

Kirsten exclaimed in astonishment, "Are you talking about *Maurice* Stanton?"

Hope lit Melina's eyes. "Yes, yes," she nodded eagerly, "the Kyrios Maurice Stanton. He is friends with the Red Cross too? You know him?"

The strangest expression had come over Kirsten's face. "Oh yes," she said with unmistakable bitterness. "I know him all right. He's a bastard. An absolute bastard."

A protest formed on Melina's lips.

Tom and Elias started in surprise.

"I loathe him," said Kirsten, "He's my father."

They could not have met under stranger circumstances. Or in a more dangerous situation. The mood in that cellar was desperate. Faces were haggard, nerves were stretched tight. Panos appeared ready to use his shotgun at any excuse.

Tom's head was spinning. "But I thought you said . . . I

mean, your name is Moutier or something? It sounded French—"

"It is," Kirsten agreed coldly. "Moutier is my mother's name. She reverted to it years ago. When he deserted us."

In that instant, he saw the resemblance. Her eyes were dark brown, almost black, exactly like her father's. And she had a way of holding her head. Once he saw it, he was surprised not to have seen the likeness before. They were even similar in character. Maurice was willful, always keen to get his own way, but nobody could accuse him of lacking compassion. Exactly like this girl. She was unmistakably Maurice's daughter. The facial resemblance was there even at that moment, when disapproval showed in the arch of her eyebrows.

"It does you no credit to be a friend of my father's," she said scornfully.

Tom stared at her. He recalled Maurice saying—*Louise has poisoned her against me.* Even now, a year later, he remembered the wistful note in Maurice's voice. *She's a lovely girl. Twenty-five now. Good God, where did the time go . . .*

Melina looked with astonishment first at Elias, then her father, before turning wide-eyed to Kirsten. "The Kyrios Stanton is your *father*?"

"It's not something I'm proud of."

"That's not fair," Tom muttered in protest. "You might change your mind if you got to know him."

"I don't want to know him."

Watching the color rise in her face, he wondered what the hell he should do? She was his responsibility. She was there only because of his insistence. And he liked her. But Jesus Christ!—Maurice's daughter! "Why didn't you say—"

"Say what? I told you who I was."

"You didn't say you were Maurice's daughter?"

"What the hell has that got to do with it?" she shouted angrily. "I didn't know he was mixed up with you . . . or Constantin . . . or any of this . . ." She gestured at Elias and the men with the guns. "Besides, I'm his *ex*-daughter. I don't have anything to do with him."

Logically, she was right. Their predicament had nothing to do with her parentage. He knew she was right. Except . . . his brain stumbled and stalled . . . it added another complication. One hell of a complication. He yearned for a stiff whisky. He would have given anything to be able to think in peace and quiet, with a glass in his hand. Instead Elias and Panos were arguing loudly, with the old man shouting interruptions for good measure. Overhearing what they were saying, Kirsten joined in, so that for several moments there was a flurry of Greek with Tom looking on not understanding. Finally Elias quieted everyone and turned back to Tom. "We make some decisions," he announced. "Point number one—the Kyrios Stanton is our friend, yes? He brings messages and money to Constantin. Okay?"

Nonplussed about Maurice's behavior, Tom responded with a nod of his head.

"Number two," Elias pointed at Kirsten, "she is his daughter."

"Oh no!" Kirsten exclaimed.

Ignoring her, Elias looked determinedly at Tom. "We can't release her—"

Kirsten interrupted, "I'm not going anywhere *near* Kariakos."

"She can't stay here, so you must take her on the seaplane. To her father. He will know what to do—"

"I am *not* going to Kariakos!" Kirsten's temper boiled over. She pointed at Elias, "Will you get that into his thick head!"

"For Christ's sake!" Tom slapped the table. "All of you—will you shut up a minute. Let me think!" He ran a hand through his hair. His forehead and scalp were damp with sweat. "Nobody goes anywhere. Nobody. Understand?" Taking a deep breath, he brought his nerves under control. "I need to know every detail of this plan first. *Every* detail," he emphasized, looking at Elias. "Now then, calmly and quietly—let's go through it again."

Panos muttered to the old man who declined to answer with a shake of his head. Melina looked frightened. Spyros retreated and scowled from his old place on the sofa. Kirsten compressed her lips into a thin line.

Savoring the silence, Tom added, "That's better. Now Elias—remember calmly and quietly."

Listening to the boy, Tom realized that the plan depended upon a number of *ifs*. The first *if* was *if* Constantin was moved to the hospital. "When will we know that?"

Elias glanced at his watch. "Costas will have spoken to Lianis by now. We should know very shortly."

"Who's Costas?"

Elias seemed surprised. "One of us." He waved a hand to include the others. Turning aside, he spoke to his father in Greek. When the old man replied, Elias nodded. "Costas was at the taverna earlier. You will know him when you see him."

Tom remembered the three men at the table. No wonder they had been so watchful. "Go on."

Elias had acquired two vehicles for the ambush, a green delivery van and a black Mercedes. "They are both a bit battered but the engines are good." After the ambush, Elias and the men with the guns would use the Mercedes as a decoy vehicle. The green van would take Constantin straight to *Helena* at Passalimani.

Elias concluded hopefully, "With luck we won't need a false trail. The police will be busy with other diversions." He recounted the details with relish. An hour before the ambush, friends would stage a protest at the Law School. "They will create such a row the police will be called in." Simultaneously other disturbances would break out in the city—students would pelt a police station with stones, and a mysterious fire would break out in the commercial district adjoining Constitution Square.

Tom felt grudging admiration. "Sounds like a whole army is working for you?"

"We can do much," Elias shrugged, his expression still anxious. "Constantin has many friends, but only you can make him disappear."

Tom chewed a fingernail.

The silence became too much for Elias. "All of this was planned days ago! We have been waiting for you."

Responsibility weighed on Tom's shoulders. "What about the ambush itself?"

"Easy," Elias answered confidently, determined to be reassuring. "I told you. Lianis has planned every detail from the inside. He will be in the ambulance. When we come on the scene . . . poof!" Smacking his hands together, he laughed. "All over!"

"What about the other ambulance crew? Doctors—"

"Lianis is a doctor," Elias announced proudly. "An Army doctor. He will be in charge."

Tom's taut nerves eased a fraction. "Will the ambulance travel alone? Won't there be an escort?"

"Maybe," Elias conceded. "A couple of motorcyclists. ESA goons. It is possible. Don't worry, we will get them." Turning to Panos he said something in Greek; Panos laughed and patted his shotgun.

The gesture was meant to reassure. But for Tom Lambert, businessman, the shotgun merely underlined how far he was from familiar territory. Unbuttoning his collar, he loosened his tie.

Realizing his mistake, Elias was quick to minimize the consequences. "Most likely just the ambulance," he added hastily. "No motorcyclists. We get Constantin and fly. Eh!" He laughed with nervous excitement. "We fly. Like birds on the wing."

Panos set his shotgun down for the first time. Leaving it with Spyros on the sofa, he collected the used glasses on the table, and took them through to the sink. Rinsing them under a running tap, he returned to put them, still wet, on the table. Stopping at a cupboard, the old man produced a bottle of ouzo.

Anxiously, Elias was still watching Tom. "The plan is good, eh?" he said seeking approval.

Tom heard the plea; it was unmistakable. *I have done all I can,* the boy was saying, *the rest is up to you.* The same thought was in the old man's eyes as he poured the liqueur. And Panos' expression betrayed his thoughts—*We've done our bit. Now it is your turn.*

Reaching for a glass, Tom drank thirstily. The proposed scenario appalled him. To take part in an ambush. To fly a hunted man to Maurice's island, in Maurice's aircraft, with Maurice's pilot at the controls. And now, possibly with Maurice's daughter along for the ride. Jesus!

The discussion about the ambush had quieted Kirsten. The flush had faded from her face. She sat across the table, biting her lip, her eyes downcast. Melina stood behind her, watching Tom as if her life depended upon his next move.

He sweated. The escape plan slid around in his mind. He pushed it one way, then another, pondering the angles. He had to do it. There was nobody else. He couldn't walk away, he was their only hope. Constantin's only hope. Poor bastard. Eyes narrowed thoughtfully, he looked up at Elias. "After the ambush, when you lay the false trail, the green van heads straight for the flying boat. Is that right?"

The boy nodded.

"Suppose the green van gets followed? Suppose someone sees Constantin boarding the aircraft? If his injuries are severe, Gregg may have to help him get aboard."

Elias glanced nervously at Melina.

Tom sensed a new problem. "Now what?"

Elias blurted out, "There will be others to help you. Melina will go with you."

"Melina?"

"You can't leave her behind," Elias said urgently.

Melina's red-rimmed eyes begged. She had no need to speak. Despair and desperation were in every line of her face.

"Constantin will need her. Besides, if the ESA get their hands on her . . ." Elias trailed off, unwilling to put his fears into words.

Involuntarily, Tom flinched. In his mind's eye he had seen Constantin slipping aboard *Helena* under cover of darkness. Alone. Now there would be two to worry about.

"And Lianis," Elias rushed on nervously. "His cover will be blown. He will have to go too."

"Three!" Tom exclaimed. "Three—"

"Four," Elias interrupted, pointing at Kirsten.

"No!" Kirsten protested.

"Yes!" Elias insisted.

Tom closed his ears. Literally. Elbows on the table, he put his hands over his ears. And concentrated. And sweated. And tried not to panic. "I need to speak to Gregg," he muttered. Then it dawned on him. "Christ!" he exclaimed looking up. Elias was still arguing with Kirsten. Tom grabbed the boy's shoulder. "My pilot. He'll be back at the taverna by now. He'll be waiting—"

"No, no." Elias shook his head. "We thought of that. The jeep would attract attention. Costas is bringing your friend here."

Tom stared, caught halfway between anger and relief; anger that he had not been consulted, relief that he had one less decision to make. Reaching for his glass, he swallowed another mouthful.

"We think of everything, eh?" Elias smiled.

Tom hoped so. His thoughts reverted to the escape plan. "Who travels in the green van?"

"We make two journeys," Elias answered. "Journey one, from here to the ambush. I drive, you're in the passenger seat and Melina is in the back on a mattress." He frowned. "Now the Kyrenia Kirsten will also be on the mattress with Melina, and then . . ." he hastened on to avoid interruption. "From the ambush to Passalimani, Lianis will drive with you in the passenger seat, and Constantin in the back with the women."

Tom hated the idea of involving the women. And the prospect of taking Constantin directly to *Helena* filled him with alarm. The trail could lead directly to Kariakos. Even if it were dark . . .

"Will it be dark? What time—"

"Past eight o'clock," Elias interrupted, anticipating the question. "Costas will confirm this when he comes."

Past eight o'clock was all right. Just. Darkness would have fallen. Even so, there was an appalling risk of leading the police to *Helena*. Lighting a cigarette, Tom pushed his chair back from the table. Standing up eased some of the tension in his muscles. There was insufficient room to pace in the cellar. Rubbing the small of his back with one hand, he took two steps to the left and came back to his chair. His very actions betrayed uncertainty. Faces were raised around the table, watching, waiting, hoping, praying. He sat down and toyed with his glass, swirling the straw-colored liqueur around and around.

His thoughts swirled in the same fashion: one idea flowed into the next so quickly that it vanished before properly formed. He rose again to remove his jacket, draping it over the back of the chair. Sitting down, he pushed the glass gently aside, sliding it carefully across the rough wooden table. The ouzo steadied in the glass. Pictures in his mind slowed to a more manageable tempo. Pushing a million doubts to one side, he searched for positive reasons of hope. Across the table, Elias fidgeted in a misery of worried impatience. In truth, Elias had done well. Tom could think of nothing more the boy could have done. He had protected Melina. With others he had planned to free Constantin. *Now it's up to me. The decision is mine . . . the responsibility is mine . . .*

His gaze settled on Kirsten. "I really am very sorry . . ." he searched for the best words, ". . . this is my fault. I got you into this . . ."

She looked up, meeting his eyes.

"Obviously I'm responsible for you, but I can't just abandon these people."

His own words made him realize that his subconscious had already made his decision. "There's not much choice. They won't let you go and you can't stay here. For your own safety, you must come to Kariakos."

Before Kirsten could respond, Melina interrupted. Dropping to her knees besides Kirsten's chair, she took Kirsten's hands in her own and beseeched her in a flurry of Greek. Even without understanding the words, Tom could follow the sentiment. With tears running down her face, Melina was entreating, persuading and begging before breaking down completely under the strain. Her father crouched beside her, putting an arm around her shoulders. Shoving his chair back from the table, Elias stood over her, his concern evident on his face. Even Panos and Spyros crowded around, anxious to provide what comfort they could.

Kirsten's expression reflected her turmoil. Hugging Melina, she helped her to her feet, uttering soft words and smoothing her hair.

"Please," Melina begged, "the Kyrios Stanton is a good man. To be trusted. . . ."

Tom added his own entreaties. "Kirsten, I promise, from Kariakos you can go anywhere. Maurice has a yacht. I'll get you to Cyprus or Italy or Malta. Wherever you want. Anywhere. After Kariakos you'll be free. . . ." The words poured out, engendered not just by a sense of responsibility. He liked this girl. He wanted her to know he was trying to protect her.

Suddenly the trapdoor opened above them. All their heads swiveled upward. A blue uniformed leg was thrust through the opening, then Gregg appeared, followed by one of the men from the taverna, the man who had put Tom's bag behind the bar for safekeeping. The bag was now in his hand. Tom guessed he was Costas.

Gregg saw Tom as he reached the foot of the stairs. "What the hell's going on?" he asked as he advanced to the table. "I got your message. This fellow came out to Passalimani. Said you'd left the taverna and gone somewhere else. I was to go with him to pick you up. We parked the jeep miles away. Gregg paused as his gaze rested on the shotguns. "You in some kind of trouble, Mr. Lambert?"

But Tom's attention was elsewhere. Gregg was talking in a vacuum. He was the only one not looking at the man who had followed him. Spyros and the old man stood transfixed, their gaze riveted on Costas. Melina's hand flew to her mouth. Elias crossed the cellar in three strides, with Panos on his heels.

A moment later Elias gave a whoop of joy. His face lit up with relief and excitement. "Costas has heard from Lianis," he shouted to Tom. "They move Constantin at eight o'clock. It's on! It's on!"

The two military motorcyclists did their ineffectual best to cut a swathe through the thick Athens traffic. Private cars and commercial vehicles edged into the curb or out towards the central reservation, but in truth they were too numerous and the dual carriageway was too narrow. Carbon monoxide belched from a thousand exhaust pipes. Acrid fumes filled the humid early evening air. The ambulance inched steadily forward, followed by a small maroon Fiat sedan and a green delivery van.

Tom glanced at Elias. The boy's hands were clenched tightly on the wheel. Even in the blue-white light cast by the street lamps the tension was clear on his face.

"You okay?"

Elias nodded but remained silent.

"Cigarette?"

The boy took one from the proffered pack. Lighting it, he drew the smoke deep into his lungs. Some of the stiffness eased from his face. "I've been thinking," he said grudgingly, "maybe your way . . . this way . . . is better."

Tom responded by reaching over to rest a hand on his shoulder. "Don't sell yourself short. We wouldn't have stood a chance without the arrangements you made. We're not doing it *my* way. We're doing it *our* way."

They had argued bitterly earlier. Elias saw everything in black and white. The rescue of Constantin was paramount, worth any risk. The plan he had devised was sharply etched in his mind. Tom had said no. He had refused despite Elias's arguments. Despite the dangerous truculence displayed by Panos. Despite Melina sobbing on bended knees.

The driver of the maroon Fiat indicated a desire to join the inside lane. Elias obliged by reducing his speed to a crawl. The Fiat edged over, leaving a space. With no wish to close the gap on the ambulance, Elias was content to allow a Lancia to push into the gap.

In his wing mirror, Tom could see Costas in the front passenger seat of the Mercedes. The street lighting turned Costas' tanned features blue, then purple. The traffic crawled onwards, increasing pace slightly, moving in an orderly queue.

Oncoming traffic was less orderly. Traffic on the far side of the road was increasingly chaotic. Cars pulled left and right, hastily making an opening through which appeared first a police car, then a fire truck. *Two* fire trucks, with bells ringing, lights flashing and horns blaring—and behind them yet another one. And *another* police car. Elias had to shout above the wail of sirens as a fourth police car mounted the central reservation. "Constitution Square must have gone up in flames," he shouted triumphantly.

Tom watched with grim approval as the police car, grinding its gears, accelerated away to the city center.

"I told you," Elias cried happily. "We create diversions all over the place. I wonder how things are at the law school?"

"I wonder," Tom echoed. Part of his mind was still back in the cellar. The women had worried him. Melina was verging on a complete breakdown. She might get in the way. Or panic. Or worse, become injured or captured. "What if these ESA outriders appear?" he had argued. "What if they open fire? Suppose Melina gets hit? Suppose we rescue Constantin and kill his wife in the process? Will you face him with that?"

Then there was Kirsten . . . so worried about Melina that concern for her own safety was forgotten. How would she react in the thick of it? Would she help? If so, the ESA might shoot her. Would she run? If so, Panos or Spyros would kill her. "No," Tom had argued, "we can't take the women."

Across the road, traffic continued to spill in every direction. A dun-colored troop carrier bulldozed its way down the center lane. Smaller vehicles scraped each other as drivers swung their wheels to escape the monster behind them. Armed soldiers waved carbines and shouted conflicting instructions. Elias shouted too. His words were drowned in the cacophony of noise, but his excitement and triumph were obvious.

There had been no triumph earlier. Elias had defended his views with tenacity. "We all know what to do," he had argued, pointing to Panos and Costas and Spyros. "New arrangements will lead to confusion. We have agreed. . . ."

But Tom had not agreed. And he refused to do so.

Gregg had helped. The little Australian's reaction had been unpredictable. Tom had flown with him often enough to know that Gregg could handle emergencies, but what few had arisen had been in the air. None had occurred on the ground. And to Tom's knowledge, nothing in Gregg's past life equipped him for the dangers they now faced.

Depressing the accelerator slightly, Elias increased speed. The traffic was thinning out. The worst congestion lay behind them in the city. "Another five kilometers and we'll know which way they are going."

Tom nodded. There were two possible routes to the military hospital. Elias had chosen ambush points on both.

Gregg had preferred Tom's plan from the outset. "I'm not worried about my own skin, don't think that," he had said quickly, "but it's the best chance for everyone." Lowering his voice, he had jerked his head at the women. "Especially them."

Melina was in a terrible state. She had sided with Elias, until Tom's implacable determination convinced her of the futility of arguing further. Accepting the inevitable, her swollen eyes had searched his face. "If we do as you say . . . you will go with Elias? You will help set my Constantin free?"

She was terrified of making a wrong decision. One wrong decision would condemn Constantin to death.

Taking her in his arms, stroking her hair, Tom had encouraged her. "Do as I ask and I'll bring Constantin to you."

"Promise?"

"I promise."

The promise had been easily given in the cellar.

Elias muttered, "They should be in the bay by now."

They were thinking the same thoughts. Not the same, Tom corrected himself. Similar. For his part he had been cataloging missed opportunities. If only he had formulated his own ideas more quickly . . . if only Gregg had been involved at the outset . . . if only Elias had been less obstinate. Gregg might have had time to fly the women to Kariakos and return to Piraeus. If, if, if . . . but it had turned five-thirty by the time Elias conceded. Time was fast running out.

Suddenly Elias exclaimed, "I've lost Spyros. Oh shit! I told him . . . where the hell is he?" Tom searched for the Mercedes in his wing mirror. There was no sign of it. Instead he saw a white Citroën, followed by a heavily laden lorry.

Elias erupted. "I told you Panos should drive! He's a better driver. Spyros is too slow. And Costas couldn't navigate his way round a—"

"It's okay." Tom sighed with relief, catching sight of the Mercedes six cars back, in the inside lane. "They're still with us."

Panos had continued to argue even after Elias conceded. It had been Melina who convinced him. She had realized by then that it was Tom's plan or nothing. Led back to the cot, she had sat down wearily, dabbing her eyes, struggling to bring her nerves under control. The old man and Costas had squatted down in front of her. Panos and Elias had followed to stand over the cot. They were all talking in Greek, Kirsten as well, clearly endorsing what Melina was saying. Watching Kirsten had caused Tom to regret his earlier doubts. She was playing her part. Whatever her personal worries, she had recognized the common danger. She was working with him, not against him.

"Look! Look!" Elias cried sharply. "He's turning. Terrific. He's going the best way for us." His voice rose with excitement. "Where's Spyros? Has he seen where we're going?"

Behind them, the Mercedes accelerated into a gap. "He's moving up." Tom tried to keep his own voice steady.

Ahead, separated by the Lancia and two other cars, the ambulance was signaling a right turn.

"But has Spyros *seen us*?" Elias demanded, feverish with anxiety.

Tom watched the Mercedes blink its indicator. "Okay. He's following."

He congratulated himself on this one stroke of luck. Learning that Panos was a fisherman with a seagoing boat had ended the argument. Tom's plan was adopted. And once everything had been agreed the two parties had left the cellar within a few minutes of each other—Tom, Elias, Costas and Spyros setting off for the city, while Panos and Gregg took the two women to Passalimani.

Elias made the right turn. "How's the time?"

Tom glanced at his watch. "Twelve minutes past."

The boy nodded. He moistened his lips. "Your friend Gregg could be in the air by now."

"He won't be. Don't worry. He'll be there."

Gregg would abide by the plan. As soon as he and the women were aboard *Helena*, he would settle them in the back seats, out of view, and prepare for take-off. Firing both engines, he would taxi a mile or so out into the bay, downwater from Passalimani toward Piraeus. Then one engine would fade, apparently misfiring. He would bring *Helena* to a stop. Leaving navigation lights on, he would clamp emergency lamps onto the wing and clamber out to work on the engine.

"He can't work on the engine all night," Elias grumbled.

"He'll make it look good. He'll climb back into the cabin, switch on, turn the props over, go back and check something else."

Meanwhile they would hit the ambulance. Then, with Constantin in the back of the van, Lianis and Tom would drive to Piraeus. They would get Constantin aboard Panos' boat, and Panos would set out for *Helena* with all possible speed. It was Tom's way to hide the trail to Kariakos.

"You're sure Lianis knows where Panos berths his boat?"

"Quite sure," Elias nodded, a grim smile on his lips. "They have met on that boat many times."

Tom tried to imagine those meetings. An Army major. A simple fisherman. And his brother Spyros. And Costas. Perhaps others. Fighting the Junta. The risks were appalling. And this boy next to him was only eighteen, yet he acted like a seasoned professional. Even so, Elias was not as tough as he pretended. He had choked up when they first saw the ambulance. His eyes had misted over. He had been on the verge of tears. Coughing to clear the lump in his throat, his whisper had turned to a sob, "We're coming, Constantin. Hang on. We're coming."

And they were.

The city now lay behind them. Street lighting was becoming less regular. Pale shadowy cubes of a small housing development showed on the left. Looking strangely sinister under the night sky, olive trees, twisted and stunted, grew in a grove on the right. The city had given way to suburbs and the suburbs were fast becoming open country.

The Lancia slowed and turned down the small road to the housing development. The tail lights of the ambulance showed a hundred yards ahead.

"What's the time?"

Tom held his wrist close to his face. "Twenty past."

"Okay. That's fine. That's good." Nodding his head, Elias was overcome by a need to talk. Nerves loosened his tongue. "We're making good time. Excellent time. Not long now. Not far. . . ."

Tom watched the road. Suddenly it seemed empty. The

traffic, so thick earlier, had either remained in the city or had carried commuters back to their homes. Here the empty road stretched before them like a ribbon, twisting and turning on its way to the hills.

"Is Spyros behind? Can you see him?"

Tom squinted into his wing mirror. "I see his lights—"

"How do you know they're his?"

"He was following us—"

"But that could be someone else. Can you see more? I only see one set of headlights. Suppose it's not Spyros?"

"It must be." Tom watched the lights. They were a long way back. Spyros, if it was Spyros, was taking his time.

"Christ! Give me a cigarette," Elias demanded. "Not so far to go now. Time for a last cigarette."

Tom's hands were clammy with sweat. Wiping them on his trousers, he reached into the glove compartment for his cigarettes. Lighting two, he passed one to the boy. Elias grunted his thanks. Crouched over the wheel, the red glow of his cigarette was reflected in the windscreen. Without the lights of the city, the night had grown darker. Black clouds scudded across the face of the moon.

The ambulance was pulling away. Glancing at the speedometer, Tom realized they had increased speed to fifty miles an hour. Yet the ambulance was losing them. The red tail lights were now a quarter of a mile ahead, maybe more. He wondered if they would be outrun. It was possible. The van rattled and shook. Elias pressed down with his foot, holding but not closing the gap. "Come on, come on," he muttered.

Behind them the lights grew brighter. Spyros, if it was Spyros, had obligingly quickened his pace.

The road flowed into a sweeping curve. Squinting into the darkness, Tom glimpsed the pencil-thin headlights of the two outriders ahead of the ambulance.

The curve favored the pursuers. Elias was closing the gap.

Another curve, this time winding round to the left. Elias stubbed out his cigarette. "Not far now," he muttered, clamping both hands hard on the wheel.

The road uncurled and straightened. Elias pressed down on

the pedal. Ahead, the red tail lights grew larger. The lights bounced, then the van bounced as it hit a pothole, jolting Tom's spine to the top of his head. His muscles knotted with tension. The van was flying, closing the gap. Fifty yards . . . forty . . .

"Get ready!" Elias shouted.

Tom braced himself. He moistened his lips. The palms of his hands were greasy with sweat. A sound roared in his ears, growing louder and louder. Suddenly the night was full of the roar of a more powerful engine as Spyros closed the gap from behind. The blaze of headlights filled the wing mirror. The nose of the Mercedes drew alongside. Tom saw the front seats, with Costas pointing the shotgun from the open window. Then the Mercedes was past, barreling along the crown of the road, tires spitting flints and pebbles like buckshot. Foot by foot, yard by yard it drew alongside the ambulance. Spyros swung the wheel. Metal scraped metal. Red and white sparks flashed in the inky night. Caught unawares, the ambulance veered to the side of the road, revealing one of the motorcyclists ahead in the widening gap. Silhouetted in the headlights, the man cast a terrified look over his shoulder. He swerved in a bid to escape. Throwing out one leg, the steel heel of his boot scraped the road. Then the Mercedes hit him. The ambulance rocked back again, blocking Tom's view. He heard the crack of gunfire, the rasp and screeching of metal, an explosion of splintering glass, tires squealing . . . and Elias screaming, "Get ready! Get ready!"

Zig-zagging wildly, the ambulance was braking. Elias was braking harder. Hands on the dashboard, Tom braced himself. The smell of scorching tires filled his nostrils. Shuddering and bumping, the van tracked to the right, then slowed, ran forward, then slowed again. Without stopping completely, Elias was already crashing through the gearbox in search of reverse. Tom was jerked backward, sideways, then forward again as the vehicle spun through ninety degrees. On the road along which they had just traveled, he could see the faraway lights of an oncoming vehicle. Reversing at speed Elias backed the van towards the rear doors of the now stationary ambulance. Tom shouted directions from his half-opened door. "Stop!" he bellowed as the gap closed. Flinging his door fully open, he leapt into the road, racing around the van to open the back doors. From the other side, Elias appeared out of the darkness, heading straight for the ambulance. Turning to follow him, Tom saw another figure from the far side of the ambulance. A uniformed figure with a revolver in one hand.

"Elias!" Tom shouted in warning.

The boy was already at the ambulance doors, struggling to turn the handle. The uniformed figure pushed him aside. Reaching out, Tom grabbed the man's shoulder to swing him around. He glimpsed a hawk nose and deep-set eyes. Elias shouted, "It's Lianis."

Gasping with relief, Tom backed away, lowering his clenched fists. Suddenly the ambulance doors burst open, kicked open from inside, swinging outward with such violence that Elias staggered backward. A figure loomed on the tailboard above them. A huge man. In the red glow of the rear lights, Tom thought it was Constantin. Then he saw chevrons on the sleeves holding the carbine. Flame burst from the muzzle. Explosions erupted. Tom felt a blow to his leg. Not pain. Hitting the ground was more surprising than painful. Pain was to come later, not while the air was full of gunfire and cordite. Rising to his knees, he saw Lianis pump away with the revolver. Then Lianis staggered. Simultaneously the big man threw his gun in the air; next moment he toppled, falling full length, crashing into the gap between the van and the ambulance. His head hit the van with a neck-breaking crack.

Tom was up, hobbling forward, intent on following orders. Under his breath he was telling himself to stick to the plan. "Transfer Constantin to the van," Elias had said. "Then go! *Go!* It will all be over in two minutes."

Elias was pulling himself up into the ambulance. "Constantin! Constantin!"

Dropping his revolver, Lianis was clutching his chest. He supported himself against the van, pausing for breath before staggering to the open front door. He slumped in the passenger seat. Tom was about to shout, "Get in the other side. You're driving," when he heard Elias crying. Wailing. The boy was sobbing inside the ambulance. Peering inside, Tom saw a shadowy figure on a stretcher. Elias was bent forward, his face contorted.

"Hang on," Tom shouted. "I'm coming." But his left leg refused to respond. He could neither lift it nor trust it to support his weight. Grabbing a rail inside the ambulance, he was about to heave himself aboard, when Spyros appeared.

Shaking his head, Spyros pointed at the van, "Go! Go!"

Costas appeared from the shadows. Shotgun in one hand, he used the other to propel Tom toward the van. Spyros was already up into the ambulance, pushing the stretcher toward the tail-board. Dropping his gun, Costas grabbed the other end, pulling it toward him.

Tom dragged himself around the van. Given no option, he squeezed in behind the wheel, glancing sideways at Lianis. The man swayed in his seat, clutching his shoulder. Reaching past him, Tom slammed the door. "You direct me, okay?" Lianis grunted. Turning, Tom saw the stretcher slide in from behind. Spyros and Costas were outlined in the opening. Then Costas slammed the doors, plunging the interior into darkness. Tom was trying to see Constantin. "Constantin! It's me. Tom Lambert." He swung round as Spyros appeared at the window. "Go! Go!" Spyros shouted, pointing back down the road. "Go! Go!"

The engine was still running. Tom let in the clutch and lurched across the crown of the road. In his wing mirror, he saw Elias. Lit by the red glow of the tail lights, Elias was being sick in the road. Turning the wheel, Tom accelerated back toward Athens. "Lianis. I need directions."

Lianis grunted and half turned to prop one shoulder against the door.

Tom was swept by a great surge of elation. "We did it!" he shouted. "We did it! We did it!" He felt an irresistible urge to laugh and sing. "Fantastic! We did it! They said it would be over in two minutes. Christ, was that all it was? It seemed longer. No, it didn't. It seemed like two seconds. Christ—"

Suddenly Lianis vomited. Still clutching himself, he slid forward. Without the restraint of a seat belt, he pitched forward until he was half on the floor. His head hit the dashboard with a sickening thump.

"Lianis!" Snatching his gaze from the road, Tom glanced sideways. Lianis was staring back at him. The man's face was lit by the green lights of the instrument panel. The blood he had vomited was over his chin. He no longer clutched his chest. His lifeless hands had fallen away.

"Lianis!" Tom screamed. Looking up, he saw tail lights half a mile ahead. He eased back on the accelerator, realizing how fast he was driving.

"Say something, Lianis, for fuck's sake! Say *something,* even in Greek!"

Headlights flashed past on the other side of the road.

"Jesus!" Still watching the road, he took one hand from the wheel and fumbled sideways. Clutching Lianis by the shoulder, he tried to pull him upright. And failed. Lianis was jammed tight. Tom worked his hand down to the man's elbow, then to his wrist. There was no pulse.

"Oh, my God!"

How far had he driven? Should he turn round? Go back? No point, Elias and the others would have fled.

He cleared his throat. "Constantin?"

The only sounds were the racing engine and the drumming of tires on the road.

He raised his voice. "Constantin!"

No answer.

He went cold. Numb. Paralyzed by fear. Without directions, he was lost. He had no idea how to get to Piraeus . . . no idea how to find Panos and the boat. . . .

His left leg was wet. He thought he had wet himself. Urinated from fear. He would not have been surprised. Or even ashamed. He *was* afraid. Christ, he was afraid. But if he had pissed himself, why was his leg throbbing with this terrible ache? Dropping one hand to his thigh, he was only mildly surprised to find his fingers tacky with blood. What did surprise him was the *amount* of blood. It was everywhere. All down his leg. Reaching forward, he groped for his ankle. Even his ankle . . .

The fear which gripped him was like nothing he ever felt in his life. Terror. Worse than a nightmare. Worse than anything he ever imagined. His mind balked. He had a gunshot wound. He was driving a stolen van. Dead men lay in the road behind him. A dead Army officer was jammed into the next seat. The most wanted fugitive in Greece lay in the back of the van. . . .

"Constantin! Constantin!"

Most chilling of all was the realization that he was lost. He had no idea where to go. Time was running out. He recalled his last instructions to Gregg. They had calculated timings. Ambush at eight-thirty. Half an hour to reach Piraeus. Ten minutes to find Panos and board the boat. Twenty minutes to rendezvous with *Helena*. "Don't wait beyond ten," Tom had instructed. "If we haven't shown by ten, something must be wrong. Don't wait a minute longer." And Gregg had nodded agreement.

Tom glanced at his watch. Eight thirty-eight. "Oh Christ!"

The groan made him jump. He was jumpy anyway. His nerves were in shreds. Mistaking the sound for road noise, he checked both wing mirrors and the instrument panel before returning his gaze to the road. Ahead of him, the rear lights were much closer. He was gaining ground on a large vehicle. A bus! High above the tail lights he could distinguish shadowy outlines of heads and shoulders of passengers. Jesus! Imagine passing a bus and someone looking down to see Lianis slumped half on the floor. His foot eased off the accelerator. He glanced in the wing mirror. Lights! Headlights! Coming up from behind. And coming fast. His foot went back on the accelerator.

The noise came again. Definitely from behind him. Unmistakably the sound of a human voice.

"Constantin!"

A groan, a definite groan.

"Constantin! Oh Jesus. Thank God! Listen, I think Lianis is dead. I dunno the fuck where I'm going. Can you pull yourself up to see over my shoulder?"

The response was neither a yes or a no. It was Constantin's voice, weak, saying something, but garbled. The words were muffled, unclear.

Adjusting his speed, Tom watched the bus in front and the lights behind. The road curved. He recalled the series of curves on the road out of Athens. Soon they would reach the city outskirts. Not long after that they would be back where they started . . . at ESA Headquarters. Swallowing hard, he tried not to panic. "Constantin. Can you hear me?"

The weak voice remained indistinct.

He risked a glance over his shoulder. Lacking windows the interior of the van was pitch-black. The stretcher was directly behind him. The back of his seat blocked his view. Craning his neck, he glimpsed a figure beneath a blanket and the pale moon of Constantin's face at the far end. And something else. A glint of light halfway down the stretcher. And he *heard* something else—the clink of metal upon metal.

He swung back to the road. The nose of the van had advanced into the orbit of light cast from the bus windows. He reduced speed. Suddenly he realized what he had seen. Handcuffs! Constantin was shackled to the stretcher. "Oh Jesus! I need directions. Constantin, I need you up here."

Street lights were beginning to appear at regular intervals. The car behind was right on his tail. His leg was dripping blood. The ache was becoming a numbness. "Constantin!" he shouted from sheer desperation.

The croaky voice mumbled some sort of reply.

"I can't hear! For Christ's sake! I can't hear!" He gulped, taking a deep breath, fighting panic. His chest heaved. His heart raced. He began to repeat over and over again, "Stay calm. Calm down. Keep calm." Beads of perspiration stood out on his forehead. "Okay, okay. Think, think! This is the situation. I think Lianis is dead. Constantin, can you hear me? I think Lianis is dead. I daren't stop to make sure in case we attract attention. I know you're hurt. I can't hear what you say. Maybe you're gagged or something. I know you're chained to the stretcher. . . ." Gulping for breath, he fought the hysteria which threatened to overtake him.

Steering one-handed, he wiped the sweat from his brow. His hand trembled as it went back to the wheel. "Wait a minute. I've got an idea. Listen, can you make some sort of noise? Hit the stretcher or something? Something? Anything? Can you do that?"

Clink! Clink! Clink!

"Oh Jesus!" A huge sigh of relief escaped his lips.

"Okay, let's try something. Here's what we do. I ask you a question, right? You hit the stretcher once for yes and twice for no. Understand?"

Clink!

Tears sprang into his eyes. Biting his lip, he recovered. "Oh thank God! *Thank God*!" He prayed softly before raising his voice, "Okay, Con. Can you hear me all right?"

Clink!

The answering sound made him light-headed with relief. He heaved a deep breath to regain control. "Oh Con! That's great. Fantastic. Keep that up and we've got a chance."

Did they *really* have a chance? Even now? The bus was pulling over. It was stopping. Dear God! He had no choice but to pass. Putting his foot down, he sped by, fearful of watching eyes looking down from the windows. Street lights were everywhere now . . . and shops and tavernas and pedestrians on the pavements. . . .

"Listen, Con. You were being taken to the military hospital. We followed the ambulance for about ten miles . . . er . . . fourteen or fifteen kilometers. We got you out on a flat stretch of road, dead straight after a series of curves. Once we got you aboard, I headed back. We've been round the curves. Now we're coming back into Athens. Traffic's getting thicker. We just passed a bus. We have to get to Piraeus. I haven't seen one sodding sign that I understand, but I think Piraeus is off to the right. Is that right? Is that correct?"

Clink!

"Oh Jesus. Oh Con! That's terrific. Just keep it up. Don't pass out on me. Don't doze off or anything. I'm looking for the first major road on my right. Okay?"

Clink!

"Terrific. You're doing great."

He drove in silence for a few minutes, his hands sweating on the wheel, his eyes darting and searching. But the silence was temporary. The need to maintain communication with Constantin was overwhelming. "Con, you still okay?"

Clink!

The reassurance was magical. He had become dependent on the sound of metal striking metal. It lifted his spirits. It gave him courage. "There's a church on our left. The road this side's all little shops . . . nothing special. Traffic lights ahead. I think I can turn right after the lights. Con? What do you think?"

Clink.

"Turn right?"

Clink.

"Okay. Lights are red at the moment. I'm slowing down. Oh shit! I'm getting funny looks from the guy in the next car. I think he's seen Lianis."

Lianis remained jammed between the seat and the dashboard. The top of his head was actually on the dashboard. His death mask was turned toward Tom, eyes open, blood all over the chin. Earlier the tunic jacket had been a blob in the darkness. Now the crowns on the epaulettes glinted in the street lights. The entire jacket was sodden with blood.

"Christ! He has seen Lianis." Tom watched in horror as the man rolled down his window. He was middle-aged; gray hair, with a mustache. A military mustache? Another soldier? A colleague, a comrade? Whoever he was, he was bloody inquisitive, peering and craning his neck for a better view.

"Come on, lights. For fuck's sake! *Change*!"

The man was actually opening his door.

The lights shone green. Tom's blood-soaked left foot squelched as it came off the clutch. The van shot forward. He swung right, narrowly missing the last car crossing the junction. Behind him, he could see the man clambering quickly back into his car. It was a smart-looking car. A black, official-looking car which, at that moment, was causing displeasure to other drivers who were honking and beeping their horns. A truck lumbered past, denying the curious driver the chance to turn right. Then the bus. Then the scene was lost from Tom's view as he followed the road.

The new road was thick with traffic. He held the inside lane. Pedestrians jostled with each other on the pavement a few feet beyond Lianis' hunched body. One of them might see something. One of them could be a policeman. Shops and tavernas and cinemas added their lumens to the street lighting, all conspiring to turn night into day.

"I can't stay on this road, Con. The whole place is lit up like a Christmas tree."

The wail of a police siren sounded in the distance. He flinched. He glanced at his watch. Eight forty-five. Fifteen minutes since the ambush. Dear God, was that all? Fifteen minutes! Elias had promised they would have half an hour before the balloon went up.

The siren grew louder. It was getting closer. Suddenly he saw the flashing blue light coming towards him. Across the road cars jinked and squirmed out of the way as the police car emerged from the pack and went screaming past.

Faint with relief, he cleared his throat. His parched mouth was as dry as scorched sand. "Con? Can you hear me, Con?"

Clink!

"I daren't stay on this road. There's more traffic lights ahead. I reckon I've got the general direction. Maybe I can find my way through the back streets. You know, do a left and a right, left, right, that sort of thing. What do you think? Con, do you think that's a good idea?"

Clink.

"Okay. We're coming up to the lights. They're still green. Come on. *Come on!* The stupid bastard in front is taking all night. Come on!"

He turned left at the lights, then right and left. It was darker. The only street lighting was an occasional lamp on a street corner. And the streets were narrow, often too narrow for two lanes of traffic, so that when vehicles met, one would pull to one side to allow the other to pass. Not that there were many vehicles, although the streets were neither empty nor quiet. Doors were open to catch what there was of a breeze. Pools of yellow light splashed out over the pavements. Youths chatted on corners. Men sat drinking in a taverna. Old women made their way to church. A radio blared from open shutters. Children called for their mothers. . . .

All of which Tom described in a continuous running commentary. He felt marginally safer. Slightly less vulnerable away from bright lights. And he was coming to terms with the horror . . . for the lights had shown him more than potential pursuers. The illumination outside the cinema had been bright enough to light even the inside of the van. He had snatched a glance over his shoulder. And seen Constantin's face. Seen what Elias had seen earlier. A face beaten and broken and pummeled almost beyond recognition . . . broken nose, missing teeth, black bruises and veined with congealed blood. Now he knew why the sounds which fell from those tortured lips were unintelligible. He tried to imagine Constantin's agony. The pain would be unendurable. He guessed Constantin would opt for unconsciousness as an escape . . . but it was not an option he could allow. Several times his questions failed to draw a response. Once he thought he had lost him for good.

"Con! Jesus, Con, will you answer me?"

Silence.

"Con! For Christ's sake! Tell me where I'm going."

No answer.

"For God's sake! We're nearly there. Panos is standing by with his boat. Gregg is in the bay with the seaplane. Con!"

Then came an answering moan, a plea for peace articulated by tone, timbre and pitch, by some trick of the larynx or curve of the tongue, which said as clearly as words "Let it be! Let me die!"

Tom shouted at the top of his voice. "You miserable bastard! Don't you dare quit. You big ape! You gutless wonder. You fucking turd. I've got Melina waiting—"

Clink, clink, clink, clink, clink, clink.

"Okay, okay!" Tom's voice was hoarse. His sweaty hands slipped on the wheel. He was losing all sensation in his leg. Changing gear was ever more difficult. Sheer concentration kept him going. And talking. He never stopped, saying anything and everything to sustain Constantin's attention. ". . . block of flats on the right. Bloody monstrosity. Architect must have been drunk. Or blind. Or both. Turning right now, Con. Another narrow street. Slight uphill gradient. Quite a long street. Con, does it sound familiar? Anywhere you know?"

Clink, clink.

"Okay. Don't worry. I'm sure this is the right direction. I'll do a left at the bottom. You all right, Con?"

Silence.

"Con!"

Clink.

"Hang in there. Melina's on the seaplane. Waiting. She's okay. She's safe. Kirsten's with her. Hey, that's something. Kirsten. You know? The Red Cross delegate or whatever? Know who she *really* is? Maurice's daughter. Stanton's daughter. What about that, Con? Can you believe that. Christ, I bet you didn't know that, did you Con? Con?"

Clink, clink.

"No. Well, there you are. I'm turning left here, Con. There's another church . . . no, hang on, some kind of school—"

Clink, clink, clink, clink, clink, clink.

"Okay, okay. It's *not* a school—"

Clink, clink, clink, clink.

"It *is* a school, right? Is that what you're saying?"

Clink.

"So we're on the right route?"

Clink.

"Thank God! Okay. Just you relax now. Stay cool. We'll get there. So what about this Kirsten, eh? She's one hell of a girl, Con. She's been a big help. Kept her nerve. Most women would have gone to pieces. And she's something to look at, eh? Shit! Looks like a main road ahead. Lots of lights. I'll go straight over. Right?"

Clink, clink.

"What do you mean? Clink fucking clink? There's *lights,* Con. All over the place. Okay, what do I do? Turn left or right?"

Clink, clink, clink, clink.

"Okay. Two questions, huh? Sorry. Jesus, I'm almost on top of it. Turn right, Con? Do I turn right?"

Clink, clink.

"Turn left?"

Clink.

"You got it. Jesus, Con, there's the sea! I can see *boats* at the end of the road—"

Clink, clink, clink, clink, clink.

"Now what? I just turned left, okay. There's lights everywhere. I'm on the main drag. Down the end of this street I can see the sea—"

Clink, clink, clink, clink.

"Don't go as far as the end. Is that right?"

Clink.

"Okay." Tom's eyes searched past the tavernas and cheap shops. "There's a garage . . . a filling station coming up. On our right. Narrow street next to it—"

Clink, clink, clink, clink.

"Go past it? Go down it—"

Clink.

"Go down the street next to the filling station. Is that right?"

Clink.

His strength was fading. He could feel it draining away. Every ounce of concentration was needed. Trying to change gear was impossible. His left foot, his entire left leg was totally unresponsive. Ramming the gear stick forward, he was punished by screeching metal. Using third gear and the brake pedal, he bounced and jerked past the garage and into the narrow street. Sweat rolled down his forehead and into his eyes. He felt giddy and faint. The dark shadows of the street closed in on him as he pushed down on the clutch with all the strength he could muster. Pain scorched up his leg making him cry out. He tried again, twisting in his seat, putting a hand on his blood-soaked thigh to add thrust to his leg. The van jumped. The engine coughed. Then stalled. The van rolled to a halt.

Panting with pain and exhaustion, he cradled his head in his arms. Tears of frustration prickled his eyelids. It was heartbreaking to be so close. They were in Piraeus. They must be within a mile of the boat . . . Gregg would still be out in the bay. . . .

Clink, clink, clink, clink.

He raised his eyes. At the end of the street, he could see dark blobs, rising and falling. Boats! And beyond them the inky black sea. Suddenly he saw two other blobs. Coming closer. Figures. Advancing up the street. Pointing at the van. Breaking into a run.

"Jesus! We've been spotted."

Frantically he turned the key in the ignition. The engine fired, then stalled, refusing to engage in third gear.

The figures drew closer. Footsteps approached from behind. Hairs rose on the back of his neck as he saw someone almost at the door. Someone *was* at the door. Someone was turning the handle, pulling it open. Constantin groaned and croaked despairingly from the stretcher.

Tom's mouth opened in protest. "Panos!" he sobbed with relief.

Other figures loomed out of the darkness, converging from both ends of the street. Men in a desperate hurry. Four, five, six of them counting Panos. They pulled Tom from behind the wheel and carried him to the back of the van. By the time the doors were open, Panos was starting the engine. Muffling exclamations, they pushed Tom inside. Three of them climbed in behind him, crowding so close that one of them sat on Tom's leg. The doors closed, plunging them into darkness. A jolting journey began. He gritted his teeth. His hands clenched. Every bump brought searing, unbearable agony. He was unable to move, they were so cramped no one could move. He almost passed out from the pain . . .

The journey was mercifully short. They stopped. The doors opened to reveal the night sky. He could smell the sea. He could *hear* the sea. Pulled from the van, he found himself lifted over a man's shoulder. Upside down, bouncing along, he saw a flight of stone steps cut into the side of the wall. The seawall. A boat . . . with Panos already aboard, looking up, stretching out both arms to help. They laid him down on the deck. A moment later Constantin's stretcher was lowered beside him. Figures scurried away. The deck boards began to vibrate, a big diesel engine burst into life. . . .

He drew a deep breath. His leg was giving him more pain than anything he had felt in his life. He fought back the nausea and tried to recover; to hang on. Turning sideways, he reached out a hand. "Con? Constantin? You okay?"

Slowly, painfully, the mutilated head turned toward him. Even the night failed to disguise the disfigurement. Constantin Peponis had acquired a face from a nightmare. The mouth opened. A faint whisper emerged, a gurgle, followed by a guttural animal sound. Then Constantin remembered. He raised one arm a few inches. Clink came the sound of metal upon metal.

The handcuffs. Tom caught his breath. He groaned, faced with another emergency. *The stretcher.* "Christ, Con, we've got to get you free of that stretcher."

Other men had had the same thought. With the darkened boat rising and falling beneath them, Panos left one of his men at the wheel. Dropping to his knees, his hands went straight to Constantin's wrists.

Tom levered himself up on his elbows. "We need metal cutters to get him free. We'll never get him on *Helena*." His words died as he saw what Panos was doing. The stretcher was a canvas sheet bound to two metal poles. Constantin's left wrist was handcuffed to the left pole, his right to the right pole. With a gutting knife in his hand, Panos was cutting the canvas. Unable to free Constantin from the handcuffs, he was intent upon freeing the handcuffs from the stretcher. The canvas was strong. Panos hacked with the knife. Swearing and cursing, he worked furiously to strip the canvas from the pole. Then he began to pull the pole through the other end of the handcuff.

A cry, muted but urgent, came from the wheel. Panos was on his feet in a flash, thrusting the knife into Tom's hand on his way past. Responding as best he could, hampered by injury, darkness and the motion of the boat, Tom attacked the canvas close to Constantin's feet. Bent low, he strained to see in the dark, realizing that the boat was running without lights.

Suddenly there *was* light. Aft of the main cabin, one of Panos' men switched on a spotlight. It flooded out over the sides of the boat, a long beam directed to starboard. It lasted a moment. He heard the shout of excitement. Then the light was extinguished. He worked on, feverishly cutting and tearing the canvas. Beneath his knees, he could feel the deck veering to starboard. Dropping the knife, he began to slide the pole through the handcuff. Behind him voices rose in excitement. Panos was back to push him aside. The boat was slowing. The note of the engine fell to a grumbling growl.

Constantin was free. Like grotesque bracelets, the handcuffs hugged his wrists, no longer attached to the poles.

Panos used every second. Hauling Constantin upright, he shouted to one of his men. Tom felt hands under his arms, helping him to his feet. A huge shadow loomed out of the water. Tom blinked with astonishment. He could scarcely believe his eyes. *Helena!* So close. The seaplane was on top of them. The boat was actually under the wing. He could see Gregg outlined in the open hatch, extending a hand toward Panos. And Panos, helped by one of his men, lifting Constantin between them . . . Panos, resting a hand above *Helena*'s open hatch . . . Panos conveying an encouraging word as they transferred Constantin aboard.

Then it was Tom's turn. Hands grasped him, lifting him up onto the gunnels of the boat. Every muscle in his body ached. The pain from his leg was excruciating. Yet pain was secondary to the exhilaration welling up inside him. He felt light-headed with joy. Tears prickled the back of his eyes. He wanted to extend the moment, to delay, to thank Panos, to praise the others . . . but he was pulled into *Helena*'s cabin as the hatch swung shut behind him. He glimpsed the back of Gregg's head as the pilot fled to his seat. For a moment he heard Melina sobbing, then the engines drowned all other sounds. His legs gave way as soft arms embraced him. Collapsing into a seat, he looked up into Kirsten's dark eyes swimming with tears.

BOOK SEVEN

1978

It's two o'clock," Alec exclaimed in surprise.

"So?" Constantin glowered. He had no wish to be reminded of the time. Most of all he specifically wished Tom *not* to be reminded of the time. It was much better to remind Tom of the old days. Better for Tom to talk, to reminisce, to sit up all hours drinking this excellent brandy. Better for all concerned if Tom got stinking, pissed-as-a-newt drunk so that by morning he would be incapable of knotting his necktie, let alone knotting a noose around somebody's neck.

It seemed unlikely. Tom was at the hearth, throwing another pine log onto the fire. His face was flushed from the heat, not from drink. Looking up, he frowned, puzzled, "Why the hell did we start jawing about this old stuff?"

The surprise in his voice gave Constantin a lift, a distinct feeling of making progress. "This old stuff is what happened to us," he mused gently. "What else do old friends talk about? Besides, I wasn't sure Alec knew the whole story."

Alec did, he had heard it many times. Surprised, he was about to say so when he caught Constantin's wink. Conspiratorially the hooded eye winked again. Alec stifled his protest. He wondered where Constantin was leading. They had spent hours covering this old ground. But did it matter? Constantin's circuitous approach might succeed where straightforward argument had failed. Anything was worth trying, even now at this late hour, *especially* now with Tom's guests due in a few hours. Glancing at the hearth, Alec watched Tom lift another log from the log basket. "No . . . well . . . I don't suppose I do know the *whole* story. Bits and pieces of course, but—"

"Huh! Bits and pieces. Hear that, Tom? That's what we were, weren't we? Bits and pieces. That night we flew into here."

Tom straightened up from the hearth. His face betrayed him. Reluctance showed in his eyes—reluctance to dwell on that night when they had arrived on Kariakos like casualties from a battlefield. He had passed out on *Helena*, regained consciousness, and passed out again. Everything was a bit hazy. He had lost a lot of blood. Kirsten had used her nail scissors on his trousers, ripping away the sodden fabric to reveal the gaping wound in his thigh. He remembered the gentleness of her fingers, the concern on her face, his blood on her hands. He could still hear the relief in her voice, "There's an exit wound . . . I think the bullet passed right through."

Constantin might have been telling a joke, "You should have seen us, Alec. He was bleeding like a stuck pig, I was delirious, Melina was having hysterics, and Kirsten kept shouting to Gregg, 'How much longer?' I tell you, it was a miracle we got here."

Alec responded quickly to keep the conversation flowing. "So what happened when you arrived? When you came up to the villa?"

"Up that path?" Constantin exclaimed, incredulous, jerking his bald head at the darkened windows and the terrace and cliff path beyond. "Gregg had more sense. We didn't come here. He took us straight to the village."

Tom could remember Maurice coming to the cottage. Strange, he had no recollection of arriving at the cottage, or even in the village, but he could distinctly remember Maurice coming through the door.

"Bits and pieces sums it up, eh, Tom?"

Still resisting the memories, Tom shrugged. "My leg wasn't so bad."

"Hah! It's a brave man who dismisses battle wounds lightly—"

"Rubbish. It was a clean wound. I was lucky. You were the one we were worried about."

Constantin momentarily fell silent. A reflective look showed in his eyes, giving a somber cast to his face. "I know," he admitted softly. "It was touch and go for a while." He rubbed his jaw with a misshapen hand. "I was in a bad way until you patched me up—"

"Me? Not me. I can't claim any credit. It was Melina and the doctors and . . ." Tom hesitated, ". . . and Kirsten."

Constantin's heart soared. Tom had said her name. He had actually used her name. That was a breakthrough. Kirsten was the reason for everything, yet until now Tom had shied away from talking about her. Constantin's voice quickened, "Ah, yes, Kirsten was wonderful. I wouldn't have pulled through without her. Neither would Melina—"

Startled, Alec interrupted. "I didn't know Melina was hurt."

"Not hurt. Not injured, no . . ." Constantin tried to find the right words. "You must understand, it was bad for me, of course, but worse for Melina. It broke her up to see the state I was in. My face was a mess, I couldn't talk, only make those god-awful sounds. I used to hear her sobbing when she thought I was asleep. My heart ached. There was no way I could console her. Kirsten nursed Melina as much as she nursed me. Isn't that true, Tom?"

Tom was pouring fresh brandies. When he looked up there was pain in his eyes, but also a deep sense of longing. He was trapped. Part of him wanted to recall those days when he had limped around on a stick.

"Maurice wanted us to come up here to the villa," Constantin continued, "but Kirsten refused. I remember her getting very angry and going pink in the face." He laughed. " 'I'm not living under his roof,' she said. So Tom came up here and we stayed in the cottage. That's what I remember most, the three of us in that cottage."

Tom remembered too. He remembered Kirsten meeting her father for the first time, clenching her fists and stamping her foot. Constantin was right, she had been angry, but temper had been only part of it. Close to tears, she had struggled to control more complex emotions.

"She didn't quit though," Constantin added hastily. "She wouldn't leave my side until proper arrangements were made."

Proper arrangements had taken time. Maurice had worked fast, but Constantin's injuries had presented huge problems. Kariakos lacked a qualified doctor, and Kirsten had refused to allow Constantin to be flown to Malta or Turkey.

Gregg had risked his freedom by flying back to Passalimani. Dragging Doug Masters from his Athens hotel, the two spent a morning working on *Helena*'s port engine, in full view of countless spectators including policemen and soldiers. No one paid the slightest attention. Relieved and satisfied, Gregg had flown *Helena* to Malta while Masters flew the Learjet to London. Forty-eight hours later he was landing at Valletta airport with a nurse and two Harley Street doctors on board. From there Gregg had ferried them to Kariakos, bypassing Greece entirely to avoid the slightest whisper from reaching the Junta.

"By the time the specialists arrived," Tom recalled, "Kirsten and Melina had turned the cottage into a nursing home."

"Not just them," said Constantin. "Everyone lent a hand. Mavros helped. All the people on the island helped. That was when we met them for the first time. They're a good crowd. They'd helped other refugees from the Colonels' regime."

A bed for Constantin was set up in the living room overlooking the sea, and the two women moved into the single bedroom. The doctors praised Kirsten for the care she had taken of her patients. Tom's wound was clean and without infection. The complications arose when they began to treat Constantin.

Tom smiled, "I thought they'd never stop."

Constantin's jaw was wired up. His entire head was encased in a protective wire basket. Limbs were sealed into plaster casts, and every part of his body was treated for cuts and burns.

"I could wiggle my fingers," Constantin remembered, demonstrating with his right hand. "That was all. I had to stay like that for a month to build up my strength before they could operate."

Alec grimmaced, "Rough."

"It wasn't so bad." Constantin shook his head. "The doctors left some drugs, so I wasn't often in pain. I suffered from nightmares, but even now I get those. No, it could have been worse. I was made comfortable. Tom came to see us every day, and I had Melina and Kirsten to look after me."

Kirsten could have left with the specialists. The nurse was willing to stay in her place. Kirsten could have flown to Malta and on to Geneva from there. . . .

"Melina persuaded her to stay," Constantin said with obvious fondness. "She and Kirsten had become friends even before I was arrested, and afterwards Melina was grateful, she trusted her, admired her. Kirsten became very special. They were like sisters, eh Tom?"

Tom nodded absentmindedly. Against his will, his thoughts had returned to the past. He had visited the cottage every day, driving the mile and a half from the villa in the ancient jeep, the only motorized transport on Kariakos. Kirsten would dress his wound. Melina would cook. The four of them became very close.

Constantin chuckled. "I remember him trying to persuade Kirsten to see Maurice. By God, that was a battle. She went up like a sheet of flames, telling him to mind his own business. Remember that, Tom?"

Tom smiled. How could he forget. Poor old Maurice was eating his heart out. Bitterly hurt by Kirsten's attitude toward him, he endured her hostility with quiet dignity, but was always ready with a battery of questions when Tom returned to the villa. Maurice would have liked to visit the cottage himself. He had every right, it was his cottage, he equipped it and supplied the food and provisions—but Kirsten kept him away. Tom had never seen Maurice so vulnerable, or so upset. They spent evenings together. Just he and Maurice. Maurice had sent his summer girls away. Two had been staying at the time—Bess, a New Yorker, and a little French girl whose name he had forgotten. Maurice had made light of it, pretending Bess wanted to see

Rome and the French girl had gone to keep her company. It had never happened before. If a girl wanted to see Rome, Maurice would take her. They would stay at the Excelsior and see all the sights. If there were two girls, so much the better, Maurice would have double the fun. The truth was he was so anxious to make a good impression with Kirsten that he had sent his summer girls away. So in the evenings he played backgammon and talked business with Tom. He listened while Tom called Alec in London, and Amiens in Geneva, or Edwards in Toronto en route for New York. Stanton Industries was expanding and a wounded leg was keeping Tom away from the action. But every evening ended with Maurice drawing the talk back to Kirsten. Did Tom like her? What sort of a girl was she?

Constantin grinned. "Kirsten used to get so mad with Tom. She would blaze up, calling her father a selfish bastard and the like, and Tom would defend Maurice by listing the brave acts he performed in the war. Naturally Melina and I had never heard such stories, but the surprise was neither had Kirsten. It wasn't easy for her, hearing these things her mother had kept from her. There was a lot of talk about gifts Maurice had sent, birthday presents during her childhood. Kirsten never received any of them, did she, Tom?"

Tom remained silent. Kirsten had been visibly shaken. She had refused to believe Maurice had sent her gifts. Tom would not accept that Maurice had lied, arguing, "Why should he? He told me this ages ago, never expecting I'd meet you."

"Tom?" Constantin persisted, seeking an answer.

Tom looked up.

"Remember those fights you had with Kirsten?"

"I remember her mother had been bloody selective with the family history."

"Even about the divorce settlement," Constantin added to keep the conversation going. "Kirsten didn't even know her father had been prevented from seeing her, did she?"

Tom remembered Kirsten's bewilderment. And her pain.

"Then there was that business about Roddy," Constantin said. "She didn't know he came out to the island regularly. She didn't know he met his father in London. It was all a big surprise to her, wasn't it, Tom?"

To avoid answering Tom sipped his brandy.

Constantin laughed. "I remember one morning. Tom and Kirsten were arguing again and Kirsten started on about Maurice's women. 'What about his mistresses?' she cried. 'They aren't figments of my mother's imagination.' So Tom says it was just Maurice's way, there was no harm in it, when Melina joins in. She blushes bright red. 'I see things in my taverna,' she says. 'These women adore him. He fascinates them. He is gentle and kind. I see with my own eyes. I don't think such a man makes a woman unhappy. Kirsten, you should be proud of your father. . . .' "

Constantin's laughter drew a quick grin from Alec and a slow smile from Tom. Still laughing, Constantin concluded, "So Kirsten throws up her hands. 'You too, Melina,' she cries, 'my God, this is a conspiracy.' "

Which it was in a way, Tom thought, looking back. Certainly Melina had helped for reasons he never fully understood. After all, she could not have known how Maurice craved to be reconciled with his daughter.

"Tom kept at her," Constantin remembered. " 'Meet him,' he would say, 'He's not an ogre.' And Melina joins in, 'How can this man be so selfish?' she asked, 'when he helps us by bringing money and letters from London?' "

Tom had asked Maurice about that. Maurice had grinned sheepishly, dismissing his role as of little importance. "A man came to see me in London," he explained. "Alexandros Dedas. I checked him out and he was what he said, a lawyer friend of Constantin's from the old days. He told me Constantin's story. I didn't mind playing courier. It reminded me of my time in the war." But Maurice had refused to become more deeply involved in the Greek crisis. "There's no comparison with the war," he said. "I'm not a young man anymore. I've no business commitments in Greece, I have no Greek friends. Perhaps most important of all, Hans Pohl isn't here to stir my political conscience."

Constantin smiled, "So that's how we passed our time. They talked while I listened. Sometimes we tuned into news bulletins on the radio. We never trusted them, the Junta controlled everything, you understand, so we had to interpret what we heard, but no arrests were reported. So we kept hoping. Then one day a fisherman brought us a message to say Elias was safe with my uncle."

"So they all got away?" asked Alec.

"Every one of them." Constantin smiled his satisfaction.

The days had flown. When Constantin was awake they drew chairs up to the bed and talked across him, to include him in what was going on. Sometimes he contributed by writing messages on a pad. In other circumstances such enforced idleness would have driven Tom to distraction, but he remembered each day as full of incident—comparing Constantin's bruises every twenty-four hours, commenting on the way his skin was regaining color and that his head was back to its proper shape—encouraging Melina, telling her not to worry—urging Maurice to have patience with Kirsten—and Kirsten herself. Not all their time was spent arguing about Maurice. She talked for hours about the ICRC. The Red Cross was much more political than Tom had imagined. It seemed that wherever dictators ruled, the ICRC could be found ranged against them. "Oh yes," Kirsten nodded, "but most delegates are much tougher-minded than me."

She had a rueful smile that he began to look out for, a self-deprecating modesty which he liked. She had sent the ICRC news of her whereabouts, along with her resignation. Gregg had dealt with it by calling at the ICRC office in London. Tom had expressed some misgivings, but Kirsten had convinced him. "Secrets are safe with them," she said.

Watchful of Tom's mood, Constantin pretended to have a sudden thought, "Know something, Alec," he said, "Kirsten wasn't just special to Melina. We all came to love her." He laughed softly. "And naturally, being a woman, Melina was quick to play matchmaker. She couldn't resist it. She liked Kirsten and Tom, the four of us were always together. . . ." His smile widened. "In any case, it wasn't so difficult. The two of them got closer every day. Even I could see it, without Melina pointing it out to me, especially when they started going off by themselves."

Tom's eyebrows rose. "That was to give you and Melina time to yourselves."

"Sure. Melina told me. She asked Kirsten to do it as a favor. But tell me, my friend, was it so hard?"

Tom stared in surprised silence.

"I'm not claiming credit," Constantin grinned. "I don't think it affected the outcome."

Tom had taken Kirsten off most afternoons. Not that they could go far. Kariakos possessed that tiny village, the villa, six narrow beaches and three pine-covered hills. There were no roads, just a few tracks into the pines, ending in clearings where trees had been felled. The least rutted track led to the villa, but Kirsten refused to go there, so usually he bounced the jeep into the uppermost clearing and parked in the shade facing the sea.

They spent hours under those trees. Talking, getting to know each other. Neither of them was prepared for what happened. Certainly not Tom. Melody was not always around when he wanted her, though she held him entranced when she was. And not only him. Somehow her lifestyle and the money she was earning conspired to endow her with even more glamour. Heads turned wherever she went. To enter a restaurant with Melody was automatically to become the envy of every man there. And they would have been even more envious had they seen her in bed—looking up at him, green eyes half closed, lips parted and her golden hair all over the pillow. Melody was a great adventure in her own right—and totally, utterly, different from Kirsten.

Of course he liked Kirsten. He felt responsible. She wouldn't have been there except for him. And now that she was there he wanted her to meet Maurice. It became important to reconcile father and daughter, to reconcile two of his friends.

And she had charm and looks and a spell all of her own. Her eyes were enchanting, deep-set and black-lashed, serious eyes, with such a startling capacity to express feelings that a glance was often more eloquent than words.

The unexpectedness of his feelings confused him, and his confusion was reflected in her. Her life was turned upside down.

Resigning from the ICRC was only a part of it. His stories about Maurice unsettled her. She believed enough of them to begin to harbor dark suspicions about her mother. Some of the conversations became painful, with Kirsten verging on tears—"How could she do that to us? All those years . . . all those lies."

He vividly recalled one afternoon. She had been stewing over his words more than he realized. Suddenly she burst into speech and once started seemed unable to stop. "You'd think there was no one you knew better than your mother. Then you discover you don't know her at all. It's like . . . you feel . . . deserted. Your whole life is based on a lie. You feel cheated. Who can you trust? Anyone? No one?"

Her bitterness was unmistakable. The prospect of facing her mother filled her with gloom—"What will I say to her? Ask her to give me the doll he sent me when I was seven? Ask why she said he never wanted to see me, when all the time she was denying him access?"

The moment passed. One of the things Tom liked about her was her lack of self-pity. The wry smile was quick to return. "So? Such a disaster," she said, tossing her head. "I am to be pitied, no? Not like Melina. She has all the luck. Her husband is tortured. She loses her home, her country, her family." Mocking herself, Kirsten sighed. "Poor, poor me. Lucky, lucky Melina."

He sat watching her, admiring the fall of her dark hair on her shoulders, and the way the quirky smile was never far from her lips. That day she was wearing a lemon shirt and a floral skirt, both borrowed from Melina.

"Symbols of solidarity," she smiled. "Conferring refugee status."

To his mind there was a bit of the refugee in her. A privileged refugee. She had never known real financial hardship—"Not that we're well off. We're penniless. Maman always had to scrimp and scrape. At least that's what she said. I always believed her. Now I don't know what to believe . . ."

She shared an apartment in Geneva with two other girls. "Just to leave home. To be independent. Stupid, really. My mother lives in this vast house overlooking the lake—"

"I think I've seen it," he interrupted, remembering Yvonne Amiens pointing it out to him. "The Château Stanton."

Her eyes widened with pleasure. "Do you know it?"

"Only from a distance."

"It's marvelous. There's nowhere like it. She ought to sell it, really. She'd be comfortably off then. I supposed she can't bear to part with it—"

"But Maurice paid her a fortune at the time of the divorce."

She looked at him. "That's what he tells you."

"Why should he lie? I'll ask him if you like. Better still, come up to the villa and ask him yourself."

"No."

"Why not?"

"Because . . ." Her cheeks colored. "It's bad enough talking to you. Not very loyal, is it? I'd feel a hundred times worse talking to him. Besides, I'm not ready to believe he's a paragon—"

"Why not talk to Roddy? He was estranged from your father in the same way. They get on fine now. Roddy's often out here—"

"That's what is so amazing." Kirsten was bewildered. "My mother can't know about that. She'd go *mad*."

Hunched in his chair, nursing his glass, Tom stared into the fire, lost in the past. Some of it seemed like yesterday.

Silence had fallen on the room. Even the wind outside had dropped to a murmur.

Constantin sensed Alec looking at him, wondering whether to speak but afraid he might say the wrong thing. The same fear prompted Constantin into speech. "We were here four weeks—or was it five? Tom, was it four weeks or five weeks?"

"What?" Tom looked up with unseeing eyes.

"I was just saying—were we here four weeks or five?"

"I dunno. A month, wasn't it?"

At the end of the month, Kirsten had pronounced on her patients. Although Tom was still walking with a stick, his wound was healing quickly. Constantin looked a terrible mess, but he was certainly stronger, and it was time to move him to London for his operations.

Maurice made the decision about travel. *Aphrodite* had been in Marseilles earlier, undergoing some sort of refit which Maurice had cut short. By the end of the month she was anchored off the island, ready to sail at a moment's notice should trouble come from the mainland.

"Why don't we send them to England aboard *Aphrodite*?" Maurice suggested one evening. He looked at Tom. "In fact you could go with them. Do you more good than flying. Set you up again before you plunge back into the fray."

Tom announced the news to Melina the next day. She was overwhelmed. Unknown to him, she had been worrying about money, fretting about paying her way. The family had converted what cash they could into gold. Melina's handbag was crammed with jewelery, gifts from Constantin in happier days, but most of it contributed by uncles and aunts. The sum total of Constantin's wealth could be laid out on a table.

Melina had become spokesperson for Constantin as well as herself, an inexperienced spokesperson deputizing for a once eloquent lawyer. Inexperience and worry led to an embarrassing moment. She pressed Tom to take a platinum ring and Kirsten to accept a gold brooch as gifts. On top of which there was Maurice to worry about. She sat shaking her head and wringing her hands. "How can we ever repay the Kyrios Stanton? All the trouble we cause. Doctors come here . . . now we go to London . . ."

To escape further embarrassment, Tom and Kirsten went off in the jeep. He drove to the clearing under the trees where they sat and talked about Melina's absurdly generous gesture and much else besides. He was desperate to get back to London and business, to see Alec, to check progress with Amiens and Edwards. His desk in Jermyn Street would be piled high with a million things to do. . . .

But Kirsten was at a crossroads. She had no compelling reason to return at once to Geneva. Duty no longer called at the ICRC. As for her mother, she shrugged. "I need time to think. Whatever I say to her will be better after reflection."

Slyly he probed for any other reasons which might draw her home. "What about friends?"

Her dark eyes met his with a look of amusement. "Men, you mean? Some. Well, two. One fun, one quite serious. But the same applies—anything said to them will be better after reflection." Her eyes remained locked into his. "And you? Who's waiting in London?"

Melody was in the States. Alec had told him that on the phone. "No one," he answered, "at least no one in London."

His suggestion was that she stay on the island for a while longer, but she declined with her quirky smile. "What's the expression?—out of the frying pan into the fire? I'm not ready for that."

"So what will you do?"

They were sitting on the grass, a few yards from the jeep. Her legs were drawn up in front of her, the hem of her skirt pulled over her knees. With her chin cupped in her hands she stared out to sea as if searching for her future on the horizon. "I was thinking about what you said about Roddy. I could go to London to see him." She sounded hopeful. "It's hard to explain, but I feel a bit disoriented, especially about my mother. Roddy must know some of the answers. Right at this moment he seems the only family I've got. We've never been close, what with the age gap and different schools and all that . . . but I'd like to see him again, to talk to him. After all, we are brother and sister. We shouldn't just drift apart the way we have. We might become friends. I'd like that . . ."

The more she talked, the more the idea appealed to her. The frown lifted from her brow and a smile returned to her lips. And a few minutes later she was making plans—"Perhaps Roddy could put me up for a while?"

Then another thought occurred. She turned to him with sudden anxiety. "What about Melina? I hadn't thought, but Constantin will be in hospital for weeks. What will she do? Where will she stay?"

Tom had no idea.

"She'll be lost, in London all by herself. If I took an apartment she could move in with me . . . ?"

And so another plan emerged. Money didn't seem to be a problem, although she did talk of seeing her friends at the ICRC in London—"Perhaps they could give me a job in the office?"

They took the decision back to the cottage. Melina was overjoyed. She hugged Kirsten. She kissed Tom. She dragged them to the bed to tell Constantin, clutching his right hand and rubbing it against her cheek. Once again they were pressed to accept her extravagant gifts. This time Tom drew a chair up to the bed and made Melina sit on the covers next to her husband. "See this?" He pointed to the medallion on his belt. "I've led a charmed life since I've worn this."

He almost believed it. His life *had* changed since Constantin gave him the medallion. He had become moderately wealthy, successful, he traveled the world. In reality he was not superstitious. Friday the thirteenth was a day like any other. Black cats were black cats. Yet he always wore that buckle. Of course he exaggerated the importance he attached to it, to emphasize how much he owed them. "But one debt cancels another," he said sternly, "so we'll have no more talk of brooches and things." He had a sudden idea. "But there is one thing you *must* do," he said to Melina, "you must give a dinner party for the Kyrios Stanton."

Kirsten was trapped. What could she do? For a month she had been Maurice's guest. She was about to sail to London aboard his yacht. To refuse was out of the question.

Constantin stirred in his chair. "Remember that dinner party?" he asked. A rueful look came to his face. "Some dinner party that was," he grumbled. "I had no teeth." He laughed and rubbed one knee with his hand. "Eh Alec, that was a sight. You should have seen Maurice and Kirsten together, and Tom with this big grin on his face, so happy . . . eh," he sighed, enjoying the memory. "Believe me, Alec, that was a night to look back on."

Maurice had been as nervous as a bridegroom on his way to his wedding. He clutched Tom's arm in the jeep. "I don't know, Tom. This could go disastrously wrong—"

"It won't. Relax. It will be a great evening."

And it was. It had been a memorable evening.

Constantin hesitated as he watched Tom stare into the fire. Such a look of sadness marked his face that it seemed cruel to go on. What profit lay in raking over dead ashes? Why cause such pain? Yet which was the lesser evil—to call up old ghosts, or watch a new specter emerge? Tom Lambert was already haunted. This madness would destroy him. Hardening his determination, he shifted his gaze from Tom's misery to Alec's look of expectation. "What a night," he said with a forced laugh, "Maurice had Kirsten eating out of his hand by the end of it. Everything went according to plan, didn't it, Tom?"

Tom remained motionless in his chair, staring into the fire. Kirsten had been charmed. Of course. Why not? Nobody could resist Maurice's charm.

Disturbed by Tom's continued silence, Constantin attempted a joke. "Melina was besotted," he growled with mock disgust. "There I was at death's door, and she's making eyes at Maurice." He threw a laugh across the room, aiming for Tom, hoping for a laugh in return and seizing on the wry smile. "See?" he exclaimed to Alec, as if proving the point.

Alec grinned, "I can't believe Melina . . . Tom?"

"Of course not."

"But Maurice and Kirsten?"

"Got on famously," Tom nodded. "Maurice made her laugh He got her talking about her life, her plans, everything really. Neither of them mentioned her mother which was a miracle considering Kirsten was going to London to escape her—"

"No, no," Constantin interrupted. "She had other reasons. You. Her brother. Even us, Melina and me, but you were the main reason." He winked at Alec. "What is it about the English? Are they afraid of their feelings? His feelings about her were written all over his face. And she was the same. Don't listen to this talk about escaping her mother—"

"Her mother was part of it," Tom insisted sulkily. "And she was keen to see Roddy—"

"Ah yes," Constantin nodded, remembering. "Didn't Maurice give her Roddy's address or something? Hadn't Roddy just moved—"

"Right. Kirsten didn't have his new address and Maurice gave it to her."

Alec said, "I bet Maurice was delighted."

Ecstatic would have been a better word. Maurice returned to the villa overflowing with excitement. Everything about Kirsten delighted him. He insisted that Tom join him in a nightcap before going to bed. "I won't sleep, Tom, not yet. Let's talk for a while . . ."

All of the talk had been about Kirsten. Maurice couldn't let the subject alone. "I would love to go to London with her. I could help her find an apartment—"

"So why don't you?"

"I'm tempted. God knows I'm tempted, but . . ." His eyes clouded with doubt. "I'd better not. I had enough trouble with Roddy about that. I daren't risk losing Kirsten, not now."

Tom waited, a look of inquiry on his face.

Faintly embarrassed, Maurice had shrugged. "It's understandable, I suppose. Kids don't want their fathers hanging around. They want their own adventures. Roddy gave it to me straight—'Don't crowd me,' he said. So I don't. I let him know in advance when I'm in London. He comes round and has dinner, he holidays out here, and such. We get on pretty well, considering . . . anyway, it taught me a lesson. I daren't smother Kirsten. I must give her space . . ." They talked until four in the morning.

Finally, when they rose to go to bed, Maurice put a hand on Tom's arm. "I'm glad you like her. It makes it easier to ask a favor. I know how busy you are, but if you could help her settle in, show her around, that sort of thing . . ."

The four nights aboard *Aphrodite* drew them not only closer to England, but even closer together. Yet they did not immediately become lovers. Things would have been different with Melody. She would have laughed and teased and flirted, so that spending the voyage in separate cabins would have seemed absurd. Whereas Kirsten's shy reserve induced a sense of caution. At times he thought she was as ready for him as he was for her, but then a distant look came into her eyes and the moment was lost. And once back in London, business took over. Inevitably. He had been away for more than four weeks. Responsibilities reached out and claimed him. The best he could do was to stay in touch by hurried telephone calls, snatched between meetings. And Kirsten was fine. She and Melina had moved into Maurice's suite at Claridge's as a temporary measure until they found an apartment. Constantin had been installed in the Brompton Road Hospital and was facing the first of his operations . . .

"In the fast-changing world of office mechanization," reported *The Financial Times*, "few organizations are moving with the speed of Stanton Industries." It was true. The collection of unrelated businesses with which Tom had started was acquiring muscle, and clout. The shipping line had been sold. So had the bottling plant in Belgium. The chemical plant had been disposed of, along with much more in which Stanton owned only a minority interest.

Yet Jermyn Street remained unchanged. The heart of the conglomerate still lay behind the small door sandwiched between the outfitters and SIMPKINS & CO., MAKERS OF BESPOKE FOOTWEAR SINCE 1808. Upstairs Barbara still ran the office, although with a much larger staff. Lack of space was becoming a problem. Alec was always complaining, "It's getting so you can't turn around in here."

Tom resisted a move. He had become adept at playing a political game. New offices would excite envy, particularly from someone as status-conscious as Andre Amiens. "It's not worth the hassle," he told Alec. "I'll stand firm on things of importance, but I'm damned if I'll fight for the size of my office."

Maurice Stanton had got what he wanted—a merger without blood on the floor. The structure Tom had created was working. Stanton Manufacturing supplied Stanton Sales with products at a price which gave the manufacturing company a profit while leaving Desmond Edwards enough margin to compete in world markets. Amiens was an efficient manufacturer and Edwards such a natural-born salesman that the bickering between them had become a thing of the past. Tom kept it that way by restricting their meetings. He and Alec were the go-betweens, assisted by the team of trouble shooters working out of Jermyn Street. They measured performance, monitored budgets and oiled the wheels.

The biggest headache was the newly formed Institute for Scientific Research. Even without the temperamental Carl Pohl, the Institute always held the seeds of conflict. Research and Development was the middle ground between sales and production. Edwards argued that he should control R&D because "We're at the sharp end, we know what the customers want." Amiens argued the opposite. "R&D is a natural adjunct to manufacturing. We have the scientific and technical skills." And Alec argued, "We're wasting money on Carl Pohl." Meanwhile the whole group was funding the Institute and it seemed to Tom that people never stopped complaining.

To catch up, he worked through a weekend and burned the midnight oil with Alec. As usual he concentrated on the item of most pressing importance. This time it was the French vineyards. Prudent management and good weather had restored them to profitability. An offer for the business was now on the table. "If I go to Bordeaux," he decided, "I might clinch the deal in a couple of days."

"Amiens is coming over tomorrow," Alec pointed out.

"We'll be finished with him by late afternoon. You can look after him in the evening. I could get across to Bordeaux and meet these people for dinner. With luck I'll be back by Friday with a sizable check."

He had a constant hunger for sizable checks. The strategy they had adopted was simple—sell everything unrelated to the core business, and use the cash to back Edwards and Amiens in a dash for growth. Stanton Industries was buying more factory space, making more products and employing more salesmen. The proceeds from the sale of the vineyards could be spent a dozen times over: competition for resources was fierce and unending.

Which was a subject Amiens raised at the meeting.

Immaculate in black mohair, he wafted into the office on a cloud of cologne. "Tom! How are you? Accidents must agree with you. You look like an athlete at the peak of his fitness."

Tom certainly looked well. The Mediterranean sun had tanned his skin and lightened his hair. Not that Amiens looked anemic. He never did. His tan equaled Tom's and his eyes were as shrewd. "Alec tells me you broke your leg. What were you doing? Chasing a girl around the pool?"

Tom had invented a cover story for everyone except Alec. He grinned. "No such luck. I slipped on those bloody steps leading down from the villa."

Amiens cocked his head. "Ah yes," he said gravely, *"those* bloody steps." His disbelief was obvious. He was not insulted, merely curious. Something had kept Tom from the office for five weeks. A broken leg wouldn't have kept him away for five days, as Amiens had remarked to his wife only that morning.

"How's Yvonne?"

"Safe and sound in Geneva," Amiens said with some satisfaction.

Tom and Alec had given up counting the different women Amiens brought on his trips to London. Redheads, blondes, brunettes: he went by age rather than type. Not one had been over twenty-five. "Full of juice," he reported with a great smacking of lips. Alec, the quintessential married man, had been mildly shocked. Tom hadn't turned a hair. "He can screw who he likes on his own time, so long as he doesn't screw up on mine." Even then Alec had argued, "But you quite like Yvonne?" Tom had laughed. "Sure, I can do business with her. But what she does with her husband is their business. She's older than him and she has the money. Maybe she keeps him on too tight a rein? Who knows? I don't care. I'm not in the business of handing down moral judgments. It's his business performance that counts."

And Amiens performed well in business. He was allowed to run Stanton Manufacturing with minimal interference, and for the most part did a fine job, as he demonstrated with his figures. His production units were keeping pace with the increase in sales.

The morning session was concluded without rancor, even with a certain amount of good humor, and not until lunch did an edge of dissension arise. The three of them—Tom, Alec, and Amiens—had strolled around to the Caprice, and the meal was almost over when Amiens fixed Tom with a quizzical eye. "What news from the boy wonder?"

"Not much. Give him time."

"Time he can have. It's the cash I resent."

Guessing what was coming, Tom tried to deflect it by comparing the wine they were drinking with that produced in the Stanton vineyards. "What do you think?" he asked, raising his glass to the light to inspect the color. "Vintage for vintage. Ours is as good, wouldn't you say?"

But Amiens refused to be diverted. "I wouldn't give Pohl one percent of my turnover, let alone the seven you deduct for the Institute."

Tom retreated behind an amiable smile. "Carl is like our vineyards. We had to nurse them along—"

"Is that how you see yourself? As a wet nurse?" Amiens scowled. "Do you have any idea when he'll deliver something worthwhile?"

"Come off it, Andre. Nothing's certain about R&D. You know that as well as I do."

"What I *know*," Amiens said heavily, "is that he's costing too much. Seven percent of my turnover would buy me that factory in Sweden this year. Instead I have to wait until next year. You're restricting our expansion by pandering to a spoiled brat."

Tom sighed, "We did *agree* to set up the Institute—"

"Not in California," Amiens retorted. "I voted against it. So did Edwards. Remember?"

How could Tom forget? Pohl's desire to establish the Institute in California had caused the biggest board room battle since Stanton Industries came into being. "You can't just ignore Silicon Valley," he said gently. "That's where it's all happening. Carl *had* to get out there—"

"No." Amiens shook his head. "We should have kept him in Europe. I expected accountability. He should be instructed to work to our priorities . . ."

Tom didn't interrupt. He had listened before, and knew he would have to listen again. He had heard Desmond Edwards on the same subject. Even Alec had voiced some hostile opinions in private. Listening, Tom decided, was the best way to buy time and keep the peace.

With lunch over they walked back to Jermyn Street and resumed their analysis of Stanton Manufacturing, which precluded reference to Pohl, and since the figures produced were excellent, the discussions ended on a happier note.

Unprepared for what was to come, Tom breathed a sigh of relief.

The three of them had walked out to the lobby, with Amiens telling Alec about the girlfriend he had brought along on this trip. "Come and join us for a drink this evening," he was urging. "You will like her."

Shaking hands while saying farewell, Tom was glad to have the excuse of his trip to Bordeaux. "Next time, Andre. But maybe Alec could join you?"

Leaving them, he returned to his office and began to pack his case. He looked up when Alec walked in. "That went okay," he said cheerfully.

"It did." Alec nodded, and walked over to the window to stand with his back to the room. "Considering."

"Considering what?"

"He does have a point, you know. We make him produce a return on every penny invested, and he performs brilliantly. No wonder he's pissed off about Pohl. Desmond's the same. He was complaining while you were away."

"I can imagine," Tom slipped the draft contract for the vineyards into his briefcase.

"Pohl needs a good kick up the arse."

"You won't motivate him that way."

"What gets me," Alec continued, "is that you go along with it. You're as bad as Hollenberg, always taking Pohl's side. You may think he's a bloody genius, but I don't—"

"Okay, Alec, I heard it all over lunch—"

"And dismissed it as usual. It won't go away. You'll have to face it sometime and it may as well be now."

Surprised by the anger in Alec's voice, Tom paused to listen.

"Andre thinks the Institute is a lousy investment, and Desmond says the same—"

"They're managers—"

"Bloody good managers—"

"Whereas Pohl is a visionary, an original thinker—"

"Original lazy bum," Alec sneered.

Tom glanced at his watch, knowing he should leave.

Alec scowled. "Andre and Desmond haven't got together on this yet, but one day they will. Suppose they persuade Gunther to back them? Come on, admit it, that wouldn't be too hard. Gunther's a banker, for Christ's sake. All he sees is the bottom line—"

"Very well," Tom conceded irritably, "they convince Gunther."

"Then they take it to the main board."

"They'd have three votes to four," Tom said lightly. "Them on one side, Maurice, Hollenberg and us on the other."

A strange look came into Alec's face. He began to say something, then changed his mind. Shaking his head, he warned, "Don't be so sure. Maurice listens to Gunther. They go back a long way—"

"Maurice also listens to me!" Tom retorted in exasperation.

More than exasperated, Alec was losing his temper. "Seven percent of Group turnover is being wasted—"

"Invested, not wasted. Invested in research—"

"Investments yield a return." Alec's gray eyes flashed. "We get fuck-all out of Pohl. Desmond's right. It's pouring money down a bottomless pit."

Tom closed his briefcase with a snap. "Very well, Alec. I hear what you say." Standing up, he looked as his watch.

"No! You don't hear what I say." Shaking his head, Alec advanced across the office, "You assume too much. You *presume*. I'm not a bloody puppet, you know. Suppose this goes to the main board? Suppose Maurice asks my opinion? What happens then?"

Shock delayed Tom's response, and in that second the door opened. Barbara's head appeared. "You're half an hour late. The car's waiting. The driver's worried about traffic."

"Right," Tom answered, still staring at Alec.

Waiting impatiently, Barbara opened the door wide. With a pained look, Alec shrugged and returned to the window.

Barbara scolded, "You should be at Heathrow by now."

"Coming." Tom cast a look at Alec's back. "We'll talk more about this when I get back, okay?"

Alec responded with a twitch of his shoulders.

"I must go."

"Yes," Barbara agreed, "you *must*!"

Tom paused at the door and looked back, expecting Alec to turn and wish him luck.

But Alec remained motionless, standing at the window as still as a stone.

* * *

The incident played on his mind. There was no time to brood; each day was taken up with negotiations for the vineyards, but in the periods in between—traveling to and from the hotel, falling asleep, shaving in the mornings—the warning came back to plague him. He couldn't believe Alec would vote against him. Alec was just being Alec. They always argued, it was the way they worked. Alec was the best Devil's Advocate in the business . . .

Yet a doubt lingered. He cursed the enforced absence from the office. Five weeks was a long time. A lot could happen in five weeks . . . new alliances could be formed . . .

He had nurtured alliances of his own. There had been precious few at the outset, Maurice and Gunther, and then only as far as it suited them, with open hostility from Amiens, Edwards and Pohl. But times had changed. He had successfully delivered the merger. Stanton Industries had come into being . . . and he and Maurice had become friends. That was a huge, unexpected bonus. But what was it worth? Maurice still demanded results. He had not given Tom *carte blanche* to do as he liked. Policies still had to be argued out. . . .

Suppose the argument went against him? Suppose Amiens and Edwards won Gunther's support? Tom would argue "It will pay off in the long run." And Gunther would counter "We're dead in the long run." Maurice would look down the table to Alec and Alec would hold the balance of power. Tilt one way and Tom would be on the wrong end, with Amiens and Edwards, Gunther and *Alec* on the other.

Not that he believed Alec would do it. Not really. Not when it came to the crunch. But suppose Alec was lukewarm in support? What then? Maurice might side with the others . . . and again Tom would be on the wrong end, with Amiens and Edwards, Gunther and *Maurice* on the other.

When it came to the Institute, only Walter Hollenberg could be relied upon. The wily old German so fervently believed in Pohl that some of his admiration had rubbed off on Tom. Tom's own meetings with Pohl tended to be contradictory. Sometimes he came away fuming over Pohl's arrogance. Other times he left aglow with excitement, his brain buzzing with Pohl's visions of the future.

In Bordeaux, the negotiations edged toward agreement. The proposed contract was re-drafted and they began to argue their way through the clauses. Tom grew impatient with his local lawyer. He had been equally irritated in Brussels when he had been selling the bottling plant. Local lawyers were a necessity, but the ideal would be to send someone to ride herd on them, someone to deputize for him and report back at moments of progress. It was beyond Alec. Alec's real forte lay in production, not in the careful drafting and arguing of clauses.

Finally, on Friday afternoon, the agreement was signed. The new owners insisted that he stay an extra night for a celebratory dinner. "You must," they exclaimed, "to wish us *'bon chance.'* " It seemed churlish to refuse. Besides he felt like celebrating on his own account. In his hand was a bank draft for twenty-two million francs, ten percent more than he had allowed himself to hope for at the outset. They agreed to meet at his hotel, and he returned there to wash and change for the evening. Feeling pleased with himself, he took the opportunity to call Alec. "It's a deal," he announced. "We got twenty-two million. Andre can have his factory in Sweden after all!"

Even as he spoke he realized he couldn't predict Alec's reaction. The thought surprised him. He had called the office dozens of times to hear Alec's voice warm in support, "Terrific! Well done. Fantastic." Alec was always there in support. . . .

"That's two million more than our bottom line," said Alec. "Well done!"

The momentary doubt faded, bringing a grin to Tom's face.

But then came the hesitation . . . a qualification, unspoken, inaudible to a less familiar ear . . . then audible as Alec put his thoughts into words. "Andre will be delighted of course, but . . ." He hesitated. "The factory in Sweden could be bought out of income if it weren't for what the Institute is costing. You're buying it out of capital. Isn't that a bit like selling the family silver?"

The taste of success turned sour in Tom's mouth. He felt bleak with disappointment when he hung up. "For Christ's sake!" he muttered. "Two million better than our bottom line. That was some deal . . ."

Crushed and depressed, the prospect of a celebration lost its appeal. Voices floated up through the open window. Outside the evening was warm and inviting, full of soft golden light. He stared down into the grounds. The hotel staff were arranging tables on the terrace. He watched as the new owners of the vineyards arrived, each with a woman on his arm. He was reminded that even the pasty-faced lawyer was bringing his wife.

Feeling lonely, he returned to the telephone, and dialed Melody's number in Paris. As he waited, he tried to calculate the traveling time to Bordeaux. Perhaps they could meet halfway? Limoges or Bourges. Have a late supper and spend the night together. He would hire a car . . . the hotel could arrange it. His spirits lifted.

He was greeted by her answering machine, Melody speaking in her carefully correct French, promising to return his call if he left a message after the tone.

"Shit!"

She was always away! Or out. It was the same whenever he called. Always that bloody machine. The only dates they had were when she called him. Weeks on end would pass, then she would call out of the blue. "Hi. I'm in London." Or "Hi. How about dinner in Venice on Sunday?" Fine, why not, after all she was the Golden Tycoon, enjoying her bloody great adventure!

He glowered at the telephone. From his address book, he found Claridge's number in London. He dialed, mis-dialed, and dialed all over again, and a few moments later was talking to Kirsten. She sounded so pleased to hear him. And so interested in his meetings. She knew where he was, he had called her before leaving London. And she had news of her own. Constantin was recovering from the first operation . . . she and Melina were searching for an apartment . . .

Disappointment and tension drained away, washed away by the sound of her voice. He was reminded of sitting in the jeep on Kariakos, talking a whole afternoon away. Why on earth had he called Melody? Habit? Because he was in France? Why . . . when all the time Kirsten was waiting in London?

Purple shadows began to darken the golden light. His hosts were waiting on the terrace. Dammit, they could wait a while longer . . .

Afterwards he was amazed at how much they did in the following four weeks, especially considering how little time he took off from the office—three afternoons and every weekend—nothing to anyone else, but verging on absenteeism for a workaholic like him. He gave her the visitors tour of London, or at least his version of it which consisted mostly of restaurants, theaters and pubs. He did show her Hampton Court and Windsor Castle. One afternoon they watched the cricket at Lords. They walked on Hampstead Heath, had drinks at The Spaniards, went to the races at Kempton Park and boating on the Serpentine.

Kirsten blossomed. She had left Piraeus in only the clothes she stood up in, augmented on Kariakos by what Melina could lend her. In London the butterfly emerged from the chrysalis, and although her new clothes were neither outlandish nor daring, she wore them with such zest that to see her was to know she was happy. Everyone saw it. Alec saw it as soon as he met her. So did his wife Jean, when she invited Tom and Kirsten to dinner. Barbara saw it and was wise and old enough to stifle her envy. "It's what he needs," she told Alec privately, "he's the loneliest man I know."

The remark so astonished Alec that he repeated it to Jean when he got home. "Lonely?" he laughed over dinner. "I ask you. Tom's always so busy, surrounded by people—"

"Hiding himself in a crowd," Jean said tartly. "Barbara's right. He's so single-minded he never looks up."

Alec set his knife and fork down. "Nonsense—"

"Oh Alec! Of course it's true. All he ever talks about is shop. I don't mind, I've got used to it, but he lives in a world of his own. Sometimes I wonder if there's room in it for anyone else. Think about it. We're his only *real* friends. You're the only person he ever listens to. Certainly you're the only person he trusts—"

"That's not being lonely—"

"Then what is?"

Chewing his food, Alec considered the argument. In a way it made him feel guilty. He felt bad about pushing Tom so hard about the Institute, but something had to be done about Pohl. "I dunno," he said, "Tom's so bloody stubborn. Sometimes he won't even listen to me—"

"So let him listen to Kirsten. She might be good for him—"

"She doesn't know the first thing about business."

"Oh Alec!" Jean flushed. "Does it always have to be business?"

"It always has been with Tom."

"Then it's time he learned better," Jean said with some irritation. But after a while her bad temper faded. Curiosity got the better of her and later, sipping coffee, watching the television news, she returned to the subject. "Kirsten speaks excellent English. There's no trace of an accent."

"I think she was at school over here."

"Really? Then she scarcely knows anyone in her family. I mean not only her father, she couldn't have seen much of her mother, not if she was sent away to school. And she was telling me about her brother . . . what's his name—"

"Roddy."

"She was saying she hasn't seen him in years. I think she plunged herself into the Red Cross much in the way Tom plunged into business."

Setting his cup down, Alec crossed the room to switch off the television. "Didn't you like her?"

A pensive, thoughtful look came into her eyes. "Yes," she said, weighing her words. "I think so. She's bright, intelligent and attractive. But I still think I'm right about her being lonely. She's as lonely as he is. They make a good pair."

"You're jumping the gun, aren't you?" Alec grinned. "What about the Golden Tycoon?"

After a moment's hesitation, Jean shook her head. "I think she missed her chance. It's Kirsten's turn now."

They had become lovers on his return from Bordeaux, in Maurice's suite at Claridge's, while Melina was visiting the hospital. They made love there again the following evening, but the prospect of Melina's imminent return created too many inhibitions for the venue to be considered as anything more than temporary.

The following night, after taking Kirsten out to supper, Tom took her back to his apartment.

Financially he was comfortably off, but he had not thought to move or even redecorate. Little had changed since his days at Bolton. The furniture was the same, and most of that had been bought second-hand. The original curtains, faded and dusty, hung at the windows. The fridge contained only butter and cheese. Bread shared the larder with a collection of canned goods. The only bottles on the sideboard were of his favorite whisky. The airless cubbyhole of a bedroom was clean but overflowing due to inadequate wardrobe space.

Kirsten tried to contain her surprise. The apartment told her everything and yet nothing about him. Shelves were crammed with books on business management. Trade magazines were stacked in a corner. The kitchen wall bore a calendar sent from a bank. "Cosy," she said dryly. "It's the most welcoming atmosphere I've experienced since I went to my dentist."

The truth was he was rarely there. He spent his time at the office or talking business in restaurants. Such was his traveling schedule that he even spent more time in hotel rooms. The flat was a delivery point for mail and the laundry.

Kirsten moved in without quite leaving Claridge's, spending two out of three nights with Tom and the third with Melina. "To make sure she's okay." During the day she looked at apartments, again with Melina, went shopping, and occasionally dropped by the office to see if Tom could join her for lunch.

One evening they went to find Roddy, driving over to the address in Islington which Maurice had given Kirsten on Kariakos. They found the house, but nobody answered the door. A neighbor volunteered the information that Roddy had been away for weeks. Kirsten sighed with disappointment as they drove away. "Oh well, at least I know where he lives. I can keep trying."

Tom's life changed. He had never had a regular time for finishing work. It could be eight or nine or even later. He finished when he finished. Yet the changes were so imperceptible that he enjoyed them too much to notice, for even with Kirsten, walking on the Heath or talking over dinner, most of the conversation was about business. Of course he was always anxious for news of Constantin, he always asked about Melina, he took an interest in the apartments she saw, but nine times out of ten the talk strayed back to Stanton Industries. And because she was so interested he found himself describing his problems.

One evening Desmond Edwards was in town and they took him out to dinner. Kirsten delighted Tom. She was modest and charming, while at the same time asking some very pertinent questions. Afterwards, when he complimented her, she laughed. "Why so surprised? Didn't you know? I'm taking a crash course in business."

He stared in astonishment.

"From you," she laughed in explanation. "You get so excited that I'm beginning to think there's something in it."

Convincing her was not always easy. She was skeptical of the world of Big Business. "There must be more to life than chasing a profit," she said. And Tom agreed. He explained about investing the profits in factories to create employment, in training to give people greater opportunities, in mechanization to eliminate drudgery. When she still resisted, he laughed. "Arguing with you is like talking to Carl Pohl."

She raised an eyebrow. "You mean there's a kindred spirit in this camp of Philistines?"

"I can't see you and Carl Pohl as kindred spirits."

"Then I'll make do with the one I've got," she said, squeezing his arm.

They had become companions as well as lovers. He knew he would miss her when he set off on his travels—as he would have to at the end of the month. Apart from business in New York, he was due at the Chicago Trade Fair with Desmond Edwards. And then there was Pohl. Most of all there was Pohl. *Something* had to be done about Pohl, even if it meant spending a couple of weeks in California. Adding it all up, he realized he would be away for over a month.

He discussed it with Alec one morning. "Of course, I *must*

go. I know that. You've got too much on your plate as it is—"

"Not only that," Alec shook his head, "I can't deal with Pohl. He won't listen to me. You're the only one who might talk some sense into him."

Tom's reluctance to go to the States was about more than just missing Kirsten. There were business reasons as well. It meant deferring meetings with Haller and Maurice. He had promised to visit Sweden with Amiens . . .

"And what about Australia?" Alec asked. "I'll have to leave that until you get back."

They had spent months evaluating the Australian market. A local production unit would help their business not just there but throughout the whole Pacific Basin.

The truth was that running Stanton Industries was running them into the ground. "We need someone to share the load," said Alec, and not for the first time. The problem was—who? To invite Amiens into the head office would provoke rebellion from Edwards, and vice versa. Beside they were both working flat-out running their own divisions. And then there was the matter of trust. Tom would never trust Amiens or Edwards with more power than they had. He delegated real authority only to Alec, and he had given up hope of finding another Alec. So the matter was left unresolved. But the pressures upon Tom grew all the time until—during those four hectic weeks—everything came to a head.

It began at the office one evening. It was past seven o'clock. Alec had just left and Tom was waiting for Kirsten. More times than not she collected him from the office at the end of the day.

She swept in wearing a white linen suit, slightly breathless from hurrying up the stairs. "I bumped into Alec outside." she said, "Nice man, Alec. I do like him."

The exertion of climbing the stairs had brought a bloom to her face, tinting the golden skin a pale shade of rose. After kissing her, he stood back to admire her. He frowned at the faint shadows beneath her eyes. "Had a busy day?"

"Sort of."

"Been looking at apartments?"

"You could say," she answered, banishing the suspicion of tiredness with a mysterious smile. "Ready?"

"Sure. I thought we'd have dinner at The White Tower?"

"Not tonight." As she shook her head, a mischievous look lit her eyes. "Tonight's my treat. I'm taking you somewhere quite different."

She took him home to his own apartment. She was right. It *was* different. The scruffy, seedy little flat had been transformed. New curtains hung at the windows. Colorful scatter cushions covered the lumps in the sofa. A Chinese rug occupied pride of place in front of the hearth.

Astonished, he went from room to room. "I don't believe it."

A bottle of wine stood on the table, a delicious Boeuf Bourguignonne simmered on the stove . . .

Kirsten hugged herself as she followed him around. It turned into a memorable evening. The gifts, the food, the wine, and the subsequent lovemaking made it the best surprise of his life. But the real surprise came at one in the morning.

"I have a theory," she said, raising herself on one elbow and stroking his face.

"Oh?"

"Want to hear it?"

Cupping her breast, he kissed her nipple and circled it with his tongue. As it hardened, he turned his face up to hers, seeking her lips, but very gently she pushed him away. "Later. When I tell you my theory."

"That's blackmail," he groaned.

She squirmed away to the end of the bed and reached for his shirt on the chair. Slipping an arm into a sleeve, she wrapped it around her. "It's a theory about you," she said with a teasing look.

"Then I'd better hear it, I suppose."

"Well . . ." She drew her legs under her and sat crosslegged at the end of the bed. "It began on Kariakos when I saw you with Maurice. You two get on so well, did you know that? Like father and son. I thought . . . well, you know what he's like—"

"But you liked him?"

"I know, that was the surprise, but I thought you were

another one like him. With women, I mean. You know, girls all over the place. I didn't quite trust you . . ." Shaking her head, she smiled ruefully. "Then I came to London and met Jean and Alec. I saw the office and everything. I knew I was wrong, especially when I saw this place." Her smile widened to a grin. "It's hardly conducive, is it? Not like Maurice's suite at Claridge's . . . marble bathrooms and wall-to-wall luxury. That suite would turn anyone on. It's a sex trap. This place is . . . well, more like a mouse trap. I've never seen anything less romantic. And this bed!" She bounced on the mattress, creaking the springs. "It would be easier to make love in the back of a car!"

"That bad—"

"I had a wonderful lover."

Mollified, he smiled. "So what's this theory?"

She hesitated. "This is the tough bit, okay? I haven't been prying or anything." A blush crept up her neck. "Honestly. I haven't searched through cupboards or drawers, I wouldn't do that . . . but this place is a shell. There's nothing here. No pictures, no photographs. Like you materialized out of thin air. You must have a home *somewhere*."

"It's here," he said, not understanding.

She searched his face. "I got to thinking. Maybe there's a wife somewhere? You know, a wife and six snotty-nosed kids—"

"You think I'm *married*?"

"I think I could handle it," she said quickly. "It wouldn't make any difference. I'd still want to sleep with you, but . . . but I'd rather you told me the truth."

He was sitting upright, unaware that he had even moved.

"Honestly," she said, her face glowing with color, "it wouldn't change a thing. It's just that . . . I'd hate it if you lied to me—"

"You've got to be crazy!"

The quirky smile returned to lift the corners of her mouth. "Does that mean I'm wrong?"

That Saturday afternoon he took her to a small house in the suburbs. An elderly couple waited at the door. "My grandparents," he explained as he opened the gate. "They brought me up. My parents were killed in a car crash when I was three."

Over tea and scones in the tiny garden, Kirsten learned all there was to know about Tom Lambert—school, qualifying as an accountant, starting at Bolton. Tom's grandfather smiled. "I'm telling you all this because Tom told us what you said to him."

Kirsten blushed.

Tom's grandmother reached over to take her hand. "You were quite right, my dear. I'd have said the same thing. It's unnatural. Work, work, work. That's all he does. We keep telling him, it's time you settled down, find a nice girl and raise a family." She looked at her husband. "That's what we say to him, isn't it, George?"

Kirsten blushed to the roots of her hair.

Later, in the car on the way back to the West End, she punched his arm. "You bastard! You didn't *have* to tell them I said you were married."

He grinned.

"I suppose you also said we were in your bed at the time?"

"I forgot that bit."

"Oh, thanks. I'm glad I was so memorable."

But she had liked his grandparents, and by the time he was edging the car along Brook Street, she was reprimanding him for not seeing them more often. "They're so proud of you. It would mean such a lot. Your grandmother said you hadn't been—"

"I know. It's finding time. I'm always so busy."

They were meeting Melina for dinner, but when they asked the Concierge to ring up to the suite there was no answer. Tom glanced at his watch.

"She'll be on her way back from the hospital. Let's have a drink at the bar."

They had one drink, then another, and still there was no sight of Melina. Not that they were worried, she was often late coming back from the hospital. Meantime they had plenty to talk about. They were deep in conversation when she arrived. As soon as they saw her they knew something was wrong. Usually she was full of smiles after seeing Constantin. His huge strength was pulling him through. He had been making excellent progress. The dental work was finished, his jaw mended, he could talk.

Melina had returned from past visits with her spirits uplifted, but she came to their table looking very upset. The flurry of Greek with which she greeted them was further cause for alarm. She had worked hard on her English. Ever since Kariakos and her arrival in London, she had made it a rule—"English is spoken here" she would smile. But such discipline was abandoned in moments of crisis.

They made her sit down. Tom ordered her a drink, while she poured her heart out to Kirsten. He feared the worst. Constantin must have suffered a relapse. Everything had been going so well. He had asked every day. The news had been good. . . .

Something happens to people who share great danger. Soldiers under fire, miners trapped in a pit—those who survive see each other differently. A bond is established. Tom would trust Constantin with his life. "What's up?" he kept saying. "How's Constantin? What's happened?"

He felt a great surge of relief when Kirsten put her hand over his. "It's okay. He's fine . . ." Slowly she began to explain.

Alexandros, Constantin's lawyer friend in London, had been to see him.

Melina interrupted, reverting to English. "He comes to the hospital with me," she said.

Alexandros had offered Constantin a partnership in the law firm he had established since coming to London. Melina's face contorted with worry. Her head shook from side to side. "Constantin refused. He says he will never be a lawyer again. I say to him, 'Constantin, you love the law. It's your whole life.' But he says no, his mind is made up. I pleaded with him. I say 'Constantin, what will we do? We are refugees. Most of what we own we left in Piraeus . . .' "

Tom remembered the pitifully small pile of jewelry. Kirsten had told him that Melina had already sold the best pieces. What remained would soon go.

They did their best to comfort Melina. Eventually Tom suggested that Kirsten have dinner with her up in the suite. Leaving them, he returned alone to the apartment. Pouring a whisky, he stretched out on the sofa which Kirsten had made more comfortable with her cushions. Both his heart and his head told him it was time to make changes.

Eating grapes, Tom sat at the bedside in the private hospital room. "What happened to your hair?"

"They shaved some off and the rest took fright."

Except for tufts around his ears and neck, Constantin's hairline had slipped back over his scalp.

"Makes you look younger."

Constantin laughed. "Melina says I will frighten the babies when I get out of here."

"Will it grow again?"

"No one can say," Constantin shrugged. "Not even the specialists. Apparently some things are decided only by time." He grinned. "There are compensations. If it doesn't grow, it can never turn gray. I'll stay this good-looking for the rest of my life."

Tom smiled. Melina had warned him about the loss of hair, but had said nothing about Constantin's loss of weight. The huge frame seemed to have shrunk.

Constantin read his mind. "The weight I will only recover with steroids and exercise. The question is, why should I bother? When I was young, working in the meat market, I grew into a giant. I needed my strength. But now. . . ." As he spread his hands he revealed scarred fingers. "I don't want to be a meat porter again, and I don't want to take steroids. My weight has stabilized. I think I'll stay slim." Grinning, he patted his chest. "It will make less work for my heart."

"Your heart's okay?"

"Sure. As strong as ever."

"Who would doubt it?" Tom put the bag of grapes on the bedside table. "I've left you a few—"

"Please. Eat them. They're no good to me." Constantin tapped his new teeth. "They get under the plate."

"Shit! Sorry. I should have thought—"

"No, no, it is I who should apologize for being rude about your gift—"

"Next time I'll bring a bottle of retsina."

"Hah! Better still I'll buy you a crate of whisky when I leave here."

Both grinned to cover the moment of embarrassment.

"I would have come before," Tom began.

"I know. Melina told me, but I wanted to be able to express myself when you came." Constantin's expression became serious. "I have so much to thank you for that—"

"Leave that until you get out of here," Tom interrupted. "Any idea how long that will be?"

Constantin brightened. "Quite soon. I'm walking and doing exercises for three hours every morning. They have some more tests, but it won't be long now."

"Then what?"

Constantin's eyes narrowed with quick understanding. "Ah," he said softly, "Melina's been talking—"

"She's worried, that's all. And I'm surprised. I thought you couldn't wait to practice law again."

"A man can change his mind. I have, and that's all there is to it." There was no mistaking the note of finality.

Tom looked at him. "You planning to return to Greece?"

"To do what? Give myself up? Let them finish what they started?" He shook his head. "No, I will not go back. I could do little before, but now, with them looking for me on every street corner . . ." He sighed. "One day perhaps, when those scum have gone, but not now."

"Meanwhile?"

Constantin shrugged, "I'll find some honest work—"

"Good. That's what I came to discuss. How about joining Stanton Industries?"

Even when he overcame his surprise, Constantin resisted. For half an hour, he protested, "My friend, you've already done so much for me—"

"This isn't for you. It's for me."

Tom explained how Stanton Industries operated, with him and Alec at the hub of the conglomerate. "The truth is we're run off our feet. We need someone to share the load—"

"But I know nothing about the business—"

"Even better," Tom grinned. "I've got experts on business coming out of my ears. What I need is your analytical mind."

"Ha! Melina's been boasting again." A look of fondness came into Constantin's eyes. "You mustn't listen to my wife. She exaggerates—"

"Does Dedas?"

Constantin stared in astonishment. "Alexandros. You've spoken with him?"

"I spent half the morning at his office. He tells me you graduated at the top of your class at Athens Law School. As a lawyer there wasn't a brief too complicated for you to handle. He's devastated by your refusal to join his firm." Tom hesitated. "I must tell you this. Dedas checks out. He's making a name for himself as one of the best commercial lawyers in London. You know what he told me? You're twice the lawyer he'll ever be. He can't get over you giving it up."

Propped up in bed, a look of pain lit Constantin's eyes. "Alexandros might change his mind if he knew my reasons." For a long moment he stared at Tom. Then he reached a decision. "I am honored, my friend. You pay me a great compliment. This position you offer is one of great trust. Is that so?"

Tom nodded.

"You would expect me to keep nothing from you?"

"Of course not."

Constantin nodded slowly, as if the answer was as expected. "Then before we go further, there is something you should know. Something I have told no one, not even Melina." His eyes focused on Tom. "I am a murderer."

Listening to the story of Petros and Anna and young Andreas filled Tom with conflicting emotions. Horror, of course, and fear along with it. He wondered what he would have done. But most of all he felt a warm sense of kinship. Constantin had no need to confess. He could have kept quiet. Instead he was entrusting Tom with a secret kept even from his wife, and from his lifelong friend Alexandros Dedas.

When Constantin finished, Tom remained silent. Then he sat back in his chair. "I'm glad you told me," he said quietly. "I'd have wanted to tell someone if it had happened to me. For what it's worth, I don't think it would stop me from carrying on with my profession. Dedas asked me to tell you that his offer remains open."

Constantin's eyes clouded with disappointment. "And your offer?"

"Well . . ." Tom hesitated, "I do have a question."

"Yes?"

"When can you start?"

BOOK EIGHT

1978

The fire was almost dead. The pine logs had been reduced to a heap of silver ashes on a few orange embers. The sky was lightening outside. Soon pale sunshine would creep across the gray waters of the Aegean and the gibbet would show stark on the skyline.

Time was running out . . .

"Best thing we ever did," Alec told Constantin. "That's when Stanton Industries really took off. Until then Tom and I were like two blue-assed flies, never with enough time to think. We couldn't have built up so fast without you."

Constantin tried to hide his pride. "You two made pretty good teachers."

"We had a bloody good pupil," said Alec.

Constantin remembered a picture of a magazine cover. *Management Today,* showing Tom's face, with smaller pictures of himself and Alec in the background. TRIUMPH FOR STANTON'S TRIUMVIRATE ran the headline. He could even remember the feature lead inside. *Lambert has more than a right-hand man. He has a left-hand man too. Between them Alec Hargreaves and Constantin Peponis cover their Boss all the time . . .*

Most of the time, Constantin thought bitterly, *we covered him most of the time.*

"Talk about being thrown in at the deep end," Alec grinned. "You'd only been in the office a week when Tom went off to the States. Remember?"

"Taking Kirsten," Constantin nodded. "We were left to do the work while he went off on honeymoon."

"Hardly a honeymoon," Tom retorted. "I worked every day."

"For five weeks?" Constantin winked at Alec. "You and Kirsten must have had *some* fun. Weekends, evenings—"

"Sure, it was great—"

"A *sort* of honeymoon?" Constantin compromised.

"I suppose so," Tom conceded with a faint smile. "It was the only one she ever had. Even after the wedding all she got was a weekend here on the island. I remember flying out on the Monday morning with Alec—"

"That's right," Alec interrupted. "On the way to Australia. Christ, that was a trip. Remember that day in Melbourne? We were taking a dozen dealers out to lunch. . . ."

Alec's reminiscences gave Constantin a chance to marshal his thoughts. He was making progress. Tom was no longer holding him at arm's length, no longer snarling, "It's none of your business, it's my problem, I'll deal with it my way." Friendship had been restored. The trick now, Constantin decided, was to keep him talking. "What about Maurice?" he asked suddenly. "Sorry, I didn't mean to interrupt. It just occurred to me. When did you tell Maurice about you and Kirsten?"

Diverted from what Alec was saying, Tom took a moment to answer. Then he remembered, "A couple of weeks before we went to the States. I spoke to him for an hour on the phone. Mostly about you, as a matter of fact."

"Me?"

"Sure. About trusting you with our secrets. I wouldn't have gone ahead if he had objected."

Constantin blinked his surprise. Until then he had believed that Tom had discussed his appointment only with Alec. "Okay, so you talked about me. Then what did you do? Ask permission to marry his daughter?"

Lines crinkled around Tom's eyes. "Nothing like that. We didn't decide to marry until we came back from the States, but we never made any secret of being together. I thought Maurice should hear it from me before anyone else told him."

"How did he take it?"

"I think he was pleased."

"Surprised?"

"No, I don't think so."

Constantin grinned at Alec. "What did I tell you? Anyone who saw them on Kariakos could have predicted the outcome."

"Even I predicted the outcome when they went to the States," Alec retorted.

"And how do I score? For my predictions about you two?" Tom commented dryly. "Anything could have happened. I half-expected Barbara to call me to say you were knocking the shit out of each other."

"Quite the opposite," said Alec. He and Constantin had got on from the start. "I never knew anyone who asked so many questions."

"Except Amiens," Constantin murmured almost to himself.

But his voice had carried. "Christ!" Alec exclaimed. "That's right. I forgot. That was the first time you met him. Tom was away and Amiens came over for the regular meeting. He took against you from the start."

"He resented me," Constantin shrugged. "He made that pretty clear. Mind you, he resented you more. He thought he should be sitting in your chair. Minding the shop while Tom was away."

"He probably could have done it too," said Alec with grudging respect. "Say what you like about him, he's bloody efficient."

"Yeah," Tom agreed harshly. "He's efficient."

The note of bitterness made Constantin hurry on. "I didn't mind all the questions. He got nothing from me, but he did worry me, he worried me sick."

"Oh?" Tom cocked an eyebrow.

"I'd just joined, remember? Alec was giving me this crash

course. I was learning all about our products. Boning up on our share of the market."

Tom's eyes glimmered with amusement.

"I was back at school," Constantin grinned. "Walking like an old man. It used to take me half an hour to climb those stairs at the office—"

"He got in at six every morning so we wouldn't see him," Alec interjected.

"I thought I was getting the hang of things until I met Amiens—"

"He wanted to know where you were," Alec looked at Tom, "I told him you'd gone over to see Pohl—"

"And that opened the floodgates," Constantin added dryly. "I got to hear about all the money being wasted. Amiens went on and on about Pohl. He made a good case too, especially to someone like me, new to the business—"

"Don't blame yourself," Alec admitted, shamefaced. "I had my doubts. Everyone had doubts. Tom and Hollenberg were the only ones with real faith in Pohl."

"I don't know about faith," Tom smiled, remembering his arguments with Pohl. "Know what Carl's favorite insult was? He used to say 'You guys date from B.C.' I thought it meant Before Christ. He meant Before Computers."

Alec laughed, "You couldn't argue. We weren't into computers then."

"Nobody was," Tom shrugged. "Except IBM and the other big boys. They had the game to themselves. Computers were made *by* Big Business *for* Big Business. It was all so . . ." he searched for the best description, "dehumanized and faceless. You know, the whole scene was spinning tape banks and batches of cards fed into machines in a certain sequence to execute a program. Air conditioned rooms with technicians wandering around in white coats. The whole thing is out of date now. Yet this was only a few years ago. Makes you realize how fast things have changed."

Alec beamed. "B.C."

"Wrong," Constantin said. "B.P.C. Before Personal Computers."

"Shit," Tom laughed, "we never stopped arguing about that. Carl had this vision of everyone in the world owning a computer. Every household. Can you imagine? I couldn't see it. I kept asking, why? What *use* would people make of it? Okay, I could understand all those guys in Silicon Valley wanting a PC in their homes, but they were enthusiasts. I couldn't see the average guy buying one."

"So why pump all that cash into Pohl?" Constantin asked quickly.

"Instinct. Gut feeling. I dunno." Tom shook his head. "One thing kept me awake nights. The technology Carl was dreaming about could wipe us out. We had twenty percent of the typewriter market in Europe, and fifteen percent of the desktop calculator business. Carl wasn't business-oriented. He saw people using these machines in their own homes. I saw them using them in offices, and that brought me out in a cold sweat. Amiens was investing in plant and machinery to make products which could become obsolete if Carl's dreams came true. That would make our plant and machinery obsolete—"

"But Edwards backed Amiens," Constantin prompted.

"Be fair. Desmond was putting twenty percent on sales every year. He was doing a good job." Tom shook his head. "Correction—he was doing a ***marvelous*** job. So was Andre. They were both bloody good at—"

"But they lacked your vision?" Constantin asked sharply.

"Most of it was Carl's vision—"

"So confrontation was inevitable?"

Tom flushed, suddenly angry. "Come on, Con. You were there. I broke a gut trying to keep the peace. I spent my life trying to give Maurice what he wanted—one big, happy family—"

"Ah! The family," Constantin pounced. "Maybe that was your downfall. Roddy and Kirsten—"

Blood rushed into Tom's face. "Leave Kirsten out of it!" His eyes blazed. "I told you before—"

"Okay, okay," Constantin raised his hands in surrender. "I didn't mean—"

"Steady on, Tom," Alec placated. "Con wasn't saying—"

"Then what the hell did he mean?" Tom snarled.

"Not that she plotted against you," Alec said hurriedly, "no one believes that."

Tom hesitated, pain and anguish in his eyes. "I don't know what to believe anymore—"

"Not that," Alec insisted. "You can't believe that. Think of all the good times you had. You were so close—"

"Remember that party?" Constantin interrupted. "When you came back from the States? Kirsten was so excited about California. Remember?"

Tom's sharpest memories were of the day after the party. It was a Sunday and they spent most of it in bed. . . .

Time must be getting on. What is it?"

Stretching from the bed, Tom reached for his watch.

"You won't believe—"

"I will. I'm getting hungry."

Shaking the watch, he held it to his ear. "It says three-thirty. That can't be right."

"Why not? We started to get dressed earlier, remember?" Kirsten's dark eyes shone mischievously. "Twice, as a matter of fact." Drawing him back into her arms, she stroked his face before sliding her hand over his chest and down between his legs. "Oh dear," she laughed, feigning despair as her coaxing fingers failed to arouse him. "May as well get dressed now. At least for a while." Escaping his embrace, she wriggled to the edge of the bed. "I'll get some food while we indulge your other passion."

In California she had told him, "Talking business and making love are the only things that hold your attention."

At that moment his attention was held by her as she walked across the room. She had a beautiful body. From the bed he admired her strong full breasts, and the way the flat line of her stomach rose over her pubis before tapering gently into the thighs and long, slim legs. The sunshine of California and before that of Greece had colored her skin a curious dusky gold which seemed almost Polynesian, an impression heightened by her dark eyes and abundant chestnut hair.

America already seemed a long time ago. They had spent the first ten days seeing distributors in New York and Chicago, before going to California. For a week Kirsten had remained in San Francisco during the day, exploring the city, while he drove the forty miles to see Pohl. Then he had rented a cottage up in the hills and the magic of the canyons and arroyos of the Santa Cruz Mountains had held them both spellbound. Most evenings he was back by seven, often with Pohl, and the three of them had sat on the patio watching the sun set over the hills.

Pohl had become more Californian than the Californians. In his jeans and open-necked shirts, outwardly all that remained of the truculent young German was the thick, heavy-rimmed glasses. But his character was unchanged. He was still dogmatic and contemptuous of social convention, still anti-Establishment. Above all, he was consumed by his dream of the future. He saw the Institute as a cross between the ultimate university campus and a company town. "By the time we finish," he told Kirsten, "there'll be nothing like it in the whole world."

Pohl encouraged Kirsten to study hundreds of sketches of lecture halls, laboratories, design studios, condominiums, recreational facilities, tennis courts, swimming pools, even a monorail to transport people around the grounds.

"My head's spinning," she complained ruefully after Pohl had left one evening. "I'm drained from concentration."

Tom was exasperated one minute and enthralled the next, for while Pohl's visions captured the imagination, it was easy to see what Amiens had witnessed on his single visit—a half-finished building project populated by three hundred young people, mostly men, long-haired, wearing sandals or tennis shoes, dressed in sweatshirts and jeans. "Fucking bunch of hippies," Amiens had growled, "sitting around smoking pot contemplating their navels."

Kirsten emerged from the bathroom wearing one of his shirts. Crossing to the wardrobe she pulled a blue wraparound skirt down from a hanger and began to button it around her waist. Watching her dress without underwear brought the heat rushing back into his loins. "Uh-uh," she laughed, backing away. "Food first, play later."

He fell back onto the bed and watched her go through the door. She and Pohl had got on really well. His visions of the future had captured her imagination. "He's a genius," she pronounced after one of their meetings.

The thought of what the "Genius" was costing brought a frown to his face. Expenses for the Institute had spiraled. Every time he went there, Pohl wanted more money. Tom doled out the cash, pulling the purse strings as tight as he dared. When he pointed out that every dollar deprived Amiens of more plant, or Edwards of more salesmen, Pohl merely shrugged. "What will Amiens make? Today's technology. Where will we be in five years? Edwards will change his tune when he's trying to peddle outdated products. I'm their future. Without me, they're dead."

"Arrogant bastard," Tom muttered under his breath.

Night after night Kirsten had calmed him down, "Be fair, Tom, you couldn't ask for greater commitment. He's dedicated to what he's doing. It's not as though he spends the money on himself."

That was true. Pohl disdained the "perks" other men would have seen as their due. There was no grand house for Carl Pohl. No expensive limousine. He rode a BMW motorcycle and lived with about thirty of his recruits in "Opus One"—a sprawling, prefabricated single-story building divided into suites each of two rooms, a kitchen and a bathroom. "He shares his whole life with them," Kirsten said after being shown around, "and it works. Did you see their faces? They believe in him. They can see what he can see. All they ever talk about is computers. It's like a religion with them."

And Kirsten had become a disciple. Tom remembered one evening. They were on the patio and Pohl, as usual, was doing the talking. "People get computers all wrong. They see machines performing huge mathematical tasks. The abacus of the twentieth century. It's about much more than that. Tomorrow's child will tap into the great libraries of the world from his own home.

He'll stare into a screen and see history, science, the story of the universe, everything. He'll acquire knowledge at the touch of a button."

Tom remembered the rays of the setting sun glinting on Pohl's glasses as he leaned forward. "Knowledge is wealth, Kirsten. Karl Marx got it all wrong. We will redistribute wealth on a scale he would never have believed. Knowledge will become available to everyone, not just the privileged few. We will change the whole world."

Kirsten had hung on his every word.

When he left they went to bed and made love. Afterwards Tom had fallen asleep, sleeping soundly until three in the morning, when he had stirred and reached out for her, only to find the bed empty beside him.

Wrapped in a robe, she was on the patio, staring up into the night sky. "He's convinced, isn't he?" she said when he joined her. "He's like some messiah. He really thinks he'll change the whole world."

"Maybe he will," Tom answered, still drowsy from sleep.

But Kirsten was wide awake, full of questions. "Is it possible. Will he do it?"

"I dunno. Part of me goes along with him. He's right—knowledge, information, whatever you call it—is wealth. I agree, but . . ." He shrugged. "Home computers? Maybe in the long run, but Gunther's got a saying—'In the long run we're dead.' "

"Meaning?"

"I can't wait forever. He can't just spend, spend, spend without giving me some sort of return."

"But if it comes off?"

"If? It's a gamble. My gamble. I can buy him time, but not forever. Amiens and Edwards are together on this. If they convince Gunther and Maurice . . ." he sighed and drew a finger across his throat, "I'm dead."

Her face was pale in the moonlight. "Would Maurice do that?" she asked, eyes rounding with surprise.

"I think he'd resist it, but if the time comes when he thinks I'm totally wrong, he won't have much choice."

"Poor darling." She snuggled against him. "What would you do? I mean, this is your whole life."

"I don't intend it to happen. I've told Carl he's got three years to make this thing pay."

She had learned to read his voice. "And has he?"

He smiled. "If I keep making profits I can give him four, maybe five. A lot depends on other factors."

She fell silent for several minutes. Then she said, "Five years is a long time to walk a tightrope."

"Not if you love the circus," he grinned.

She looked up at him. "I think you believe in him too."

He sighed. "Part of me does. He's onto *something.* I can't see him being that wrong. The question is, who will buy these ideas if they ever work?"

"You don't think he's right about parents buying them for their children?"

"To do what?" he laughed. "Carl describes a society that doesn't exist. Even if he's right, there has to be a stage in between." Falling silent, he thought for a moment. "I wish he'd stop calling them home computers. It sets the mind off on the wrong track. If he's right, I can see a million uses for them outside of the home."

It was past four when they returned to bed. He was dozing off when she snuggled into him. "Tom."

"Mmm."

"What sort of wife do you want me to be?"

His eyes snapped open. "What sort of question's that? You're you, aren't you?" He grinned into the darkness. "You mean there are other versions? I get a choice? Fine, I'll have the sexy one and we'll eat out every night."

"I can cook as well."

"As well as what?"

She held his hands to restrain them as they began to explore her body. "Do you think I should get a job?"

"What for? We don't need the money."

"Maybe if I went to see the Red Cross in London—"

"Is that what you want?"

"No."

"So what the hell are we talking about?"

"Us." Propping herself up on one elbow, she stared at him, her serious eyes huge in the gray light. "I'm trying to imagine it, that's all. What we will do. What it will be like."

"You know what we'll do. We talked about it the other night."

"So tell me again."

"It's five o'clock," he protested.

"So humor me. Won't you humor me when we're married?" Leaning over, she kissed the tip of his nose. "Repeat after me, I vow to love, cherish and humor this woman all the days of her life—"

"We'll go back to London," he sighed. "You'll find a house and I'll sell that crummy flat. Okay?"

"Then what?"

"What do you mean, then what? Then we get married and live happily ever after."

"But what sort of a wife do you want?"

"Jesus!" He sat up, abandoning hope of sleep. "Will you tell me what this is all about?"

"Steady." Laughing, she admonished, "You sound like a bad-tempered husband."

"I sound like a man deprived of his sleep."

"It's an important question. I've given it a lot of thought." She slid to the far side of the bed. "You couldn't have a career-girl wife, could you? It wouldn't work. You're so wrapped up in what you're doing and she'd be the same. You'd never talk to each other. We'd drift apart . . ."

He wondered if she was talking about Melody. He had never mentioned Melody. Maybe Jean had said something? Or Barbara? Women talk. No, not Barbara. Barbara was as close as the grave.

"So I couldn't be a career girl. Not that I want a career—"

"Kirsten!"

"Okay, don't get impatient. I'm coming to the point. The point is I've learned a lot on this trip. Now I know why you work so hard. It's exciting. Carl and everything. It's fantastic. The thing is, I'd like to be part of it. I don't mean a job in the office or anything, but . . . I don't want to be excluded. It would be better for us, our marriage, if I knew what went on. Especially if you're walking a tightrope—"

"Okay," he laughed, "we'll fall off the tightrope together."

"Oh no, I'll be there to catch you," she said, the quirky smile back on her face.

Now, in bed in London, with the aroma of coffee coming from the kitchen, he smiled at the memory. He marveled at how his life had changed. Stirring himself, he went into the bathroom. He washed and shaved, thinking of the house they would buy. Kirsten was right. The flat was pokey and cramped. Too small to live in for any length of time . . .

Dressed, he went into the kitchen. The table had been laid. Kirsten was at the stove. "Good party last night?" she said over her shoulder. "Did Constantin tell you about their new house?"

"Jean did. She found it for Melina."

"They'll be neighbors. I bet you never thought they'd get on so well."

A look of surprise came into his eyes. "Con wouldn't have got the job if I hadn't."

"Oh . . ." She hesitated. "I thought you did it to help him?"

"No way. I did it to help me."

Sliding steaks onto plates, she brought them to the table, a puzzled look on her face.

"I need Alec on other projects. He's wasted in Jermyn Street. I want him to look at Australia. Con's legal mind is exactly right—"

"Are you saying you wouldn't have helped him?" She sat down, sounding shocked.

"I would if I could. Some other way, but Con only got the job because it was a good move for us."

A knowing look replaced the surprise in her eyes. "The ruthless Tom Lambert," she mocked. "I suppose it was another ruthless decision to smuggle Melina's parents out of Greece?"

Grinning, he reached for the salad. Bringing Melina's parents to London had been a secret hatched by him and Maurice and Gregg. "No heroics," he had told Gregg. "Get them out if it's possible, but I don't want you risking your neck." It had proved very possible. Melina's parents had boarded *Helena* under cover of darkness and within minutes were on the first stage of their journey to London. The party Alec had organized to welcome Tom and Kirsten back from the States had turned into a tearful reunion.

"I thought Melina would never stop crying."

"You're ducking my question. Why not admit it? You did it for love and friendship."

The grin remained on his face. "Con can't work flat-out with an unhappy wife on his hands. Answer, make the wife happy. Simple as that."

"Says you," she scoffed.

A companionable silence descended as they devoured the steaks. He had never felt so relaxed or comfortable with anyone. It was no longer a question of whether there was room for her in his life, she had become *part* of his life, almost part of him. Pouring the wine, he caught the smile in her eyes. "What's up?"

"Nothing. Just enjoying myself." She raised her glass, *"À votre santé."*

Sipping his wine, he was reminded of Maurice. "Maurice always says that. More style than cheers, I suppose."

"I wonder what he'll say about us getting married?"

"He knows you came to the States—"

"That's different. He would have seen that as fornication. He approves of fornication—"

"With *his* daughter?" Tom shook his head. "Don't you believe it."

"Hmm," she sounded doubtful, "then there's my mother. You'll have to meet her."

"Sure."

"And Roddy. We must go and see him. It's so stupid, he only lives a few miles away—"

"We did try. He was out. It would help if we knew his phone number."

"Let's go tonight?" she suggested, brightening at the idea. "We're not doing anything. If he's not there, I'll leave a note." Seeing his hesitation, she reached for his hand. "Please, Tom. After all . . ." she smiled, "he'll be your brother-in-law."

* * *

He was reluctant to go. Crazy really, he could think of no reason. But something about Roddy jarred. He told himself he was being unfair. Unreasonable. He had only met Roddy on three or four occasions, brief encounters on Kariakos, with Roddy making himself scarce to allow Tom to talk business with Maurice. Roddy's partner had been there. Tom had disliked him too, again for no reason. They were always polite, if a bit distant, and . . . he suddenly realized . . . faintly condescending. That was what irritated him. It was as if, beneath their impeccable politeness, they were sneering at him. Laughing up their sleeves. He remembered meeting them for the first time. One of them called him a *Consigliori,* the right-hand man of a Mafia Don.

"Do you know if Roddy's still making films?" Kirsten asked as she got into the car.

"I think so. With his partner Hugo."

She laughed, "Weird, isn't it? You know more about my family than I do."

"I don't know much about Roddy." *Except I dislike him. Except I think he's a supercilious little creep who sponges off his father. I know that much.* Months before, on Kariakos, he had come down from his room on the way to the terrace. As he passed the study door, he heard Maurice, sounding angry. "If Hugo's such a fucking genius, how do these films lose money?"

The answering voice had been Roddy's. "Father, you must understand. Hugo's an artist—"

"He's a parasite. How much is it this time?"

"We thought . . ." Roddy faltered, almost losing his nerve. "We thought sixty. Seventy if you could manage it—"

"Manage it! Seventy thousand pounds is a lot of money even these days. Maybe I should ask Tom to look at this—"

"What does he know about films?"

"He knows about business—"

"This is art—"

"Don't tell me about art. Art I know about. *And* I know artists. Hugo's no artist . . ."

The temptation to eavesdrop, especially after hearing his own name, had been strong. Tom might have succumbed except for the sound of footsteps. Turning, he saw Hugo descending the stairs, leaving him no choice but to hurry out. Some twenty minutes later, Roddy and Hugo had crossed the terrace on the way down to the jetty. Roddy had looked green, almost ill. Hugo's face had worn a look of absolute triumph.

Kirsten said, "It will be like meeting a stranger. I'm just trying to think when I last saw him."

Concentrating on the traffic, Tom remained silent.

"Do I look all right? she asked suddenly, tilting the sun visor downward and touching her hair.

"You look great."

The white lace dress, bought in New York, was molded to her body and set off her tan to perfection. She straightened her collar and smoothed her skirt. "He was always so critical of what I wore, of what everyone wore really, even my mother." She laughed. "And that was when he was a kid. God knows what he's like now."

Tom found the right street. The Victorian houses were large, tall four-story buildings set over sub-basements in a long curving terrace. A pleasant road in a newly fashionable area. Expensive. He wondered if Roddy had squeezed Maurice for the money . . .

"I hope he likes me," said Kirsten. "I know we'll be away a lot, but . . . well, living in London, we could see something of him in future, couldn't we?"

Searching for a parking space saved Tom the need to give an answer. The curbside was a continuous row of cars, most of them expensive. Finally, fifty yards beyond the house, he was able to reverse into a gap between a Porsche and a Ferrari. Kirsten took a last critical look at her hair.

"Sounds like a party," said Tom.

Roddy's house was the end one in the terrace. A short path from the gate led to wide stone steps which climbed to a half-open door. Sounds of heavy rock music escaped from within. Seeing no point in ringing the bell, Tom pushed the door which swung open to reveal a hall crowded with people, talking, laughing, glasses in hands, most standing but a few sprawled on the stairs. Crossing the threshold one became engulfed by the noise.

Scanning the faces, they saw no sign of Roddy. Tom raised an eyebrow at Kirsten. "Better find him," she shouted. Nodding, he took her hand and began to shoulder his way through the crush, drawing her along in his wake. To the left of the hall were a pair of big double doors, thrown open. The crowd in the hall had overflowed from the room. Tom pushed onward. The farther he went, the harder it was to see where he was going. The light in the hall had been dim; it was almost nonexistent in the big cavernous room. Thick velvet curtains blotted out the evening outside. At the distant end of the room, narrow shafts of red light as thin as pencils fell from the high ceiling, their glow augmented by a spotlight which flashed intermittently like the beam of a lighthouse. Music thumping in the background was so resonant with bass that vibrations jarred through the carpeted floor.

The smoke-laden air was heady with pot. Tom wondered if they were in the right house. The heat was stifling. Oppressive. Peering into shadowy faces, he edged forward, with Kirsten behind him. A vague thought began to stir in his mind when suddenly a hand fell on his shoulder. "Hello. You're new. I haven't seen you here before."

Turning, he looked into eyes heavy with mascara above full pouting lips. A strong face, smiling approval. "You're nice, aren't you. Don't spoil it by saying you're taken."

A masculine voice from a male face.

The thought, vague only a split second before, crystalized in Tom's mind. "We're looking for Roddy," he said. "Roddy Stanton. Do you know him?"

"And who's *we* when we're at home?" Squinting over Tom's shoulder, the painted eyes widened. "Oh my! What's she doing here?"

"I'm Roddy's sister," said Kirsten, squeezing into full view.

"His sister!" The thickly coated lips broke into a smile. "I didn't know Roddy had a sister." Knowing eyes examined Kirsten. "Oh my. And we just dropped in for a visit, did we?"

Tom wondered if Kirsten realized she was the only woman there.

"Out of the blue, so to speak."

"Yes," Kirsten agreed, "on the off chance."

"Oh my! How priceless. Hugo! Hugo darling. Where's Roddy?"

Tom gripped Kirsten's elbow. "I think we'll go—"

"Look who's here!" exclaimed a voice as Hugo squeezed past Kirsten to stand before Tom. "How extraordinary. If it's not the *Consigliori* in person. What a rare and unexpected honor." His gaze fell upon Kirsten. Eyebrows rising, he cocked his head. "And you are?"

"Kirsten. Roddy's sister."

"Ooh! I don't believe it! Roddy's sister! Kirsten!" Hugo's eyes rolled. He began shouting to make himself heard. "Quiet! Quiet everyone, *please*! Terry, get them to turn that bloody noise down, there's a pet. Quiet everyone—"

Tom tugged at Kirsten's elbow. "Come on—"

"No, no!" Hugo shouted. "You came to see Roddy and Roddy you shall see. I know *exactly* where the little slut is. I shall take you to him." Gripping Kirsten's hand, he dragged her into the crush of people. "Gangway!" he shouted. "Make way for the *Consigliori* and the little Swiss virgin!"

Cursing under his breath, Tom had no choice but to follow. He wondered if Hugo was drunk? Or stoned? But a second glance told him that Hugo knew exactly what he was doing. There was something malevolent about him. The vicious look on his face was obvious even in that shadowy light. Dressed in a loose silk shirt with long flowing sleeves, one silken arm waved before him while the other towed Kirsten behind him. Responding to his cries, people fell back, creating a pathway. "This is darling Roddy's little sister," he shouted, leading the way back into the hall.

Somehow Tom lost his grip on Kirsten's elbow. People got in his way. He now realized several men were wearing makeup. One was in the arms of a sailor at the foot of the stairs. Hugo dragged Kirsten past before Tom could reach her. The music became louder and louder as they ascended. Tom was less than halfway up when Hugo and Kirsten reached the landing. Stepping over couples embracing or drinking, he hurried after them. He called her name but his voice was drowned in the music.

He caught up with them on the threshold to the bathroom. It was a huge, mirrored room, with the door open wide. Inside he glimpsed people crowding the walls, all shouting and roaring with the fervor of a crowd at a racetrack. He sensed rather than saw them, his gaze drawn directly ahead. With his trousers round his ankles, Roddy was pressing a figure against a washbasin. The figure was a boy, naked from the waist down. Roddy's fingers were splayed across the bare buttocks. The boy's leg was cocked up into the wash basin. Rhythmically, Roddy moved into him. The crowd screamed their excitement. The boy rode up and down, gasping and panting. Their breath-smeared reflections showed in the mirror. The boy looked no older than twelve. On his shoulder, Roddy's face was contorted with lust.

The telephone was ringing when they returned to the flat. It was Roddy, begging to see them.

"I don't think that's a good idea," said Tom, holding the telephone with one hand while reaching for a cigarette with the other.

"I'm coming anyway. I've got your address. I've sent for a cab—"

"No!"

But the connection was broken.

"Damn and blast!"

Kirsten was slumped on the sofa, her face as white as when they stumbled down the steps outside Roddy's house. He poured her a drink and sat down beside her. When she looked up he could see the shock in her eyes. "You knew," she said, "didn't you?"

"Not before tonight. I've never given Roddy much thought."

Sipping from the glass, she turned her gaze away to stare at the floor. "It was such a shock. I never knew. It's not that I . . . I suppose I've never really thought about it. Homosexuality, I mean. It's something other people get involved in. I suppose I understand it. I think. . . ." Staring at her glass, she twisted it around in her hands. "God knows. If I've thought about it at all, I suppose. . . ." Her voice faded as she shook her head. "But that was so *bestial* . . . so degrading. Like animals." Disbelief echoed in her voice. "That was Roddy, my brother—"

"He's on his way over."

"What, here?" The glass almost slipped from her hands. "Oh no."

"I tried to stop him."

Roddy was there half an hour later. He brushed past when Tom opened the door and stormed into the small sitting room. Following him, Tom mistook belligerence for an attempt to conceal embarrassment, until he looked into his eyes. The pupils were contracted to pinheads. "Sit down, Roddy. You look half stoned—"

"What if I am? I needed something, for fuck's sake! You come barging into my life, snooping for my father—"

Kirsten flushed crimson. "We weren't snooping. We came to see you, that's all."

"Yeah? So you saw me. What are you doing about it, that's what I want to know?"

Tom guessed what he meant, though Kirsten looked mystified. "Doing? What do you . . . I mean, it's your life—"

"Oh, like that, is it?" Roddy sneered as he slumped down into a chair. "Live and let live. Some hopes. I've seen the way he sucks up to my father." He stared accusingly at Tom. "Wouldn't surprise me if you've called him already. Well, *Consigliori?* I bet you've been on the phone to him—"

"No." Tom struggled to curb his irritation, "and if I had it would have been to discuss something important."

"Oh clever!" Roddy brushed a strand of hair away from his eyes. "It was all Hugo's fault anyway," he said petulantly. "He knew I was paying him back. He has it away with every bit of rough in the neighborhood—"

"We don't want to know," Tom interrupted as he collected Kirsten's empty glass. "It's none of our business. Okay?" As he crossed the room to the sideboard he thought of the cruel irony of Maurice's son being gay.

"Well?" Roddy persisted. "Will you tell him?"

It became easy to understand why Roddy wanted advance

warning of Maurice's visits to London. Tom asked, "Doesn't he know?"

"What do you think?"

"I think you're a fool not to tell him. I've always found Maurice—"

"Oh yes," Roddy sneered waspishly. "We all know you think the sun shines out of his arse. And he's the same. All I ever hear is Tom this and Tom that. He was full of how you've shacked up with my sister—"

"If you're here for my help," Tom said evenly, "you're going a funny way about it."

Roddy's mouth closed into a thin line.

"I'll make a deal with you," Tom said.

A look of hope flickered across Roddy's sulky face.

"I won't say anything to Maurice, but I won't tell him lies. The best thing you can do is make sure I know nothing about you. So you stay out of my life, and I'll stay out of yours."

Kirsten caught her breath as she looked up.

"If you want to see him, that's up to you," Tom said to her, "but don't involve me. Don't *ever* involve me."

"Oh, hark at that!" Roddy cried. "Laying down the law. I wouldn't take orders from him. Who does he think he is? Telling you who you can see—"

"No, Roddy," Kirsten's face was grave. "You don't listen. He's not *telling* me. That's the whole point." Standing up, she smoothed the crumpled white dress. "He's saying the decision is mine—"

"Of course it's yours," Roddy nodded. "So you tell him. We'll see each other whenever we want."

"No." Kirsten joined Tom at the sideboard. "I mean it's true, I did want to see you, but . . . I don't know, I need to think. We'll see. Let's leave it at that. Now I think you should go."

Roddy sat completely still for a moment. His gaze focused on her face, and look of hate came into his eyes. "Smug little bitch," he said, rising to his feet and turning for the door. "Why didn't you stay in Geneva. I warn you. . . ." He paused with his hand on the door. "You say a word, that's all. You say one fucking word about me and I'll kill you!"

Kirsten did go back to Geneva, the following week, not to stay but to invite her mother to the wedding. Twenty-four hours later she returned to London, looking despondent. "Oh dear," she tried to hide her disappointment behind her quirky smile. "First Roddy, now my mother. This marriage isn't exactly being blessed by my family."

Tom didn't give a damn about Roddy or her mother. "Maurice approves. I spoke to him on the phone. We're invited to St. Moritz for the weekend."

Maurice more than approved. He was delighted. He never looked happier. He hugged Kirsten, he kissed her, he slapped Tom on the back, wrung his hand and tousled his hair. "When is it to be?" he wanted to know.

They had planned to marry quietly in London. "Sometime around Christmas," Tom said. "That gives Kirsten a few months to find us a house."

"Christmas?" Maurice pulled a face. "But London is miserable at that time of year. This is a red-letter day. I shall be giving the bride away. We must have the wedding here, in St. Moritz. It will make the perfect setting. Tell you what, let's have it Christmas Eve. We'll make it the glitziest wedding in Europe this year."

In full spate, Maurice was an unstoppable force. Grinning hugely, Tom did not even try to resist. Neither did Kirsten. She was swept away by the idea until she remembered her mother. "It was awful last week," she confessed. "I'm not even sure she will come to London. She'll never come here. Once she heard Tom runs your businesses, that was that. It's so stupid when she's not even met him."

"Don't you know your mother yet?" Maurice asked gently. "She's consumed by this hatred. She hates anything connected with me. It rules her whole life. You could hold the wedding outside her front door and she wouldn't come out."

Kirsten's eyes clouded. "I think you're right, but we must try. Tom agrees. He's coming with me to see her on Monday."

Maurice looked at Tom. *"Bon chance,"* he said, "I mean it. If you persuade her, I'll fall in with whatever arrangements you decide upon, but . . . meanwhile, why not indulge me? Let me make plans to hold the wedding here on Christmas Eve."

With irresistible charm, he sold Kirsten the idea. Watching him coax her into agreement was an object lesson in the art of persuasion. Later, when she left them to finish their brandies, Tom grinned. "God knows why you employ me. You're better at closing deals than I am."

Maurice laughed. "Don't be so modest." Wrapping an arm around Tom's shoulder, he led him to the windows overlooking the valley. Lights winked in the distance. The moon and stars shone down on the snow. "See that? I used to ski on clear nights like this. I'd go ten, twenty miles, just for the hell of racing through the night. The thrill of danger was sensual. The curves of these mountains gave me as much pleasure as the curves of a woman's body." A look of amusement came into his eyes. "Well, not quite. Now it's enough for me to look." His smile faded. "One day it will be like that with women. Not yet, thank God, but one day."

"A long way off."

Maurice looked melancholy. "Closing business deals is a young man's game. You need to look at a proposition and say, 'What can I make of this in five years?' Or ten. Even twenty. Make plans to live forever—"

"That's not what Gunther says."

"Ah! Gunther is a banker. They see life differently. But we need them, you and I. They remind us of the passing of time. There's a date when all bills become due . . ."

Listening was to hear Maurice talk in a different voice, one Tom had not heard before. He always thought of him as indestructible, as possessing infinite vitality. He remembered once saying to Alec, "If you could plug into Maurice, you'd have enough power to light a small town."

Maurice laughed. "Anyway, you're not so bad at closing deals. You proposed to her, didn't you? She accepted. Seems to me you got what you wanted."

"I did."

"And me," Maurice smiled. "Who would have thought," he

mused, "first you bring Kirsten back to me, then you two get married. You and Kirsten. . . ." He beamed his delight.

Glowing from the brandy and reciprocated affection, Tom went to bed, happy except for one thing. Never before had he known Maurice talk, even indirectly, about mortality. Maurice was a titan, immortal . . .

Next morning such gloomy thoughts seemed to have passed with the night. Maurice was as vital as ever. After breakfast, he settled down to his favorite game of charming Kirsten. He took her on a tour of the chalet. He explained the views from every balcony. He told her the history of every painting. He sat down at the grand piano and recalled the famous people who had played it over the years. He took her down to the cellar to examine his vintage wines. Returning to the vast living room, his eyes twinkled. "So you see. There is everything here a man could wish for. Well, almost everything. Perhaps one thing is missing."

Her eyes sparkled. She needed no prompting. It was as if she had grown up with him and those empty childhood years had never existed. "Only one?" she laughed. "From what I've heard two or three would be more likely."

"Perhaps," he agreed ruefully. "When I was younger, but soon I'll be a father-in-law, then perhaps even a grandfather. Two or three might be unseemly."

She regarded him in silence, the quirky smile on her lips.

He steepled his fingers. "But one," he mused, "someone I don't have to hide away when you come on a visit . . ." his face brightened, "that might be an idea. Amusing for me and extra company for you. Someone to take you shopping when Tom and I talk business."

"Are you asking my permission?"

"Did you ask mine before you slept with Tom?"

"No."

"But you're glad I approve?"

Tilting her head, she pretended to consider. Finally she laughed. "You know I am. It's marvelous that you two are friends."

"Exactly." He nodded sagely, "it's a comfortable feeling

when friends and family accept each other's domestic arrangements. Don't you agree?"

"Oh I do." Kirsten nodded earnestly. "A very comfortable feeling."

"So you won't object, if when you come on a visit, someone . . ." His eyebrows twitched.

"How could I object? I'm living with someone—"

"Ah," he interrupted. "But I might, er . . . just fancy this someone. Marriage isn't on my agenda."

"I fancied Tom. Marriage wasn't on my agenda to begin with."

Veronica Taubman arrived in time to join them for dinner. She was tall, slender, full-chested, with corn-colored hair and eyes as blue as the Mediterranean—similar, in fact, to several of Maurice's girls, except for one thing. Veronica Taubman was nearer forty than thirty. In conversation over dinner other differences from the norm began to emerge. She had been twice married—an early marriage which had ended in divorce, and a second which had lasted until the death of her husband two years before. Originally from New Jersey, she had lived in most parts of the world. She owned an apartment in Paris and a summer home on Majorca. Clearly, Veronica Taubman had already experienced life's "great adventures"—even before she met up with Maurice.

Tom talked about her all the way to Geneva the next day.

They flew from St. Moritz in the Lear, with Masters at the controls and Gregg serving coffee. Kirsten had already become his favorite passenger.

Tom's every sentence began, "In all the time I've known Maurice—"

"Why so concerned?" asked Kirsten. "Didn't you like Veronica?"

"Yes, she's fine. It's not that . . ." He frowned. "It's Maurice. I know it sounds crazy, but I always think of him as immortal. Now, suddenly, he takes up with an older woman—"

"Don't worry," she grinned. "He's growing up, not growing old."

He supposed she was right, but his late-night conversation

with Maurice stayed in his mind. It seemed to him that Maurice was feeling his years.

"What I can't understand," said Kirsten, "is how anyone could *hate* him so much. He's right about my mother. She's wasted her entire life, just hating him."

The nearer they got to Geneva, the more fretful she became. She even had second thoughts about taking Tom to meet her mother. "Perhaps you shouldn't come up to the château? Could you lunch at the airport? Or go and see Amiens—"

"No, no. I said I'd come."

"It's bound to be awful. She'll probably be rude to you."

He laughed, "I'll survive. If you go, I go."

Gratefully, she squeezed his hand. "I must try. She is my mother. If she won't come to the wedding, she won't. I can't force her, but I must ask her."

They took a cab from the airport. Tom had seen the Château Stanton before, from a distance. Yvonne Amiens had pointed it out on his very first visit to Geneva. The château was only a couple of miles from where the Amiens lived, but set higher up and farther back from the lake. From afar the high walls and turrets looked decorative, giving the place a picturebook charm, but as the cab turned into the front gates the turrets loomed above them like the battlements of a fortress.

Kirsten saw the look on his face. "I know. It doesn't look very welcoming, does it? But the other side of the house is marvelous, you'll see. And even this side was pretty at one time. Apparently Maurice had lights everywhere and urns of flowers and things. Some were still here when I was a child." She shrugged. "One by one the lights stopped working and weeds overran the flower tubs. One day I came home and everything had gone."

The housekeeper answered the door; an elderly woman, dressed in black, with an unhappy face, who smiled briefly at Kirsten while ignoring Tom.

As their footsteps echoed in the vaulted hall, he thought about Kirsten coming home to find the lights and flower tubs missing. There wasn't much left. Then he corrected himself. What was left would fill a normal house a dozen times over. The size of the place deceived the eye. The stone-flagged hall would house a party for a hundred people. Everything was larger than life. Like Maurice. He could see Maurice here. Maurice would fill the house with people and laughter and music.

His gaze followed the wide sweep of the staircase as it climbed past the huge chandelier.

"That's Maman when she was young." said Kirsten.

He turned to confront the huge portrait over the fireplace, recognizing Maurice's type—hair so blonde as to verge on platinum, eyes of cornflower blue.

"She was said to be the most beautiful woman in Switzerland."

"I can imagine," he murmured politely, staring at the portrait. The woman *was* beautiful. The cheekbones, the finely honed features were all perfectly proportioned . . . yet something jarred. Perhaps everything was *too* perfect? Looking at those blue eyes he was reminded of Veronica Taubman whom he had met the previous day, also for the first time. Her eyes were as blue, but somehow quite different. Of course she was older, her looks flawed by comparison, but her eyes held a warm and welcoming look. The eyes in the portrait were watchful and cold.

Kirsten laughed. "Maman always said the family tragedy is her looks went to Roddy instead of me."

Then he saw it. Roddy's face. The too perfect face. The spoiled, spiteful look.

"Come on. This way."

Gladly he left the portrait to follow her through an arched doorway at the end of the hall. They entered a wide, spacious room, dominated by a superb view of the lake. Kirsten hurried eagerly to the middle of three sets of French windows. Stepping through onto a terrace, she turned to him proudly. "Eh voilà!" she cried, looking pleased. "The best view in Switzerland!"

The view was quite astonishing. Breathtaking. He realized the architect had designed the entire house to capture this view. The disappointing front entrance suddenly ceased to have importance. Cantilevered into the rock, the wide terrace curved all the way along the ground floor. A long row of French windows, all shaded from above by blue roller blinds, stretched down the terrace to suggest that all of the principal reception rooms shared in the view.

"Fantastic," he murmured, walking across the terrace to stare out at the lake.

"Careful," she cautioned as he approached the edge, "the balustrade is very low."

Startled, he realized that the stone balustrade scarcely reached his knees.

"It was designed that way," she explained. "Any higher and it would interrupt the view from the room. When you sit in there and look out it's like being in an aircraft. Some people get a bit queasy, but I love it." She laughed. "When we were children a metal railing ran along it to stop us from falling over."

Craning his neck, he peered down at the rocks below. Without being sheer, the drop was sharply angled. His gaze followed the rocky, uncultivated ground. He squinted, "There's a path—"

"It goes all the way down to the lake. It starts near the other end of the terrace. I spent my life climbing that path. I've been up and down a thousand times and never got tired of it. It's very steep, you have to be careful." She smiled, "I couldn't do it in these heels."

He shook his head in admiration. "It is fantastic," he said, "quite, quite fantastic."

Eyes shining, she hugged his arm. "I'm glad you like it. To me it's always been so special—"

"Kirsten," a voice interrupted.

They turned. Madame Moutier was framed in the French windows, dressed all in white; white shoes and stockings, white skirt and high-collared blouse—even white-haired, although as Tom advanced he realized her hair was more silver than white.

"Maman," said Kirsten, "this is Tom Lambert."

Tom extended a hand. "I'm pleased to meet you, Madame Moutier."

Ignoring him, she spoke to her daughter in French. *"Tu es en retard. Je t'attends depuis une demi-heure."*

Lowering his hand, Tom remembered being snubbed by Roddy in the same way. Like mother like son, he thought as he studied her. The portrait in the hall had been painted a long, long time ago. She was an old woman. She looked much older than Maurice. An old woman who had aged without grace.

"Not half an hour," Kirsten corrected calmly in English. She glanced at her watch. "A few minutes perhaps, but we have flown the length of the country to get here."

"Je pensais que tu venais de Londres?"

Kirsten colored. "Please speak English, Maman. No, we haven't come from London. We flew from St. Moritz."

The blue eyes glinted. "You've been to see him?" she asked, speaking English for the first time.

"He's not the devil incarnate," Kirsten protested gently.

Madame Moutier's mouth tightened. Distaste and displeasure showed in every line of her face.

"Maman," Kirsten said softly. She stretched out a hand but the old woman drew away, cold and furious. For a moment Tom thought she would turn on her heel. He half expected the meeting to end there and then. Instead Madame Moutier drew a deep breath while her small, clawlike hands clenched into fists.

"Very well," she said more in anger than acceptance. "You came for lunch. We'd better eat." Turning, she began to walk along the terrace. "I've no idea what it will be like," she said over her shoulder. "Lunch was ready to be served half an hour ago."

Throwing Tom a look of apology, Kirsten followed her mother. The next set of French windows opened into a dining room, confirming his guess about the main reception rooms all looking out over the lake. It was a well-proportioned room, with a vaulted painted ceiling above a long rosewood table capable of seating at least twenty. Three places had been set at the far end. A sullen-looking maid, bearing a covered tureen on a tray, entered from the hall.

Madame Moutier swept to the head of the table and sat down before Tom had a chance to pull her chair out from the table. She said, "Serve the soup, Estée. It should still be warm."

Taking his place, Tom wondered about a hostess who failed to ask her guests if they wanted to use the bathroom before lunch, especially guests who had flown three hundred miles. For Kirsten's sake, he made an effort to be pleasant. "I must say,

Madame Moutier, your house is quite beautiful. The views are superb. Kirsten was saying—"

"Yes," Madame Moutier interrupted, "the views are superb, but the house is not mine." She looked him full in the face for the first time. Her eyes glinted with malice. "Surely you know? The Villa Stanton belongs to your employer."

Tom bit his tongue. Feeling he should have been warned, he cast an aggrieved glance at Kirsten, only to catch her look of total astonishment. "I didn't know that," she gasped.

Madame Moutier dipped her spoon in her soup. "Why should you? When that man deserted us, my duty was clear. To bring up my children in a secure environment. Would you have felt safe knowing you were living under his roof? Of course not! You wouldn't have slept at night. You hated him, remember?"

Kirsten's face was full of pain and confusion. "There was a lot I didn't know then, but . . . I always thought . . . you always said—"

"*Naturellement!* Should I have given you nightmares every night?"

"You gave me nightmares about him."

"But not about the château." Madame Moutier sounded triumphant. A gloating satisfaction showed in her eyes. "He desperately wanted this place, *desperately,* but my lawyers were too clever for him. 'You walked out,' I told him, 'and you won't walk back in until the day I die.' "

It took Kirsten a moment to recover. "I see," she said sadly. "Well, it's all over with now. I don't think this is the proper time—"

"Why not? Because you've been to see him? Because you believe him and not me?" Pushing her soup bowl aside, Madame Moutier looked up angrily. "Estée! This is cold. Take it away." Her spiteful gaze returned to her daughter. "So he didn't tell you everything, did he? He didn't tell you how he begged and begged me for this house. All of Geneva was laughing at him. Maurice Stanton, thrown out of the family home. That's why he moved to St. Moritz in the first place. To escape the laughter. So don't come here with your head full of his lies—"

"Please, Maman," Kirsten interrupted, "it was all a long time ago—"

"So I should forget it? I should pretend—"

"You pretended about other things. About money. You had a *fortune*. And every year he pays—"

"He pays. Of course he pays. Why shouldn't he? He walked out leaving me with two young children—"

"He wanted to take us. He told me—"

"To raise you in a brothel!" Madame Moutier spat the word onto the table. "Bring you up as a whore. Raise my son as a pimp. Oh no! I wouldn't allow that." Her eyes gleamed, "We fought him and beat him. We made him sign—"

"Maman, *please*," Kirsten begged, "we don't have to talk about—"

"You're a silly, impressionable young girl. You always were. Look at all that idealistic nonsense with the Red Cross. You're a fool. Not like Roddy. Roddy saw through him. He can—"

"Roddy did?"

"Oh yes!" The triumphant gleam became a smirk. "I know he went out there. To this island place. He told me. 'Never again,' he said. All that debauchery. He came away sick to the stomach. He was disgusted—"

"Roddy was disgusted!" Unable to disguise her disbelief, Kirsten's eyes found Tom across the table.

Following her daughter's gaze, Madame Moutier swung around in her chair. "And I suppose you condone your employer's way of life? Perhaps you even participate in what goes on . . ." She broke off as the maid returned with a tray laden with dishes. "Take it away. I'm too upset to eat."

Hesitating, the maid glanced at Kirsten, who shrugged and cast an embarrassed look of enquiry at Tom. He shook his head. "I don't know what you've heard, Madame Moutier," he began, "but I think you've been misinformed—"

"By my own son!" A look of outrage leapt into her eyes. "You forget yourself, Monsieur. Just because you're a guest at my table—"

"Please!" Kirsten cried. "We came here to invite you to our wedding—"

"I hope it's a long way off. I told you the other week. You're far too young—"

"I'm twenty-eight!" Kirsten's cheeks burned.

"Better to be thirty-eight. You'll have enough sense then to avoid such an unsuitable marriage." Shaking with temper, Madame Moutier whirled round on Tom. "Any friend of . . . of that man can't have a thing to recommend him—"

Kirsten leapt to her feet. "How *dare* you be so rude!"

"Sit down at once. Don't be so stupid. I'll say what I like in my own house—"

"It isn't your house!" Kirsten's dark eyes smouldered. "You just said so. It's Maurice's house. You live in Maurice's house on Maurice's money, and you could live damn well if you wanted to—"

Tom pushed his chair back from the table. "I think we should go—"

"Go now and never come back!" Madame Moutier flung at her daughter. "I did it to him and I'll do it to you!"

Kirsten stopped as she turned for the door. She was trembling.

Madame Moutier half-rose from her chair. "Leave now and you'll never get a penny from me. Never! Not even when I die. Roddy will get it all. I'll see to that."

Tom felt Kirsten shaking as he put a hand on her arm. Her eyes brimmed with tears. "You don't understand, do you? I just . . ." she gulped, "for once in my life I wanted you to be happy for me." Swallowing hard, she took a deep breath. "It was a waste of time to come. You'll never be happy, for me or anyone else, not even yourself. I've changed my mind. I don't want you at my wedding. It will be Christmas and . . . you'll spoil it for everyone. Goodbye, Maman. You'll never see me again."

Back at the office the following morning, Tom took a call from an old friend, Bill Watson, who worked for *The Times*. Bill had just returned from covering a story in India. "I heard something that might interest you," he said. "The Indian government is developing local industry by handing out interest-free loans and subsidies. There's a rumor that the office equipment industry could be the next beneficiary. Someone told me there's a huge new factory planned for Calcutta. They're looking for a partner to bring in expertise . . ."

Three days later Tom was in Delhi, only to find the Germans and Japanese already negotiating with the Indian Government.

So began seven months of dashing from London to Delhi, Delhi to Calcutta, Calcutta to Geneva . . . seven hectic months to try to win Stanton Industries a foothold in Asia.

Within two weeks, Tom had involved Alec and Amiens in the talks. Within a month they had established a small office in Delhi, staffed with twelve production engineers flown out from Geneva, all working on costings with Indian officials. The streets of Delhi were to become as familiar to Tom as those of London. Amiens came to know Calcutta better than Zurich. Even so, as days slipped into weeks, the Japanese seemed too far ahead to be caught.

Tom telephoned Kirsten every evening from the hotel. "We're giving them a hell of a fight. They had this sewn up until we arrived."

In London, Kirsten looked for a house and did what she could to prepare for the wedding.

"I'm not sure when I'll be back," Tom confessed on the phone. "Why not go across to St. Moritz and plan the wedding with Maurice. You'll have more fun . . ."

Kirsten hesitated. She had imagined flying into St. Moritz with Tom at her side . . . but time was getting short. Next week would be December. There was a lot to do.

Meanwhile, unexpectedly, there was trouble with Amiens. He had picked up with a local girl and was bringing her back to the hotel every night. "You'll have to stop him," Alec complained to Tom. "We're negotiating with government officials, for Christ's sake! What will they say if it gets back to them?"

The following day, Tom took Amiens to lunch. The Frenchman protested. "So what? Is it affecting my work?"

"No—"

"Then it's none of your business."

"Sorry, Andre, business makes it my business. Usually I don't say a word. You know that. You can bring who you like to London, but out here it's different."

Amiens shook his head, "It's the same all over the world. Women are women. They're all whores."

"I'm not asking you," Tom said quietly. "I'm *telling* you. Stop seeing this girl. You're to have nothing more to do with her or any other Indian girl. Is that understood?"

A mixture of anger and contempt came into the Frenchman's face. "You wouldn't say that to Maurice," he sneered. "Maurice screws around all the time. You wouldn't dare say anything to him." Tossing his napkin onto the table, he stood up, "You're a hypocrite, but then double standards are expected from someone as two-faced as you."

Tom would have liked to send Amiens home, but the technical side of the negotiations hinged upon production techniques. Alec was good, but Amiens was better. When it came to planning automation on the factory floor, Andre Amiens was in a class of his own. And it was true what he said—his sparetime activities never for a moment impinged on his work.

His remark about double standards stung. Of course there were differences between him and Maurice. Tom could make a whole list, beginning with the fact that Amiens was married; but the biggest difference of all lay in the remark Amiens had made, "All women are whores." Maurice would never have said that, Maurice wouldn't even have thought it.

Three nights later Tom and Alec were in the hotel bar, having a drink before dinner. "Is Andre joining us?" Alec asked.

Tom was unsure. Amiens tended to dine with them every other night. It was the nights when he was missing that concerned Tom. He was just beginning to feel anxious when Amiens came into the bar. On his arm was a blonde.

"Ah Tom, Alec." He smiled, "Let me introduce Gabrielle." Hugely pleased with himself, he watched Tom's face. The girl was obviously not Indian. "Gabrielle is a compatriot of mine. She works for Air France."

Afterwards, Alec shook his head. "Why does he do it? It's like he's trying to prove he can screw every bird in the world."

Tom thought of Yvonne in Geneva. Old man Bouvier's

daughter. The Boss's daughter, or she had been when Amiens married her. Yvonne with the big nose, who dressed too youthfully in an effort to please her husband. Was that what Amiens was trying to prove—don't judge me by my wife? With my looks and charm I can have any woman.

"You could be right," Tom agreed. "But don't let it bug you. Just as long as he gets on with his job."

And Amiens did get on with his job, and Tom and Alec got on with theirs, and with each day they were closing the gap with the Japanese.

Kirsten, meanwhile, had taken Tom's advice and gone to St. Moritz. St. Moritz proved merely the starting point. Maurice took her shopping in Paris and Rome. She updated Tom with regular calls. "Maurice is a whirlwind. He knows everyone. He's done everything and can't wait to do it again. Veronica and I collapse every night . . ."

Sweat-stained in Delhi, Tom smiled, "It's all a great adventure."

". . . And you should see him and Veronica. This could be a double wedding, do you know that?"

"Not Maurice," Tom chuckled.

"Tom . . ." Anxiety crept into Kirsten's voice. "It's the twelfth of December tomorrow. When are you coming back?"

It was hard to say. The Indian officials were holding talks with Stanton Industries and their Japanese rivals on alternate days, and Tom was busy playing politics on the days in-between. He had recruited three members of the Indian Parliament as consultants; their help and advice was making a difference.

"Maybe next Monday."

"That's the eighteenth. It's getting close."

"I know . . ."

After the conversation, he went down to join Alec in the bar. Amiens was with him, and they were discussing the same subject. Alec came straight to the point. "You're kidding yourself if you think they will let up for Christmas. They don't celebrate it here."

Amiens agreed. "But the Japs will celebrate right back to Tokyo if we go home."

"Go and get married," Alec suggested, "Andre and I will keep the flag flying here."

But the Okaki team was being led by the company's president. If Tom left less senior colleagues to negotiate for Stanton Industries, the Indian government might feel slighted. They would suffer loss of face; Stanton Industries would be at a disadvantage. Besides Alec was supposed to be best man at the wedding. And with Pohl and Edwards invited, Amiens felt he should be there as well.

By the following evening it was clear that the talks would extend through Christmas and beyond.

Tom returned to the hotel, unsure of the best way to break the news to Kirsten. Deciding there was no such thing as a best way, he swallowed a whisky and reached for the phone.

"If we win this it puts us into a different league," he explained to Kirsten. "It's a turning point—"

"Whereas you can marry me whenever you want."

"I didn't say that."

"Why not? It's true." Kirsten retorted, hurt and upset. "Maurice and Veronica have gone overboard on this wedding. You know how many are coming? Nearly four hundred. Everyone will be here except you."

Wrestling with the decision, Tom felt desperate. He shouldn't have left things to the last moment. He should have decided before. He wavered. Nobody was indispensable. He *should* go. Maybe he could go. "Let me talk it through with Alec again. I'll call you back. Okay?"

But it was Kirsten who called him half an hour later. He returned to his room to take the call. "I've been thinking," she began.

"Yes."

"Lose this deal and you'll never forgive me. It could ruin our marriage—"

"No, no—"

"Will you listen to me! If I'm going to be noble, you can sit there and listen."

He fell silent.

"You can have a postponement on one condition."

He waited.

"You owe me one hell of a wedding present, Tom Lambert."

"I'll say. Anything—"

"Good. I want that contract. I won't have my mother saying I married a failure."

He was still laughing when he rejoined Alec and Amiens in the bar. Alec whistled. "Wow. Jean would have gone berserk."

Amiens smiled with approval, "*Formidable,*" he said, using the French inflection.

"That's my wife," Tom agreed. *"Formidable."*

They won the contract on the fourteenth of January. Tom had the documents copied and bound into a tooled leather case made by the finest craftsmen in Calcutta. Like a knight in shining armor, he carried it back to St. Moritz and laid it at Kirsten's feet.

Everything was coming right. He could *feel* it. They had established a presence in Asia. Constantin had emerged as a superb administrator in London. Desmond Edwards was setting sales records. There were encouraging prospects for a joint venture in Australia. A new date was set for the wedding. It was all coming together.

The only fly in the ointment was Pohl. The Institute was still soaking up huge sums of money.

On the second of February, Tom flew to California. This time Kirsten went with him. "I've been left at the church once," she said ruefully. "I'm not letting you out of my sight until the end of the month when we walk up the aisle."

But even that prediction failed to come true.

The news reached them two days after they returned from the States. The telephone rang in the flat.

"I'll get it," said Kirsten.

Tom had only moments before arrived home from the office. He was at the sideboard pouring a drink. The architect's plans for their new Hampstead house had arrived in the post, and he carried them eagerly over to an armchair. As he sat down, Kirsten returned from the telephone in the hall. "That was Roddy."

The name and the tone of her voice jerked his head up from the plans. She was standing in the doorway, white-faced and shaking. On faltering legs she stepped forward to grasp the back of a chair. "It's Maman. She's dead."

The papers spilled off his lap as he rose to go to her. Taking her arm, he eased her gently down into a chair.

"She died last night," she said, staring with blank eyes.

He poured her a drink and squatted down beside her to take her hand in his. Then he realized—the wedding was only seven days away. Once shock and surprise were assimilated, it was his first conscious thought. *What bloody perfect timing. The bitch!* He had despised the woman in life, he hated her in death; she seemed determined to blight her daughter's happiness.

Ten minutes later, the telephone rang again. Tom answered it this time. Maurice came on the line. He had heard the news. Whatever he felt about his former wife he kept to himself. His questions and concerns were solely for Kirsten. "How is she? Did she take it badly?"

She was more affected than Tom would have expected. Not tearful, at least not immediately, but dazed and shocked by the unexpectedness of the news.

"Oh God, I wish I'd never said that," she said, twisting a handkerchief around in her hands. "You know, when we stormed out, and I said I never wanted to see her again. Oh Tom . . ."

He tried to comfort her, but with little success.

"Perhaps she was ill, even then. Oh Tom. That might explain—"

"Maurice said she died in her sleep. You've nothing to reproach yourself—"

"Oh I just thought . . ." Her eyes brimmed with sudden tears. "I know it's selfish, but the wedding . . . we can't."

"I know." He cradled her like a child in his arms, stroking her hair, "We'll fix another date. Don't worry. Maurice already has it in hand." He tried to soothe her, "You know what they say? Third time lucky. It will make it a very special wedding."

They were up until two in the morning, talking and drinking coffee. Kirsten did most of the talking. Her thoughts jumped around like a grasshopper. One minute she was reminiscing about her childhood, the next wondering about the funeral arrangements. One moment wringing her hands with reproach, the next bemoaning the cancellation of her wedding. Tom did his best to let her talk herself out. Eventually he persuaded her to go to bed, where he lay awake until she fell into a fitful sleep.

He was up at six. His first meeting was at seven, in the office with Constantin and Alec. Kirsten was still sleeping. He left her a note, telling her to call him when she awoke.

Constantin had scheduled meetings on the hour every hour through the day, and it was past ten before Tom remembered. Excusing himself from the meeting, he called home from Barbara's office.

Roddy was at the flat. The name was enough to make Tom's nose crinkle. But Kirsten sounded calmer and more in control. "Roddy's flying to Geneva tonight," she said, "he's spoken to the lawyers and between them they can organize the funeral and everything. He says I should stay here and let them make all the arrangements . . ."

Listening, Tom was surprised. And relieved. He had never expected to have reason to thank Roddy for anything.

The next surprise occurred at midday. Barbara slipped a note in front of him. *Kirsten phoned. She's gone out to lunch with her brother. She wanted you to know in case you called and worried about not getting an answer. She says she's feeling better.*

It was nine o'clock when he got home. Kirsten, still looking very pale, was over the worst of the shock. During dinner, she told him about Roddy. "He was here until four," she said. "I'd wish you'd seen him. He was a different person from . . . well, you know, when he came here before."

"He was stoned before," Tom said bluntly.

"I know and he knows too. He's very ashamed about what happened."

It had been a long day. Tom was tired. He wanted his dinner, a few drinks to unwind, and bed. He felt grateful to Roddy for nursing Kirsten through a bad day, and relieved about her staying in London until the funeral. But nothing would convince him that Roddy was genuinely repentant. Not that he said so. Kirsten had just lost her mother. Now was not the time to tell her he thought her brother was a louse. So he remained silent, letting her tell him about her day, letting her talk herself out.

". . . he's terrified you'll tell Maurice he's gay."

"I said I wouldn't."

"I know but some men are so anti-homosexual. I said you weren't one of them. I said you believe in live and let live . . ."

She seemed to have forgotten what they had seen. The appalling part had not been the homosexual act. It would have been just as horrifying had the young boy been a young girl. What they had seen was one step away from a gang bang. That mob in the bathroom, shouting and screaming. And that boy had looked very young.

". . . he thinks Thursday for the funeral. I'm so relieved that I haven't got to go through everything with him. It is good of him, isn't it?"

"Very," Tom said dryly. He wondered what was in it for Roddy. He remembered eavesdropping on Kariakos: Roddy whining and pleading for money. The first vulture always got the best pickings.

". . . anyway," said Kirsten, "I feel a bit better."

But he could still see shock in her eyes.

The following day was another bruising stint at the office, but he managed to get home by seven.

"Roddy called," she said, "he says everything is under control."

"Good."

Wednesday passed with his rearranging his diary, and on Thursday the Lear flew them to Geneva. Kirsten was quiet and solemn, but had regained her color.

There were only a few mourners gathered at the château. Roddy was standing on the top step, the big front door half-open behind him. Dressed in a black suit and tie, with his fair hair brushed down, he looked older, and his grave expression added to the image of a responsible, caring young man.

The hearse was waiting outside. Chauffeurs stood talking in low voices next to three black limousines. Inside the house Estée the maid was taking coats. Tom met the elderly housekeeper and a man called Henri Monet who apparently tended the gardens.

Two middle-aged women were introduced as cousins of the deceased. And Yvonne Amiens was there. "As a friend and a neighbor," she explained. Tom hadn't expected her, but then he hadn't known what to expect. He kissed her dutifully, thinking that even at a funeral she dressed too young for her age. Her black dress was too short, and somehow too smartly fashionable: more appropriate for a cocktail party than a funeral.

When Roddy came over, his manner was almost deferential. "Hello, Tom," he said gravely, extending his hand, "thank you for coming."

Tom murmured his condolences, which Roddy accepted. Then Roddy said, "It will be a very simple affair. I only ordered three cars. I thought the family in the first, you and Yvonne in the second, and the rest in the third."

Tom glanced enquiringly at Kirsten. Her face looked pale beneath her black hat. "Don't worry. I'll be all right."

Tom wondered if it was Roddy's idea of a snub. Even with little idea of the etiquette of funerals, he would have thought he counted as family by now. Not that it worried him. He doubted he would ever be family with Roddy. Looking at him, he tried to read his expression, but the blue eyes were guarded, hiding his thoughts. Tom turned away, concerned only with Kirsten.

They set off for the cemetery, with Tom in the second car with Yvonne, while Kirsten rode with the cousins and Roddy ahead. The servants traveled behind. *Get this over,* Tom told himself, *and then we can get on with our lives.*

Geneva was at its worst. The day was cold and blustery, with a hint of rain in the air. Dark, brooding clouds rolled over the snow-covered mountains. The open air cafés along the Quai du Mont Blanc were all boarded up. Hotels were bereft of their smart summer awnings. The lake was as gray as the sky.

Yvonne mused, "I wonder what Maurice will do with the château? He always loved it. Perhaps he'll take up residence in Geneva again."

Looking at her, Tom realized she knew far more of the family history than he did. Where he had come in halfway through, she had been there at the beginning.

Yvonne watched the hearse leading the slow procession.

"What a wasted, pitiful life," she said softly. "She went quite ga-ga you know, for a while. My father thought she'd kill herself. Instead she settled down into a lifetime of hate." Sighing, she shook her head. "The things women do for a man."

He wondered if she was thinking of her own life. She had kept her man, but most people thought Andre stayed more for the Bouvier name and the Bouvier money than for her. Now that he knew Andre, he could imagine him as he had been, young, good-looking, and fiercely ambitious. He would have prospered on his own account, given time. He had the ability. Instead he had taken the short cut of marrying the boss's daughter. Maurice's goddaughter.

"Was she your godmother?" he asked with a sudden thought.

"I suppose she was, but when they broke up she automatically saw us on Maurice's side. I was discouraged from visiting the château. But later, when Andre and I became virtual neighbors, I saw a bit more of her. I took her books and things, I did what I could, but she was always a difficult woman."

It struck him that beneath Yvonne's veneer of toughness lay a kind woman. He remembered their first meeting, when he had stayed with Amiens after visiting the Bouvier plant. Yvonne had seen him as an enemy then. She had fought to protect Andre's best interests. Everything she did was for Andre. Even the absurd way she dressed was to catch his eye. He wondered if she knew how often Andre's eye strayed elsewhere? All that loyalty, so poorly repaid. He felt a sudden admiration for her, even affection. Reaching across, he surprised himself by squeezing her hand. "I'm glad you're here," he said.

As always her large nose seemed smaller when she smiled. "I told you before. This is my town. There are certain duties attached to being a Bouvier. My father would have wanted me to pay my respects."

Monsieur Rochere, the lawyer, was waiting at the cemetery in Petit-Sacconex. He was a small, timid-looking man who hurried forward as the first limousine rolled to a halt. After a whispered conversation with Roddy, he went forward to offer his condolences to Kirsten.

Pall bearers carried the coffin into the church, and the

ceremony began. Mercifully it was soon over. Half an hour by Tom's watch. Thirty minutes later the coffin was lowered into the ground and the short service was concluded. The handful of people began to return to the limousines. Taking Kirsten's arm, Tom searched her face. Her eyes were dry, but her pallor concerned him. Every scrap of color had gone. There were no words he could say. She knew his opinion of her mother. Extravagant condolences would have been hypocritical. He hoped his presence helped, that the ordeal had been lessened by his being there.

Her eyes found his with a fond look of thanks. "Roddy says Monsieur Rochere wants to read the will back at the château."

Inwardly he groaned. He had hoped to flee to the airport as soon as they decently could.

"He says it should be done with everyone present."

"I understand." He wondered who was meant by everyone. Glancing at the handful of people, he walked Kirsten back to her car. Roddy was already there, holding the door open. His face was blank, yet Tom sensed his impatience: Roddy's left foot tapped on the gravel. It stopped when they arrived, but not before Tom had seen it.

The gesture stayed in his mind on the way back to the château. Yvonne might have glimpsed it as well, because at one point she murmured, "Roddy seems to have taken charge. His moment of glory, I suppose. Must make a change to see himself as the man of the house."

He wondered if she was making a reference to Roddy's private life. He tried to encourage her with a sideways glance of enquiry, but she only added, "He always was Mother's Little Darling."

Yet Mother's Little Darling had not looked unduly upset. Merely impatient.

"Do you see much of him?" he asked, probing.

"Roddy? Not much. He called a year ago when he was over to see his mother. I think Andre bumped into him in London once, but no, we hardly see him. What about you? Living in London—"

"No. I mean what with one thing and another, we're hardly there."

He was reminded of Roddy again as soon as he entered the

house. The blue eyes greeted him from the huge portrait up on the wall. Beneath it a dreary fire smoked in the hearth.

As he helped Yvonne off with her coat, Kirsten emerged from a door at the side of the hall. "Tom. Monsieur Rochere has asked that you be present when the will is read."

"Me? He doesn't need me. I'll stay here with Yvonne. We'll keep each other company."

"Yvonne is to be present as well," said Kirsten, "and he specifically asked for you to be there."

"Surely that's unnecessary?"

"Apparently those were Maman's instructions."

They exchanged bewildered looks as Estée passed by with glasses of wine. Tom took one, wishing it were whisky. Something was wrong; he had a feeling of impending disaster. His gaze roamed the hall, hunting for clues. Roddy emerged from the side door in earnest conversation with the lawyer. They stopped when they saw him. Roddy managed a faint smile, while the lawyer looked distinctly embarrassed.

Kirsten said, "There's a buffet laid out in the dining room. I'm not hungry, but—"

"Me either," he said. He felt troubled. "Do we have to stay? If we go now—"

"Oh Tom. We can't just walk out."

"Certainly not," Yvonne murmured with obvious curiosity. "Especially when your presence is demanded—"

"I can't believe . . ." Tom began as Roddy came over to join them.

"Not eating? There's a buffet—"

"We know," Yvonne smiled sweetly, her shrewd eyes searching his face, "but no one is hungry."

Roddy could see that for himself. The gardener and the housekeeper each had a glass of wine, but neither took any food. Nor did the middle-aged cousins. "Perhaps it's best if we eat afterwards," he decided. "I know Monsieur Rochere is anxious to start. He has to get back to his office. I'll get everyone organized."

Watching him walk away, Yvonne's eyes lit with a speculative gleam. "He can't wait, can he?"

Alarm bells rang in Tom's brain. Why was his presence required? It didn't make sense. He hated the old bat. And she had made her opinion of him very clear.

"Kirsten," he said, but Kirsten was already moving toward the door at the side of the hall. Yvonne had gone too. Everyone was filing through the door. Kirsten and Yvonne turned, waiting for him to join them. Even as he walked toward them, he had the strongest feeling of impending calamity.

The room was a library, the only ground floor room without a view of the lake. Books covered every wall. Daylight filtered down from a domed glass ceiling, but the sky was so gray that someone had switched on the lights. Kirsten sat down in the second row of chairs. He sat down beside her. Roddy was a few chairs away in the front row. The housekeeper, the gardener, Estée the maid, the cousins and Yvonne, everyone had sat down.

Seated at a table in front, Rochere began to read the will.

Tom had to concentrate. His French had improved a good deal, but speed of delivery could sometimes defeat him. His eyes followed Rochere's lips. He understood that the housekeeper was to receive five thousand francs. The gardener was given the same. Estée got two thousand. The cousins received most of the books in the library. Yvonne was left some pieces of jewelry. . . .

Rochere spoke as distinctly as his thin reedy voice would allow, and at a steady pace which permitted Tom to follow the proceedings quite well, even so it was a surprise and a relief when the lawyer switched to English.

"This last clause," Rochere said, glancing up, "I have been specifically asked to read in English, to avoid any misunderstanding." A troubled, uneasy expression came into his face as he looked first at Roddy and then at Kirsten. "You understand that it is my strict duty to obey Madame Moutier's wishes? A lawyer has no choice in these matters."

As he spoke he drew out a small chamois leather bag from the attaché case in front of him. He hefted the bag in his hand for a moment, then set it down on the table with a clunk.

Clearing his throat, he picked up the will, and read: "With the exception of the foregoing and one special bequest for my daughter Kirsten, I leave the entire balance of my estate to my beloved son Roddy who has been a comfort to me throughout my entire life. Alas, where my son has been constant, my daughter has been fickle. Where my son has been loyal, my daughter has betrayed. To her, therefore, I leave the traditional reward for a Judas. Thirty pieces of silver, to be given to her in front of the man she is to marry so that he may know her true worth."

"I didn't know!" Roddy's voice rose almost to a scream. "I swear I didn't know."

Reluctantly Tom lifted his gaze from his desk. Two weeks had passed since the funeral. It seemed longer. Kirsten had been distraught. He had led her weeping and humiliated from the library in the château. To save waiting for a cab, Yvonne had driven them to the airport.

"You've got to believe me," Roddy insisted.

"Why?" Tom's voice was hard. "You lied to your mother. You lie to your father. Probably you even lie to yourself."

"She'd have gone mad if she knew I was seeing him. You don't know what she was like—"

"I met her. I was there when Kirsten told her she was seeing Maurice. Kirsten told her the truth. You were the Judas—"

"Please, Tom. I'll do anything—"

"Just leave Kirsten alone. Leave *us* alone. You go your way and we'll go ours—"

"It's not as easy as that." Roddy shook his head. "My father called last night to tell me the new date for your wedding."

"Ah!" Tom sat back in his chair. Now he knew what had brought Roddy to the office.

"You won't tell him, will you?" Roddy pleaded, "I know you despise me because I'm gay—"

"You can fuck kangaroos for all I care. I told you before—"

"But what about Kirsten? Will she tell him? After the funeral, I was afraid she'd get so mad—"

"Don't judge others by your standards. Kirsten won't say anything to your father—"

"Not even at the wedding?" Some of the anxiety faded from Roddy's face, "I mean, I'll have to be there, won't I?"

Tom sighed, "Yeah. You'll have to be there." Roddy was right, he thought, I do despise him. Yet at the same time, I'm afraid of him for Kirsten's sake. He's so like his mother—the same blue eyes and spun-golden hair, the same delicately formed, regular features. Most of all, the same character—waspish and spiteful. Vindictive enough to scar someone for life, the way his mother had scarred her own daughter.

Kirsten had cried herself into exhaustion on the Learjet coming home. Seething with frustrated anger, Tom could scarcely credit such cold-blooded cruelty. What sick, twisted mind led a woman to do that? To her own daughter! His mind was still in turmoil when they landed at Heathrow. Normally decisive, he was unsure of what to do. They were halfway to the flat when he changed his plans. Afterwards he wondered why he hadn't gone to Alec and Jean, or Constantin and Melina. They would have helped. As it was, some deep, buried instinct caused him to give the cab driver different instructions. Half an hour later they drew up outside the small suburban house in which he had grown up, and while his grandmother put Kirsten to bed, he drank half a bottle of his grandfather's best whisky.

"I've never known such wickedness," his grandmother pronounced when she came down to join them.

For the first time in years, Tom asked their advice.

"Keep her busy," said his grandmother. "You'll never take the hurt away. She'll live with that for the rest of her life. But you can't let her brood. Whatever you do, keep her mind occupied."

Occupied how? Tom was at a loss. Kirsten's days were divided between rearranging the postponed wedding and organizing their new house. Then it came to him. That was it! The house! Within minutes he was calling his architect, Bill Walker, at his home number.

"It's ten o'clock," Walker grumbled. "I've had a long day and I'm off to bed soon."

But he changed his mind when Tom explained about Kirsten—half an hour later Bill Walker became party to a conspiracy.

Next morning, Tom's grandfather carried a cup of tea into Kirsten. "Do you know someone called Walker?"

Kirsten looked up with dull eyes. "Bill Walker? He's our architect."

"That explains it. He wants to see you urgently. I'm afraid something's gone wrong with your house."

By eleven o'clock, Kirsten was in Walker's office. Pinned on the wall were plans and elevations labelled NEW HAMPSTEAD RESIDENCE FOR MR. AND MRS. LAMBERT. Kirsten had seen them before. She was not sure which gave her the greater pleasure, the words "Mr. and Mrs. Lambert" or "new Hampstead residence." And it was "a residence." A large Victorian house set in a walled garden, at the foot of which was an old coach house Walker was converting into a guest cottage. The cottage was almost complete, but work had yet to start on the large derelict house. "It will take a year," Kirsten had told Tom when she found the property, "but we can live in the cottage to begin with. I'll be on hand to supervise everything. It will be terrific fun. By the time I finish we'll really have a residence worthy of the CEO of Stanton Industries."

Walker got straight to the point. "What I'm about to tell you is strictly confidential. I'll deny I even said it if ever anyone asks. But I've heard a rumor . . ." He paused, as if doubtful about confiding in her, then made up his mind. "As you know, there's a chronic shortage of housing in London. Councils are considering making compulsory purchase orders for derelict properties. Somebody told me yesterday that this may come into force on the first of May. If it does—" he shrugged "—I'm afraid you may lose your new home."

Kirsten was living through a nightmare: everything was going wrong. After the shock of the funeral the day before, her brain was slow to respond.

Walker spelled it out for her. "If the house is still derelict on the first of May, it will be liable to a compulsory purchase order. It's as simple as that. There's nothing we can do—"

"But that's monstrous!" Kirsten gasped, finding her voice.

He sympathized. "Of course you could appeal, but I have to tell you that appeals can take a couple of years."

"Can't we do *anything*? Suppose it's not derelict?"

"But it will be. It's February now—"

"We wouldn't have to complete *everything*, would we?" Kirsten's brain was beginning to function.

Walker appeared to consider. "Anything short of total completion would leave you at risk—"

"Could it be done?" Kirsten asked urgently.

He was very doubtful. "We'd have to employ extra craftsmen. There can be no skimping on a house like this." He sighed. "I'm sorry, but clients never realize the extent of these things. We haven't even designed your kitchen yet. There are four bathrooms. Have you decided on tiles and fittings and all the rest of it? Of course you haven't. I'm not blaming you, I'm just saying—"

"But suppose I did all those things?"

Walker laughed. "You'd be working full time. Honestly, it's not on, you've no idea what's involved. Suppliers break promises on delivery dates, I simply haven't the staff to chase them all day—"

"I'll do the chasing."

He shook his head, "It wouldn't work. You would have to be here every day, helping to coordinate—"

"Do you have a spare desk and telephone?"

Kirsten left Walker's office an hour later. As soon as she was out of the door, he put a call through to Tom. "She's on her way over to tell you—"

"Did she buy it?"

"Lock, stock and barrel. And congratulations. Your bride-to-be is a very determined young woman. I'm going to enjoy working with her."

"So am I," Tom said softly with a sigh of relief, "so am I."

He knew his grandmother had been right—"She'll live with that hurt for the rest of her life." Sometimes, in the evenings, a look of pain and sadness filled Kirsten's eyes that made Tom's heart ache. But for the most part she was too tired to brood. Walker kept her hard at it—visiting manufacturers and builders merchants and tile makers and countless other suppliers.

And, very quickly, it seemed, the day for the wedding drew nearer.

After the big event Kirsten laughed. "The whole world came to my wedding." And if that was an exaggeration it seemed only slightly so at the time. Maurice exceeded himself. And Veronica egged him on. For the first time in his life he was partnered by someone who had thrown bigger parties than he had. When one of them came up with an idea, the other set out to cap it; while Maurice borrowed notions from British coronations and royal celebrations, Veronica fell back on pure Hollywood. The result was a glitzy extravaganza which lasted forever in the memories of those who attended.

Not that Tom and Kirsten knew in advance. Until two days before, she was working feverishly on the house, and he was traveling on business, that week to the Pohl plant in Germany.

Kirsten never discovered that the specter of compulsory planning orders had been invented by Tom and Walker. Walker neatly avoided further complications by remarking one day, "I was at the Council Offices this morning. They're backing away from the idea." With color charts in one hand and a measuring stick in the other, Kirsten simply shrugged, "Who cares—by the first of May this place will be a palace."

Everyone who enquired about the wedding was given the same answer. "Maurice and Veronica have it in hand. All Tom and I have to do is be there."

Then the surprises began.

Roddy was the first. Knowing nothing of his meeting with Tom at the office, Kirsten hadn't heard from him since that black day in Geneva. Then, the week of the wedding, he arrived at the house in Hampstead, which at the time looked more like a building site than a home.

In checked shirt and blue-jeans, she was halfway down the stairs. The house rang with the sounds of hammers and roared with transistor radios at full blast. The ground floor was chaotic. Timbers were piled in one corner, and pots of paint were stacked high in another.

"Hello!" Roddy shouted from the open front door. Hugo

was behind him, impeding two plumbers who were carrying a pink porcelain hand basin over the threshold. Roddy was delivering his wedding gift. "It's too big to take out to Kariakos," he said, tugging Kirsten by the hand. "Come and see for yourself."

And there, at the curbside, stood a gleaming red Mercedes sports car.

Tom saw it the next day when he returned from Germany. "Isn't it pretty?" Kirsten enthused.

What could he say? Yes it was. Yes, it was a very generous gift. Yes, perhaps he had misjudged Roddy after all. In order not to spoil her pleasure, he said all the right things, though nothing changed in his heart. He was determined to keep Roddy at arm's length in the future.

They dined with Constantin and Melina that night. The single disappointment about the new wedding arrangements was that Constantin and Melina could not attend. With the Colonels still ruling Greece, everyone said the same thing, "Don't risk it." When Constantin wavered, Melina insisted, "No, no, no. We dare not go—for your sake, for my sake, and for Kirsten and Tom. Will you spoil their wedding by getting yourself arrested again? Never!"

And that settled it.

They came to see them off from Heathrow the next day. Melina was tearful, and Constantin hugged Kirsten as if it would be years before he saw her again. She squealed as he lifted her up from the ground. "Put me down, you big ape. You're crushing my ribs!"

Melina waved until the Learjet was a dot in the sky.

Even then, neither the bride nor the groom had much idea of what lay ahead. They knew Alec and Jean had traveled to Kariakos the day before, taking Tom's grandparents with them. They knew Carl Pohl had flown there from the States. They expected Andre and Yvonne Amiens to be there, and Desmond Edwards with his new wife.

In their minds, they played the wedding down. "After all," said Kirsten, "it's only a long weekend."

Tom nodded, "And the villa can't accommodate much of a crowd. There's only eight bedrooms."

Neither of them minded. Six months before they would have settled for a quiet wedding in London, and with two postponements behind them they were simply glad that they were to be married. "Third time lucky," Tom grinned.

Even lack of time for a honeymoon failed to blight their spirits. By the time Tom returned from Australia, Kirsten would have furnished the house.

"We'll have a holiday then," she smiled, "just for a few days. Don't worry, I won't let it interfere with your schedule."

The first hint of what was to come came when *Helena* dipped in the evening sky on her approach to Kariakos. The sun was well down on the horizon. The darkening sky was turning the Aegean a deep, inky blue. Verdant pines stood like gray and black sentinels in the fading light. The island seemed to be peacefully slumbering.

Suddenly a flare arced high up into the sky. Then another. And a third and a fourth; Kirsten grabbed Tom's arm in alarm.

"It's okay!" Gregg shouted. Twisting in his seat, he grinned. "I'm coming in close to the village. Look!"

Even as he spoke, the whole sky lit up. Tom had never seen so many fireworks. Huge colored bursts of light patterned the sky. A rainbow of reds and greens appeared over the pine trees. Gregg waggled *Helena*'s wings in response. Then they were past, parallel to the next cove, with the villa coming into sight, with more fireworks painting the cliff, white one moment and red the next. Flares and lanterns lit the silver strand of beach. More fireworks burst up from the jetty. The bay was full of boats. *Aphrodite* was ablaze from stem to stern. And so were other yachts. And fishing boats. . . .

Gregg made no attempt to put down. Instead he dipped *Helena* into a gentle curve and turned back out to sea before coming in once more over the island. This time the fireworks were more brilliant than ever. For half an hour Gregg flew up and down the coastline—and for half an hour the show continued. Then the boats cleared a path in the bay, and *Helena* brought Tom and Kirsten safely into Kariakos.

Bride and groom were parted that night. Kirsten stayed up at the villa, while Tom was billeted in the village. The place had been transformed. Everyone on Kariakos was to take part in the wedding. Tables were set out in the square. Lanterns swung in the breeze. Bouzouki bands never stopped playing and people never stopped dancing . . .

Afterwards, looking back, so many memories were fixed in Tom's mind that he had difficulty deciding which took pride of place. Even so, one scene was totally unforgettable. He was standing on the steps of the tiny church the following evening. It was ten minutes to nine. Alec stood beside him, both looking up toward the villa. Everyone in the square was staring in the same direction, peering into the darkness. It was quiet, astonishingly quiet, considering the size of the crowd. Suddenly a shout rang out. The crowd stirred. Voices rose in a murmur of excitement. An arm pointed. Tom craned his neck. Next to him, Alec made binoculars of his hands as he stared upward.

Flickering pinpoints of light appeared a mile away. Like a glowworm, the torchlight procession began to wind its way down the track from the villa to the village. For several moments the flares themselves, dancing in the breeze, were all that could be distinguished. Then, as the procession drew closer, shadowy figures of men carrying the torches could be seen; two files of men on either side of the path, flanking the horse-drawn vehicles between them.

Suddenly, from the church tower above, came the sound of a bell. Then another bell, and a third and a fourth, until the air shook with the pealing of bells. And into the square filed the procession, with Maurice leading the first garlanded horse by the bridle, and Kirsten looking serene and beautiful on the seat of the trap just behind.

BOOK NINE

He coughed to clear the lump in his throat. "We had it all, didn't we? Health, wealth and happiness." The bitterness in his voice was unmistakable. Distracted by memories, he ran a hand through his hair. His other hand searched for a cigarette.

Alec stirred in his chair. "It was an incredible wedding. Kirsten looked radiant. Everyone said so."

Tom's hand shook as he raised the cigarette to his mouth. Constantin, watching in sorrowful silence, could think of no words which might ease the pain.

"Five years," Tom said softly, "you know each other inside out when you're married five years. Half the time we didn't even have to put our thoughts into words, we just knew what the other was thinking. We were so close."

Alec struggled to find suitable words of comfort. "Anyone could see that," he said. "It was the perfect marriage—"

"Then why that?" Tom shouted so suddenly that Alec jumped. "Why *that*?" Tom repeated, pointing to the projector. "If the marriage was so bloody perfect. Why? Why? It doesn't make sense."

Alec could have torn out his tongue. He scowled at the projector, angry with himself for saying the wrong thing.

"She wasn't like that!" Tom's face twisted with pain and frustration. "She wouldn't get involved with that sort of thing. I just can't understand—"

Making placating gestures with his hands, Alec half-rose from his chair. "Perhaps it's not Kirsten. I've been thinking. Okay, I know it *looks* like her—"

"Don't be a fool! You think I wouldn't know my own wife?"

"Maybe it's trick photography," Alec blundered on, "you know superimposing one face over another—"

"Bollocks!" Tom said in disgust. "That's crap and you know it."

Alec cast a look at Constantin, a mute appeal for help, but with the briefest shake of his head, Constantin rose from his chair. "I could use some coffee and a breath of fresh air."

The terrace outside was no longer gray. Early morning sun was finding spots of color. The marble balustrade was turning from pale oyster to pink. Terra cotta pots became brown, not black. Bougainvillea showed purple and gold, and even the pearly white sky was beginning to turn blue.

Tom glanced at his watch. "God! We've been up all night. We should get some rest—"

"Fresh air will do you more good," said Constantin as he slid back the glass door. "Ah! Smell that." Sucking air into his lungs, he cursed Alec's well-intentioned clumsiness. Of course it was Kirsten in the film. It was obvious. Watching it once was enough to remove any doubt. And Tom had watched it a hundred times. But now wasn't the time to discuss the film. Now was the time to coax Tom into telling what was left of the story while there was time left to search for some clues. "Know something," he asked with a laugh, "Greek air is the best air in the world. It's a fact. Greek air and Greek coffee."

"I'll make some," said Alec, taking the hint and glad to escape. "Why don't you go and sit by the pool? It won't take a minute."

"Tom?" Constantin cocked an eyebrow. "It will blow the cobwebs away."

Tom ran his tongue around the inside of his mouth. It tasted foul. "I wouldn't mind some coffee."

"Alec will bring it out to us. Come, let's go and look at the glory of Greece."

"You can't see the mainland from here." Surprise getting the better of him, Tom rose to his feet, stifling an absurd urge to point at the empty horizon.

Constantin laughed as he walked out onto the terrace. "I know." He waved an arm, "But that's where it is. Over there. My beautiful homeland, restored to democracy." Leading the way to the chairs, he sat down next to the white table. "Come on, Alec will bring the coffee."

Unsure of what to do next, Tom followed.

"Funny," Constantin mused, staring out to sea. "All this looking back sets you thinking. It makes you count the years. Seven years and two months. That's how long the dictatorship lasted. To achieve what? Know what they said when they seized power? They were saving the country from the Communists. Hah! Twice as many people called themselves Communists by the time the Junta was ousted. They claimed they would restore the economy. Balls! They left Greece with the highest inflation in Europe and a two hundred percent increase in debt. Meanwhile they murdered and tortured and plundered. . . ." Shaking his head, he looked at Tom. "We saw it all, eh, Tom? We saw it all."

"I didn't see much of it—"

"You saw enough. And you saved me from seeing the rest."

Alec crossed the terrace to join them. "Coffee's on. Won't be long."

Constantin caught his eye. "We were talking about Greece," he said quickly, "and the fall of the Colonels."

Nodding his head, Alec responded, taking his cue, "Ah yes. When you went back to give evidence at the Trials. I thought we were going to lose you. All the big jobs you were offered." He looked at Tom. "Remember that? When was it? Seventy-four or five?"

"The Trials?" Constantin answered. "They began in '75 and

lasted a year. But I already had a big job, thank you very much. Helping you two run Stanton Industries."

Alec grinned. "I remember you being disgusted with the sentences."

Constantin pulled his lower lip and remained silent. Initially the Colonels and their henchmen had been sentenced to death. Subsequently the sentences were commuted to life imprisonment.

A thoughtful look came into Constantin's eyes. "Yes, I was disgusted. I wanted to see them dead, all of them. I wanted vengeance. But now. . . ." he shook his head, "I think it was a wise decision. Following all that bloodshed, Greece had to face the rest of the world. Despite what had happened, we had to prove we were a civilized people. The ancient Greeks had a word, *thikaosini*, meaning justice. Unfortunately they often confused it with *ekthikissis*, meaning vengeance." His gaze rested upon Tom. "It is the civilized man who can distinguish one from the other."

Tom knew the remark was meant for him. "You wouldn't be so bloody philosophical if Melina had been in that film."

"No," Constantin admitted, "I would have felt pain and torment and agony, just like you—"

"And betrayal!" Tom's voice was harsh.

"Yes, betrayal too," Constantin said gently. "Certainly, to begin with. But something here doesn't make sense. We will get to the bottom of it—"

"Damn right—"

"Meanwhile, I'd try to cling to all the good things. I'd say to myself: This awful thing that has happened, this terrible incident, for that is what it is—an incident, cruel and disastrous—is *part* of my life, but not my *whole* life. I'd cling to the good things for fear of driving myself mad."

Tom stared at him. "Is that what you think? I'm mad."

Sadness showed in Constantin's eyes. "Of course not." He shook his head. "But what happened to you would have destroyed many strong men." He smiled. "You, thank God, are indestructible."

Absentmindedly, Tom watched Alec go back inside the villa. "I used to say that about Maurice," he said.

"He was one of the good things. Think of the times you shared with him. He was so proud of you, you know that?"

Tom nodded. "I know," he said, husky-voiced.

"And so was Veronica. By the way, I saw her last week. She sends her love. She's worried about you." Constantin's lips twitched into the ghost of a smile. "But then, we're all worried about you."

The faraway look remained in Tom's eyes. Maurice and Veronica. What a pair they had made. They never stopped having fun. Maurice had finally found a woman who could keep pace with him. Correction, sometimes he'd had to run to keep pace with her. Hunched in the chair, with the morning sun warming his skin, Tom was quite unaware that the memories had brought a smile back to his lips.

But Constantin saw it. His hooded eyes never strayed from Tom's face. Deliberately he pressed home his advantage. "Veronica got to talking about all the good times. Parties, Christmas holidays spent in St. Moritz with you and Kirsten. She was telling me about when she taught you to ski."

Tom laughed. He actually laughed. A proper laugh without bitterness. "She almost killed me. She and Maurice between them. They were a mad pair. Jesus! I remember falling into a snowdrift. I was up to my armpits in snow, and Kirsten was laughing until the tears rolled down her face . . ." The ache returned to his voice, the words faded away.

"It was the same for Veronica, you know," Constantin said quickly. "You and Kirsten were married five years. She and Maurice were together the same length of time."

Tom began to pat his pockets, searching for cigarettes. He cleared his throat. "I know. I used to tease them. I used to tell Maurice he might as well get married. Veronica had become the only woman in his life. She always gave me the same answer. 'Maurice is still on approval,' she would say." Looking up, he saw Alec returning from the villa. "I think I left my cigarettes—"

"They're here," Alec nodded at the tray in his hands.

"Veronica asked if I had seen Roddy," said Constantin.

All signs of affection vanished from Tom's face. His eyes went cold. "Veronica did? Why? She didn't like Roddy."

"I didn't say she did. I suppose . . . well, we got talking, looking back . . . you know what it's like."

Tom watched Alec set the coffee tray on the table. He reached for his cigarettes.

"She did say something I didn't know," Constantin continued. "Roddy was broke last year. He went to Maurice for money."

Tom absorbed the information without surprise. "Roddy was always broke. Hugo's ripped him off all these years, persuading him to invest in their stupid bloody films. Not one film ever made money. Not one! Christ! You'd have thought he'd wise up by now. His mother left him a fortune. And all he did for Kirsten was buy her a car. Big deal. That red Mercedes. Blood-red. Blood-red for blood-money. That's what I thought at the time. Not that I said so to Kirsten—"

"But you argued about Roddy," Constantin prodded, his voice suddenly hard.

"No, we didn't," Tom retorted, "we disagreed. I didn't want to get involved with him, that's all. But it was never an issue. She saw him now and then. He *was* her brother. But I don't think she saw him often and I hardly saw him at all—"

"So what did you and Kirsten fight about?"

"When?" Tom blinked with surprise.

"What did you fight about?" Constantin demanded.

Tom was taken aback. Constantin had changed tack. Warm and friendly moments before, suddenly his voice had become loud and insistent. "Hey? What is this—"

"Time!" Constantin tapped the watch on his wrist. "Come on, Tom." He leaned forward in his chair. "We're running out of time! Your whole life blew up in your face last year. It blew up in our faces too. I want to know why. You and Kirsten had a big fight—"

"Who said so? What the hell makes you think—"

"Was it about Melody? Did you fight over her?"

Tom looked at him in astonishment.

"Was Kirsten jealous? It would be understandable. Melody is very attractive—"

"What the hell is this?" Tom's startled gaze went to Alec. "For Christ's sake! What's he going on about?"

Alec shrugged, "You and Melody."

Tom was too amazed to lose his temper. "What do you mean? Me and Melody. I've only seen her about four times in the last five years. Kirsten was there for half of them—"

Constantin interrupted, "Did she know you and Melody had been lovers?"

"It was over and done with. Melody's been married and divorced since then."

He had run into Melody on a flight from New York. That was when he learned that she had married shortly after he married Kirsten. But her marriage had lasted only two years. "And I was away most of the time," Melody had said, making a joke of it.

Following that reunion, Tom and Kirsten had bought some paintings from Melody's gallery in Albemarle Street. They had lunched together afterwards. All three of them. Without becoming friends, Kirsten and Melody seemed to have liked each other.

Glaring at Constantin, he said coldly, "Kirsten never had any reason to worry about Melody."

"I know," Constantin nodded. He sounded resigned. "Melody told me."

"You mean you asked her? You've got a nerve—"

Constantin shrugged, "She's very fond of you—"

"I don't get this. I can't see what you're driving at—"

"Last year. Before the world blew up in your face. You went to California. Right?"

"You know I did—"

"Kirsten always went to California with you. It was her favorite place. You always took her." Constantin pointed an accusing finger, "Every trip. Until last year. All of a sudden you're going to California without her. Why? You must have had a fight or something."

A look of understanding grew slowly in Tom's eyes. He remained still for a moment. Then he shook his head. "You couldn't be more wrong," he said sadly.

"So tell me!"

Sipping his coffee, Tom regarded his friends over the rim of the cup. He set it back on the saucer. "We didn't have a fight," he said quietly. "We were trying to start a family. It hadn't happened, so Kirsten was seeing a gynecologist. The gynecologist felt it was best if she stayed in London those weeks." A wry smile touched his lips. "We were hoping for some good news by the time I came home."

"Shit," Alec muttered half under his breath.

Constantin sat back in his chair. Pain and defeat showed in his face. "Forgive me, my friend. I didn't know."

For several moments not a word was spoken. Rubbing his knee, Constantin rose and limped along the edge of the pool, then turned and came back to the table. He looked baffled, bewildered and old. Frowning, he lowered himself carefully into his chair. "Very well," he said wearily, "if we cannot find answers one way, we'll try another. Concentrate on the business end. The battle started with your plan to take over Apple Computer. It all stems from the same place and time. Your trip to California last year. . . ."

1977

Lulled by the steady drone of aircraft engines, Tom closed his eyes with a sense of satisfaction. New York was fine. Good marketing, good distribution, excellent profits. It was always a pleasure to work with professionals. He wondered if he would find such professionalism in Vancouver. Two Canadian manufacturers were planning to merge and had invited him to join them for three days of talks, secret talks to explore the possibility of Stanton Industries joining them in a Canadian venture. . . .

His mind drifted. The Vancouver arrangements were already in place when the call had come through from Carl Pohl. A strange disturbing call, urgently requesting a meeting without giving reasons. "Just bring your check book," Pohl said.

"Some hopes," Tom muttered under his breath. Especially with Amiens in the States, looking for trouble. Amiens had been singing the same song for five years—"Pohl has failed . . . the Institute is a white elephant . . . Research and Development should be under my control in Geneva." He raised the matter at every board meeting. Nag, nag, nag. Like a dripping tap. Chinese water torture. It had worn Desmond Edwards down.

Edwards now supported him, and Gunther Haller was beginning to waver.

He had known Amiens was in the States, specifically in Chicago buying machine tools, but the proposal to visit the Institute had come out of the blue. Amiens had called him in New York. "While I'm over here I thought I'd call on Pohl to see how things are going."

Or *not* going, Tom reflected darkly. Absurd really, because there was much to be pleased about. Stanton Industries was established as a force to be reckoned with. In India and Australia, despite intense competition from the Japanese, Stanton operations were expanding. In Europe, sales of Stanton equipment had risen twenty percent a year, year upon year.

Maurice Stanton's dearest wish had been achieved. The son of Hans Pohl was still part of the business. Old man Edwards had died knowing that Desmond was secure. Yvonne Bouvier's interests had been protected. Every single one of Maurice's promises had been honored. And, no matter what Amiens said, the Institute *had* achieved some successes. Stanton pocket calculators were sold all over the world. Five years ago they were an inferior product, now they could compete with the best. And a myriad of minor product improvements had flowed from the Institute. . . .

He wished Kirsten was with him. It would seem strange to visit California without her. Carl would be disappointed. Still unmarried, Carl had difficulty relating to women. Kirsten was the exception. Perhaps because she made her liking for him so obvious. "I'm your biggest fan," she would say, grabbing his arm and insisting that he show her around. She shared his dreams. She had bought his ideas about home computers. She sat and talked with him about small computers being used in schools all over the world.

Yet the dream remained a long way from reality. Pohl's little computers were toys. Toys using a television screen. A white dot representing a ball could be batted back and forth in simulation of tennis or football. Other games had been devised depicting crudely designed figures. "Infantile pastimes for infantile minds," Amiens sneered.

Tom searched in vain for business applications. He had never shared Pohl's dream about *home* computers. Small computers, yes. Small computers could be used in business. That was his market. Get there first and Stanton Industries could rival IBM.

Strange the way he and Pohl now got on. Kirsten's influence, no doubt. But in addition, Pohl had changed. California had smoothed the rough edges. He was less arrogant, less dogmatic. Yet his commitment remained total. "We will get there," he was always saying, "be patient, Tom, we will get there."

Meanwhile the Institute was costing a fortune.

And now Pohl wanted more money. Tom sighed. He knew what he would do. Listen carefully and then cut the figure in half. He had done it before. These days he could reason with Pohl. Not that he fooled himself. Whatever regard Pohl had for him was due to Kirsten. She was the one who had won him over. Pohl had come to like her, then to trust her. In his own awkward way, he was even a little in love with her. Kirsten blushed when Tom said so, but they both knew it was true. "So don't bully him," she scolded when he kissed her goodbye.

Tom wished she were with him. She would soften Pohl's disappointment. Not that she could help with Amiens. She disliked Amiens—"He undresses me with his eyes," she once said.

"So do I," Tom grinned.

"I like it when you do it. Andre has got dirty eyes."

Tom had not pursued it. Dirty eyes or not, Amiens was still good at his job.

They did want a child. The gynecologist was optimistic. Kirsten's hopes were sky-high when he left. "This time it's going to happen. I can *feel* it. You could be an expectant father by the time you get back."

A father? He wondered what it would be like. Marion, Desmond's wife, had had triplets. Desmond had been delighted. "We planned on three. Now it's over and done with."

A child would make Maurice a grandfather. He would like that. He was good with kids. Desmond and Carl and Yvonne all talked about the happy times spent on Kariakos when they were children.

He felt a hand on his shoulder. Opening his eyes, he saw the stewardess. She smiled, "I have to ask you to fasten your seat belt, Mr. Lambert. We're beginning our descent. We land in San Francisco in five minutes."

"Thanks."

He glanced at his watch. Seven-fifteen local time. He wondered what time Amiens would arrive from Chicago? No doubt they would have their usual argument about the Institute. Some of what Amiens said was true—money could be saved by closing the Institute and establishing a Research and Development Center in Geneva. They would lose Carl in the process. Amiens would see that as a bonus. But they would lose something else as well. By moving to Geneva they would turn their backs on the electronics culture of Silicon Valley. Kids working in garages on new ideas. Dozens of them. "Wireheads" who spent every spare hour designing circuits for this and circuits for that. Local electronics clubs abounded in California as nowhere else in the world. Bright minds coming together. If the breakthrough ever came, Tom had a gut feeling it would come here.

Pohl was waiting in the handsome lobby of the St. Francis. He had dressed for the occasion, which meant he was wearing a tie. After watching Tom enter, he shifted his myopic gaze over Tom's shoulder.

"She's not with me this trip," Tom said, shaking hands. "She sends her love."

"Oh." Pohl looked crestfallen. He glanced down at the sofa on which he had been sitting. Wrapped in cellophane, the bouquet of flowers contained every color in the rainbow.

Tom smiled. "She'll be sorry to have missed those. They're terrific. I'll tell her."

"Yeah, well . . ." Pohl fidgeted, embarrassed. "It was just a thought."

"That's what counts. You know what they say."

There was a message from Amiens at the desk. *Arrive ten-thirty. Have dinner without me. Catch up with you later.*

A look of relief came into Pohl's face. "That's good. I can tell you my news without being interrupted all the time." While Amiens never missed a chance to denigrate Pohl, the German hated him back with a vengeance. Tom had given up hope of their ever seeing eye to eye.

Still carrying the bouquet, Pohl accompanied him up to his suite. "Don't mind, do you? We can talk while you wash up. In fact . . ." lowering his voice, he studied the other occupants in the elevator, "it'll be better up here instead of the restaurant."

Tom had known him in various moods—angry, bitter, excited, depressed—but never mysterious. Usually he blurted out what was on his mind in five minutes flat.

Intrigued, Tom tipped the porter who had carried up his case. "Wait a minute," Tom looked at Pohl, "Want to eat up here, or what?"

"I'm too tensed up for food." Dropping the bouquet onto the small sitting room table, Pohl turned to the window. "Let's decide later—"

With a knowing glance at the flowers and a quick look at Tom, the porter departed with a smirk on his face. Tom grinned ruefully as he took off his jacket. "Kirsten will never believe this," he muttered under his breath. Raising his voice, he said, "You pour me a Scotch and I'll have a wash. Then we can talk. Okay?"

"Tom." Pohl turned from the window. His voice was urgent. "We need two million dollars. Maybe three million. Can you fix it?"

"Oh boy," Tom groaned. He sat down in the nearest chair. Pohl had no understanding of the meaning of money. Financial calculations were beyond him. Usually he explained his plans and left others to calculate what they would cost. Loosening his tie, Tom unbuttoned his collar, and kicked off his shoes. Grinning, he tried to turn the request into a joke. "Is this for anything special, or are you just changing your lifestyle?"

Pohl's sense of humor was never strong. At that moment it was nonexistent. "I want us to buy a company," he said. "It's called Apple Computer."

Tom breathed a sigh of relief. He had imagined the Institute's operating costs had got wildly out of line and that Pohl was looking to make good a shortfall. "Buying companies is a bit out of your line, isn't it?" he said softly, raising his eyebrows.

"Besides, the Institute's Articles expressly prohibit the purchase of commercial ventures—"

"You could fix it."

Tom stood up. His worries had gone. "Why don't you fix me that drink?" he said with an easy smile. "I'll have a wash and you can tell me all about it."

They were still talking two hours later. Carl Pohl would never make a businessman. Even as a manager he had some glaring weaknesses. He possessed few organizational skills and the Institute suffered from his lack of them. He could be stubborn, obsessive and temperamental—but he did have vision, and on some matters Tom had total faith in his judgment.

"That's it. They've jumped the whole field. They've got this thing called Apple Two and . . ." Pohl's face glowed with admiration. "It's out of sight. State-of-the-art doesn't come into it—"

"Can't you copy what they've got? Can't you catch them?"

"Sure. A year, maybe two. We'll catch Apple Two. So will other people. The question is, where will Apple Computer be then?"

Pushing the remains of his room-service steak to the edge of his plate, Tom dabbed his mouth with his napkin. "What makes you think we could buy them?"

"They're looking for backing. The word's out. It's all around the Fair."

Tom reached for the cheaply printed pamphlet on the table. *The West Coast Computer Faire.* The very title filled him with misgivings. "Faire" was spelled with an "e." Just like in Ye Olde English Tea Shoppe. He looked at Pohl. "You really think this could be a business machine? Not just another computer freak's toy?"

Without agreeing on the subject, they had discussed it endlessly. While Pohl still clung to his belief in home computers, he had listened long and hard to Tom define what he called a personal computer with business applications. "It won't do everything you listed," Pohl admitted, "but it's halfway there."

Tom's excitement grew. "Tell me about them again. What were their names?"

"Jobs, Steve Jobs. And Wozniak. His name's Steve too, but everyone calls him Woz. Then there's someone called Markkula. I don't know much about him. Jobs and this Woz seem to be the main technical guys."

"Where did your figure of two million come from?"

"Someone said that's what they're trying to raise."

Tom smiled. Typical Carl. It didn't occur to him that borrowing money and selling the company were two different things. Not that it mattered. Everything was negotiable if the deal was right. "You really think this is it?"

Pohl grinned for the first time since they had met in the lobby. "Wait till you see it in the morning. You'll wet yourself."

There was a knock at the door.

"That'll be room service," Tom paused on his way across the room. "Sure you don't want anything more to eat?" Pohl's meal had consisted of an open sandwich and a glass of milk. He shook his head.

It was Amiens. Out of the corner of his eye, Tom glimpsed a female figure standing a few yards down the corridor, a girl wearing an air hostess' uniform.

"Tom! You are well, I hope." Shaking hands, Amiens advanced smiling into the suite. When he saw Pohl he merely nodded, before peering around the sitting room. "And where is the lovely Kirsten?"

"In London. She's not here this trip."

"Oh?" Amiens cocked his head. "Nothing wrong, I hope?"

"No, she's fine."

The amiable smile had already returned to the good-looking face. "And you have eaten, I see. I am so famished that I booked a table on my way in. Will you join me anyway?"

"No. You go and eat. We'll meet up in the morning."

As Amiens turned away, he saw the bouquet of flowers.

"A mistake," Tom explained, in response to the quizzical look.

"Then may I?" Amiens picked up the bouquet. "It would seem a pity to waste them."

Tom looked at Pohl, who shrugged.

"Until the morning then," said Amiens, sweeping out with a

bow. As the door closed, Tom heard a squeal of delight in the corridor. "Oh Andre. They're lovely."

Later, when Pohl had gone, Tom sipped a last Scotch as he prepared for bed. It was almost midnight. Tired from traveling, he was still slightly disoriented from crossing the time zones. Kirsten was right. He was due for a rest. He felt vaguely resentful of Amiens; not for the girl he had taken to his room, but for his unflagging stamina. "But then he only came from Chicago," he remembered, consoling himself as he climbed into bed. Yawning, he switched off the light. Figures floated around in his mind. Two million. He could fund that out of cash flow. Silly bloody name though, he thought, I'll have to change that. Nobody in business would pay serious attention to a name like Apple Computer.

Whatever Amiens' mood the night before, he was all business at breakfast. Tom found himself envying the man all over again. Amiens had the ability to live his life in compartments. He could switch off one activity and forget it, plunging himself into the next without a second thought. Maurice had the same knack, to some extent. Tom had never been able to do it. He had tried. He did try. Many an evening he would say to Kirsten, "Okay. No shop tonight. We'll talk about something else." But even visits to the theater or the cinema failed to absorb his total attention. In the intermission, at the bar, or on the way home, suddenly something about the business would enter his mind. Kirsten would scold, "Isn't there *any* way I can make you switch off?" Then he would grin and she would smile, and a few minutes later they would be undressing each other.

"So what's this exhibition?" Amiens wanted to know as they left the hotel. "I'm only here for the day. I thought we'd go straight to the Institute."

"Carl wants to show me something. We're meeting him there. We'll go out to the Institute this afternoon if you like."

In the cab, Amiens set the pattern for the rest of the day. "We've got to stop this madness. It's holding us back. All this money we're wasting on the Institute. You've got kids up there playing Ping-Pong. You know that? That's all they do. Sit around all day batting a white dot across a screen. It's got nothing to do with business machines. Even at that they're not very good. There's this outfit Atari. You seen their stuff? Okay, I see where they're going. Putting machines into arcades and cheap restaurants and places. That's their business, but it's not ours. Go on like this and we'll end up making jukeboxes. Is that where you're taking us? I tell you, Tom, we must call a halt. . . ."

The West Coast Computer Faire made Tom's heart sink as soon as he entered the hall. Exhibitors' stands were so lacking in professionalism that most of them had hand-painted signs. Products were displayed on cheap folding tables.

"Amateur night at the village hall," Amiens said scornfully, rolling his eyes. Soon he was stopping people in the aisles. "Excuse me, could you direct me to the IBM stand? Oh, they're not here. Really? Well, perhaps Olivetti? No? What about Xerox? Or Canon? Or . . ."

"Okay, you've made your point," Tom conceded wearily. "Let's go and find Carl. He wanted us here for a reason."

They found Pohl among the crowd around Apple Computer. It was the only stand in the place which looked modestly professional. The booth announced itself with an elegantly smoked and back-lit plexiglas sign sporting the name Apple Computer next to a colorful logo. Equally colorful were the images on a large screen monitor which flickered through a range of demonstration programs. Amiens held his nose and pulled an imaginery lavatory chain. "More games," he sneered as he edged away into the crowd.

Gripping Tom's elbow, Pohl whispered, "When this dem is over, I'll show you under the lid. You won't believe it. They've crammed this whole package into sixty chips. Wait until you see their board. It's so neat . . ."

But Tom was watching the graphics. A spectacular kaleidoscope of color swirled across the giant display screen. For expanding cubes and boxes, he was seeing bar charts and pie charts. How far could they take it? Rotate a cube, slice it, explode it? Reformat data into matrix designs? Animate statistics on screen? Managers manipulate options. Business is about comparing cause and effect. How will a price increase affect profits? What will delays in customer payments do to cash flow? What will happen to inventories if production takes a week longer?

Such thoughts were not new. He had long since decided what small computers had to do to become tools of business. Many would have to co-exist with mainframe computers to provide information to a whole network of managers . . .

Pohl dragged him away, not wanting to display a too obvious interest. Touring the hall, Tom studied faces. They were kids. Teenagers. Half of them talked a language all their own. But these kids would be working in commerce in a few years. They would bring their ideas with them. They would adapt and refine them.

Halfway around the hall they bumped into Amiens. He was laughing. "I'll tell you something," he said, "these freaks are something else. Know what a company back there calls itself? The Kentucky Fried Computer Company. It's true. They got a sign up. Come on, Tom. What the hell are we doing here? This isn't serious business."

"Give it time," Tom said watching Amiens stuff leaflets into his briefcase.

"Mementos," Amiens grinned. "People won't believe me when I talk about these nuts." He patted the briefcase, "I'm collecting the evidence." He checked his watch. "I've had enough of this place. I can make some calls back at the hotel. See you in the bar around lunchtime."

They left him and went back to Apple. Tom studied the three demonstration machines. Instead of metal cases with sharp, ugly corners, he saw beige plastic boxes. They looked more like the latest design typewriters than engineers' toys.

"Hey," shouted a voice from the crowd, "there's a bigger computer hidden under the table." The demonstrators disproved it by pulling the draperies away from the tables.

Tom walked down the aisle and watched from afar. Three people were manning the Apple booth, demonstrating the equipment and taking orders. He watched them sell ten Apple computers in half an hour.

Pohl polished his oversize spectacles with a grubby handkerchief. "What do you think?"

"We're watching history," Tom said softly, "the dawn of the age of the personal computer." Further confirmation came when they left the hall. Waiting patiently for admission, lines of people snaked around the building.

They found Amiens in the bar at the St. Francis. "Well, now," he beamed at Pohl, "here comes the boy wonder back from the toy fair."

Pohl ignored him.

They went into the restaurant for lunch. Amiens was still laughing when he slid into the booth. "I asked some guy back there what he did with *his* home computer. Know what he said? He's got it linked up to the sprinklers on his lawn. Oh yeah, I forgot. It also opens his garage door." He rolled his eyes. "Disneyland's got nothing on this lot."

Pohl continued to ignore him. He and Amiens had not exchanged one word all morning.

Amiens flushed and leaned across the table. "You programmed for speech?"

Pohl turned away and asked Tom, "Shall I try to set up a meeting?" Wishing Amiens was somewhere else, Tom responded, "How long does the show last?"

"Closes tonight. The organizers are kicking themselves. They could have run it for two weeks."

Tom watched Amiens study the menu. "I take it you weren't impressed by this morning, Andre?"

Amiens scowled. "Kids playing with toys," he said dismissively.

"I don't agree. In fact there's a company there I wouldn't mind buying."

"You're out of your mind."

"Not if I can buy it at the right price."

Amiens set the menu back on the table. Already flushed after several drinks at the bar, his face went red as disbelief turned to anger. "The whole lot's not worth a light! Which company? How much?"

Ignoring the first question, Tom shrugged, "Hard to say. Maybe three million dollars."

"You're not serious?"

"I am."

The waiter arrived at the table. "Later," said Amiens, waving him away. When the man remained where he was, Amiens shouted, "I said come back later!"

Flushing with embarrassment and surprise, the waiter retreated.

Amiens pointed a finger across the table at Tom. "You spend even three dollars and it's the last money you waste for this business. We've put up with this long enough. Too long. You and this clown . . ." he jerked his head towards Pohl, "and your crackbrain ideas. I'll tell you something: you think Stanton Industries is big? I could have made it ten times bigger. All the money you've wasted—"

"Andre!" Tom's interruption was chilling. "This isn't the place—"

"Fuck the place!" Amiens pushed his chair back from the table. "And fuck you. Three million dollars. Then another three million for working capital. Then more money for some other half-baked idea." Shaking with fury, he rose to his feet. "Not this time. Not anymore. Haller won't stand for it. Neither will Desmond. Neither will I." He tossed the unused napkin onto the table. "And I wouldn't be too sure of Alec if I were you. He doesn't believe in this farce. He won't vote with you forever." He turned for the door. "I want a meeting on this. You, Maurice, everyone. Then we shall see." He stuttered with temper. "Then we shall see."

Most of the restaurant watched as Amiens barged past a waiter and made for the door.

"Christ," Pohl muttered under his breath.

Tom had seen Amiens lose his temper before, although never in so public a place. "I think you got under his skin."

"Me? I didn't speak to him."

"Exactly," Tom agreed, trying to appear calm. In fact he was embarrassed and a little shaken. Previous outbursts from Amiens had been different. Outbursts of temper in the past had been more controlled. Amiens could simulate rage for effect. Tom had seen him do it. But today, stung by Pohl's refusal to be drawn into an argument, and with a drink too many under his belt, the frustrations had boiled over. *I could have made it ten times bigger.* And he believed it. The old resentment about losing the top job was still there.

The waiter appeared at Tom's shoulder. "Excuse me, Mr. Lambert, will your friend be returning, or shall we clear his place at the table?"

Tom sighed, "I think you can clear it."

Amiens had checked out. After lunch, Tom stopped by the desk, thinking he might have gone to his room. "No sir," said the clerk, "he left half an hour ago."

"Where do you think he's gone?" asked Pohl, looking worried.

They went up to the suite and Tom called Alec in London. "My guess is he's already on his way back to Europe. He'll go and see Haller and stir up more trouble . . ."

Even as he talked he remembered the leaflets Amiens had stuffed into his briefcase. Ammunition for the battle. And Alec wasn't too pleased when he heard the full story. "Three million dollars. Jesus! Tom, we must call a halt *sometime.*"

"But not now . . ."

They talked for half an hour. Inconclusively, with Alec still expressing concern. Pohl watched and listened, fidgeting and twitching.

Afterwards Tom felt drained. He looked wearily at Pohl. "What is the flight time to Vancouver from here?"

"Want me to check?" Pohl reached for the phone.

Tom nodded. Leaving him, he walked into the bedroom and stretched out on the bed. Arguments buzzed around in his head. Amiens was right. Three million would become six with working capital. That would create a hell of a row. But now was the time. Like no other time. Pohl sensed it. Tom sensed it himself. Apple was close to getting it right. Get in on the ground floor, and six million dollars would be peanuts.

"There's a flight at four and another one at seven," Pohl said from the door. "Flight time is three hours."

He made up his mind. "Get me on the early flight. Hang on . . ." he said, seeing Pohl's look of disappointment. "I'm convinced about Apple, don't worry. But there's no point in trying for a meeting tonight. Those boys will be whacked after the show. And they'll be on a high. If they think they've got the world by the balls, they won't even think about selling their business. Savvy?"

Pohl nodded.

"I'll be in Vancouver for three days. That should give them time to calm down. I'll get back here at the end of the week, *then* we'll go and see them. Okay?"

He slept all the way to Vancouver. Dozed, more than slept. He would have rested more fully had worries about Amiens not kept him awake. He could see Amiens flourishing the contents of his briefcase under Haller's nose. The crunch had to come soon. They couldn't go on like this. The fights were becoming too frequent and too bruising. Amiens would have to be told once and for all—"Shut up or get out." But only Maurice could tell him . . .

Tired and worried, he went straight to bed when he reached the hotel. Within minutes he was asleep. For a few hours he slept undisturbed. Then the nightmare began. The faces were so vivid . . . Maurice was at the head of the table. Hollenberg was on his right, Amiens on his left, and Edwards and Alec sat close to Tom at the foot of the table. Amiens' words rang in his ears. *I wouldn't be too sure about Alec if I were you. He doesn't believe in this farce . . . he won't vote with you forever.* And Alec was doing the unthinkable. Alec was voting against him. Hands were raised around the table. *Everyone* was voting against him.

In the morning, as he showered and shaved, he put the dream into perspective. He rationalized, reminding himself that he had fallen asleep with the argument with Amiens still on his mind. He told himself it was stupid to brood.

Yet, as he went down in the elevator to meet his Canadian host, he had the strangest feeling of impending disaster.

Of course nothing happened. He laughed about it when he called Kirsten, "Next thing you know I'll be consulting fortune tellers."

Most important of all, Kirsten was feeling well. The gynecologist was pleased with the tests. "I'm due for another examination on Monday. Then we should know." The excitement in her voice carried him through the rest of the day. And the day after. And the meetings went so well that by late afternoon on the third day, most things had been agreed. "In principle," Tom grinned, "Now it's up to the lawyers."

It was a good dinner that night, a cautious celebration, toasting the future. Tom went to bed at just after eleven, content with the progress they'd made, and looking forward to flying down to San Francisco to meet Pohl in the morning.

At two A.M. the telephone rang at his bedside.

"Tom!"

He came awake with a start. "Kirsten? What's the matter?"

Her voice quivered. "It's Maurice. He's had some sort of attack. Veronica thinks it's a stroke."

He sat up in bed, coming awake. The telephone felt suddenly clammy in his hand.

Kirsten sounded more frightened than tearful. Veronica had called her from Kariakos. ". . . there's no qualified doctor on the island. Gregg's flying one out there from Athens—"

"Jesus! I can't believe it. Not Maurice . . ."

Kirsten was coping better than he was. Roused from a deep sleep, his brain kept rejecting the idea. Nothing ever happened to Maurice. He was indestructible.

". . . Veronica was hysterical. Tom, I must go. Alec's at the door. He's taking me to Heathrow. There's a flight out to Athens at noon. Oh, Tom . . ." her voice broke, "Come as soon as you can. . . ."

He was in the wrong place at the wrong time. On the other side of the world. On the wrong continent. With the help of the night porter, he tried to hire a private jet. They made dozens of calls. Greece might have been on another planet. "Yes," he kept repeating, "Athens, Greece. In Europe." The best he got was a half promise of an aircraft late the next day. "Can't you be *sure*?" he bawled down the line. "Sorry, but we cannot confirm until later this morning." How much later? They came back to him within ten minutes. "We should be able to confirm at nine in the morning." Not before? Was there *nothing* before? Could they fly him to London, Paris, or at least as far as New York. "Sorry sir, we can't arrange anything until nine in the morning."

Air Canada had a flight leaving Vancouver at eight. It would reach Toronto in the afternoon, fly over the pole during the night, and arrive in Athens late the following morning. He booked on that and called Constantin in London.

"Alec's out at Heathrow with Kirsten—"

"Is he going with her?"

"No. I've spoken to Doug Masters in Athens. He'll be at the airport to meet her. Don't worry. They'll look after her."

"Do you know any more about Maurice? What's happened—"

But Constantin could only repeat what Kirsten had told him.

Two hours had passed since her call.

The porter made him coffee and toast. He returned to his room to shower and shave. He was still trying to absorb the shock. Maurice! It wasn't possible. Maurice always looked so well. So fit. Maurice was a titan who bestrode the world like an ancient god.

He was in the cab, on his way to the airport, when he remembered the baby. My God! Kirsten was supposed to have plenty of rest. She wasn't *supposed* to fly. Oh Jesus! He hadn't thought to say anything. She hadn't given him the chance. He should have thought. . . .

He checked in, waited, boarded the aircraft. Part of his brain functioned, but his movements were automatic, reflex actions developed over the years.

The steady beat of the engines got on his nerves. Drone, drone, drone. The least urgent sounds he had ever heard in his life. Rev them up, for Christ's sake! Couldn't they go faster? He toyed with his breakfast. He drank four cups of coffee. Dear God, he should have remembered the baby. Everything had happened so fast. The counseling from the gynecologist went out of his head. But he should have remembered. A more caring man would have remembered. A proper husband would have told Kirsten to stay where she was. Not that she would have taken a blind bit of notice.

He tried to work out where she was. London to Athens took

less than four hours. She had called him at ten o'clock London time. The plane was leaving at twelve noon. He checked his watch. She would be there soon. In Athens. It would be late afternoon in Athens. They would be two hours ahead of London time . . .

God! He should have asked about the baby. Not that it *was* a baby yet. Just an embryo. An egg.

"More coffee, please," he said.

Masters would meet her. Masters and Gregg. They would look after her. Good old Gregg. They had known each other a few years now. Ever since . . . Poor Maurice. What was it? A stroke? Heart attack? Gregg might know. He could tell Kirsten. To prepare her. . . .

Kariakos! Living like Robinson Crusoe is all very well, until something goes wrong. They should have known. They should have been *prepared*. Maurice ought to have hired a doctor years ago. There should be a doctor on the island at all times. At *all* times!

Alec should have gone with her. Not just to Heathrow. Bloody hell! He should have flown out there with her. . . .

It was mid-afternoon when they landed in Toronto. Rain splashed down on the runway. Gray clouds scudded low overhead. Tom hurried into the first class lounge in search of a telephone.

Alec was at home. "Where are you?"

"Toronto. We're here for an hour. What's the news?"

"Kirsten arrived safely—"

"You should have gone with her. Honestly, Alec—"

"There was no point. Calm down. I took her to Heathrow. Gregg and Masters met her on the other end—"

"Okay," Tom conceded grumpily. "What's the news on Maurice?"

"He's stable. According to the doctors Gregg took across—"

"That's something." Tom began to feel better.

"Don't celebrate yet. Maurice is stable inasmuch as the doctors preferred not to move him. That's why they let Gregg go back to collect Kirsten—"

"So he's critical?"

"I'm not saying that—"

"You holding something back?"

"Tom, I'm telling you all I know. I haven't been able to get through to the villa. You know what it's like."

Tom did know. For reasons he had never understood, making calls out from Kariakos was usually fine, but getting a call into the island could take hours. "Okay," he sighed, "we seem to be doing all we can." He ran a hand through his hair. "Listen, you'd better call Pohl—"

"I already did. Hours ago. Now calm down. Take it easy."

Alec sounded so calm. Alec *always* sounded calm. Hugging the telephone between his chin and his shoulder, Tom reached for a cigarette.

"Tom." Alec hesitated. "Have you thought what will happen? I mean if the worst happens . . . you know, to Maurice? Have you thought what happens then?"

He was slow to see where Alec was leading. "How do you mean?" he asked, lighting the cigarette.

"To Stanton Industries. What happens to the business?"

"Jesus! You're a cold-hearted bastard at times. For God's sake—"

"Steady on. I'm merely asking. I know how close you are to Maurice. I thought you might have discussed it at some time."

"No, Alec," Tom's voice went cold, "we've never discussed it."

"I see," Alec said slowly.

He knew that tone of voice. It was Alec's "bad news" tone of voice. Alec said, "Well, let's hope for the best."

He was still working out the sums when he reboarded the aircraft. Part of him was ashamed. Part of him condemned what he was doing as cold-blooded and callous. He loved Maurice. Maurice was the father he had never had. He wanted Maurice to live. He wanted to reach Kariakos to find Maurice as vibrant as ever, laughing about the way he had scared them half to death.

But what if . . .

Stanton Industries had six shareholders. When the amalgamation was finalized, Pohl, Edwards and Yvonne had each held five percent of the shares. So had Haller. Maurice held the remaining eighty percent. But much had changed. Maurice's generosity in rewarding his executives with part of his business had allowed Tom to convert his every bonus into shares. He now held eleven percent. Yvonne, on her husband's advice, had increased her shareholding to keep pace. Edwards had increased his to seven percent and Haller increased his to six. Only Carl Pohl, supremely uninterested in financial matters, had left his shareholding where it was. And Maurice now held only sixty percent.

What would Maurice do with his shares? Would he leave his entire fortune to Veronica? Property perhaps, and money. But shares in the business? Veronica took no interest in the business. And she was independently wealthy . . .

Alec had no reason to come on like a prophet of doom. But that was Alec. He spent his life looking at the down side. . . .

Whatever happened, and please God Maurice lived, but whatever happened, Maurice would look after Kirsten in death as he had in life. He doted on her.

Tom saw no reason to worry. Kirsten might, probably would, become a wealthy woman, but little would change. He felt sure she would wish to continue to live as they lived now, especially if they started a family. She was happy with the house. She was happy with her life.

He was tired. He had been up half the night and been traveling all day. Now it was night again. Fatigue set in; he banished Alec from his mind. He dozed . . .

"Excuse me, sir, would you like a drink?" The stewardess smiled down at him. "We're just about to serve dinner."

He ordered a Scotch. He ate another airline meal. He drank another whisky. He thought about the North Pole in the darkness below. Taking a copy of *The Crash of '79* from his briefcase, he tried to read, but not even Paul Erdman could engage his attention.

Maurice was reported to be in stable condition. That *had* to be good news. That was the first step to recovery. Look at Constantin. Kirsten had nursed him . . .

She'd be on the island by now. She would have reached Kariakos hours ago. That would cheer Maurice up.

What would he do with his shares? Tom knew Maurice well.

He probably knew him better than anyone else alive. Maurice would do the fair thing. Whatever happened, he could be counted upon to be fair. Fairness was his hallmark.

What would a fair man do with his shares? There would be no spiteful nonsense with Maurice. Not like Kirsten's bitch of a mother.

Maurice would give half to Kirsten and half to Roddy. That's what Maurice would do. It was fair. It was predictable. Born lucky was Roddy. Born with a silver spoon in his mouth. The dividends would make Roddy rich. No doubt Hugo would waste all the money on those bloody films, but that was up to Roddy. . . .

Suddenly Tom was wide awake. Suddenly he realized what had been worrying Alec.

Suppose . . .

Most of the other passengers were asleep. Or trying to sleep. The lights had been dimmed.

Tom switched on his overhead light and beckoned a stewardess. "Could I have some more coffee, please. And another Scotch."

If Maurice left Kirsten thirty percent of the shares, with Tom's eleven percent, they would have forty-one percent between them. They would be the largest shareholders by far.

Amiens wouldn't like that. And without Maurice to protect him, Amiens would be vulnerable. For the first time ever, Tom would be able to tell him, "Do as I say or get out." Amiens would need another protector. *Roddy!* Amiens would go running to Roddy.

Suddenly Tom felt clammy with sweat. If Roddy had thirty percent of the shares and voted them with Yvonne's eleven, Amiens would control forty-one percent. Exactly the same as Tom and Kirsten mustered between them.

Stalemate.

It would be up to the others. Carl Pohl could be relied upon. He would vote his five percent with Tom and Kirsten. That would give them forty-six percent.

But Edwards would vote with Amiens. And Edwards had seven percent. Amiens would control forty-*eight* percent.

"Oh Jesus!"

"I beg your pardon." With a startled look the stewardess paused as she passed him his drink.

He stared at her. "Bring me the bottle, will you."

"Sorry, sir, we only have miniatures, but I can come back."

He looked at her with unseeing eyes.

"Is anything wrong, sir?"

"What? No, fine. Thanks."

It would be up to Gunther. His six percent would swing the vote either way. Gunther would control Stanton Industries.

He remembered Amiens shouting with temper in San Francisco—*Haller won't stand for it. Neither will Desmond. Neither will I!*

It was true. Gunther had expressed alarm about the costs of the Institute. Gunther was a banker. He would play safe. He would consider further investment in personal computers as too great a risk.

Frightening thoughts came thick and fast. Gunther had an easy way out. He would say that as a non-executive director, he felt obliged to vote with the majority. And that would be with Amiens.

Tom's hand trembled as he lifted the coffee cup. He could not see a single alternative scenario. If Maurice divided his shares the *fair* way, equally between Roddy and Kirsten, that was the way it would go. And not just about personal computers. Everything would be put to the vote. Tom's days as CEO were over.

All those years of work. Suddenly he remembered when the Brierleys told him they had sold Bolton. All that time ago. He had held Tim Brierley with his left hand before belting him with his right.

Alec had spotted the pitfall. Alec had a nose for such things.

He was dead tired. Exhausted. But sleep was impossible. Like a trapped animal his brain hunted and searched for a way out . . . and the only way out was Roddy.

Roddy would laugh in his face. Roddy knew he despised him. "I've made it plain enough over the years." And Roddy hated him in return.

It was morning outside. Blue skies. The cabin staff began to serve breakfast. He ate a croissant, drank some coffee and smoked cigarettes.

He stared out of the window, thinking that among the millions of thoughts which had occurred to him about Stanton Industries over the years, one thought had eluded him. That Maurice would die.

Greece lay below them. He thought of Constantin and Melina. Con had turned down some very big jobs when he went back for the Trials. The new government had been anxious to recruit him.

He hoped the jobs were still open. Amiens wouldn't stop with him. Constantin would go. Alec would go. Pohl would go. Amiens would rid himself of everyone loyal to Tom Lambert.

A cold wash freshened him physically but not mentally. His brain was numb.

"Local time is ten forty-five," the flight steward announced over the intercom. "As you can see, ladies and gentlemen, it's a beautiful morning. Please fasten your seatbelts. We land in Athens in five minutes."

Doug Masters was waiting at the gate in the arrivals hall. Bad news was etched into every line of his face. Tom's fears deepened as soon as he saw him.

"Let me take the case, Mr. Lambert."

"How bad is it?"

The pilot avoided his eye. "Someone's holding a table for us at the bar. Let's get out of this crush."

Tom caught his arm. "How bad?"

Masters hesitated. "I'm afraid you've got to prepare yourself for the worst."

Tom sucked in a breath. He felt his stomach contract. *Maurice was dying.* Thoughts and fears felt during the journey were nothing compared to confronting reality. Raw-eyed from lack of sleep, he was in a daze as he followed Masters. The pilot led the way to the bar where a waiter stood guarding the table. Masters slipped him a note and sent him away. Tom stared at the table: a full bottle of Scotch stood next to a pitcher of ice and two glasses.

"I'm not flying today," said Masters, waiting for Tom to sit down.

"We can't hang around here—"

"He's dead, Mr. Lambert. Maurice Stanton is dead."

"Oh Jesus!" Tom put his head in his hands. Hot tears stung his eyes. All the breath was knocked out of him by the shock. He sucked air into his lungs; once, twice, three times, taking deeper breaths to recover. He groaned with pain and self-recrimination. "Oh Jesus. I came as soon as I could—"

"Here." Masters pushed a full glass of Scotch across the table. "I couldn't think of how to break the news."

Believing the news was the first step. Just to *believe* that Maurice was gone. No more great booming peals of laughter, no more warm slaps on the back, no more huge cheerful grins. Tom felt so alone.

"Kirsten!" Her name was torn from his throat. He raised eyes moist with tears. "She'll be destroyed. She'll be—"

"She's okay," Masters said quickly. "Gregg's bringing her over from Kariakos."

It was three or four minutes before he could think straight, before his breathing felt even half normal, before he began to ask questions. "How's Veronica? Is Kirsten with her—"

"Mrs. Taubman's at the Hilton. I booked half a dozen rooms. I didn't quite know—"

"She's here? In Athens? She's not on the island—"

"Please, Mr Lambert. Let me explain. Gregg got the doctors and a ton of equipment over there fast. The doctors decided not to move him—"

"I know that, I know—"

"Please," Masters interrupted. He looked very tired, and deeply upset.

"Sorry."

"I got a message about Mrs. Lambert coming in, so I'm here waiting to meet her, when Mr. Amiens comes through the barrier—"

"Amiens was here?"

"Yesterday afternoon. He flew in from Geneva. He hadn't heard about Mr. Stanton, so I had to tell him." Masters shook his head. "He looked agitated when he came through the gate. He got worse when he heard the news. He wanted to go straight over to Kariakos, but I explained your wife was due within half an hour so we sat around and waited—"

"Bastard!" Tom's hands clenched on the table. No doubt having complained to Haller in Geneva, Amiens was on his way to stir up more trouble with Maurice. "If he did anything to worsen Maurice's condition, I'll kill him."

Masters shook his head. "Gregg flew him over with your wife. Mr. Stanton suffered a massive heart attack just before they got there. He was unconscious, on a stretcher with a mask over his face, oxygen cylinders, the lot. They had to move him. The only chance was to get him to a hospital."

Tom groaned. Rubbing his face with his hands, he imagined the difficulties of carrying a stretcher down the cliff path.

"Gregg said the people from the village were marvelous. *Everyone* helped. They thought a lot of Mr. Stanton on Kariakos." When Masters looked up, tears blurred his eyes. He cleared his throat, "Seems to me everyone thought a lot of Mr. Stanton. There'll never be anyone like him."

Swallowing hard, Tom agreed, "No, Doug," he said quietly. "There won't be."

A moment passed before Masters could continue. He blew his nose, puffed on a cigarette, and coughed several times to clear his throat. Then he said, "Gregg ripped out the back seats and they got Mr. Stanton on board. That was a miracle by itself, what with Mrs. Taubman refusing to let go of the stretcher. He pleaded with her to stay behind with your wife, but she wouldn't have it. I know it was understandable, but what with the doctors and the oxygen cylinders to cope with, Gregg could have done without her being there." He shrugged. "Anyway I'd got an ambulance waiting at Passalimani. The local hospital was on red alert. . . ." Anguish contorted his face. "Believe me, Mr. Lambert, we did all we could—"

"I know—"

"But he died on the way. He was dead when they got here."

Tom sipped his drink and said nothing.

Masters continued, "We went up to the hospital. That's

where he is now. In the morgue. One of the doctors came back with us. He gave Mrs. Taubman a sedative. I hired a nurse to stay with her. She's still with her now . . ." He dragged on his cigarette. "It must have been about eleven by then. Gregg and I hit the phones. We called Herr Haller in Geneva and Alec Hargreaves in London. That's how we found out what time you'd be here. There seemed no point in going back to Kariakos, not at that time of night. It would be past one by the time we got there. Gregg was on his knees and I wasn't much better. It wasn't as if anyone could do anything—"

"I understand," Tom said quietly.

A look of relief came into Masters' face. "Gregg is taking Mrs. Lambert directly to the Hilton when he gets back from Kariakos. They should be there soon. I booked half a dozen rooms. I wasn't sure how many we'd need, but it seemed best to be on the safe side. Then I came down here and waited for you." The relief in his eyes echoed in his voice. "You'll take over now, won't you, Mr. Lambert?"

Weary from lack of sleep, and suffering from shock, Tom nodded. "Yes, Doug, I'll take over now."

Roddy strutted into the Hilton like a little Hitler. Spoiling for a fight, he marched up to Tom. "You've no right to organize this. This is a family affair and none of your business."

Tom walked away. Otherwise he would have hit him. He did hit him later.

It happened that evening. Kirsten was still in their room, so distraught that he could find no words to console her. He had expected her to fall into his arms. He had imagined himself hugging her, holding her, sharing her misery. United in their loss, he had seen them facing the bereavement together. Instead, she had pushed him away. He spent the afternoon trying to comfort her, but grief buried her in some black pit of depression from which he was excluded. He was not wanted. Rejected. Sobbing into her pillow, she shouted, "Go away! Leave me alone."

Eventually he went to Veronica's suite in search of the nurse. Veronica herself opened the door. Swollen-eyed and white-faced, she was more in control than he had expected. Seeing him gave her a shaky moment, but they clung to each other while she shed a few tears. She seemed to recover. She had dispensed with the nurse—"Who wants a nurse at my age?" she sniffed. Her first question was, "Where's Kirsten?" When he told her, she said, "Come on, we should be together at a time like this."

But Kirsten preferred to be alone. Even when they tried to comfort her, sitting either side of her bed, she remained inconsolable. Verging on hysteria, at times she was angry. "You should have been there," she flung at Tom, burying her face back in the pillow.

After twenty minutes Veronica returned to her room. She came back holding a white paper packet. "It's a sleeping draft," she said to Tom. "It worked for me last night."

A moment later she emerged from the bathroom, mixing the powder into a glass. Kirsten sprang from the bed and knocked it out of her hand. "Get away from me with that!" she screamed. "Get away!"

It was a scene Tom wanted to forget. Even allowing that grief affects people differently, Kirsten's behavior was completely out of character. She seemed to blame Tom for Maurice's death. Tom's protest, that he had flown halfway around the world to get there, only fueled her anger. They calmed her eventually, but Veronica did most of the calming. She sent Tom back to her suite to wait for her there.

Half an hour passed before she joined him. She looked drawn and worn out. "She's quieter now. I think she'll soon be asleep. Don't worry, it's the shock. I fell apart myself yesterday."

Having someone else to worry about helped Veronica to pull herself together. "Maurice wouldn't like this," she said a moment later. "Just look at us. Like survivors from a shipwreck. I haven't eaten in thirty-six hours and I've been cooped up in this room all day. Come on, you can take me to dinner. Maurice would approve of that."

She wanted to get out of the hotel, anxious for a breath of air. "Let's walk down to Constitution Square. It's not far. We can eat in one of the cafés. I'm too scruffy to go anywhere else." Her only clothes were what she stood up in; a navy blue dress, creased and soiled from traveling. But once she had washed and brushed her hair and put on some makeup, she was feeling and looking much better.

They checked on Kirsten before they left. As Veronica had predicted, she was sound asleep. Veronica squeezed his arm. "The worst should be over by the morning. She'll begin to accept it."

In the lobby, he stopped at the desk to exchange some Canadian dollars for Greek drachmas. He was just putting the money away when Roddy and Hugo came through the front door. Veronica must have sensed something unpleasant was about to happen, because she stood stock still, watching Roddy approach.

Roddy might have been a bit drunk, or stoned. Or perhaps Tom walking away from him earlier had given him courage. "Ah, Veronica," he said, "I trust you're paying your own bill if you're staying here? After watching you sponge off my father for years, I'm not having you sponge on his estate."

Grabbing his collar, Tom pushed him up against the wall. His fist exploded in Roddy's face. Hugo shouted, but ran when Tom swung at him. Roddy slid from Tom's grasp with blood streaming from his nose.

"Tom!" Gripping his arm, Veronica pulled him to the door. "Come on."

He was still trembling with anger as he stepped into the street. Clinging tightly to his arm, Veronica made him turn to the left. Trembling herself, she muttered through clenched teeth, "God! He really is a little shit."

Walking dispelled some of their nervous tension. They had stopped shaking by the time they reached the Square. Veronica pecked at her food, but drank fairly steadily. Having cried herself out, she wanted to talk herself dry. Naturally most of the talk was about Maurice. Her eyes misted at times and her voice trembled at others, but for the most part she kept her grief under control.

A cab carried them back to the hotel. Tom felt drained and exhausted. Lack of sleep was taking its toll. "That's good," said Veronica, "you'll crash out tonight and Kirsten will be over the worst by the morning."

He suspected she had insisted on dinner more for his sake than her own.

Gunther Haller was waiting in the lobby. Maurice's oldest friend had never looked older. A strong robust man, Gunther looked drawn and weary to the point of collapse. He rose and came to meet them, shaking Tom's hand and kissing Veronica's cheek.

"Have you come to take charge?" she asked.

Gunther, executor of Maurice's estate, nodded soberly. "If you want to put it that way," he sighed, "though it's a duty I had hoped to be spared."

"It's what Maurice wanted," she said, "and he was the best picker of men I ever met."

"And of ladies," Gunther responded gallantly.

Her eyes glimmered. "He had enough practice. Blast those virgin angels in heaven. They're in for the greatest adventures they ever had."

So, as Maurice would have wanted, the long day ended with a smile, not a tear. But there were plenty of tears still to come.

By the time they landed in Geneva, the world and his brother knew that Maurice Stanton was dead. The press had picked up the story. STANTON INDUSTRIES UP FOR GRABS ran the lead headline in *The Financial Times.* The local press ran a similar story: *Speculation is already mounting that Stanton Industries, the Swiss-based office machinery empire, thrown into turmoil by the sudden death of founder Maurice Stanton, may be the target of takeover bids . . .*

Reporters crowded around Tom as he led Kirsten and Veronica through the airport. Angrily, he pushed them aside. "This is neither the time nor the place to talk business."

More reporters and cameramen were waiting outside the Château Stanton. Tired and distressed, Veronica and Kirsten retired to their rooms.

Tom went to the library and called Alec in London.

Alec was at his wits' end. "The papers are on the phone every five minutes. We must tell them *something.*"

"Such as? We can't say a thing until we know what happens to Maurice's shares—"

"Didn't Gunther tell you? He's the executor. He must know."

"If he does he's keeping it to himself. He didn't say a word last night."

"Did you ask him?"

"For God's sake," Tom groaned wearily. "We were tired and upset. I figured if he wanted to tell me he would—"

"You'll have to ask him."

"No," Tom said firmly, reaching a decision. "I'm not doing that. It's a matter of respecting Maurice's wishes. We'll have to wait until after the funeral."

Alec fell silent for a moment. Then he said, "Didn't Maurice ever say *anything* about what he would do with his shares?"

"Not to me."

"What about Roddy and Kirsten? Did he tell them? Can't you ask them?"

"I can hardly ask Roddy," Tom said dryly.

First there had been the fracas in the Hilton; then another embarrassing scene had occurred before they left Athens. Roddy had expected to stay at the château when they reached Geneva. But Gunther had ruled otherwise. "Why?" Roddy had complained bitterly. "I grew up there as well as Kirsten." Gunther had been resolute. "I'm empowered to make all the arrangements. I've booked you and Hugo into the Hotel Bristol."

Alec groaned, "You actually thumped him. Christ! We can kiss goodbye to his support."

"We never had it."

"Maybe, but if timing is everything, you sure picked a bad moment to remind him."

Afterwards Tom went into the kitchen. Having set coffee on to percolate, he picked up the telephone and called the Robinsons. Maurice had often joked about them. "The Swiss Family Robinson" he called them. They were an English couple he had recruited when the château had reverted to him.

Totally renovated, the château was a different, smarter, prettier house than it had been five years before. It had become a home away from home, a base available to Tom and Kirsten as well as to Maurice and Veronica on visits to Geneva. A permanent housekeeper was not needed. Instead, Mrs. Robinson came in for an hour every morning to clean, and she and her husband cooked and served evening meals when required.

It was Mrs. Robinson who answered the phone. She had heard the bad news. Tom thanked her for her condolences and said the three of them would be there for a few days. As he put down the phone Veronica came in. He said, "I've organized dinner here tonight. I didn't think you'd want to go out."

She sat at the table and he poured her some coffee. He wondered if Maurice had spoken to her about the shares. He wanted to ask, but the words stuck in this throat.

"Where's Kirsten?"

"Still upstairs," he said. "I was going to take her some coffee."

"She looked awful this morning. She hardly spoke on the plane, and she didn't touch her lunch." Veronica looked at him. "Has she eaten at all?"

He shook his head. Kirsten seemed to have withdrawn into herself. There had been no tears that morning, but neither were there any words. When he had explained the arrangements, she had listened with a blank look of indifference.

"She must eat," said Veronica.

He found some biscuits and took them up with the coffee. The room was in semi-darkness. Drapes were drawn over the windows. Fully dressed, Kirsten was stretched out on the bed, staring up at the ceiling.

"How are you feeling?" he asked.

Instead of answering, she turned her back to him and began to sob into the pillow.

That became the pattern for the next two days. Nothing he said seemed to reach her. Engulfed in a pit of remorse and depression she rebuffed his every attempt to get near her. He pleaded with her, "Let me call a doctor. He'll give you something to get through it. At least until after the funeral—"

"I don't want a doctor!" she screamed.

She refused to leave the bedroom. And it became *her* bedroom, not *their* bedroom when she asked him to move his things down the hall. They had not so much as embraced since meeting at the Hilton in Athens.

"Is it because of the baby?" he asked. "I'll fly the gynecologist over from London—"

She shot up in bed. "I'm not pregnant! Can't you understand? They were only tests. And if I were pregnant I'd have an abortion."

For the past year she had wanted a child. Their child. For the past *year*!

"It just isn't Kirsten," he blurted out to Veronica. He had not meant to add to her misery; she was holding up remarkably well.

"You forget," she said sadly, "I've been through all this before."

He had overlooked the fact that she was a widow. "The funeral is the final farewell," she said. "Be patient. Get her through that, and she'll come back to you."

Meanwhile, Alec seemed to call every five minutes asking if there was any news on the shares.

By the morning of the funeral Tom was fighting a battle with his nerves. Then the miracle happened. Kirsten took a step back toward him. When he went to her room she looked somehow brighter. Some of the despair had gone out of her eyes. She had eaten a light breakfast and was getting herself ready. Sitting at the dressing table, she was fixing her hair. She wore a black skirt and blouse. Her black jacket lay on the bed.

He sat down in a chair and watched her. "How did you sleep?"

"All right," she said, turning to him. He saw the dark circles beneath her eyes. Then the familiar, much-loved quirky smile touched the edge of her lips. "I'm sorry. I know I've been an absolute bitch."

Leaping up, he took a step toward her.

"No," she said quickly. "I'm all mixed up at the moment. I need time to think it all out, time by myself. Get this . . . get this morning over, and I think I'll go away for a few days."

He was so full of relief because she was talking again, because of her apparent recovery, that he said the first thing to enter his head. "We'll go to Kariakos. I'll tell Doug Masters . . ." and stopped as he saw the horror on her face.

"I can't go there. I can't *ever* go there."

Staring at her, he cursed his clumsiness. He should have realized. Kariakos would remind her of her last sight of Maurice . . . on a stretcher . . .

"No." Her voice had turned cold. "I need time by myself."

"Yes," he agreed. "Well—"

"What are you doing? I mean where are you going . . . after today?"

He wanted to talk to her about the shares. He wanted to say, *I could be fighting for my life if Maurice has divided his shares between you and Roddy.* But her expression stopped him. He was losing her again. A haunted, almost frightened look was growing in her eyes. Quickly he said, "I expect I'll go back to London. Alec and Constantin are here for the funeral. I ought to go back with them."

"Then I'll stay here."

"But—"

"For a few days." Her voice softened again.

He was walking a tightrope. One wrong word would plunge her back into depression. There was still the funeral to get through. And the reading of the will after that. "If that's what you want," he said carefully, "Veronica is going tomorrow—"

"That's all right."

"Mrs. Robinson could get your meals in the evening."

Kirsten nodded.

He searched her face anxiously. "If you're sure you'll be all right?"

"I need time to think. By myself."

"I'll come back at the weekend, of course," he said, humoring her. He might have said more but the depression was already clouding her eyes. "That's settled then," he smiled. He picked her jacket up from the bed and held it out to her. "I think we should go."

Standing up, she turned her back to him and slid her arms into the sleeves. He held the jacket close to him and let his arms continue around her. He could see their reflections in the mirror, his face on her shoulder. She reached for his hand. Her long eyelashes glistened with tears. "I'm sorry, Tom," she whispered.

Squeezing her gently, he kissed the nape of her neck. "Nothing to be sorry about. We'll all miss him. Desperately. But he wouldn't want you to be unhappy. Everything will be all right, believe me."

The feeling of dread which had been with him ever since Athens began to lift. Relief surged through him. Veronica was right, Kirsten was coming back to him.

Everyone was there. Pohl had flown in from the States. Edwards was there. Alec and Constantin had arrived from London. Bill Rodgers, who ran Stanton Australia had arrived from Sydney the night before. Melody was there, with Jasmine and at least two dozen other beautiful women whom Tom had never set eyes on. Veronica gave them a curious look; then her face softened and her eyes warmed. "My, my," she said softly, pulling in her stomach. "Pick of the parade at my age, and that's *some* parade." Jimmy Carrol and Rahji Singh, joint managing directors of Stanton India, had flown in from Delhi. A complete *Who's Who* of Geneva was there, including of course Yvonne and Amiens. "A cast of thousands," Hugo was heard to remark with his usual sneer. He had actually asked Gunther if he could make a film of the proceedings. Gunther refused with a curt "No" and a look of chilling contempt.

And so they gathered to pay their last respects to Maurice Stanton. Gunther, as Maurice's oldest friend, delivered a eulogy in which he described Maurice as "a lover of life." And as Tom choked back his tears he thought of how much Maurice was loved in return, and how they would miss him.

The king was dead. Long live the king. But who was to be the new king? As the line of black cars wound its way through the streets of Geneva, thoughts returned to the living; and by the time Maurice's inner circle began to assemble at the Hotel Bristol, a noticeable tension marked some of the faces.

Alighting from the limousine, Kirsten hesitated and turned back. "No," she choked, "I'm going home." She had borne up well during the service, but tension and hysteria were mounting once more in her eyes. Her pale cheeks were wet with tears. She began shaking her head.

Tom remembered her mother's funeral and the spiteful insult contained in that will. "Darling," he took her arm. "Everything will be all right—"

Avoiding his eye, she stared down at her feet. "You said I could be by myself," she muttered, "you *promised.*"

"But—"

"I want to go home," she repeated.

Home at that moment did not mean *their* home in Hampstead, London, but the old château overlooking Lake Geneva in which she had grown up. He could feel her slipping away all over again.

"Tom," Veronica rested her hand on his arm, "the poor girl is worn out. Of course she should go back to the château. I think I might even go with her—"

"No!" Kirsten shook her head, her eyes still averted.

"Okay then," Veronica said calmly, her voice soothing. "Why don't you go home now and I'll come on later. I promise I'll be as quiet as a mouse."

They returned Kirsten to the back of the limousine. Tom crouched down by the open door. "I'll come back at the weekend. All right?"

She was weeping. He crouched there with a heart as heavy as lead. He was on the point of getting into the car with her, when Veronica's hand tightened on his shoulder. "Leave her be, Tom. Let her cry herself out."

He stood up.

The chauffeur closed the door and gave him an enquiring look. "Okay, Monsieur?"

Tom nodded and stepped back onto the pavement. "Okay," he said softly, "okay." Something in his heart said it was far from okay. But Veronica tugged on his arm.

"Tom. We must go."

He turned to see Amiens and Roddy entering the hotel together. The sinking feeling in the pit of his stomach said his worst fears were about to be realized.

* * *

The lawyers conducted the proceedings in English, appropriately, given the fact that the deceased client had been English-born. There were four of them—the four senior partners of the most respected firm of lawyers in Geneva—gray-faced, elderly men who had known Maurice Stanton for the best part of half a century. They sat with Gunther Haller at a table at the front of the Blue Room.

It was a large, ornately furnished room, only slightly smaller than the one adjoining in which the rest of the gathering had assembled. People had been discreetly divided upon arrival: beneficiaries in one room, those who had attended the funeral merely to pay their respects, in the other. Joining Alec and Constantin, Tom was about to leave Veronica to go her way while he went the other, when one of the lawyers' clerks redirected him: "We'd be grateful if you would join us in the Blue Room, sir."

Tom sat beside Veronica, not knowing what to expect. Carl Pohl slouched untidily at the end of the row, polishing his oversized glasses with the tip of his tie. Yvonne, swollen-eyed and distressed, sat next to Amiens who scarcely stopped whispering to Roddy. Conspirators plotting: they glanced over at Tom at one point. He met their stares, feeling their hatred. He was left in no doubt that they had made the same calculations about the shares. And reached the same conclusions. That he was vulnerable, that one concerted attack would see him defeated.

He wondered what he would do? Stanton Industries had become his whole life. Stanton Industries and Kirsten. Life would have no meaning without them, somehow one went with the other; they were intertwined; in her own way Kirsten was as committed as he was to building the business. Or she had been. And surely would be again? Once she recovered from this terrible, all-consuming bout of depression. She would come back to him. They would be together once more . . .

The lawyers droned on. They took it in turn. The tallest of them was on his feet at that moment, listing various charities to which Maurice had made substantial donations.

What wealth! And what generosity, for everyone seemed to have been remembered, so many people whose names meant nothing to Tom. An artist in Nice. A tailor in London. A restaurateur in Paris. A doctor in Rheims. People who had rendered service to Maurice in life were rewarded with small gifts on his death.

The tall lawyer sat down. His colleague on his left, shorter, plumper, rounder of face and deeper of voice, rose to his feet and took over.

Yvonne was left some jewelry.

An early Picasso was left to Melody.

Desmond Edwards inherited a pair of French dueling pistols. The lawyer smiled—"With the strict instructions never to use them."

Bequest followed bequest, until it seemed that almost everyone in the room had received something. Then the lawyer sat down. For a moment his colleagues conferred in whispers, shuffling papers on the table in front of them, seeming to consult Gunther on a technical matter. Nodding agreement, the senior partner rose to his feet. Short-sighted, he peered at the sheet of paper held rather shakily in his blue-veined hand.

"To my darling daughter Kirsten," he read, "I leave the Château Stanton complete with contents, together with sufficient monies to pay for ten years' upkeep of the property."

Setting the paper back on the table, the lawyer peered into the audience, searching for Kirsten. Heads turned, Tom felt eyes focus on the empty chair to his left. Warm with gratitude, he thought how clever of Maurice: the château was the one thing in his vast fortune which Kirsten truly loved. The house overlooking the lake had become hers forever.

"To my son Roddy," continued the lawyer, bending over the paper, "I leave the yacht *Aphrodite,* together with sufficient monies to pay for five years' crew and maintenance."

Tom watched the flush of excitement rise in Roddy's face. There was no doubting Roddy's love of the boat. He was forever giving parties afloat.

"And to my good friend Tom Lambert," continued the lawyer, "I leave the lease and contents of the villa on Kariakos, with sufficient monies to pay upkeep for ten years, together with the following very strict instructions—" The lawyer smiled and read: "That you take sufficient time from your labors to enjoy it."

Tom blinked back the tears. Kariakos was his! *Oh Maurice! You stupid, magnanimous wonderful old bastard. There was no need. No need at all. God, how I'll miss you.*

"And to my beloved Veronica," read the lawyer, "I leave the chalet at St. Moritz, together with its contents and monies for the upkeep of the property for the rest of her life." The lawyer paused and looked up. "There's a message," he said. "It reads, 'Thank you, my darling. You were my greatest-ever adventure.' "

Big tears coursed down Veronica's cheeks and fell like raindrops on her tightly clasped hands. Biting her lips, she trembled as Tom drew her toward him, then she buried her head in his shoulder and wept.

The lawyer sat down.

For a moment the only sounds in the room were of Veronica weeping.

Then Gunther Haller pushed back his chair and rose to his feet. In his hand was an envelope. Veronica gulped and clung to Tom as she struggled to recover.

Gunther cleared his throat. "We now come to Maurice Stanton's principal assets. I mean, of course, his shares in Stanton Industries."

Tom felt drained. He had already received more than he expected. Far more. He had loved Maurice as a son loved a father. He found himself wishing only one thing, *Do what gives you the most pleasure, Maurice. That's all that matters . . .*

"This envelope," said Gunther, tearing it open, "has been in the bank vault ever since Maurice handed it to me . . ."

Whatever gives you most pleasure.

"I have no idea of its contents," said Gunther.

A movement over Veronica's shoulder caught Tom's attention. Roddy had leaned forward, biting his nails.

Gunther unfolded the single sheet of paper. Clearing his throat, he looked out at his audience. "I divide my shareholding equally among my children," he read.

Turning to Roddy, Amiens hugged him with joy. Triumph in

their eyes, they turned to look over at Tom. His face masked his feeling. Exactly as he had expected: Maurice had done the fair thing. And if that was what Maurice wanted. . . .

"Therefore," Gunther read on, "I bequeath one-third of my holdings to my son Roddy, one-third to Kirsten my daughter, and one-third to my son-in-law Tom Lambert."

Tom's heart leapt. Maurice had seen him as a son. He had treated him equally with his blood children. One-third? One-third was twenty percent of the total. Adding to his existing eleven percent, he owned thirty-one percent of Stanton Industries. He had become the biggest single shareholder. And Kirsten owned twenty percent. Between them they had fifty-one percent. They had control!

He stared blindly as Gunther sat down.

Control! Jesus! I've got control.

The senior law partner once more rose to his feet. "In view of this development," he said, "we would recommend an extraordinary general meeting of the shareholders be called, for the purposes of confirming the appointment of the company's officers."

Amiens slumped forward in his chair.

"We would suggest as quickly as possible," said the lawyer. "Shall we say in three days?" He was looking at Tom.

Tom cleared his throat, "Er yes . . . that's fine."

The lawyer looked around the room. "I believe all but one of the other shareholders are here. Are there any objections?"

Not a voice was raised.

"Very well," said the lawyer. "An extraordinary general meeting of Stanton Industries will take place at our offices, being the company's registered office, at two P.M. on Friday."

It took Tom what was left of that day and most of the next to appreciate how totally things had changed. Ever since he had amalgamated Excel with Pohl and Bouvier to create Stanton Industries he had been forced to play a political game. The management team had been cobbled together from obligations, not from choice. But now—having discharged his promises in life—in death Maurice had written a new mandate. Tom had control.

He felt like a new president, or a prime minister coming to power. For the first time he could pursue his own policies without worrying about trouble from this one or pressure from that one. This one and that one could be changed. For the first time he could pick his own team.

In Jermyn Street, an atmosphere developed of a new broom sweeping clean. Celebrations were out of the question, but nothing could disguise the air of growing excitement.

Tom could now discuss Apple: Pohl had stopped over in London and was in an hotel nearby waiting instructions.

"The point is," said Tom, "whether we get Apple or not is almost irrelevant. This will be the age of the personal computer: the growth will be explosive. We can't wait any longer, we're going to throw everything we've got into this."

Obviously Amiens would be against it.

"I'd fire the bastard," Constantin growled. "He's always resented you."

Alec agreed, "He's a first-class production man, no doubt about that. But he'll never go along with your policy. He turns everything into an issue, a bloody great argument—"

"Now he's thick as thieves with Roddy." Constantin shook his head. "I don't like it. They own almost a third of the company between them. Those two will always give you trouble."

"A house divided," Tom mused softly.

"Exactly."

They were all of one mind. Amiens had to go. The sooner the better.

"I'll tell him at the shareholders' meeting on Friday," said Tom.

Alec cocked a speculative eyebrow. "Strictly speaking, Yvonne owns the shares."

"I think Amiens will be there with Yvonne's proxy vote." Tom shrugged, "If he's not, I'll tell her." He pulled a face. "The shame of it is I quite like Yvonne. She deserves better."

With every decision, restrictions began to melt away; a great sense of freedom grew, a feeling of power. "For instance," Tom said at one point, "now that we're not hampered by political infighting, we might consider closing these offices and moving to Geneva?"

"All of us?" Constantin said in surprise.

"Alec will have to go. Alec's the only one who can step into Amiens' shoes."

"You mean *live* in Geneva?" said Alec.

"You can't run Stanton Manufacturing from here. And it always made sense to make Geneva the head office. We couldn't do it at the outset for fear of giving Amiens an advantage. But if we get rid of him, we don't have to worry."

It was like drawing on a blank sheet of paper. Everything could be looked at afresh. And one decision led to another. Moving Alec would cause problems—Australia and India had answered to him.

"I know," Tom nodded. "But I think we should promote Bill Rodgers to the main board. He's ready for bigger responsibilities."

And so it continued all that day and all of Thursday. Tom's team, molding his policies. Constantin was to fly to California with Pohl to establish contact with Apple. Pohl was delighted. He sat in the office and grinned like a schoolboy. He was itching to get started. "Do I *have* to come to this shareholders' meeting? If it wasn't for that, Con and I could leave in the morning." He thought for a moment, "Tom, I'll give you my proxy vote. Whatever you do is okay by me."

Carl Pohl had become part of the team: Tom's team, pursuing Tom's policies.

Desmond Edwards was left until Friday morning. He was flying to Geneva with Tom for the shareholders' meeting. Tom had him come to the office first.

"You backed the wrong man," he said bluntly.

Desmond fidgeted in his chair. "Backed is a bit strong," he demurred. "I merely agreed with Amiens about the Institute. It *does* cost a lot of money—"

"So does your sales force but we can't do without it. Neither can we live without Research and Development . . ."

He had no intention of dismissing Edwards. Desmond was an excellent marketing director, universally liked and respected. But Desmond had to choose, either to follow Tom's policies or get out. Tom and Alec had discussed the best way to proceed. "You won't need to knock him over the head," Alec had counseled. "Desmond can figure out what fifty-one percent means along with everyone else. He knows you've got control, he knows he can't fight you. But if you want to keep him, my advice is don't bully him. Win him over. Persuade him, sell him the idea."

"Know something," Tom mused, looking at Desmond across the desk. "Words are dangerous things. All this talk about *home* computers. Okay, maybe . . . Who knows? Frankly, who cares? I'm not interested in *home* computers any more than you are—"

"You're not?"

"Never have been. That's not our market—"

"That's what I've been saying."

"Exactly. But *small* computers. *Personal* computers . . ."

Tom scarcely paused for breath in the next hour. He was as persuasive as he knew how, and Edwards was there to mend fences. So agreement was not long in coming. "What I want you to do," Tom concluded, "is to get out to California as soon as you can. Con and Carl Pohl are already on their way there. Go and see this Apple equipment."

"Okay."

Tom paused. "Do you really want to come to the shareholders' meeting? I'm just thinking, it could be embarrassing for you."

Ten minutes later, he had all he wanted. Another act of faith. Another supporter joining the team. His team, to pursue his policy.

Running late, he grabbed his case and coat to go to the airport. Alec was in Barbara's office, selling her the benefits of living in Geneva. "You'll love it," Tom grinned. "Oh, do me a favor. Call Kirsten for me. Tell her I'll be up at the château right after the meeting."

He had expected Roddy to be there. In his mind's eye he had seen Roddy and Amiens on one side of the table, Gunther on the other, with himself at the head and the lawyer's clerk to one side taking the minutes.

It was a gloomy room on a gloomy day. Geneva had been bathed in sunshine for Maurice's funeral, but even as the Lear flew over the lake, spots of rain slashed the windows and were falling steadily by the time he reached the center of town.

Not that Tom cared. This was his day and nothing could spoil it.

Gunther was crossing the street as his cab drew up at the door. He waited for him in the lobby. For a moment Gunther stood in the entrance, folding his umbrella, not seeing Tom. Then he looked up and a sad smile came to his face. Shaking hands, he said, "I was just remembering our first meeting on Kariakos. When I said I hoped you'd run Stanton Industries for the rest of your life."

It was a long time ago. "Don't worry," said Tom, "I won't let you down."

Smiling his sad smile, Gunther led the way into the old-fashioned elevator and they went up to the third floor.

It was ten minutes to two P.M.

The clerk escorted them from reception to the gloomy conference room. Coffee and mineral water stood on the sideboard. Paper and pencils had been set out in six places around the big table. "We won't need all of those," said Tom. "Carl and Desmond won't be here."

Gunther listened to what had happened in London. Tom smiled. "I know you still have your doubts, but trust me. I know what I'm doing."

Gunther took his place at the table. "Personal computers," he mused, shaking his head. "It's a different world." At Tom's grin, Gunther shrugged. "Well," he said, "it's your business now. You've got control."

Tom took the chair at the head of the table as the clerk opened his pad and sat down near the sideboard. Tom glanced at this watch. Five minutes to two. His stomach churned.

Gunther speculated, "Perhaps the others won't come either? After all, Andre will guess what's in your mind."

On his last word the door opened and Amiens walked in. His

flushed look might have come from hurrying, but not the gleam in his eyes. Everything about him spoke of a man who had come to do battle. "Gunther," he nodded, "Tom." Noting where Tom was sitting, he walked to the far end of the table and sat down. Opening his briefcase, he took out a paper.

"Here is Yvonne's proxy for eleven percent of the shares," he said. "That establishes my right to be at this meeting."

Tom smiled grimly. Amiens was a fighter all right. He was clearly ready to battle to the last ditch. Reaching down, Tom opened his own briefcase. "Carl and Desmond won't be here," he said, as his hand found the papers. "Here are their proxies. Both made out in my favor."

He slid them across to Gunther, who inspected them with a cursory glance before passing them down the table to Amiens.

Tom watched him. He wondered what he was thinking. He must have counted upon Edwards for support. Now even that had collapsed around his ears. In other circumstances, for another man, Tom might have felt sympathy, even pity. But Amiens had been a thorn in his flesh for too long.

Gunther said, "It's past two. I don't know how long you want to give Roddy—"

"He won't be coming," said Amiens.

So even Roddy had deserted him.

Tom shrugged. "Very well," he said. "Let's start the meeting."

He saw no point in beating about the bush. "This isn't a matter of being vindictive," he said evenly to Andre, "it's simply that you and I have differed in the past and I'm quite sure will differ again." He quoted examples from over the years, including the recent clash in San Francisco. "Consequently," he concluded, "I think it is in the shareholders' best interests if you resign. Therefore I formally propose that you be dismissed as an officer of this company unless you resign with immediate effect."

Amiens sat perfectly still. He watched Tom with a curiously unblinking stare. His concentration was intense; not a muscle moved in his face. He might have been a condemned man watching the hangman put a noose around his throat, determined to remember his executioner's face for all eternity.

Then he said, "I oppose the motion."

Tom sat back in his chair. "Don't be a bloody fool. I control the company."

Gunther Haller looked as if he suspected Amiens had taken leave of his senses. "I'm sorry, Andre," he said gently, "there's nothing you can do—"

"On the contrary," said Amiens, "I would like to put an alternative motion to this meeting. That Mr. Tom Lambert be dismissed as chief executive officer of this company."

Tom looked at Gunther, then at the clerk, then back down the table to Amiens. "Have you gone mad?"

"It's a perfectly reasonable proposal."

"For Christ's sake!" Tom slapped the table. "I've got fifty-one percent of the shares. Then these on top." He pointed to the proxy votes from Pohl and Edwards. "You can't propose anything, you bloody idiot. You're out. Finished—"

"Shall we put it to the vote?" Amiens interrupted.

The faintest of alarm bells rang at the back of Tom's head. So faint it might have been the bell on the ambulance coming to carry Amiens off to the asylum. "Andre," he said, "you know perfectly well that Kirsten and I—"

"Do you have her proxy votes? In writing?"

Tom looked wildly around the room for a telephone. Seeing one, he pointed. "I can have her down here herself in ten minutes. What's the bloody point?"

Amiens looked at the clerk. "Please record that two motions are on the table and I wish a vote to be taken. Shareholders may only vote the shares which they own and any written proxies they may have in support. Is that not so?"

"Oui." The clerk nodded and glanced nervously at Tom. "Yes," he said, reverting to English, "that is correct."

"This is a bloody farce," said Tom, looking to Haller for support.

"I agree—"

"Shall we vote?" Amiens interrupted, injecting a note of authority into his voice. He stared up the table at Tom. "How many votes do you have to support your proposal?"

Tom felt the meeting slipping away. He had all the trump

cards, yet he was defending. "Thirty-one percent in my own name," he said coldly, "plus . . ." he reached for Pohl's proxy, "five percent from Carl Pohl, and . . ." he fumbled with the other sheet of paper, "seven percent from Desmond Edwards."

Amiens wrote the figures down. "A total of forty-three percent," he said, looking at Gunther. "And how do you vote?" he asked crisply.

"I vote with Tom."

A cruel, thin smile came to Amiens' lips. "Six percent from Gunther Haller," he said, making a note on his pad. He looked up at Tom, "That gives you forty-nine percent."

"Exactly," Tom nodded, pointing at the telephone, "and that's *before* I call Kirsten."

Amiens dipped his hand back into his briefcase. "I have here two documents," he said. "One is a share transfer from Roddy Stanton to my wife. As you will see, he has transferred his entire shareholding to her. And here is her authority for me to vote on her behalf."

Haller took the two pieces of paper, studied them briefly, and passed them up the table.

Tom pushed them aside without looking at them. He knew the figures by heart. "So what? That only gives you thirty-one percent."

Standing up, Amiens placed his briefcase on the table. "Here are two more documents," he said. "The first is a share transfer from Kirsten Lambert to my wife. Transferring her entire twenty percent. And this is my authority to vote those shares on my wife's behalf."

Tom was out of his chair and down the room. He snatched the papers from Amiens' hands. Kirsten's signature leapt off the paper. It couldn't be true. It was impossible. He cried out, "No! I don't believe it. This can't be right."

Amiens said, "Which gives me fifty-one percent and control—"

"This must be a forgery!" Tom shouted. "It must be a trick. Whose name is this here?" He waved the paper in front of Amiens. "This bloody witness—"

Amiens said, "Don't worry. The share transfers were properly witnessed. Monsieur Lapierre is one of Geneva's leading lawyers."

Tom looked at Haller. "Gunther?" he said, thrusting the share transfer under his nose.

Haller looked dazed. His head nodded with reluctant agreement. "That's Lapierre's signature. I'd know it anywhere. I do a lot of business with him."

Amiens was saying, "Motion one is defeated and motion two carried. Mr. Lambert is dismissed as chief executive officer with immediate effect."

"I demand an adjournment," Tom gasped, gripping the back of a chair. He looked at the clerk, at Haller and Amiens. For a split-second their faces swam out of focus. When his vision cleared and the buzzing in his ears stopped, he heard Amiens saying, "There are no grounds for an adjournment"—and Gunther and the clerk were nodding agreement.

None of it made sense. Kirsten would never do this to him. She wouldn't do it to herself, to Maurice. She just wouldn't do it.

They were all on their feet. He thought of telephoning but dismissed the idea. Kirsten would have to *be* here, to tell them, face to face, to explain it was some kind of trick.

He forgot his briefcase and his coat. Running from the room, he raced along the corridor to the elevator. Not finding it there, he ran down the stairs, jumping them two at a time. He collided with a girl in the lobby, almost knocking her flying. Shouting apologies, he ran through the door and into the street. The pavement was wet with rain. He slipped, stumbled, and righted himself. He made for the cab rank; running, bumping into people, scurrying around them, brushing the rain from his eyes.

The cabdriver saw him coming and started the engine. Tom threw himself into the back seat and shouted the address. "Hurry up," he shouted. "Get there as fast as you can."

Catching his breath was easier than catching his thoughts. They were all over the place. A jumbled kaleidoscope of images raced around in his brain. Fumbling for his wallet, he waved some Swiss francs over the seat to the driver, urging him to go faster. Gunther might stall. Gunther would argue, play for time.

Gunther might win an adjournment. "Hurry," he shouted to the driver, "hurry!"

They roared up the hill, climbing and climbing. He glanced at his watch. Three o'clock. What time was it when he ran out of the meeting? How long had it been? How long would they wait?

The turrets of the château loomed into view through the trees. "Come on," he shouted, "come on!" They rounded the familiar curve in the road. Then they took the curve to the left. There was the entrance. Throwing francs onto the front passenger seat, he opened the door as they rolled to a halt. "Wait," he ordered, "wait for me. Understand? It's important."

Before the man nodded Tom was out of the car and bounding up the front steps. His keys were already in his hand. It took him a moment to find the right one. "Kirsten!" he shouted as he opened the door. "Kirsten!"

Not finding her in the big drawing room, he tried the kitchen. Not finding her there he tried the sitting room, the library, then the dining room. "Kirsten!" he shouted as he ran back into the hall.

Hauling himself on the banister, he raced up the stairs. "Kirsten!" He tried every bedroom. Then all the bathrooms. "Kirsten!"

She was not there. Doubled up, catching his breath on the landing, he racked his brain to think where she might be. He ran back to their bedroom, trying to remember what clothes she kept in Geneva. Her black suit was in the wardrobe. So were two of her coats. And a raincoat. He looked at the rows of shoes, trying to remember, trying to think. . . .

Running downstairs, he searched the rooms all over again, his eyes darting everywhere, looking for clues. There was a film projector in the library, pointing at a small canvas screen. He had not noticed it there before. Hurrying from one room to the next, he called and shouted. The French windows were open leading out onto the terrace. Kirsten would never leave the house without closing and locking the French windows. "She *must* be here." he muttered, stepping out onto the terrace, turning his gaze right, then left, then right once again. The terrace was empty.

He stood there, trying to think. The rain had stopped. He stared aimlessly out at the view. Then he saw her. She was down on the rocks. Wearing a yellow skirt and a white shirt. Stretched out on the rocks. Face downward. Not moving.

His heart stopped. For a moment he froze. Then he shouted. "Kirsten!" He stepped perilously close to the low balustrade. "Kirsten!"

He ran. Past the dining room, past the kitchen, past the staff quarters. He ran the length of the terrace. He shouted again as he raced across the rough ground and onto the path. Loose stones slid and scattered under his feet. The gradient worsened and became even steeper. Running was impossible. To run meant falling headlong. He descended sideways, crablike, struggling to maintain balance. Hands outstretched, grabbing rocks to remain upright. Hurrying as fast as he could, faster than he dared. Shouting. Panting. Shale slithered and slipped under his feet . . .

Then he was on his knees, crouching beside her, touching her gently with the tips of his fingers. Whispering her name. She was wet from the rain. And cold. Very cold. With infinite tenderness he turned her over onto her back. The bruise on her forehead was more than a bruise. Her temple was crushed at the hairline. Without feeling for a pulse he knew she was dead.

He was weeping, sobbing, repeating her name over and over, "Kirsten . . . oh Kirsten. . . ."

The rain started again.

Blinded by tears, he slid his arms beneath her, intending to lift her. His fingers touched metal. Moving her gently, his hands closed around a flat, narrow canister.

BOOK TEN

Constantin looked a hundred years old. Badly in need of a shave, stubble grazed his chin and the sides of his face up to his cheekbones. His eyes were full of sadness. Next to him, Alec sat as still as a stone, haggard with pain and sorrow.

Tom swallowed hard and ran a hand through his hair. "You know the rest. The police raised hell because I carried her up to the house. I didn't think. For Christ's sake, it was raining. Did they expect me to leave her there. It was—"

"I'd have done the same," Constantin interrupted quickly.

"And me," Alec nodded.

Tom's hands were trembling, and a nerve twitched so badly in his leg that he had to stand up. He walked to the edge of the pool, stamping his left foot as if to rid himself of cramp. Returning to join them at the table, his face bore the blank look of a sleepwalker. "They took me to the central police station and kept asking questions. They thought I'd killed her. Nobody said so, but their faces were full of suspicion." He sat down, elbows on his knees and his head in his hands. His fingers kneaded his forehead so vigorously that white trails appeared across the furrowed brown skin. "The cabdriver didn't help. He said I was in a hell of a temper when he picked me up, and that I'd made him drive like crazy." He shrugged. "I didn't give a shit what they thought. They could suspect what they liked. They were very polite. No rough stuff, no shouting. Then at about nine or ten o'clock, something like that, their attitude changed. I suppose they'd established time of death by then. She died at about one-thirty. I was at the airport, then in a cab on the way to the lawyers' office. They found the cabdriver and he confirmed we went straight there." He looked up. "She could have seen the plane. She used to do that, stand on the terrace and watch for the plane . . ."

Restlessly he rose from the chair and began to pace up and down. "They started asking a different sort of question then. You know the kind of thing. Has she been under strain? Has she been worrying about anything? Of course they knew all about Maurice and the funeral. It had been in all the papers. I said she had been deeply upset—"

"You had a right to a lawyer," Constantin pointed out.

Tom agreed. "I'm not saying they refused one. I don't remember. Most likely they played it by the book. You know the Swiss. Very correct. Anyway, by now it was about eleven o'clock. They'd taken my passport away and told me not to leave Geneva, but they were obviously going to let me out. Then Gunther arrived. I didn't call him or anything, but Geneva's a small town and Gunther owns his share of it. The police fell over themselves when he appeared. He wanted me to stay at his place for the night, or book into an hotel, but I insisted on going back to the château."

"Gunther called me," said Alec to Constantin. "I couldn't believe it. Any of it. The whole thing was a nightmare. I spent the rest of the night trying to trace you in California."

Tom stared into the swimming pool. "Gunther stayed with me for nearly an hour, sitting around, drinking. I drank a lot more when he left. Then I remembered the can of film."

"The police didn't know about it?" asked Constantin.

"I forgot about it. Genuinely. I honestly didn't remember until—"

"Didn't they search the place?"

"What for? There hadn't been a break-in or anything. They went down onto the rocks and examined the terrace, but everything in the house was normal enough."

Constantin nodded. "So you remembered the film."

"Not where I put it. I knew it was somewhere. I remembered carrying Kirsten in from the terrace, putting her down on the couch, going to the phone. . . ." Tom shook his head. "I had to retrace my steps. By now it was three or four in the morning. Finally I found it on one of the bookshelves. Of course I didn't know it was a can of film until I opened it. Then I remembered seeing the projector in the library . . ." His voice tailed off to a whisper. "That was the first time I watched the film."

Constantin closed his eyes. Imagining the scene in the small hours of the morning. For Tom it must have been the final blow, the ultimate stupifying horror.

All three of them fell silent. The morning sun had climbed high in the sky, warming the terrace and bringing all the colors to life. Out at sea the haze on the horizon warned of another hot day.

"It's been eight months, Tom," Alec said softly.

"Seems more like eight years."

Constantin frowned. "I wish we'd known about the film. I wish you'd told us before—"

"Why?" Tom looked up, anger in his eyes. "What difference would it have made?"

"It would have helped us understand, especially about the funeral."

Friends had rushed to Geneva. Alec and Jean arriving that morning. Melina and Barbara had followed on the next flight. Constantin and Carl Pohl arrived late in the evening. Veronica had come on one plane, and Melody on another.

Tom had refused them admittance at the château, not answering the door or the telephone. Constantin had been on the point of forcing entry when Alec remembered "the Swiss Family Robinson."

Tom was drunk. Blind drunk. Paralytic drunk. With the help of a doctor they had sobered him up, but it took the best part of two days. By which time the inquest was upon them. He gave his evidence steadily enough, and listened in stony-faced silence to the verdict of suicide. People had remarked upon his dry-eyed lack of emotion. Friends were surprised, but they were shocked to the core a day later.

Alec said, "I wish you'd been there, that's all. Everyone loved her."

With his passport returned to him, Tom had packed his bags and left, not waiting for the funeral. He had flown Swissair directly from Geneva to Athens. No ride in the jeep with Gregg. No *Helena. Helena* belonged to Stanton Industries and Stanton Industries belonged to Amiens. Instead, with a sad look upward to seek Maurice's forgiveness he had chartered a helicopter.

"We got the same pilot yesterday," said Alec. "He remembered bringing you over."

"You shouldn't have come."

"Melody was coming with or without us," Constantin said heavily. "Besides, we shouldn't have listened to you. We should have come over before."

They had tracked him down within a few days. Then the phone had started to ring. For the first few months he had promised to return to London. "Soon," he kept saying.

"Why did you stop answering the phone?"

"I was getting too many calls. Anyway I had nothing to come back for, I was still thinking things out."

Consumed by bitterness, he had suffered bouts of physical illness during those first few months. Not caused by grief. He had not mourned Kirsten then. He had hated her. Picturing events, trying to piece them together, he had seen her leading a double life. Transferring the shares had been bad enough. To have actually sat down in a lawyer's office and signed their lives away—how could she do that? He thought he had known her, known everything about her. But there had been secrets. And then that film . . .

Alec cleared his throat. "A lot's happened," he said. "Jermyn Street has been sold. Everything is run from Geneva."

Tom shrugged his indifference.

Alec, Constantin, Carl Pohl and a dozen others had all

resigned within a week of Amiens' taking control. The Institute had been closed. Talks with Apple Computer were stopped before they had even started.

Alec said, "Apple got their finances sorted out. They've got an order book from now until Christmas. They're working all around the clock and still can't keep pace. It's incredible. No one in the business has seen anything like it. Stanton's pulled out, of course. They're not into personal computers."

A flicker of anger showed on Tom's face. His fists bunched and he was on the point of responding when footsteps sounded behind them.

The sun caught Melody's hair as she walked out on the terrace. Dressed in a white linen suit, she looked as elegant as a fashion plate, and just as beautiful except for the signs of strain in her face. She managed to greet Tom with a weak smile. "Sorry about last night. I got all tired and emotional. Alec was right to put me to bed." She gave them a curious look as she sat down. "You guys look like you've been up all night?"

"We have," said Alec.

Her eyes searched his face. She turned to Constantin who responded with an almost imperceptible shake of his head. With a sigh, she glanced at the coffee pot. "Is that hot?" Alec poured her a cup.

"That film got to me," she began, and then corrected herself. "No it wasn't the film. It was the look on your face as you watched it. Tom, I *saw* you and Kirsten together. I saw the way she looked at you. She didn't just love you, she adored you. I can't make any more sense of it than you can, but I wish to God you didn't hate her so much."

"I don't," he said quietly, "not now."

In a strange way the people from the village had helped. They all knew Kirsten. They had been guests at her wedding, and before that they remembered when she first came to Kariakos, with Tom wounded and Constantin at death's door. Simple Greek fishermen and their families. Men like Mavros and Petsas. They refused to believe ill of Kirsten. When Tom ranted and raved during those first couple of months, they had closed their ears to all that he had said except when he cursed Kirsten. Then they had closed ranks. "No," they said with one voice, "we knew her too."

Such faith. And he had lacked faith.

Held by Melody's green eyes, he said, "I did hate her. Now I'm ashamed, but I'd be a liar to deny it. Now I hate them. I'll destroy them as they destroyed her."

Constantin protested, "Not this way—"

"There's no other way. You think I'd get them in court? With what? You're a lawyer. You know I'm right."

Constantin subsided, defeated.

"Why did they agree to come?" asked Alec.

A grim smile flickered over Tom's face. "Amiens is coming to buy thirty-one percent of Stanton Industries."

"Why? You're locked in."

Tom pulled a face. "Because I could cause trouble with that many shares. Because he hates the thought of paying me dividends. Because he thinks he'll buy them for nothing."

"And Roddy?"

"Ah," Tom mused reflectively. He looked out at the horizon. "Roddy sails *Aphrodite* up and down on that blue sea. At times he comes in close to the shoreline. He and I look at each other through binoculars. I can see him watching me, envying me. I've got something he wants. Kariakos. *Aphrodite* isn't half as much fun without Kariakos."

"And he thinks you'll sell it?"

"That's what I told him on the phone."

Constantin stood up and rubbed his stiff knee. "All of this is only conjecture. Even if you're right and they did it, you don't know *how*. You can't prove a thing. You'll *never* prove a thing."

"I'll make them tell me," Tom said with chilling conviction. "Then I'll kill them."

Melody shuddered. "Please, Tom, I don't care about them, perhaps they deserve to die, I don't know. But I care about you and this will destroy you—"

"And not knowing won't?" Tom flared. "Living with this doubt. Not knowing. Never being sure." He shook his head. "This is the only way I'll ever live with myself."

They all knew it was true. Persuasion had failed. Further

argument was as futile as the wasted night. Constantin accepted the inevitable with a deep sigh. "What time are they coming?"

"This afternoon." Tom rose to his feet. "The helicopter can take you off before *Helena* arrives. You have a choice. Go or stay. But if you stay, you stay on my terms. You don't raise a finger to help them."

They looked at each other. Constantin made up his mind. "I'm staying."

"And me," said Alec.

Melody looked at Tom. "You might need me afterwards."

He nodded. "Very well. I'm going to get some rest. I suggest you do the same. Mavros will wake us when *Helena* is sighted."

He watched them climb the rise from the villa. Standing ten yards down the path, the clearing and everything in it was concealed by the final bend behind him.

Yvonne's presence was a surprise. He had not expected her. Not that it changed anything. Nothing would weaken his resolve. She walked in front with Melody. They were the same height, despite Yvonne's high heels and Melody's flat sandals. A contrast in styles: Yvonne overdressed in a silk floral dress, with gold glittering on a wrist and more at her throat, and Melody in the simple white suit. He wondered about Yvonne. How much did she know? How much was she a part of it? She had written a touching letter of condolence about Kirsten. He had thought it genuine when he read it, but then he had always found Yvonne to be genuine, not least in protecting her husband.

Amiens walked several paces behind. In an immaculate gray suit and Gucci shoes, he was dressed even more expensively than his wife. His handsome tanned face was set in a scowl. Then came Roddy and Alec, with the ubiquitous Hugo behind them, and Constantin bringing up the rear.

They were later than he had expected. The sun was already casting long shadows. The faint breeze stirred the pine cones and dried beads of sweat on his face. Underfoot the parched grass was the color and texture of straw.

He harnessed his hatred. It would be easy to become angry. The very sight of them made the gorge rise in his throat. His hands clenched and unclenched at his sides. Taking a deep breath, he walked down to meet them.

"Tom!" cried Yvonne. She came forward to put her hands on his shoulders and kissed him on both cheeks. She stepped back, her shrewd eyes raking his face. "You don't look well. I heard you'd been ill. How are you?"

"Better now, thanks."

Linking her arm through his, she stepped forward to continue the climb. "What are we doing up here?" she asked. "Alec said something about a surprise—"

Amiens shouted from behind, "This was supposed to be a private meeting."

Tom stopped. "You knew Roddy and Hugo were coming."

"Of course I knew. They came with us."

Tom responded with a wintry smile, "You have your friends and I have mine."

Yvonne laughed softly. "Hardly friends," she said in a low voice, "personally I've always thought—"

"Get on with it," Amiens complained from behind. "You're holding everyone up."

Tom turned to lead the way. As he did so, Roddy called out, "No need to show us the view. You don't have to go to so much trouble. I know every inch of this place."

Hugo laughed.

"It's changed a bit," Tom replied, ignoring the gloating looks. "Come and see for yourself."

As he led the way, with Yvonne still clutching his arm, he heard Amiens grumbling behind them, "You brought me here to talk business—"

"We will," he reassured over his shoulder.

"Specifically, we agreed to talk about your shareholding."

"Absolutely," Tom agreed as he walked into the clearing.

Yvonne stopped so abruptly that her husband trod on her heel. She dropped her hand from Tom's arm. Amiens cursed as Roddy in turn bumped into him.

Stepping around Melody, Hugo advanced into the clearing. "What the hell?"

For a moment everyone stood stock still, staring at the sight which confronted them.

Hanging low over the horizon, the sinking sun was directly behind the gallows. The grim outline was etched stark-black upon the blood-red orb of the sun. The breeze caught the noose and moved it gently to and fro. Ten chairs, in two rows of five, were set sideways to the gallows, facing the trees on the opposite side of the clearing. The screen had been erected in the trees, shaded from the sun by a rough partition which Mavros and his men had constructed from old packing cases. Next to the screen was a table. Tom swiftly advanced to it.

"Please sit down," he said loudly. "Then we can get started."

"What is this?" Amiens demanded.

"Sit down and I'll tell you."

Alec responded on cue. Pushing past Roddy he took Melody's arm and led her to the second row of chairs.

Roddy continued to stare at the gallows. "What the fucking hell are you playing at?"

"Not playing, Roddy. This is for real."

Yvonne sucked in her breath. "I'm going back to the villa," she said, turning quickly. Stepping around Constantin, her eyes suddenly widened. She screamed with terror.

Mavros and Petsas stood shoulder to shoulder on the path. Both were armed with Lee Enfield rifles, well-maintained relics of World War II.

"Andre," Yvonne cried, retreating to clutch her husband by the arm.

Amiens wrenched his gaze from the armed men and back to Tom. "Have you gone mad?"

"I nearly went mad," Tom admitted, "but I'm quite sane at this moment."

"I came to talk business!"

"So did I," Tom nodded.

"Well, I bloody well didn't," Hugo exclaimed suddenly. "Whatever this is about, none of it concerns me. I'm going—"

The shot was deafening. A spurt of earth flew up a yard ahead of Hugo's feet. The acrid smell of cordite filled the air. Sound waves hit the trees and reverberated around the clearing.

"Jesus Christ!" Hugo stood still, shock all over his face.

Mavros pulled the bolt of his rifle and ejected the spent shell.

"Bloody hell." Roddy's voice rose querulously as he swung back to face Tom. "I don't get this. You said you wanted to sell this place. That's why we came. To help you—"

"You'll help me most by sitting down."

Amiens advanced to the table. "Tom," he said, sounding faintly bewildered, "what is this? I've got a busy schedule. You wouldn't believe—"

"Sit down, Andre," Tom ordered.

"I shouldn't even be here. Yvonne and I came all this way to see you—"

"Sit down!"

"Tom—"

"Sit down."

Defiance flashed in Amiens' eyes for a moment, but he quickly brought his anger under control. "Oh, well," he said, turning to Yvonne, "why not sit down?" He loosened his tie. "I got hot walking up from the villa." Turning his smile back to Tom, he said, "I hope you're going to offer us some refreshments? A picnic or something?"

Tom let his stare roam from Yvonne to Roddy to Hugo.

Yvonne sat down beside her husband. "This isn't like you, Tom," she said with a look of reproach. "Frightening people. Being discourteous. I can't imagine what's come over you."

Looking vaguely uneasy, Roddy sat down behind her. Hugo affected a show of indifference as he shuffled over to join him.

At that moment two more of Mavros' men emerged from the trees. Both carried rifles.

Amiens tried to make a joke of it. "This is beginning to look like an armed camp," he said, but his voice contrasted with the anxiety in his eyes. He twisted around in his chair. "Is this for one of your films, Hugo?" He laughed loudly; Hugo responded with a stony-faced stare. Amiens turned back to Tom. "Well? We're all in our seats. Now what?"

Tom looked fixedly at him. "I want you to tell me how you and Yvonne obtained Kirsten's shares."

A look of understanding came into Amiens face. "Oh, so

that's it." He waved a hand at the clearing, "There was no need for all this. You could have asked on the phone."

"I'm asking you now."

"Sure," Amiens nodded.

"Well?"

"I can understand your curiosity, of course, but, sorry"—he shrugged—"the transaction must remain confidential. It was part of the deal—"

"And I insist on an answer."

"Insist?" Amiens half-rose from his chair. "Now look here, I gave Kirsten my word. I can't go back on that, can I? Especially under the circumstances. Surely you understand that? I mean . . . you could have asked her if she were alive—"

"But she's dead," Tom interrupted bitterly, "conveniently for you."

Yvonne sucked in a breath. "That's a wicked thing to say—"

"Not if someone here were responsible—"

Yvonne's hand flew to her mouth, "You're distraught. You don't—"

"There was an inquest," Amiens reminded him. "Pull yourself together, Tom. I can understand how you feel—"

"Can you?"

"Of course. We can all understand. But there was a proper investigation. The poor girl committed suicide."

Tom nodded. "A couple of months ago I thought she was murdered. But not now. I think she either committed suicide or her death was accidental."

"There you are then." With a look of relief, Amiens sat back in his chair. He injected a note of sadness into his voice. "A terrible, tragic thing—"

"But the inquest got it wrong," Tom interrupted, "with all those suppositions about her being deranged by Maurice's death." Shifting his gaze, his eyes rested upon Roddy. "Naturally she grieved for her father. A daughter would. So would a son, eh, Roddy?"

Roddy looked ill. He picked at a silk thread on his expensive cream blazer. His blue eyes looked away, avoiding Tom's gaze.

"Kirsten was waiting for me," Tom said. "She often waved

from the terrace when the Learjet came down the lake." His voice faltered. Resting his hands on the table, he stared down at his fingers. "I hope I can say that usually she looked forward to seeing me. But not that day. She must have been very upset. Possibly in tears. She would have been agitated and distraught. She threw something over the balustrade, meaning to get rid of it, and then . . ." he swallowed, "she went over after it. I don't know whether she meant to or not, but I'm sure that's what happened." Patting his trouser pockets, he searched for his cigarettes.

"Tom," said Yvonne, stretching out her hands. "You mustn't blame yourself—"

"I don't," he said sharply. Cupping his hands, he shielded the flame of his lighter as he lighted the cigarette. Exhaling, he looked up, his dark eyes searching her face, "How did you get her shares, Yvonne?"

"How did *I* get them?" Rocking back in her chair, she cast an anxious look at her husband. "I just paid for them. You know how we are, Tom. Andre arranges our business affairs. But if he gave Kirsten his word—"

"How much did you pay?"

Amiens snorted. "That's none of your business. I told you before. The arrangement was strictly confidential."

Ignoring him, Tom continued to stare at Yvonne. "I've checked Kirsten's bank statements. She didn't receive any especially large amount—"

"Especially large!" Yvonne flashed. "I'll say it was especially large. Everything I own went into raising that money. Everything!"

"It's none of your business," Amiens shouted, "it was all legal and aboveboard. That's all you need to know—"

"Is it?" Tom cut in. "A court might say differently if there was no appropriate consideration. Ask Constantin. He's a lawyer—"

"But we paid," Yvonne exclaimed. "We paid a fortune." Looking bewildered, she clutched Amiens by the arm.

"Of course we paid." Amiens squeezed her hand in reassurance and turned back to Tom. "For the last time—everything was legal. If you think otherwise, bring an action. That's what I'd do. Can't say fairer than that, can I?" Patting Yvonne's hand, he concluded, "Meanwhile I'll honor my bargain. I gave Kirsten my word and I'll keep it." He looked at his wife for approval. "I don't see why I should break it, do you?"

"No." She shook her head. "No, I don't. We paid the money."

A shadow passed across Tom's eyes. Keeping a rein on his anger was testing his strength. And his patience.

Roddy said, "There must be another bank account. After all, she didn't tell you everything, did she?"

"Meaning?" Tom glared at him.

"It's obvious," Roddy sneered spitefully. "If she didn't tell you she was selling her shares, why should she let you know what she did with the money?"

Still staring at Roddy, Tom chose his words carefully. "There was something else she didn't tell me."

Roddy smirked. "Proves my point."

"I found something close to Kirsten's body. Something I kept from the Swiss police."

Amiens cocked an eyebrow. "Withholding evidence," he murmured reprovingly.

"It's not something I'd like people to see," Tom retorted. He wondered if Hugo was smirking, then decided it was merely Hugo's usual sneering arrogance. Looking over their heads he signaled to Constantin.

Lifting the projector out from under the trees, Constantin checked the connection to the temporary line Mavros had laid earlier.

Amiens turned in his chair. "You going to show us a film?"

"That's right," Tom nodded.

"Okay," Constantin called. The images which flickered onto the screen were pale and shadowy. Distorted by sunlight, they lacked definition. Stopping the projector, Constantin picked it up and carried it forward, setting it down again next to Melody's chair. Meanwhile Tom had angled the plywood partition to shield four square feet of white canvas from the sunlight. Satisfied that the screen was in shadow, he stepped back to the table. Constantin depressed a switch, and rewound the film.

"Ready?" He looked at Tom.

Tom nodded.

This time the images were clearly defined. They seemed larger than life. Gritting his teeth, Tom vowed he was watching the film for the very last time. He watched the pink marble terrace come to life on the screen. Kirsten made her entrance, clad only in the skimpy bottom half of a bikini and that ridiculous mask. She was dancing. A slow, sensuous dance. Her full breasts swayed in time with her hips. By now she was very close to the hooded man in the chair. Naked except for his mask and the towel over his lap, the man sat back and watched her approach. He raised his drink in a toast. Kirsten smiled. Her lips moved in speech, or even in song. She threw her head back, laughing. . . .

Tom's fingernails dug into the palms of his hands. He had seen Kirsten laugh a thousand times, but never the way she laughed on the screen. Never so completely abandoned, never so . . .

He tried to imagine how her laughter would sound. So much would have been revealed by a soundtrack.

Kirsten thrust her pelvis toward the man in the chair. Her hands fondled her breasts in obvious invitation, oil gleamed on her skin. Putting his glass aside, the man reached for her with his left hand. She moved into his embrace, holding him in return, clasping the ugly hooded head to her breast, shifting her balance to allow him to suckle a nipple . . . and all the time she was laughing and laughing . . .

The towel fell away from the man's naked lap, revealing his right hand stroking his erect penis.

Tom studied the black mask. Concealment was total, there were no clues. The material clung to the man's scalp and fell loose to his throat, leaving only eyelets and a gash for the mouth.

Kirsten rubbed her body against him as he slid his hands up her thighs and into her crotch. Her nails raked his back as he pulled her bikini down over her hips to reveal the pale moons of her buttocks. Stepping out of the bikini, she parted her legs . . . and all the time she was laughing and laughing . . .

Yvonne drew a sharp breath; her eyes were fixed on the screen as the masked man thrust upward. Kirsten stood over him, straddling him. Opening herself with one hand, fondling her breasts with the other, she lowered herself onto him.

Pale sunlight caught the sheen of sweat on Amiens' face.

Tension in Roddy's expression drew the skin tight over his cheekbones.

Hugo's lips parted as he held his breath.

The man on the screen thrust up and up. Suddenly another figure appeared. A man danced across the picture, naked except for a grotesque mask. Made of skin and bone, it looked like the head of an animal. Another man appeared, wearing the painted face of a clown, prancing into the picture, masturbating with both hands. The camera drew back to reveal other figures—four, five, six, all nude and masked, one of them female, a negress squatting like a dog while a man sodomized her.

Suddenly Constantin stopped the film. The muted whirring of the projector ceased abruptly, leaving only the sound of the sea splashing onto the rocks.

Yvonne was dabbing her upper lip with a handkerchief. "I don't understand. Are you saying you discovered this awful film . . ." Her voice stopped as she turned to Tom. In that moment she saw beyond him to what was happening at the edge of the cliff. Eyes wide with horror, her mouth opened in a scream which pierced the air and soared up into the trees.

A figure, naked except for the black mask, swung from the noose.

Mavros grasped the wheel at the base of the scaffold. Cogs meshed and the gibbet turned until the figure hung suspended over the sea.

"It's a dummy," Amiens shouted, drawing Yvonne into his arms to quiet her screams. "It's a dummy, for Christ's sake!"

Sobbing, she buried her face in his chest.

Mavros moved to the lever at the side of the gallows. With both hands, he pulled it toward him. The rope rattled. The pulleys raced. Spinning giddily, the figure jerked and fell with the end of the rope whistling through the air.

Pushing Yvonne aside, Amiens leapt to his feet. "What in God's name is this?" Trembling, he took a step toward the table next to the screen.

The two men behind Tom raised their rifles.

Amiens stopped.

"I'll ask you again," Tom said harshly, "how did you make Kirsten part with those shares?"

"Me?" Amiens prodded a finger into his own chest. "All the time me. Why me every time?" Glancing over his shoulder his arm began to rise, as if to point a finger. Recovering, he regained control. "I told you before—"

"Roddy?" Tom interrupted. "Do you know the answer?"

"Me? No—"

"Hugo?"

"I don't know anything about shares—"

Amiens spread his hands to convey the dilemma of a reasonable man. "Tom, I gave my word. The whole thing was confidential."

Suddenly Roddy screamed. "Get away. Get off me . . ." Struggling violently, he tried to break free of Petsas and Mavros as they looped a rope over his shoulder. "Bastards! Get off! Let go . . ."

They were too strong. Kicking and struggling Roddy was pulled toward the scaffold. Knees buckling, he tried to fall to the ground. They dragged him. The toes of his white shoes scuffed up puffs of dust from the ground. Mavros leapt onto the scaffold, heaving Roddy up behind him while Petsas secured the rope around Roddy's chest and under his arms.

Melody cried out and buried her face in her hands.

Yvonne was screaming and sobbing.

Amiens stood as still as a rock, his eyes on the gallows.

Hugo glanced at the path to the villa. He seemed set to make a run for it, until he looked back at the men at the table. Both had their rifles pointing at him.

Pulled up onto the scaffold, Roddy fell to his knees.

Throwing the rope over the pulley, Mavros leapt down to secure the other end to the winch. Grabbing the wheel, he began to turn. The rope tightened under Roddy's armpits, dragging him up on his feet. A stain appeared on the front of his trousers. He screamed. "Stop! Please! Oh God, stop!"

Mavros took his hands from the wheel.

Arms pinioned behind his back, Roddy stood there and wept.

Amiens began to shout. "You're mad, Tom! Stark raving mad. You'll never get away with this. People know where we are—"

"What do I care?" Involuntarily Tom started to shake. He pressed his hands palm down on the table, making his arms rigid while he fought for control. "You destroyed her," he stuttered, "somehow you did it. You didn't push her, I know that much. You simply left her no place to go—"

"He's only guessing!" Hugo blustered. "He doesn't know. He *can't* know." He shouted to Roddy, "He's bluffing! He can't prove a thing!"

In answer, Tom signaled to Mavros. Responding at once, Mavros began to turn the wheel. Roddy's feet lifted from the scaffold.

"Please!" he screamed. "No! Oh, God. Please . . ."

The cogs meshed. The gibbet began to swing out over the drop. Roddy's legs were making cycling movements in the air. Mucus ran from his nose. Attempted speech produced only gibberish. He still screamed. Beyond his dangling feet, he could see the spume-tipped waves of the Aegean as they washed over the rocks below.

Tom shouted to him, "You shot that film, didn't you?"

Roddy might not have heard. He raised his eyes to the rope. "Please! Please. I'll do anything. Oh no! Christ, no!" A putrid smell fouled the breeze as he emptied his bowels. "Don't kill me. *Please,* don't kill me—"

Tom bellowed the question again.

"Oh God! You can have all the money. I'll do anything—"

"Did you make that film?"

"Yes . . . no . . . it wasn't my fault . . . it was them." Roddy's words jerked out in terrified gasps. Grimacing, he pleaded, ". . . Anything . . . don't kill me, please don't kill me . . . I'll tell you—"

Suddenly Hugo moved. Flinging his chair aside, he hurled himself toward the scaffold. His hands were on the lever before Mavros realized what was happening. Constantin flung himself forward as Hugo's fingers slipped. The rope rattled. The pulley rolled. Roddy began to drop. Mavros lashed out with his boot. Hugo sprawled to the ground with Constantin's hands at his throat. The pulley stopped. The winch held. The rope jerked. Roddy hung suspended in space, screaming with all the strength left in his body.

Mavros was already turning the wheel, bringing the gibbet back to the scaffold. Lowered by a few feet, Roddy's legs smashed into the woodwork as he fell onto the gallows. Dropping forward onto his knees, the rope saved him from falling flat on his face. He screamed at Hugo. "You tried to kill me!" For a fleeting second, his shock and fear gave way to a look of sheer disbelief. Then of loathing. "I did it for you . . ." Roddy gulped, "everything was for you . . ." He choked on his tears, ". . . everything . . ." He sobbed as his head fell forward.

Mavros and Petsas dragged Hugo, half senseless, to a chair.

Leaving the table, Tom advanced on Roddy. "What happened?"

Sniffling piteously, Roddy pleaded, "No one thought she'd commit suicide. Please, Tom. Don't hurt me—"

"How did you make that film?"

Hugo struggled upright. "Keep your mouth shut," he shouted. "Don't—" He choked up as Petsas hit him full in the face. Petsas struck again and again until Constantin pulled him away.

Tom stepped close to the scaffold. He felt no pity. They had shown no pity for Kirsten.

Roddy flinched. "Don't," he cried. "Please . . ." He gulped. "It was . . . when my father was taken ill. We got back on *Aphrodite.* Kirsten was in a hell of a state . . ."

When Maurice was taken ill! So that was when it happened!

". . . we were all stoned. We'd been having a party on board. When we got up to the villa we found Kirsten in tears." Roddy threw Hugo a look of pure hate. "It was Hugo's idea. He had some Triple E's. He put them in her drink—"

"Triple E's?"

Roddy looked at him. "E's. Ecstasy. Three times as strong. MDMA. Hugo's got a supplier . . ."

Tom's eyes lit with understanding. He knew about Ecstasy.

MDMA. And this stuff was three times as strong. Christ! Ever since his first suspicions that Kirsten had been on drugs, he had researched the subject by every means open to him. An entire library on drugs had been assembled at the villa.

"Go on," he commanded in a voice harder than steel.

Roddy sniffed, "She kept drinking—"

"That's no surprise. Even ordinary MDMA dehydrates—"

"Yes . . . well, Hugo gave her a couple of drinks . . . she just sort of went crazy . . ."

Tom's fists bunched at his sides. MDMA elevates mood, brushes off inhibitions. Even a mild dose stimulates sexual arousal. He remembered reading an account written by a first-time user: *Suddenly I was in love. Starting in my toes a tingle shot through my whole body. Laughing gas coursed through my veins, making me sparkle and fizz . . . hot shivers ran through my head . . . my skin felt like silk . . . I had to have sex . . .*

". . . It was a joke," Roddy was saying.

A joke! Tom remembered reading: *MDMA starts to poison the brain at a dose of 1.7 milligrams for every kilo of body weight . . . a hundred times more dangerous than amphetamine . . . an above-average dose will cause permanent brain damage.*

Three times as strong!

Roddy was sniveling, ". . . It developed from there . . . I'd been snorting, someone began rolling the camera—"

"Your father was dying!" Tom shouted. "Dear God! You did that to your own sister while your father was dying!"

Roddy wept, he tried to speak but choked on his words.

Tom turned away. For a moment disgust outweighed even hate. He could smell Roddy's shit. He could see the urine-stained trousers, and hear the sniveling contrition . . .

But he felt self-disgust too. Had he trusted Kirsten so little? When he saw the film he had felt outraged. Betrayed. Now he was ashamed. He had been too quick to doubt, so fast to judge.

Everything added up. Kirsten's behavior at Maurice's funeral. Her black depression. *The day after taking the drug, subjects woke feeling drunk. But the real down hit them the day after, and in some cases, the day after that . . .*

In her grief for Maurice, the down would have been like falling into a bottomless pit.

Roddy was whining, ". . . Anything, anything you want. Have mercy. I've still got most of the money—"

"No!" Hugo cried out. "Roddy! We need it for the film—"

"Bastard! You just tried to kill me. I hate you, you and your fucking films. Everything was for the films. They were all you ever cared about. You made me go to Andre in the first place. Blood-sucking bastard!"

Hugo's shouted response was throttled by Petsas. The hairs rose on the back of Tom's neck. He slid a sideways glance at Amiens. The Frenchman was on the edge of his chair. Sweat showed on his face. Beside him, Yvonne watched Roddy with a mixture of revulsion and incredulity.

Tom looked back at Roddy. "So Hugo sent you to Amiens to raise cash for a film—"

"He's lent us money before—"

"And then Maurice left you the shares—"

"Andre wouldn't buy them. He laughed in my face. 'They're no good to me,' he said. 'They won't give me control of the business. Get your sister's shares as well,' he said. 'Then we've got a deal.' "

Another piece of the jigsaw fell into place, but Tom's brain stalled on the biggest piece of all. "Kirsten wouldn't sell you her shares," he said, staring at Roddy.

"I know," Roddy gulped. "When I told Andre, he said 'Show her the film. She'll change her mind when she sees that.' "

Tom's mind was so fixed on Roddy's blackmailing Kirsten that other implications passed him by. "When?" he shouted. "When did you do this?"

Roddy, terrified, stuttered into gibberish.

"When?" Tom roared.

". . . You were in London. After the funeral. Veronica had left. I went up to the château. She was by herself . . ."

Tom groaned, "She *wanted* to be by herself. Oh God!"

Roddy was blubbering, "I told her I'd show you the film—"

"What about the witness?" Tom interrupted. "This lawyer—"

". . . He waited in the car. I called him in when she was ready to do it."

Turning away in disgust, Tom caught the look on Yvonne's face. She was staring at Roddy. "How did Andre know about the film?" she asked.

Amiens jumped up. "How do you think? He told me, of course. He came to the office—"

"No!" Roddy howled, straining against the rope as he looked at Tom. "Didn't you know? Didn't I say? He was there . . . when we got there on *Aphrodite*—"

Amiens was on his feet, pulling Yvonne up with him. "Come on. We've heard enough of this—"

She pulled away, "Wait a minute—"

"We've waited long enough. Come on. I've got a business to run." Pulling her by the arm, he began to lead her past the second row of chairs.

Yvonne struggled. "No, Andre, wait—"

"He was there," Roddy screamed. "In the mask, fucking Kirsten."

Tom's heart missed a beat.

Jerking against the grip on her arm, Yvonne almost broke free.

"Come on!" Amiens shouted furiously. Tugging her forward with his left hand, he swung his right, intending to grab her shoulder. The blow caught her full in the mouth. Crying out, she stumbled. "For God's sake!" he shouted, stooping over her, putting both hands under her arms. Which was when Mavros hit him, a huge blow which landed behind his left ear. Dropping Yvonne, he buckled and fell to one side, just as Petsas came up from behind. They dragged him to a chair.

Alec helped Yvonne to her feet, while Melody dabbed Yvonne's lip with a handkerchief. Together, gently, they sat her down between them.

Roddy was babbling, "Andre always fancied Kirsten." He cowered, pleading to be believed but fearful of the consequences. "It was a joke, her being your wife—"

"Liar!" Amiens shrieked before Mavros pulled him backward and knotted a handkerchief around his mouth.

"It's true." Roddy's eyes were a blur of tears as he looked at Tom. "That's how it all happened. I swear it's the truth."

Tom knew it was the truth. He could have killed Amiens, strangled him with his bare hands. He knew he would if he looked at him. He lowered his gaze, clenching and unclenching his hands as he thought of Kirsten's torment. He imagined her bracing herself to tell him, losing her nerve, pacing the terrace, then seeing his plane coming in . . .

Hot tears stung his eyes. It *might* have been an accident. She *might* have meant only to throw the film over the balustrade, not herself. He would never know. He would live with the doubt for the rest of his life.

Nauseated by the smell and spectacle of Roddy, he walked back to the table and slumped into a chair. He had been so *sure* of what he would do if he discovered the truth. He reached for his cigarettes. He felt sick, tired of the world, of the lies and deceit and the greed and cruelty which had driven Kirsten to her death. He drew the smoke deep into his lungs and directed his gaze out to sea to avoid the watchful eyes around him.

Lost in thought, he sat there for several minutes, smoking the cigarette.

"I think we know the truth now, don't we?" said a voice.

Startled, he turned to find Yvonne behind him. A cut marked her lower lip, which was beginning to swell. Her floral silk dress was crumpled and soiled. But most of all she looked as tired and ill and old as he felt.

"I said I think we know the truth," she repeated. Her eyes were full of pain as they searched his face.

He nodded.

"You always were resourceful," she said with the shadow of a smile. Her gaze drifted past him and out to sea. The sun had fallen below the horizon, taking the heat from the day and leaving the shadowy cool of evening. The sea was turning gray.

"Not that it makes any difference," she said, "but I didn't know."

"I never thought you did."

She looked at Tom. "Thank you for that."

He shrugged.

"He told me you and Kirsten had quarreled, that you would probably split up. She wanted to sell her shares. That's what he said."

Tom drew on his cigarette without answering.

"I've wasted my life trying to prove a point," Yvonne said quietly. "My father said Andre only wanted my money. I so wanted to prove him wrong that I've spent years turning a blind eye. Of course there's always been someone, I've know about various women . . . but not that"—she gestured with disgust at the screen—"I never thought . . ." Her voice trailed off, leaving an echo of contempt. "Don't make my mistake, that's what I'm saying. Don't ruin your life to prove a point, Tom,"

He looked at her.

"How much vengeance do you want?"

The question confused him. Shylock's pound of flesh? Was that what she meant?

"That spineless little creep and Hugo came here as lovers," she said. "Look at them now."

Without looking, he could hear Roddy sniveling.

"They hate each other. Leave them alone and they'll do your job for you. Only more slowly." Yvonne covered his hand with her own. "No matter what you do, nothing will ever be the same for any of us."

Looking down at her hand, he was vaguely aware of the rings on her fingers.

"I'd be even more contemptuous of them if I wasn't so contemptuous of myself," she said. "You've done that, opened my eyes, made me look at myself. I don't much like what I see." Removing her hand from his, she loosened the rings on her fingers. "Can you get my money back from him?" she asked, her nose crinkling with distaste as she looked at Roddy.

On his knees, soiled by his own excrement, Roddy's eyes lit with hope. "You can have it. Everything—"

"Take it," said Yvonne.

Walking away from the table, she pulled the rings from her fingers. There were three of them, including the wedding band. Pausing a few yards from the edge of the cliff, she tossed them over without a hint of hesitation. As she walked back to him, her eyes were clear, free of doubt. "I'll hand over the shares for whatever you get out of him. His shares, as well as Kirsten's. You'll have more than seventy percent. Stanton Industries will be yours without strings."

He would have given his right arm to hear that, at one time. Stanton Industries had been his life. When Maurice was alive . . . and he had met Kirsten and fallen in love and married her . . . Stanton Industries had been part of them and they had been part of it.

Yvonne said, "Would you mind if I keep my eleven percent of the shares? I let my father down by allowing Andre to get anywhere near them. It would please him to know that Andre's gone and I've managed to hold onto them."

Tom's gaze drifted past her to the others waiting and watching as, face mottled with fury, Amiens tried to bite through his gag; Hugo's head was slumped on his chest, and Roddy continued to plead from the scaffold.

Catching Tom's eye, Constantin limped forward. "Yvonne's right, nothing will ever be the same. Those two will destroy each other"—he jerked his head at Roddy and Hugo. "And him," he said, looking at Amiens, "he's lost his wife, Stanton Industries, everything." He looked Tom in the eye. "Isn't that vengeance enough?"

Alec added, "It's a vengeance you can live with."

Looking at him, Tom knew he was right. Wise old Alec. Always there. Ever since the grim days at Bolton. For some reason he remembered the two of them walking up Jermyn Street that first time, searching for Maurice's office.

"Tom?" Constantin persisted, seeking an answer.

When he looked at Constantin Tom recalled that nightmare drive through Athens . . . and Melina's tears when they were pulled aboard *Helena*.

He made up his mind. "You can have the shares," he said. "You and Alec between you. Kirsten and Maurice would approve."

He felt very tired. Drained. Turning to Yvonne, he said, "Come on. Let's take Melody back to the villa. Alec and

Constantin can finish up here." The path was in shadow as they walked from the clearing. The day was drawing to a close, taking with it part of his life. Soon it would be a memory.

Tomorrow would be time enough to think of the future.

HarperPaperbacks *By Mail*

Explosive Thrillers From Three Bestselling Authors

LEN DEIGHTON

Spy Sinker

British agent Bernard Samson, the hero of *Spy Hook* and *Spy Line*, returns for a final bow in this thrilling novel. Through terrible treachery, Samson is betrayed by the one person he least suspects—his lovely wife, Fiona.

Spy Story

Pat Armstrong is an expert at computer generated tactical war games. But when he returns to his old apartment to find that someone who looks just like him has taken over his identity, he is thrust into an international conspiracy that is all too real.

Catch a Falling Spy

On the parched sands of the Sahara desert, Andrei Bekuv, a leading Russian scientist, defects, setting off a shadow war between the KGB and the CIA. Yet, nothing is what it seems—least of all, Bekuv's defection.

BERNARD CORNWELL

Crackdown

Drug pirates stalk their victims in the treacherous waters of the Bahamas, then return to their fortress island of Murder Cay. Then comes skipper Nicholas Breakspear with the son and daughter of a U.S. Senator. What should have been a simple de-tox cruise soon lurches into a voyage of terror and death as Breakspear is lured into a horrifying plot of cocaine, cash, and killings.

Killer's Wake

Suspected of sailing off with a valuable family treasure, sea gypsy John Rossendale must return to England to face his accusing relatives. But in the fog-shrouded waters of the Channel Islands, Rossendale, alone and unarmed, is plunged into someone's violent game of cat-and-mouse where a lot more is at stake than family relations.

CAMPBELL ARMSTRONG

Agents of Darkness

Suspended from the LAPD, Charlie Galloway decides his life has no meaning. But when his Filipino housekeeper is murdered, Charlie finds a new purpose in tracking the killer. He never expects, though, to be drawn into a conspiracy that reaches from the Filipino jungles to the White House.

Mazurka

For Frank Pagan of Scotland Yard, it begins with the murder of a Russian at crowded Waverly Station, Edinburgh. From that moment on, Pagan's life becomes an ever-darkening nightmare as he finds himself trapped in a complex web of intrigue, treachery, and murder.

Mambo

Super-terrorist Gunther Ruhr has been captured. Scotland Yard's Frank Pagan must escort him to a maximum security prison, but with blinding swiftness and brutality, Ruhr escapes. Once again, Pagan must stalk Ruhr, this time into an earth-shattering secret conspiracy.

Brainfire

American John Rayner is a man on fire with grief and anger over the death of his powerful brother. Some say it was suicide, but Rayner suspects something more sinister. His suspicions prove correct as he becomes trapped in a Soviet-made maze of betrayal and terror.

Asterisk Destiny

Asterisk is America's most fragile and chilling secret. It waits somewhere in the Arizona desert to pave the way to world domination...or damnation. Two men, White House aide John Thorne and CIA agent Ted Hollander, race to crack the wall of silence surrounding Asterisk and tell the world of their terrifying discovery.

MAIL TO: **Harper Collins Publishers**
P. O. Box 588 Dunmore, PA 18512-0588
OR CALL: (800) 331-3761 (Visa/MasterCard)

Yes, please send me the books I have checked:

- ☐ SPY SINKER (0-06-109928-7) $5.95
- ☐ SPY STORY (0-06-100265-8) $4.99
- ☐ CATCH A FALLING SPY (0-06-100207-0) $4.95
- ☐ CRACKDOWN (0-06-109924-4) $5.95
- ☐ KILLER'S WAKE (0-06-100046-9) $4.95
- ☐ AGENTS OF DARKNESS (0-06-109944-9) $5.99
- ☐ MAZURKA (0-06-100010-8) $4.95
- ☐ MAMBO (0-06-109902-3) $5.95
- ☐ BRAINFIRE (0-06-100086-8) $4.95
- ☐ ASTERISK DESTINY (0-06-100160-0) $4.95

SUBTOTAL .... $______

POSTAGE AND HANDLING .... $ 2.00*

SALES TAX (Add applicable sales tax) .... $______

TOTAL: $______

*(ORDER 4 OR MORE TITLES AND POSTAGE & HANDLING IS FREE! Orders of less than 4 books, please include $2.00 p/h. Remit in US funds, do not send cash.)

Name ____________________

Address ____________________

City ____________________

State ______ Zip ______

Allow up to 6 weeks delivery.
Prices subject to change.

(Valid only in US & Canada)

HO271